FALLIBLE JUSTICE

LAURA LAAKSO

BLOODHOUND
— BOOKS —

www.bloodhoundbooks.com

Print ISBN: 978-1-916978-61-4

For Andrew Rogers, who showed me I could and told me I should.

SUNDAY

BRIEF ENCOUNTERS

T am running. The foot that touches the ground is a deer's hoof, the foot that propels me a wolf's paw. Between strides, the wings of a seagull hold me aloft. The wind is against me, whipping through the horse's mane that is my hair. With the wind come the smells of the land and the sea, and I sift through them with the nose of a badger. In the distance, a magpie takes flight and the ears of a dormouse pinpoint the source of the sound. My foot lands in a grassy depression, but with the balance of a squirrel I change direction and keep going.

I am running through the wilderness and the wilderness runs through me.

The hills follow the curves of the coast, and from a sheltered cove, I smell decay. My stomach growls and it's the hunger of a vixen stalking a chicken coop; a pine marten pouncing on a shrew; a striped dolphin chasing a school of cod. As soon as the thought registers, the smell has gone.

A hound bays in the distance. It is downwind from me and has recognised my scent. I bay back. Kin recognises kin.

Although I move with the grace of a pond skater, there comes a point when I have to stop. I brace my hands against my knees, breath coming in gulps. In that moment, I am all human – only human. There is no sorrow in the change; the wilderness hovers on the edge of my consciousness, ever-present and comforting. I wipe a sheen of sweat from my forehead, a mixture of beads of dew and salt from the sea. Everything is connected. I smile at the thought as I begin the long walk back to my car.

From my backpack, I pull out a large sack. Once it is unrolled and slung over my shoulder, the work begins. My steps take me in a zigzag pattern down to the wide, flat beach. The receding tide has left plenty of driftwood behind on the damp sand, and the waves have not yet begun to creep closer. The rain at the ebbing of the tide will have washed much of the salt from the wood. I collect the smaller pieces into the sack and use a length of rope to gather together longer branches, dragging them behind me.

The waves call out to me. They invite me to join them, to dip, dive, and dance in the water. My kin is there: the fish, the cetaceans and the crustaceans. I am connected to it all, even the algae and the sea plants. Part of the infinite being of nature, I can feel the cycle of life and death all around.

It is this understanding of our place in the unity of the world that is the greatest gift and the greatest curse of Wild Folk like me.

The temptation to accept the waves' invitation is great, but there is a hint of autumn chill in the air. Perhaps another time. Even on a day like this, surrounded by the wildness I love and crave, I dare not throw caution to the wind.

The hairs on the back of my neck prickle a warning: I am being watched. While I pick up the next piece of driftwood, I look along the beach. A figure is standing on a hill up ahead. The distance is too great for human eyes, so I borrow the sight of a red kite and the figure comes into focus. It is a woman; her navy-blue jacket, white blouse and skinny jeans seem out of place on a windswept hill. She is looking towards me through a set of binoculars. Is she watching me? More likely she is a businesswoman taking a break at the seaside to fit in some birdwatching. Except it is Sunday and something about the image jars.

I continue my walk, puzzled by the presence of a stranger on a beach I have come to consider as mine. My kind understands our place in the world and how we never truly own the land we inhabit. Nevertheless, I feel a sense of intrusion.

When I next look up, the woman is gone. Pausing to brush my fingers along a strand of seaweed, I wonder if she found what she was looking for.

Halfway back to my car, my steps slow and I rest on the edge of a grass-covered dune while I eat an apple and a handful of nuts. The fatigue from the run and the walk back is warring with my recharged power, leaving me restless. As reluctant as I am to leave the beach, I know that I must return to Old London while I can still drive safely.

Ignoring my protesting muscles, I stand and gather my belongings. My car is parked by a narrow service road snaking through the dunes, and when I arrive at the crest of the hill, I see there is another car behind mine. The woman from earlier is leaning against the bonnet of a black Mercedes, eyes glued to her phone. She does not look up until I disengage the central locking of my car and she appears startled by my silent approach. The phone disappears into the pocket of her jacket and she pushes herself off the bonnet to face me.

At first, I think she is human, but then I catch the scents of frost, moss, and autumn leaves. A North Mage. Interesting. Mages are far more likely to wield their magic in libraries or laboratories than on a deserted beach. As much as there is a stereotype about uncultured Wild Folk living in forests, so there is one about North Mages occupying lofty towers that bring them close to wide open skies and the power behind weather patterns.

Without the binoculars covering her face, I see she is beautiful. Blonde hair, forget-me-not-blue eyes and pale skin suggest Scandinavian origin, which fits with her school of magic. Minimal make-up enhances her beauty, and she moves with an elegance that is part breeding and part learned.

Next to her, I feel gangly and unsophisticated. I have no curves to match hers and I have never worn make-up. Whatever beauty I may have comes from the way I wield my powers.

'It's quite something, seeing one of the Wild Folk running,' she says.

Feeling self-conscious, I tuck a lock of my wind-snarled hair behind my ear. Her hair streams behind her, and in the sunlight, the strands glow gold and honey. Distracted by her beauty and thrown by her comment, I cannot think of a suitable response. I say nothing.

'I apologise. It was not my intention to make you feel uncomfortable.'

Her concern seems genuine and I force a smile. 'It's fine. I'm not used to people being here, let alone watching what I do.'

'I didn't mean to spy on you, but your command of nature is a thing to behold.' She laughs and the sound eases the loneliness in me. 'Sorry, I'll stop gushing now.'

'It's fine,' I repeat. The situation feels bizarre, and something she said troubles me. 'But I don't command nature, I borrow that which is freely offered. It's an exchange, something is always given for something received. We strive for harmony in all things, never mastery.'

She smiles, and I see curiosity warring with something else in her expression. I wonder if it is desire, but I dismiss the thought as wishful thinking.

'In case the conclusion I jumped to didn't make it clear, I'm a Mage,' she says. 'Alas, my kind is all about mastery and control.'

'I recognised you as a North Mage, yes.' I offer nothing further. We Wild Folk are private about our abilities, especially with curious strangers.

Silence stretches between us. The wind carries a myriad of scents, tempting my attention away from her. My chin lifts of its own accord so that I may better sample the air. I become aware that the stranger is leaning forward, staring at me with intent eyes. Not wanting to show her my powers again, I relinquish the threads of magic that would have unlocked the secrets of the wind.

'Well,' she shifts her weight, and I realise she is nervous, 'I won't intrude upon your day any more than I already have.'

Despite her words, she remains where she is, invitation and expectation in her expression. It's my move, but fatigue washes over me while I try to determine what she wants from me. In the end, all I can do is offer her a smile that is a little more genuine than my first.

'Sorry to have trespassed on your beach,' she says, and takes a step back.

'It's not my beach. This place, this world, belongs to everyone in equal shares. You are as welcome here as I am.'

'I'm not sure that's true. My understanding is that a beach would take a Wild Folk over a Mage any day.'

'Why would the beach judge you based on the source of your power?'

She opens her mouth to reply, but all that comes out is a laugh. It is her turn to be caught unawares. 'I suppose it's really only people who judge and feel the need to own things. Though is it not true your kind owns vast swathes of the North Country?'

I concede the point with a nod. 'Under English law, we can own land, but what it gives us is the right to occupy. The land itself is not affected by an entry of ownership in the Land Registry.'

'I'll bear that in mind.' She rests her hand on the car door-handle. 'Thank you. This has been... enlightening.'

Her choice of words gives me pause, but she slides into the driver's seat before I have a chance to ask what she means. As she does so, the mask of light flirtation slips and I see fear and anguish in her expression. The door closes, and I am left watching as she turns the Mercedes around and heads away from the sea.

My curiosity is aroused by the unexpected encounter and there are things that do not add up. The interval between my spotting her on a dune and finding her next to my car was long. Was she waiting for me? If she was, to what purpose? The brief conversation was general at best and gave no indication she was here for me. As a Mage, she is unlikely to harbour any ideas about my being able to teach her or lend her power. It does not work that way, and she will have learned that early on in her training. What did she want?

Thoughts of her preoccupy me as I load the driftwood into my car and ready myself for the long drive home to Old London. I linger a moment longer than necessary, drawing in the power from all around. A surge of wildness rushes over me and I am tempted to become lost in it. But danger lurks behind the temptation, and I resist even as my legs merge with the sand dunes, my fingers become crashing waves and my hair morphs into threads of the sea breeze. As the moment passes, I am left full of power and yet curiously hollow.

This is no life for one of the Wild Folk.

A flash of anger burns away the traitorous thought while I take my place behind the steering wheel. Sand sprays behind me as I turn the car and accelerate faster than necessary. My choice was a difficult one, but it was the right thing to do. I am living on borrowed time and every second ticking by brings me closer to the inevitable.

The arrival of pain is as predictable as the rise and fall of the sun. It begins as a burning pressure in my hips, which pulses down to my knees and ankles. An ache settles in my pelvis, then in my shoulders, my elbows. I crank up the heating and direct it at my feet. It provides temporary respite, but an hour into the drive, my world has narrowed until nothing exists except the pain and the road in front of the car. I allow the agony to consume me, to pulse through my core in time with my heartbeat. It is either that or scream until my throat is raw.

Arriving home, I have no memory of the journey beyond the fire in my limbs. The lack of recollection is a frightening thing, but one I have grown used to.

A narrow alleyway runs between the houses, and I park my car next to the back gate to the garden. The sound of a door opening nearby catches my attention. Swivelling towards the sound, I see my upstairs neighbour, Jans, walk down the steps. He waves to me as he heads towards the corner shop.

It takes a matter of moments to unlock the back gate and the large shed where I keep the firewood. Tall piles line the walls, leaving the centre of the shed free for a circular section of a tree trunk on which I chop wood. The ground is littered with woodchips, and there is a large basket for smaller twigs and kindling. Another basket contains fir branches in three-inch pieces. The neighbours all donated their Christmas trees to me in January.

Moving as fast as the pain allows, I transfer the wood from

the car to the garden. Next to the shed, driftwood from the week before has been exposed to the elements. It has rained enough for much of the sea salt to have washed away and I take the older wood into the shed. The branches fall into an untidy heap, but I cannot will myself to organise them now. There is always tomorrow.

When the new batch of branches has been spread on the grass, I move the car around the corner to my allocated space. Instead of using the front door, I return to the back gate, lock it behind me and go in through the back window. Daylight is fading fast, and I switch on the light in the kitchen.

On the counter, two pills and an empty glass are waiting for me. I swallow the pills with some water and eat a sandwich I also prepared this morning. While I wait for the medication to take effect, I walk to the fireplace. It is constructed from the same grey bricks as the house and the inside is black from frequent use.

Kneeling in front of the raised brick edging, I stack small twigs and strips of bark in the centre of the fireplace, followed by thin branches. My lighted match flares in the gloom of the lounge and shadows dance at the back of the fireplace. Once the branches have caught the flames, I stack more on top until the fire is strong enough to add logs. Tiny blue and lavender flames flare from the blaze, and I lean away to avoid the toxic fumes of sea-salt residue.

Next to the fireplace, away from the reach of wayward sparks, is a clay bowl. I pick up one of the short lengths of fir it contains. My hold on the offering is reverent as I bring it close to the fire, where it flares bright at the first lick of flames and burns with a crackle of sap. Heat against my fingertips is my cue to let it fall on to the body of the fire and begin the prayer.

'Hearth Spirit, ward this home and its inhabitants, who give thanks for the light and heat you provide, for the life you sustain. Accept our offering and guard these flames for another night.'

The words are spoken without conscious thought, the thanksgiving and the prayer learned as a child but appreciated only as an adult. When I was growing up in a conclave of my kind, protection and heat were a given. Alone in Old London, I am far away from everything familiar, and the old rituals offer more than just spiritual reassurance. Here, it is my deep belief that a Hearth Spirit is watching over my home, granting me safety in return for faith and offerings.

With the fire going strongly, I throw in more logs and set up the spark guard. My bed, nothing more than a double mattress on the floor, is near the centre of the room, and I push it closer to the fire. Tonight the heat will be a blessing. The layers of blankets will absorb the warmth from the flames and offer comfort against the pain.

As I stand, the painkillers take effect and numbness settles over my limbs. The relief is welcome, though beneath it the pain has not relinquished its hold.

Footsteps sound above me as I slip between the warm blankets. Jans must have returned. The building is old, full of creaks and sighs that come with age. Added to the natural sounds are echoes of the people who lived here before me. Their magic has left behind a residue in the very foundations of the building, and there are moments when I catch a fleeting impression of a Shamanistic ritual or a Mage spell. A human may think the house is haunted, but the physical manifestations of its history are an integral part of what makes Old London so special.

All the familiar sounds and whispers of power comfort me as I roll on to my side, my back to the fire. Heat washes over me in waves, reaching into tired muscles and sore bones. The warmth does more to ease the pain than any amount of medication, but only while I stay still. The embrace of the fire is the safest place in the world for me, and that knowledge eases the last of the tension from my body.

Right before sleep claims me, I recall the woman from the beach and the contradiction of her ringing laughter and her fear as she departed. The feeling that she was there because of me lingers, but why would a North Mage seek out one of the Wild Folk? Was she watching me to see someone who, even in Old London, amounts to a fairy-tale figure – or was her interest more personal? If it was the latter, why did she not tell me what she wanted? And at the end of it all, did she find what she was looking for?

MONDAY

2

A HELPING HAND

My dreams of sea and shore are disturbed by a regular thwacking sound. It is at odds with the crash of the waves, and my consciousness stirs. The noise abates, but before I can drift off, it begins again.

It is no use trying to get back to sleep. I push myself to a sitting position and disentangle the blankets from my legs. The fire has reduced to a pile of ash overnight and the air carries the chill of autumn. I reach for the socks next to the mattress, followed by a second, thicker pair. The rest of my clothes are in a pile by the fireplace. Wasting no time, I get dressed.

Standing up, I bite back a groan. My muscles are stiff and sore after yesterday's run. It is an expected consequence; as predictable as the immediate pain. The first steps are the hardest, but once I get going some of the discomfort will disappear.

As I zip up a fleece, the thwacking sound continues. It is coming from the garden. I unlock the lounge window and slip on a pair of sandals. Two rows of bricks outside the window provide a step for me.

The garden is little more than a patch of lawn bordered on two sides by shrubbery. A winding path of patio stones leads from the back gate to the shed. It is my tiny haven. The threads of power from the garden tug at the edge of my consciousness, but without regular trips out of the city they would be insufficient to sustain me. Therein lies the conflict between my nature and my chosen abode.

Once outside, I pause to draw a deep breath. The air is crisp, and even to my human nose it is sharp with the stink of cars, machines, and people. Already I can feel my power faltering, hemmed in on all sides by buildings, technology, and pollution. A small voice at the back of my mind pleads with me to run, to return to the place where I belong, away from Old London. But I cannot go back, not yet, and I silence the voice.

A pigeon is ambling near the open shed door, aiming idle pecks at the gaps between the paving stones. Drawing on the threads of power from the garden, I coo a greeting. It glances up, puzzled, for it sees a human but hears another pigeon. The coo I get in response is hesitant but polite enough.

The thwacking from the shed ceases and a voice calls out, 'Do us both a favour and tell the pigeon to fuck off.'

Stepping around the pigeon, I cross to the shed door and lean against the doorframe. 'That would be impolite.'

Karrion, my best friend – my only real friend in the city – is standing next to the wood-chopping block, my axe in his hand. Black trousers adorned with metal studs and chains and an artfully torn black T-shirt look at odds with the piles of firewood that surround him. Sweat has plastered locks of black hair on to his forehead. Reproach battles with frustration in his brown eyes, and his teeth are worrying a lip piercing as he stares at me.

'Why would you care about hurting the feelings of a pigeon?' he asks.

Wrapping my fleece more tightly around me against the chill, I remind Karrion that all things are equal and deserve equal respect.

'Now you're beginning to sound like my mum.' Karrion's shoulders hunch a fraction and he turns away to pick up the next length of wood. With the rearing of his emotions, his power flares before returning to roil around him like a murder of crows.

'Perhaps that's because she's right. It's not the pigeon's fault that it's drawn to your power.'

He offers no response, but the axe lands on the branch with more force than is required and the wood is cut in half. I dodge the end that flies out of the shed. The unexpected missile scares the pigeon into flight, and for the moment we are alone in the garden. Soon another pigeon will come.

My movements are sluggish as I retrieve the piece of wood and stack it on top of the nearest pile. I return to leaning against the doorframe, watching him.

Karrion is a Bird Shaman going through a goth phase. His preference is to associate only with ravens and crows, but to his chagrin, pigeons seem attracted to him. Wherever Karrion goes, it is guaranteed that at least one pigeon will be hovering nearby, watching him with placid, friendly eyes. It causes him to have occasional outbursts about killing all the pigeons in the city. Of course, he could never do such a thing. Despite his tendency towards melodrama, he has a good heart. A wicked sense of humour is a bonus.

Shamans like Karrion draw their power from a specific type of animal and the spirits linked with that animal. A Wolf Shaman can not only borrow the senses of a wolf, but with the collective wisdom and instinct of millennia behind them, they are the best trackers in the world. Bird Shamans never get lost and they possess an innate sense of position that makes them superb pilots. If ever there is a job that requires working with animals, a Shaman of the right type is the obvious choice.

It takes a sizeable pile of branches for Karrion's anger to die down. By then, he is warm enough to discard his T-shirt in a careless heap on top of the chopped wood and I see that he has added nipple rings to his collection of piercings. No doubt that has caused additional tension with his mother, who has traditional views. My words earlier touched a nerve and while I am not going to apologise for them, I have no desire to fuel his anger. I stay silent until the furrows on his forehead smooth and his movements with the axe calm to efficient blows.

'Why are you spending Monday morning chopping wood in my shed?'

Resting the axe against the chopping block, Karrion wipes sweat from his forehead and gives me a pointed look. 'Come on, Yan. We both know you're in no shape to chop anything after yesterday.'

It is my turn to feel defensive and I cross my arms. 'I might have waited until later in the week. It's easier to chop the wood when it's begun to dry.'

'Yeah, like I believe you,' Karrion scoffs.

He is right, of course, and my silence confirms it. His expression softens as he scoops up a handful of wood and adds it to the existing pile of logs that are still drying. Karrion understands my need for independence, but has figured out that the easiest way to get around it is not to wait for me to ask for help. This is not the first time I have found him chopping wood for me, or mowing the lawn, or picking up heavy bags of shopping before I have a chance to grab them. Although I always object, he knows the gestures mean more to me than I can say. He accepts my implied gratitude without making anything of it.

I am blessed to have a friend in Karrion. Who knew that a

chance encounter on a roof one night would lead to such friendship? Karrion saw me jump between two buildings, borrowing the wings of a bat for gliding, and he struck up a conversation. His unguarded enthusiasm for what he described as "wicked powers" was a nice change from most of the Old London folk treating me like a country bumpkin. We talked until the early hours; and a week later, I realised that Karrion had become a permanent fixture in my life, changing it for the better.

Some of my thoughts must be reflected in my expression, for he rubs his neck and hangs the axe on the wall. 'Besides, Mum's been on my case about getting a proper career again, so I told her I was assisting you with your new investigation.' A grin makes an appearance. 'I might also have suggested you were taking me on as an apprentice.'

'My *apprentice*?' I get no further with the teasing when the rest of his words register. 'Wait, what new investigation?'

'Didn't you get my note? I was here avoiding Mum and church yesterday morning and I took a call from a woman who wants to hire you to investigate something. She didn't go into detail, but when I told her you were out, she made an appointment for this morning and is coming by...' he pulls his phone out of his back pocket and checks the time, 'in an hour. I left a note on your desk. I figured you would have seen it when you got back last night.'

'No, I came in through the back.'

Karrion looks me up and down. 'You better take a shower and try to make yourself look professional.'

'Right back at you. And maybe wear a shirt that doesn't have holes in it.'

'Don't worry, I brought a spare with me. I'll finish here and jump in the shower once you're done.'

'Sounds good. I'll make some toast while you shower.'

I turn to leave and get no further than three paces when Karrion's voice stops me.

'I wasn't entirely joking when I said I could be your apprentice.'

Looking at him over my shoulder, I feel a smile tugging at the corner of my mouth. 'I know. Note how I haven't said no.'

As I move towards the house, my weight shifts off balance and pain lances down my leg. A gasp escapes my lips. Karrion is by my side in an instant, a hand on my elbow. A year ago, I would have dodged him and gritted my teeth. Now I lean on him, grateful for the support while I wait for the pain to fade. Karrion lets me breathe through it in silence. When only a throb remains, I glance up long enough to flash him a smile.

'Is it the knee again?' he asks.

'No, my hip this time. Life's never boring with EDS.' I make no effort to hide my frustration with the connective tissue disorder. 'But never mind that, I'm okay now.'

'Will you manage the window?'

'Should do. If I don't, I'll only fall flat on my face.'

He takes his phone out and waves it with a grin. 'For the photos.'

I decide not to answer, but test my leg to see if it will hold my weight. The throb intensifies, but I can walk. As I head towards the open window, Karrion maintains his hold. But when he sees I'm fine, he allows his fingers to slip away.

'Leave the log basket outside the window and I'll fill it for you.'

Pausing with my foot on the makeshift step, I look back at him.

Knowing I am about to argue, he beats me to it. 'I know you can manage on your own, but with me around, you don't have to.'

Although we have had similar conversations in the past, Karrion's honest affection reminds me it has been some time since I felt cared for. Karrion is worlds apart from the Wild Folk and the conclave that was once my home, and his youthful certainty is a comfort. His concern is genuine and not an attempt to garner favour, standing, or power. The friendship he offers holds a simplicity I thought was lost forever. But old habits of wariness die hard.

I slip in through the window.

My flat is the lower half of a house at the end of a terrace of six. The entrance is on the lower-ground floor, where the bedroom and the bathroom are, with a narrow staircase leading up to a small lounge and an even smaller kitchen. The décor is old, with high ceilings and moulded cornices. On both levels, the floors are wooden, which I like. The stairs creak, the taps can be temperamental, and the boiler rattles when it is switched on. Still, I love my home. It is the place where I can hide away from the rest of the world, from the memories that threaten to take me back to the conclave.

Given how expensive office space is in London, I use what should have been the bedroom as my office. It is not a large room, but there is enough space for a desk with two chairs in front of it, the compulsory filing cabinet harking back to older times, and my coat stand in the corner. A door leads to the corridor and stairs. While the rest of the décor may give the room an old-fashioned feel, the laptop on my desk is new and hooked up to fast broadband.

Another reason to sleep upstairs, in the lounge, is the damp. It clings to the walls and hovers near the floor, always ready to trigger the ache in my bones. I dislike the damp chill of London winters, and in the office the damp lingers all year round. So I sleep upstairs, in front of the fireplace. It is where I feel the safest as well as the warmest.

A hot shower refreshes me, dispelling some of the lingering ache from my legs. Karrion is lifting a basket full of logs through the window when I return upstairs. In his other hand, he is carrying the T-shirt he discarded earlier as well as his rucksack. I fetch him a towel from the wardrobe and he heads downstairs.

I twist my hair into a braid before I make toast, and weigh a foil strip of painkillers in my hand. The thought of taking a mild painkiller is tempting, but I decide against it. It is better to keep a clear head for a meeting with a prospective client.

My private investigator business has been going for a little over a year and although it will never make me rich, it pays the bills. The work itself is not as exciting as the name suggests; it is mainly due diligence checks for businesses and personal transactions that involve an element of magic. Occasionally, there are bursts of action when things do not quite go according to plan, such as a few cases of spouses hiding infidelity with spells. In many ways, I am still finding my bearings and building my list of contacts within both Old and New London.

Old London is the magic folk name for what humans know as the City of London borough. Magic thrives in an island in the middle of London. At the borders, there exists the friction of constant struggle between magic and the mundane, but the boundaries have remained largely unchanged for decades. Most people living here have power or have family with power. Something draws us together, to find strength in numbers and comfort in neighbours who understand. The more we gather, the more we are drawn together, I believe, though it is just a theory. We are attracted to the landscape shaped by centuries of spells, rites, and raw power. Even for someone who grew up surrounded by wilderness, Old London holds a resonance that calls to some primal part of my blood.

The surrounding city is known as New London and that is where the non-magical people live. Some come to Old London to gawk, though most of us look no different from the average human. Others come in search of power, some trinket or potion that will make them feel special, not understanding that magic is in the blood. I imagine there are plenty of other humans who prefer to ignore the existence of Old London altogether.

With my thoughts lingering on the difference between a city full of people and a close-knit conclave in the wilderness, I am leaning against the counter when Karrion comes up. The fresh shirt has no artful holes, and it hugs his lean figure. When he reaches past me for a slice of toast, I smell my mint shower gel. Beneath it are the familiar scents of wind and feathers which mark him as a Bird Shaman, and a blend of pheromones that are unique to him.

We eat in silence, standing side by side in the kitchen. Our friendship has progressed beyond the need for small talk, which suits us both.

'We might as well go down,' I say, once the plate is empty.

Karrion studied fine art at university and he has taken it upon himself to decorate my office. As a result, framed on the walls are old-fashioned Wanted posters, each with a twist. One shows a drawing of a wolf, tongue lolling out in a canine grin, and the caption below reads, '*Have you seen this werewolf?*' Another is a blank square where the picture should be, with a caption, '*The Invisible Man still at large*'. A third depicts a child's bedroom and the punchline is, '*We can find the monster under your bed*'.

When we get to the office, there is a moment of shuffling. Karrion has brought down another chair from upstairs, and he shifts the electric heater next to my desk to make room for it. I switch on the laptop, so Karrion can take notes for me, and I rest my free hand on top of the heater as it warms up. Together we wait for the arrival of the woman we are to meet.

3

A CLIENT AND A CASE

We have been in the office long enough for me to check my emails when the doorbell rings. According to Karrion's note, this prospective client is punctual. I skirt around Karrion's chair and walk to the door.

Standing there is the woman I encountered yesterday on the dunes. She smiles at my look of surprise, but there is something forced in her expression; a pain that she is trying to hide.

She is dressed in a cream skirt and a matching jacket, her white blouse revealing her curves while remaining tasteful. A pale-green scarf adds the only splash of colour to the outfit and brings out the blue in her eyes. That she and I live worlds apart is as obvious now as it was yesterday. Yet here is a North Mage standing at my door, and from the way she carries herself, she is from one of the aristocratic bloodlines.

Aware that I have stared at her longer than is polite, I step back. 'Please, come in.'

As she walks in, she takes in the posters, and for a brief moment, a brighter smile lifts the lines of worry on her face.

She is not alone. An older woman follows her in. I catch

fleeting scents of nectar and meadow grass underneath Chanel No 5. She has Feykin blood in her, although I cannot tell how much. I wonder if the perfume is meant to disguise her bloodline. Aloof eyes meet mine and I know I am right. The Feykin are even more careful with their secrets than the Wild Folk.

With her long chestnut hair and green eyes, she would be a striking woman even without the magical blood. My first estimate puts her in her late thirties, but her eyes reveal her true age to be greater. How much longevity her ancestry provides her I am not certain, nor is it something I could ask without risking great offence.

There have been no confirmed sightings of the Fair Folk for decades. For most people, the only evidence of the existence of the Fey on the British Isles is the birth of children who are gifted with inhuman grace, beauty, and charm. They are known as Feykin. On the flip side, they are also known for being cunning, irreverent, and unconcerned with social norms; and, unlike other magical people, they rarely congregate.

It is harder to manipulate one of your own kind.

Closing the door behind them, I offer my hand to the younger woman. 'Yannia Wilde.' I pause. 'Obviously.' Did she know who I was yesterday when she watched me through the binoculars?

'Ilana Marsh.' Her hand is soft in mine, but the grip is firm.

She shares a name with the accused in a recent murder case. The charged man was due to appear before a Herald on Saturday morning. Not having had the chance to read the news since then, I am unaware of the verdict. Could that be what has brought her to my door?

Ilana motions to her companion. 'And this is Tanyella Fernlea. She's a... family friend.'

Tanyella remains silent as she too shakes my hand. My

power stirs at the touch of a Feykin, but I keep my expression neutral. Nature lends us both some of her power, though it manifests in different ways. If Tanyella feels the connection, she gives no indication of it. I recall old Wild Folk stories of my kind seeking to take Feykin lovers to feel the merging of our compatible magic. It must be an extraordinary experience.

'Please, sit,' Karrion says as he steps closer and indicates the chairs in front of the desk.

'Meet my apprentice, Karrion.' His pleasure at the title shines in his eyes and I smile at him.

'Aren't you a little young to have an apprentice?' Tanyella asks.

Ilana casts an apologetic glance in my direction. 'I don't think there's an age limit to taking on an apprentice.'

'Karrion has been helping me for some time and he is keen to learn.' I walk around the desk as Karrion shakes hands with both women. From the way he stands up a little straighter, I can tell Ilana has made quite the impression on him. He is not the only one.

For the most part, Karrion's power manifests as an aura around him, which flows and ebbs with his moods like a murmuration of starlings. Detecting the strength of someone's power is a Wild Folk ability, an innate skill rather than something learned. I never knew it was possible until I came to Old London and came into contact with so many different magic users. Now I sense a tempering in Karrion's magic, as he instinctively responds to the social hierarchy within Old London.

While magical folk may be progressive in some ways, such as recognising women as being of equal power with men, in other ways our existence is governed by medieval norms. Old Mage families have held power and authority in Old London since we first emerged as separate races from humans. Paladins, the keepers of order and justice, are a rung lower in the hierarchy. At the bottom are Shamans, regarded as lesser because of the limited scope of their powers, and finally Mages who cannot trace their lineage back through noble houses. Feykin claim individual superiority over others, but as a race, they are too divided to establish a place in the overall hierarchy. And Wild Folk, we are seen as the savages who hide in the remaining forests and eat our kills raw.

While the women are taking their places on the other side of the desk, I sit and tuck the blanket that was on the chair over my legs. Ilana notices this and I look away, unwilling to explain myself.

Once everyone is seated, I lean forward to rest my elbows on the desk. Karrion opens a new document on the computer, fingers poised over the keyboard to note down the conversation.

'What brings you to me?'

Ilana gives me a wan smile. 'I assume you are aware of the murder of Gideor Braeman, the Speaker of the High Council of Mages and the First among the Light Mages?'

'Yes.'

'A Herald of Justice declared my father, Jonathain Marsh, guilty of the murder on Saturday.'

Now her anguish makes perfect sense. Her father will be executed soon. The punishment for a murder committed with the aid of magic is always death.

'I'm sorry.'

She brushes off my condolences with a shake of her head. 'No, you don't understand. My father is innocent.'

Of course, she would want to see her father as innocent, regardless of the Herald's judgement. 'What is it that you want from me?'

'I want to hire you to prove my father's innocence,' Ilana says. 'And to find the person who framed him for the murder.'

'Your father must be guilty. The Heralds are never wrong.'

'I know. But in this instance they are. My father is innocent.'

How many others has she tried to convince? 'What makes you so sure?'

'Because he has an alibi for the time of the murder.'

'But the police ruled it out as unreliable?'

'He has not told the police he has an alibi.'

'Why ever not?'

Ilana's huff indicates that she too has asked that question. 'Apparently, he saw no reason to do so, given that he was innocent. In his mind, there was never any question that he would not be acquitted of all charges. And given that his alibi was of a sensitive nature, he chose to keep quiet.'

Karrion and I exchange a glance. It sounds like odd behaviour from a guilty man. In Marsh's position, most people would have done anything to avoid coming face to face with a Herald of Justice. Not presenting his alibi is scarcely believable. Ilana will need to give me something much more convincing before I believe in Marsh's innocence. The Heralds are infallible.

'What was his alibi?' Karrion asks the question that is on the tip of my tongue. Perhaps the apprenticeship proposal has potential.

'He–'

'Jonathain was with me,' says Tanyella.

I meet Tanyella's stare head on, and her calm eyes invite me to jump to conclusions.

Ilana shifts on her seat. For old Mage families, adultery is still a cause for a major scandal and something to be hidden at all costs. I assume she has not known about the affair long and I direct my next words at her.

'I take it your father is married?'

'Yes.' There is shame in her eyes as she looks at me. 'You

must understand it has for a long time been a marriage of appearances only. But they are appearances my father is keen to maintain, for his own reasons. Had he told the police of his alibi, no doubt word would have reached my mother. There are plenty of people in Old London with sharp hearing and keen tongues.'

She is not wrong. 'But are they appearances he wishes to maintain even now when his life hangs in the balance?'

'He will not be swayed, even though I have implored him to tell.'

'He's always been stubborn,' Tanyella says to Ilana. 'The judgement hasn't changed that.'

From the consternation on Ilana's face, it is clear she wishes it were not so. But if her objections are not enough to change Marsh's mind, there is little she can do.

'He was with you all evening?' I ask Tanyella.

'Yes. He arrived about nine thirty and didn't leave until the following morning. His wife was away visiting relatives in New London. I understand that some of her family have chosen to marry humans.'

Ilana nods to confirm this.

'Is it possible he could have slipped away while your attention was diverted?'

'No.' It is Tanyella's turn to look uncomfortable. 'I assure you that he was fully occupied until the early hours of the morning, long after the murder had been committed.'

'Can you prove it?'

'No.' Tanyella hesitates, but continues. 'He switched off his phone, I did the same, and we took full advantage of his wife being away. We didn't fall asleep until gone three in the morning. Neither of us spoke to anyone, went anywhere, and we were not seen by anyone else.'

'The word of a lover is not much of an alibi.'

Two auras of power flare with their anger, but that was the reaction I was expecting. As far as I can tell, their indignation is genuine. Not for the first time, I wish for a Wild Folk ability that would allow me to sniff out deceit. But in that, I am no different from an ordinary human. Only Paladins can call upon the divine powers to distinguish truth from lies, and even they are constrained by the subject's willingness to speak.

'Jonathain was with me all night, I swear,' Tanyella says.

'Accepting that's the case, why haven't you come forward before now?'

'It was Jonathain's decision. He told me not to. And I admit there are certain factors that mean it was beneficial for me to stay silent.'

From the look Ilana gives Tanyella, I gather this is news to her. I also wonder about Tanyella's motives. Feykin are not known for altruistic actions. She must have an angle in all this.

'Do you have anything else, any concrete proof that your father is innocent?' I ask Ilana.

'No.'

Next to me, Karrion sighs, and although he tries to hide his emotions, I know he feels for Ilana and her father's predicament. But from the tone of his notes, he too is far from convinced. Time to be more direct.

'You must realise how this looks, especially given that it's all happening after the verdict. A mistress coming forward with an alibi to cast doubt over the judgement simply doesn't work with the Heralds. They are never wrong.'

'I will take any lie detector test you want me to, submit to any spell.' Tanyella hesitates, then squares her shoulders and says, 'I'll even declare it publicly for all of Old London to hear.'

A promise like that from a Feykin is far more than I would have expected. Were she to follow through with it, I have no doubt she would lose the benefit of those "certain factors" she is keen to keep hidden. This indicates she has something to gain from Marsh staying alive. Could she care for him, or does he have some other value? Either way, if she is willing to risk that much to stand by an alibi, she may just be telling the truth.

'Why would you, if it harmed your other... interests?'

Tanyella offers me a thin smile. 'I'm well aware of my kind's reputation, but not all of us are heartless monsters. Have I got something to gain by Jonathain avoiding execution? Certainly. The affair has been mutually beneficial, and his political influence has opened many doors for me. Nor has he outlived his usefulness. Likewise, he would not have his seat on the Council without a careful word here and the right introduction there. But ultimately, I have as little desire to see an innocent man executed for murder as you do. And as it wasn't Jonathain who committed the murder, I too wish to know who did.'

It is a shot in the dark from her, but it hits its mark.

'And you would be willing to swear to it in the presence of a Paladin?'

'Gladly,' Tanyella says.

'Let's, for a moment, assume that I believe the alibi. Is your position, therefore, that Jonathain Marsh would have to have been in two places at once to kill Gideor Braeman?'

I notice on the laptop screen that Karrion has written *"Evil twin syndrome?"* and I have just enough self-control to keep my lips from twitching.

'That's right.' Ilana nods. 'At the time of the murder, he was with Tanyella so he cannot be guilty. I've no doubt this is the truth.'

I am still not convinced, but I am intrigued. A lover vouching for a suspect is a weak alibi. The police would have been unlikely to give it much credence. But to not offer it at all is beyond comprehension, and that is what intrigues me the most. A man found guilty will gain nothing by the revelation of an alibi after the judgement, for the indisputable fact is the Herald has declared his guilt.

Jonathain Marsh has been judged guilty.

Leaning back in my chair, I scrutinise the women. This is a much bigger case than I have handled before. Am I up to the challenge? To prove the Heralds wrong? It seems impossible. Just as impossible is the notion that the Heralds could be wrong. They are the very foundation of our justice system and the key to maintaining peaceful cohabitation with humans. Through their infallibility, we can demonstrate that no amount of magic can influence the process of justice. The guilty are punished, the innocent exonerated.

As much as my upbringing rebels against the notion of the Heralds being mistaken, Ilana and Tanyella have sown the seeds of doubt in my mind regarding the Marsh judgement. I want to know more. The thought of failure is a worry, but the opportunity to prove myself as a private investigator tempts me.

When I was growing up, everything I did was defined by the wider context of my family and the conclave as a whole. This could be my chance to show what I can achieve as an adult and a person in my own right. But given my relative inexperience, why did Ilana choose me?

I think I know.

'How many other private investigators in Old London have turned you down?'

Ilana flushes and I know my suspicion is correct. The silence hangs between us.

'Most of them. They all told me the Herald's verdict is unquestionable and that I'm deluding myself about my father's innocence.' There is a tremor of anger in her voice and a glimpse of steel beneath the polished exterior. My curiosity about her intensifies.

'Let me guess: I'm your last choice.' There is no accusation in my tone. I am stating a fact, nothing more.

'I am aware you have less experience than many of the others,' Ilana hedges.

'And that's why you were at the beach yesterday.'

Karrion's head whips around to look at me, and I ignore him.

'Yes. I wanted to learn a little bit more about you first, to see what you were like. I apologise for the subterfuge.'

'You're putting a lot of faith in me. It's understandable that you would do some homework first.'

It is Ilana's turn to lean forward in her chair. 'Will you help me?'

'Yes, I'll take the case.' Ilana opens her mouth to speak, but I stop her by raising my hand. 'Wait. I'm willing to take the case, but you must know that I remain unconvinced regarding your father's innocence. To disprove the infallibility of the Heralds, I'm going to need far more than an alibi from a lover. Indeed, it may be that all I find is that the Herald was right and your father is guilty.'

'He's innocent.'

I shake my head. 'You're not listening, Ms Marsh. What if I spend the next few days scrutinising every aspect of the case and the judgement, only to discover irrefutable evidence of your father's guilt? Will you accept that as the conclusion of my investigation?'

Ilana hesitates, and I see she wants to continue protesting Marsh's innocence. To her credit, she squares her shoulders and meets my gaze. 'If you can disprove his alibi and show beyond any doubt that he's guilty, then yes, I will accept it.'

Perhaps she will, though I doubt in truth she would. But the assurance helps and I nod.

'You must also accept that once I start digging into your lives, there's no guarantee that the things I uncover will be pleasant.'

'I do. Whatever it takes to clear my father's name.'

'In that case, you have yourself a private investigator.'

The relief in Ilana's smile tells me that I have made the right choice. All I can hope for is that I will not have to give her the bad news I fear; that in proving my worth, I can help her and her family.

'What are your rates?'

'Five hundred a day, plus expenses.'

'I'll pay you fifteen hundred a day, plus expenses, if you work for me to the exclusion of all other clients.' Ilana offers me a tight smile and sits up straighter. There is a gathering of power in the room and the hairs on the back of my neck stand up. 'There is little time for my father and this must be done.'

My skin itches at the display of Mage power, but I accept her point and the subtle assertion of authority. From the way Tanyella is keeping a discreet eye on Ilana, I expect she too can sense something of the power next to her.

'When is the execution due to take place?'

'Friday, at noon.'

She is right, there is little time. That gives me only four days to succeed or fail in the assignment. On the other hand, six thousand will pay the rent and the bills for a good while, and I have very little scheduled for this week. I can give Ilana's case my undivided attention without alienating my other clients.

'Deal.' I stand and offer her my hand. She also stands and the gathered power fades away. I wish I could prolong the handshake, but as both Tanyella and Karrion are watching us, I let go and return to my seat.

'What evidence did the police have against your father?' Karrion asks.

'They found a shirt and a ritual dagger covered in Gideor's blood at the back of my father's wardrobe, in a plastic bag.

Gideor phoned my father shortly before he left our home that night. It is my understanding that they argued.'

'About what?' I ask.

'About me.' Ilana's teeth begin to worry her lower lip.

Tanyella leans towards her to rest a hand on her arm. 'This is not your fault.'

'I know that,' Ilana says, but she sounds far from convinced.

I am intrigued by the exchange, but I hold back the questions and wait for one of them to elaborate. Once she has regained her composure, Ilana does so.

'As I'm sure you know, we Mages receive most of our training from the elders of our own school of magic. Towards the end, there is a secondment period during which we learn from the other types of Mages. When it came to Light, I was one of a select few to receive tuition from the Head of the school himself.'

'Gideor Braeman?'

'Indeed. My father holds one of the North Mage seats in the Council and as such has considerable influence when it comes to tutors. He wanted nothing but the best for me.' Ilana's expression twists into a grimace as she runs a hand over her eyes. 'That was when the trouble started.'

'What do you mean?'

'It turns out Gideor favours a certain type of student: young, beautiful women. They would receive... private lessons.'

'He wanted to sleep with you?'

'He did. I said no.' Her lips tighten into a thin line, colour bleeding from them. 'And I told my father about his advances.'

'What happened?'

'Pretty much what I expected. My father pulled me from Gideor's lessons, threatened exposure of his appetites to the Council if Gideor did not leave me alone, and found me a less lecherous tutor. And that, I thought, would be the end of it.'

'Until Gideor was murdered and your father was arrested?'

'Yes.'

'Did Gideor try to contact you after he came on to you?'

'He tried, but I refused to see him or accept his calls.'

I glance at Karrion and see in his eyes that we are thinking the same thing. 'Did you tell your father?'

'No. I didn't want to cause any more trouble since I had already resumed my studies under a different teacher.'

'Is it possible someone else told your father?'

She opens her mouth to answer, but reconsiders her words. 'I suppose one of the household staff could have told him.'

'Your father has motive.' Again, Ilana's and Tanyella's anger flares, but it does little to deter me. 'Either your father is guilty or he is the perfect scapegoat.'

'Jonathain may have had motive for murder,' Tanyella says, 'but not for the theft. He had no financial problems.'

'Theft?'

'The night Gideor was killed,' says Ilana, 'certain magical artefacts were stolen from his study. And two days after the murder, ten thousand pounds was wired to my father's personal account from an offshore bank. The amount matches the price that two protection scarabs were sold for in an online auction earlier that day. But my father didn't steal anything; he's not a thief, or a murderer.'

'What about the fees?'

'What fees?'

'Auction fees. If something was sold for ten grand, the seller would get the sale price less the auction fees.'

'Perhaps the buyer paid for them?' Ilana suggests.

'Perhaps.'

Ilana glances at the gold Cartier watch on her wrist and opens her purse to get out a chequebook. 'Is an advance payment for the first two days acceptable?'

'Certainly.' I watch her write the cheque with a Montblanc fountain pen. This is the first time I have received such a sum. 'Thank you.'

'Is there anything else you need from me? I have a meeting with my family's solicitor.'

'Some way to contact you.'

Ilana hands me a business card printed on heavy vellum.

'I'll want to talk to the staff at your family home at some point soon,' I say as they both rise.

'What about?'

'About the shirt and dagger. If someone has framed your father for murder, they must have gained access to his bedroom to plant the evidence. Perhaps a staff member remembers seeing or hearing something.'

'The staff will be yours to interview whenever suits you best.'

'I may also need to speak to you again about the alibi,' I say to Tanyella, and she also hands me a business card.

I walk them to the door, but instead of grasping the doorhandle, Ilana lays her hand on my arm.

'Thank you for helping my father.'

'I haven't done anything yet,' I reply. 'And you must understand that I may not be able to help.'

'At least you're willing to try, which is more than can be said for anyone else I've approached.'

'I'll keep you updated with my progress,' I say. I open the door for them. Ilana's hand slips away and I miss the warmth of it.

'We'll speak soon,' she says.

I watch them as they walk up the narrow stairs and out of sight. Once again, I cannot help but wonder if Ilana found what she was looking for.

4

BACKGROUND

After closing the door, I return to my chair and collect the blanket that has ended up on the floor. Karrion is going through his notes, adding details while they are fresh in his mind. I watch him until his attention turns to me.

'Shall we run to the bank?' He points at the cheque with a grin.

I laugh at his practicality and he joins in. It feels good to lighten the mood.

'I'm more interested in hearing your ideas for our first move.'

Karrion taps his index finger against the edge of the keyboard. 'We could talk to Jonathain Marsh?'

'And what information do you think we would get from him?' I keep my tone neutral, neither approving nor condemning his suggestion.

'A confession?' At my cocked eyebrow, he rethinks his response. 'More detail about the night. And we could check whether what Tanyella says about his alibi marries with his own account.'

'Why wouldn't it, when they have discussed it during his

imprisonment? But we could ask about the phone call he had with Braeman on the night of the murder.'

'I hadn't thought of that,' Karrion says, his expression growing worried.

'Don't worry about it. That's why we're talking about this. We both have different ideas about what to do first.'

'And your idea would be?'

'Get a copy of the case file for Braeman's murder.'

'Can we do that?'

'We'll see. I know a detective inspector at New Scotland Yard who might be able to help. I'll give him a call.'

Karrion nods. 'If that's your first move, what about me?'

'I do believe you said something about going to the bank.'

He laughs, and I complete a paying-in slip for the office account. Instead of leaving, he pulls one leg up on to the edge of his chair to rest his chin on his knee.

'Do you think he's innocent?'

'I don't know,' I say, each word slow as I mirror his posture. 'It's impossible, and yet his actions don't strike me as those of a guilty man. But showing that a Herald can cast an incorrect verdict is a huge task. Proving it to the rest of the world, harder still. I suspect this will be an interesting case.'

'Do you think we'll be able to prove his innocence or guilt?'

'Again, I don't know. But you heard Ilana, we're her last hope. If we hadn't taken the case, Marsh would die for sure. The least we can do is see if there's any doubt. If there is, I'm going to try my best to find proof of Marsh's innocence.'

'Me too.' He stands and walks to the door before hesitating again. 'What happened yesterday?'

'What do you mean?' I scroll to the beginning of his notes and look at him over the laptop screen.

'You met Ilana.'

'I didn't know who she was at the time.'

'What happened?'

'She was at the beach, watching me run. We had a strange conversation, where she expressed admiration for my powers and identified herself as a Mage. She was checking out a potential private investigator.'

'Is that it?'

I frown, puzzled. 'What more should there be?'

'I don't know. I just caught the vibe that she made quite an impression on you.'

'Yes, she did. Don't you have an errand to run?'

'I'm going, I'm going.' With a wave of his hand, he slips out of the door and I am left alone in the office.

Having reviewed Karrion's notes and made a few additions, I scroll through the contacts on my mobile phone until I find the one I need. My thumb hesitates over the call button.

All police departments across the country employ Mages to detect spells and other magical effects at crime scenes. Among the human staff, there are some who focus on crimes with magical elements. Detective Inspector Jamie Manning is one of them. We have met a few times and he seems like a fair man. But from the first time we were introduced, I have known why he has chosen to specialise in magical crimes.

Whenever we meet, he looks at me with longing. It is not longing for me, but rather for what I am, what I represent. Humans want what they cannot have, even if they do not fully appreciate what it is they desire. Having magic comes with consequences they cannot fathom.

Overcoming my hesitation, I tap the button. The call connects after four rings.

'Manning.'

'Jamie, hi, it's Yannia Wilde.'

'Yannia Wilde.' He tastes my name, and I hear the longing.

'And what is it that I can do for you, Yannia? Are you calling to report a crime?'

'Nothing like that. I need a favour.'

'And what might that favour be?' There is wary curiosity in his tone.

'I wondered if you could email me a copy of a closed murder case file. It would be interesting to study it to see what the process of gathering evidence, following leads, and building a case against a suspect is like from your point of view.'

'Study, eh? Would you happen to have a particular closed case in mind?'

Crossing the fingers of my free hand, I take the plunge. 'As a matter of fact, I do. Gideor Braeman's murder.'

Jamie barks out a disbelieving laugh. 'Christ, Yannia. You don't waste time. That file is barely closed.'

'I figured it would be topical.'

'Is that so?' he begins, and I know he doesn't believe me. 'What's really going on?'

There is a pause in the conversation while I debate my options. I have to give him something. If he thinks I am lying, he will refuse to help.

'I don't know, maybe nothing. Perhaps I'm chasing a ghost.'

'Given that ghosts are real, what sort of ghost?'

'An impossible one.'

'An impossible ghost in connection with the murder of Gideor Braeman... You have me intrigued.'

Another pause follows. While I wait, I hear a door open and the noises of New Scotland Yard cascade into the office. Phones ring, and there is a steady murmur of voices in the distance. Jamie thanks someone, and the door closes. I bite my lip, hoping that the prospect of a magical murder being revisited will be too much for him to resist. It is just the sort of case he likes.

'Okay. I'll pull some strings and get you the file. Strictly speaking, I should wait until the execution has been carried out, but I don't suppose there's any harm since the verdict's been given.'

My smile colours my words. 'Thanks, Jamie. I owe you one.'

'I'll bear that in mind. It shouldn't take more than a couple of hours for the file to reach you.'

I thank him again, recite my email address and we end the call. It's a good start.

While I wait for the file, I open a browser on the laptop. Time to do some research into Gideor Braeman.

By the time Karrion returns, I know far more about the victim than I did before.

Gideor Braeman was fifty-three when he died, married with two daughters. From the photos I find, he was a striking figure with deep-blue eyes, dark hair that was greying at the temples, and a salt-and-pepper beard. He was rich, but not descended from one of the old Mage families. The articles indicate that the family's wealth came from human companies and that Braeman maintained close ties with the human communities in New London and elsewhere in Britain. He had been the Speaker of the High Council of Mages for the past six years. In that time, he used the influence of the position to campaign for better control in the use of magic.

According to a recent statement he published, his concern was a divide between humans and people with magic; between Old London and New London. I find an excerpt of it online:

> It is no secret that crimes are easier to commit with magic. The police and the Paladins of Justice are working to combat that, but when it comes to prevention, we are not there yet. As hard as we are working, what is harder to change is the perception of ordinary people. If humans believe we are above the law, nothing good will ensue. At present, we co-exist in peace, but it is the nature of people – human and magical – to fear what they cannot understand. And fear is no foundation for a future.
>
> I propose greater control and therefore greater security for us all. By working together to build trust and acceptance, we will all prosper.

He had a point. As much as humans and magical races co-exist peacefully, we are forever aware that humans outnumber us a thousand to one. Magic makes us dangerous, just as the human masses make them dangerous. To control the masses, we must be seen to control our magic.

So Braeman campaigned for greater accountability and more restrictions. From the comments I read online, it did not make him popular with everyone. But could it be motive for murder? Marsh appears to have supported Braeman's campaign. Whatever their disagreements, they did not extend to their political views.

The chill of the office seeps into my bones despite the blanket and the radiator, and I am about to move upstairs with the laptop when Karrion lets himself in. I make a show of looking at the clock on the wall and he grins.

'Was everyone in Old London at the bank this morning?'

'Nope. No queues at all.'

'What happened? Did you walk around the whole city before cashing that cheque?'

'Nope, not that either.' His grin widens, and I experience a flash of sympathy for his mother. Obtuse Karrion is infuriating.

To avoid strangling him, I leave the room. He follows me, of course, but I ignore him as I leave the laptop on an armchair in the lounge and continue on to the kitchen. I want a hot drink to chase away the chill of the office. While the kettle boils, I get a mug out of the cupboard, drop a blueberry-and-apple teabag into it and add a spoonful of honey.

Karrion tolerates the silence until I am pouring water into the mug.

'The cashier at the bank was a friend of Mum's,' he says, and makes himself a cup of English breakfast tea. My conscience twinges at not having prepared his drink with mine, but I am not feeling polite.

'Is that so?' I carry my mug to the lounge.

He follows me. 'She was keen to catch up, and she knows all the gossip in Old London.'

This gets my attention, and he laughs.

'Did you really think I would have wasted all this time chatting to someone I barely know about the weather?'

'Who knows? She could share your irrational hatred of pigeons.'

'For the record, there's nothing irrational about that.'

I raise an eyebrow, but Karrion ignores me.

'And I learned some pretty interesting things about Gideor Braeman.'

'Go on, spill.'

He makes a show of spilling some of his tea. Then he relents and carries on talking.

'His wife of more than two decades is an East Mage. Light

and East is an unusual match, but apparently, these two married for love. Whether you believe that or not is up to you. They have two daughters, but I hear only one carries magical blood and she is an East Mage. No amount of training has enabled the elder to access her power. It was a bit of a scandal some years back.'

'Inheriting powers can be unpredictable, especially if the parents carry different types of blood.' I swirl the tea in my mug. 'But it must be tough for the only person in the family without magic.'

'I guess. Carita, the elder, went to university in New London and now works abroad as part of Doctors Without Borders.'

'She has found meaning for her life elsewhere,' I say, with a mixture of sympathy and respect.

Karrion watches me over the rim of his mug. 'Sometimes you have to leave everything you know to figure out who you are.'

I offer him an uneasy smile before steering him back on track. My past is not a topic I wish to discuss. 'Did your chatty friend say anything else?'

The twist of his lips tells me he knows what I am doing. 'They are a family of appearances. Mrs Braeman spends all her time fundraising for a children's charity called Lifelines. Mr Braeman liked to be seen as a doting husband and a proud patriarch of a successful family, but the couple may not have been quite as happy as they liked to show in public. It didn't go unnoticed that when Braeman took on students, they tended to be young, beautiful women.'

'That ties in with Ilana's story.'

'She's certainly young and beautiful.'

'And a woman. Well noticed.'

'Hey, I'm just saying.'

'Me too.' I finish my tea and set the mug next to the laptop. 'So Braeman liked young women. I wonder if his wife knew.'

'If a bank teller knows, I find it hard to imagine Braeman's wife didn't. Although I suppose it's possible she chose not to listen to the rumours. But if she's well aware of her husband's adulterous nature, that could be motive for murder.'

'Indeed.' I summarise what I discovered about Braeman online.

'Speaker of the High Council of Mages must be a prestigious position to hold,' says Karrion.

'It is. Braeman held the position much longer than other Speakers in recent times. He proved to be a unifying force among the Council, even if not everyone agreed with his agenda to impose stricter controls on the use of magic.'

'From what I heard, if Braeman had got his way, we'd all have to fill out a form and apply for permission before casting even the simplest of spells.' Karrion takes our mugs to the kitchen and asks over his shoulder, 'Who's taken over from him?'

'Just a second.' I open the laptop and call up my notes. One of the articles had mentioned the name and I wrote it down. 'Lord Wellaim Ellensthorne.'

'Oh, him.' Karrion leans against the kitchen doorframe, the corners of his mouth pulling down in distaste.

'Do you know anything about him?'

'He's rich.' His tone implies that the short statement explains everything, but a pointed look encourages him to elaborate. 'He has a large house in Old London and at least one landed estate somewhere else. Lots of serving staff. Mum applied for a cleaning job there a while back and she said the whole household had a strange feel to it. She didn't get the job; maybe Ellensthorne didn't want a Shaman scrubbing his floors.

And although she needed the money, Mum told me later that she was glad not to have been hired.'

'He sounds like a real delight.'

'At least not all the old Mage families are like that. Mum found a job elsewhere and she was all the happier for it.'

I have met Karrion's mother a few times, and she has always been welcoming, if tired. Her mouth smiles as she makes tea and offers me homemade biscuits, but her eyes are haunted by too many things.

Karrion's father died when Karrion was ten. From what little he has told me, I understand it was some kind of accident at a construction site. Bird Shamans make good construction workers because they have no fear of heights, but their magic cannot turn them into a bird should they fall. His mother remarried for a time, but her second husband migrated south with the swallows, leaving her with three toddlers. Since then, Karrion's mother has worked two jobs to feed him and his siblings. They all live in a small flat on Bride Lane. Karrion as the eldest had an evening and weekend job all through his teenage years to help make ends meet. University was a bit of a break for him because an art foundation paid for his tuition, but even then he kept his job so his studies would not cause an additional financial burden. Since he graduated a month and a half ago, he has been temping while looking for a job that will pay a little more than the minimum wage, but they are not easy to come by with a fine art degree.

Which reminds me, if I am going to follow through with my hasty decision to take Karrion on as an apprentice, I will need to make sure I pay him a fair salary. He still lives at home and I know that most of what he earns goes towards paying the bills and buying clothes and books for his younger siblings. The piercings and goth clothes seem to be his sole luxury.

Lost in my thoughts, I am struck by his strength. His life has not been easy, and yet he is nothing but positive and keen to get ahead. Many would have become embittered in his place, whereas all he wants to do is help those he cares about. I seem to fall into that category. It is only fair that I return the favour.

'Do you mind running another errand for me?' I ask as I walk across the room and get my wallet out of my rucksack.

'Sure, what do you need?'

'Can you grab us some sushi for lunch?' His eyes light up at the suggestion. 'My fridge is pretty empty, and the last thing I need right now is to have to explain to your mother why I'm not feeding my apprentice properly. We have a lot of work ahead of us.'

'No problem, though I have some money–'

'My treat.' When I see he is about to object, I press the notes into his hand. 'It's your first day and all, which calls for a celebration. Get the good stuff, and I don't want to see any change when you come back.'

He slips the folded notes into his pocket. 'Thanks, Yan.'

'You know what, I think this apprenticeship business could be good for both of us.'

His smile deepens as he nods. 'I agree. And to solve our first case together, all we need to do is prove the impossible. How hard can it be?'

5

CASE FILE

We are just clearing away chopsticks and wasabi packets when my laptop pings to announce the arrival of a new email. Without a word, Karrion takes the plastic sushi platters from me and heads for the kitchen while I open my email.

'It's from Jamie,' I call out to him. 'He managed to get me a copy of the file, though he says there is a report that hasn't been released yet in their system. He will forward it when he can.'

'Can you print what you've got? That way we can scrawl our own notes in the margins and I don't have to read the whole thing over your shoulder.'

'Good idea. I'll skip the photos as my printer isn't going to do justice to those. I'll be back in a bit.' As I pick up the laptop, I reconsider my words. 'Well, given how slow the printer is, I may be a while.'

'I'll put a pot of coffee on to brew.'

By the time I return upstairs with a stack of papers and my laptop, Karrion is nowhere to be seen, but the lounge window is wide open. I look out and smile. It's a warm, sunny afternoon; the autumn is granting us a short reprieve before the turn of the seasons. Karrion has laid out a blanket on my small patch of lawn. On it are cushions off the armchairs and a tray with two coffee mugs and a packet of ginger snaps. A pigeon lands on the shed roof and Karrion glares at it. When he sees me through the window, he beckons me out.

'It's too beautiful a day to spend in your damp office.'

I pull off my two pairs of socks and swing my legs out of the window. The grass is cool and soft under my feet and I take a moment to wriggle my toes. Elsewhere, in a different life, I would spend most of the summer days walking barefoot along forest paths and meadows. But not here, not in the city. The ground is cold, unyielding; just another reminder of the differences between the past and the present.

'Are you okay?'

At Karrion's words, I yank my head up. I have been staring at my feet, rooted to the spot outside the window. A sharp shake of my head ought to dislodge my dark thoughts, but some of the disquiet lingers as I step over the paving stones to the edge of the blanket.

'I'm fine.'

'Is the pain bad? Do you want me to get meds for you?'

'The pain is fine. I was just thinking about stuff.'

'About home?'

I am about to sit down on a cushion, but Karrion's question freezes me. 'What makes you think I was thinking about home?'

He pauses, choosing his words with care. 'Because you looked completely lost.'

It is my turn to pause as I debate whether to lie. Truth wins out. 'Yeah, I was thinking about home.'

'Why don't you go back for a visit? I know it's far, but it's not that far.'

I imagine driving through the familiar countryside, leaving the car at the edge of the forest and walking the rest of the way. For a brief moment, I am back there. The trees tower over me, the wind caresses my cheek, and the path I am walking is a dappled pattern of light and shadows. In that place, no magic is required to sift through the scents in the air. They all mean one thing: home. But I need only to think of the whiff of decay on the Elderman's breath to remember why I am in London. I need only to think of the night before I left the conclave to remember why I will not return until I must.

Some of my thoughts must show on my face, for a warm hand closes around mine and tugs me down on to the blanket.

'If I go back now,' I whisper at our clasped hands, 'I'm not sure I'd be able to leave again. I must stay away while I still can.'

He understands, to some extent.

'It's not just that I miss the conclave, it's the conflict between my nature and my need to be in the city. Living here is harder than I thought.'

'There must be a compromise between the conclave and London?'

'I don't know if I have time to find one.'

'What about Dearon?'

At the mention of the name, I recoil and pull my hand from Karrion's grasp. 'Don't.'

On the night of Karrion's graduation, we drank too much cheap wine and I told him things I later regretted. I cannot, I will not, discuss Dearon with him. Karrion tries to object, but I silence him with a stern glare. 'We have a case to focus on and a man who will be executed in a few short days for a crime he may not have committed. Let's focus on what's important.'

Karrion looks like he is going to argue and I square my shoulders, ready for a fight. But he exhales his frustration, perhaps sensing that this is not an argument he is going to win. No doubt he will try again later.

'What did this Jamie bloke send us?'

I indicate the pile of papers. I glanced through the contents of the file while my printer churned out the pages and they are for the most part in a coherent order. Jamie has sent me a summary of the crime-scene findings, a key to the crime-scene photos, the coroner's report, the findings of the police regarding Marsh, a list of other suspects or persons of interest, transcripts of the interviews they conducted, and a summary of the evidence against Marsh that was presented to the Crown Prosecutor and the Paladins of Justice.

'How do you want to do this?' he asks.

'Why don't you take half of these papers and read through them, while I take the other half. We can summarise what we've read, and if needs be, swap material. Once we've gone through the file, we can take a look at the crime-scene photos on the laptop.'

'Sounds like a plan.'

He holds out his hand and I divide the pile into two, giving him the lower half. After a quick flick through the pages, Karrion stands and disappears inside, soon returning with two pens.

'We did want to make notes, didn't we?'

'Already you're doing a great job as an apprentice,' I say as I take one of the pens.

'It's the hair.' He winks at me and brushes back his black hair. His natural hair colour is dark, but he has added a blue tint to it. The colour suits him, although I find teasing him far too amusing to ever admit this out loud.

'Sure. That's why I've done so well too.' Wisps of my brown hair have escaped the braid and they tickle my nose in the gentle breeze.

'Knew it.'

I glance at the papers on his lap and he takes the hint. He

grabs a cushion, tilts back until he is lying on the blanket and begins to read.

The sun is warm on my face, and I unzip my fleece as I get more comfortable on a cushion. My feet are cold despite the warmth of the day and I tuck them under the corner of the blanket. I am tempted to curl up and take a nap in the sun, but the case is a priority and I reach for my coffee instead. After a few moments of reading, my fatigue is a thing of the past and I am fully focused on the notes.

By the time I have gone through my share of the papers, my coffee is finished and Karrion's is cold. Even the ginger snaps have not distracted him from the file, and I have demonstrated considerable self-restraint in not eating them all. When he jots down a final note in the margin and looks up, I set my pen down.

'Ready to share?' I ask.

'I think so.'

'Shall I go first?'

'Sure.' He tries to hide his nerves with a grin. 'Amaze me.'

I summarise the coroner's findings. The cause of death was a single stab wound to the heart. Magic was used to power the stab through the ribs, and several were broken. Braeman bled out slowly, too slowly to be wholly natural, though neither the coroner nor the Mage knew why. The weapon was a narrow, slightly curved blade that tapered into a tip, and one side was serrated. A series of shallow cuts were carved into the victim's chest as part of a ritual identified as a North Mage curse for a painful afterlife. Those cuts also bled less than they should have done.

'There is a note that the coroner wanted to run further analysis on the wound and the suspected murder weapon, but I can't see any results back yet,' I say.

'Isn't it strange that the case went before a Herald when there were still test results outstanding?'

'It is. There's probably a backlog at the lab and those tests weren't considered crucial for building a case against Marsh.'

'Anything else in the coroner's report?' Karrion asks.

'Spermicide from a condom indicates that Braeman had sex shortly before his death.'

'That's curious.' Karrion shuffles through the stack of papers. 'I have a statement here from Braeman's wife Viola stating that they had a lunch meeting at the Savoy to discuss an upcoming event for the Lifelines charity, and upon returning home, they went their separate ways. That was the last time she saw her husband alive.'

'Either she's lying or her husband slept with someone else that day.'

'Which do you think is more likely?'

'Without knowing much about the people involved, it's hard to say. But my gut instinct says Braeman was sleeping around.' I pause and take another biscuit. 'Well, specifically sleeping around on the day he died.'

'When did he have time? According to the statements from various people in the house that day, his whereabouts are accounted for. I don't think he had time to leave for a tryst somewhere.'

'The crime-scene photos might provide an answer to that.' I open the laptop's cover and unzip the folder of photos Jamie sent me. A quick scan through the serial numbers and I find the one I want. 'Take a look at this.'

The photo shows a view of the study where Braeman was killed. While it is difficult to get a true sense of dimensions from a photograph, it is clear that the room is huge. At the forefront are two desks facing opposite walls, a glass-fronted cabinet with its doors open, and a body on the floor. But for now, my attention is drawn to the far end, where a large bed sits next to an arrangement of armchairs, a sofa, and a coffee table. The bed has a burgundy cover across it. At a casual glance, there is nothing odd about it. Now, though, I wonder how recently the bed was used and for what.

'Who has a bed in their study?' Karrion asks, awed. 'And who calls an enormous hall like that a study in the first place?'

'Money can buy an awful lot.'

He nods. 'And both Gideor and Viola come from money.'

'Braeman might not have needed to leave the house to have an affair.'

Karrion picks out a page from his stack. 'And the Master of the House, the guy in charge of all the household staff, noted in his statement that Braeman's study had a separate entrance.'

'So anyone could have entered or left without the rest of the household knowing?'

'Looks that way.'

'Any sign of forced entry?'

'I don't think so.' Karrion checks his notes and shakes his head. I can see his small scrawl on the margins, covering most of the free space.

'Which means that Braeman knew the killer or that person had a key. Either way, there's unlikely to be any eyewitnesses to our murderer coming or going, whether it was Marsh or someone different.'

'Funny you should say that because the police received an anonymous call which stated that someone matching Marsh's general description was seen coming out of the door leading to the study, looking nervous and shifty.'

'What time was that?' I ask, and it is my turn to go through the papers.

'About ten thirty.'

'The coroner's report puts Braeman's time of death somewhere between ten and ten forty-five.'

'That's a pretty convenient eyewitness account.'

I can hear the "but" coming.

'The police traced the call to a payphone on the far side of Old London,' says Karrion.

'What sort of a person witnesses something suspicious and waits until they are miles from the scene to report it to the police?'

'Someone with something to hide?'

'How long would it take someone to walk from the Braeman house to that payphone?'

'My guess would be between twenty and thirty minutes. A bus or a taxi would be quicker. None of the Underground lines go in the right direction.'

'So someone could have witnessed Marsh or someone else acting suspiciously during the time-of-death window and reported it at ten thirty.'

'They could have done,' Karrion agrees. 'Or it's an easy way to throw suspicion in Marsh's direction.'

'Or it could be a double bluff.' My head is beginning to ache and I rub my temples. 'Any chance that the payphone was covered by a CCTV camera?'

'No, it's in a blind spot.'

'Coincidence?'

'I doubt it,' Karrion says.

'Me too.' My attention returns to the papers on my lap. 'The scenes of crime officers matched all the prints found at the scene to Braeman, his PA, his family or household staff.'

'Meaning the killer wore gloves.'

'Or he wasn't concerned with leaving prints because there would be another explanation for them being there.'

'Or that. I have here a summary of the household staff.'

I take the sheet from him and scan through it. Braeman's PA is a man called Reaoul Pearson, a fellow Light Mage who had been his student before taking up the position of assistant. He has been employed by Braeman for five years. The Master of the House, Simon Underhill, has served the Braeman family for more than four decades and his conduct has always been impeccable. There are also three maids, a chef, two drivers, and Viola's secretary, on the payroll. All the household staffs' whereabouts have been verified.

'Does the PA, Reaoul Pearson, have an alibi?' I ask as I hand back the sheet.

'He was home by nine thirty. Both his wife and a neighbour he met outside the building confirmed that.'

'And Viola?'

'She was in her office until ten thirty, speaking with the chairman of the Lifelines charity. A maid served her a cup of chamomile tea, a nightly ritual, and she went to bed.'

I am about to ask another question, but Karrion indicates that I should wait.

'Both daughters were elsewhere that night. With family and staff all having alibis, it's likely the killer was someone Braeman knew and invited into his study.'

'Someone like Marsh,' I say. 'Braeman's phone records indicate that he called Marsh at about eight forty-five. The call lasted for three minutes. That would have given Marsh plenty of time to travel across Old London and murder Braeman.'

'Except that he has an alibi,' Karrion says.

My response is a non-committal shrug.

'You're not convinced by the alibi, are you?'

'Not really. There's plenty of evidence to indicate his guilt.'

'What led the police to Marsh?' Karrion asks, and reaches for his coffee cup. I am too slow to warn him about the cold coffee and his expression indicates that he does not appreciate the surprise. He swallows with a grimace and reaches for a biscuit. 'I noticed his name came up in the PA's statement.'

'That statement pointed the police in Marsh's direction. Apparently, Marsh and Braeman had a loud argument about Ilana, like she said. And the PA thought the description given by the anonymous tip matched Marsh. After they saw Braeman's phone records, the police went to talk to Marsh. He refused to tell them where he had been during the murder and didn't appreciate the questioning, which led the police to speculate that he had something to hide. The detective got a warrant to search his home and they found a bag in his wardrobe that contained the murder weapon and a shirt covered in Braeman's blood. The assumption was that he had intended to dispose of them later, but the police got on to him too fast.'

'Even if that's the case, it's pretty stupid of him to have brought the murder weapon back to his home.'

I rub my eyes. 'I agree. From what I've seen, the police had it pretty easy with Marsh.'

'Were there any other suspects?'

'No one viable. The police also considered the other Council members, but before they got beyond the briefest of enquiries, they had begun connecting the dots to Marsh.'

Karrion picks up another biscuit, changes his mind and gives it to me. From his expression, I can tell something is bothering him.

'Is it just me or was it all a little too easy?'

'You think he was framed?'

He nods.

'Me too. Or else he's the most incompetent murderer in the history of Old London.'

There it is, the first sign of doubt I have been looking for. It is not much, but it fuels my desire to keep digging until I uncover the truth. There is more to this case than meets the eye, too many questions raised and not answered. All this when we have only skimmed the surface.

'But if he was framed,' Karrion taps his knee with the pen, 'it means someone thought about killing Braeman long and hard. Marsh makes for a pretty convincing scapegoat, but the killer must have known not just about his argument with Braeman, but also about his routines.'

'Including when he spent time with his mistress?'

'Including that,' Karrion says. 'I've no doubt there are people in Old London who know about his indiscretions. That sort of thing never stays a secret for long. Framing Marsh was a good plan and the police swallowed it hook, line, and sinker.'

I brush biscuit crumbs off my lap. 'But you're forgetting one thing: the police had their theory confirmed when the Herald declared Marsh guilty of the murder.'

'And that's what doesn't make any sense about this case. The Heralds are infallible.'

Gathering my papers, I stand. 'There's our challenge. If we want to solve this case, we'll have to find out not just who killed Gideor Braeman, but also how the Herald condemned an innocent man.'

6

EARLY STEPS

I take the tray of coffee mugs back into the kitchen and get myself a glass of water. When I return to the garden, Karrion is where I left him, flipping through the pages I had been going through.

'What does the magic report say?' I ask as I settle back on to my cushion.

'An East Mage confirmed that magic had been used for the killing blow and that a North Mage curse had been cast. She also thought there might have been some other magical interference, but she could not pinpoint the specific effect. The report notes that it was hard to identify which spells related to the crime because there was too much background power in the study. Apparently, the cabinet next to the body contained a collection of spell books, none of which had been disturbed, but it also held an unusually large number of magical artefacts, most of which were designed to store power for later use.'

'That's not unheard of with a Mage of Braeman's standing.'

'No, but the East Mage thought it was worth noting in her report.'

'I haven't seen enough Mage reports to know whether any of this is usual or not.' My doubts resurface. 'I hope I haven't made a terrible mistake in agreeing to take on this case with so little experience.'

'How else are you going to learn?' Karrion reaches over to brush his fingers across my knuckles. 'Besides, I think you're far better at your job than you give yourself credit for.'

'I hope so, for Jonathain Marsh's sake.' Fatigue washes over me, despite the coffee, but I push it aside. I have no time to be tired. 'We need to find out more about the judgement.'

'Have you ever seen a Herald of Justice?'

'Sure,' I say. 'There was a murder judgement soon after I moved to London. I'd heard stories about the courts of Old London and I went to see it. It was quite something to witness.'

'I know what you mean. I attended a judgement as soon as I turned eighteen. But I never expected to feel so small in the presence of the Herald.'

'Isn't the seating always in the upper galleries?'

'Yes. I don't mean physically. It's more that I felt as though he dwarfed everyone else in the room. I couldn't say whether it was deliberate or not, but the Herald seemed more real, more present than the rest of us. I know there are people who doubt the existence of the Heralds, but in that moment, it was my own existence that I doubted.'

'It's hard to deny the Heralds are real when you watch one of them step through a portal into the courtroom. But my experience of them was very different.'

'How?' Karrion pushes himself up until he is sitting cross-legged opposite me.

I cast my thoughts back to that afternoon in the courtroom. It had been a confusing time for me; I was new to Old London, trying to get used to the environment that sapped my power at a steady rate, to the numbness caused by the pain medication I had been prescribed, and to living on my own. Witnessing the arrival of the Herald had felt unreal. I had spent far more power than I could spare trying to catch the scent of him. Even though I had been successful to a point, the myriad of smells had defied all attempts at identification. I can still remember them, but there are no words to describe his scent, except perhaps that it was otherworldly.

'This may sound crazy, but it felt like the most natural thing in the world. He belonged, he made sense. Even if he wasn't from this plane, he was exactly what he was meant to be.' I push loose strands of hair from my face. 'It's as if the Heralds have reached a state of harmony that we are still grasping towards.'

'And therein lies the difference between a Shaman and one of the Wild Folk. You always see the bigger picture.'

'Not always.' I shake my head with a rueful chuckle. 'And sometimes the last thing I want to see is the bigger picture.'

Karrion looks like he is about to ask me to elaborate, and I bring us back on track. 'We need to find out more about that judgement. What do you suggest?'

He thinks for a moment, straightening the papers on his lap. 'We could talk to Ilana and see if she noticed anything out of the ordinary.' Although he tries to keep his tone neutral, I catch a tremor of eagerness and suppress a smile.

'And what do you think she would say? What was she focused on?'

'Her father.' He dips his chin. 'It's unlikely she noticed anything beyond him and his reactions. Not a great idea.'

'The idea is good,' I say, 'but we need to talk to someone else who was there; someone who has seen a great many judgements over the years.'

A frown appears between Karrion's eyebrows as he thinks. 'Do you think the Mage presiding over the judgement would talk to us?'

'It's possible, though I was thinking more about getting in touch with the Paladin who summoned the Herald. If there was anything fishy about the judgement, he ought to know.'

Karrion nods, eyes growing distant as he pulls his phone out and begins tapping. I am assuming he is doing something other than checking his emails, so I wait and watch. After a while, a grin lights his face and he puts the phone away.

'I was right.'

My only response is a tilt of my head, inviting him to explain.

'There was a news article about the courts of Old London a little while back and I've just found it online. A section of it talks about accountability, about how magic shouldn't be able to sway the judgement. To satisfy the government in New London and New Scotland Yard, the courtroom has CCTV. Every judgement is recorded.'

'Fantastic.' My grin matches his. 'We get hold of the recording and see for ourselves.'

'As soon as we figure out how. I don't know if the Paladins keep the archive of footage or if it's stored somewhere else.'

'Let that be your next challenge. Find out who we need to contact and what hoops we need to jump through to get the recording. While you're doing that, I'll track down the name of the Paladin at that judgement and try to set up a meeting with him or her.'

'Check us being all Roman,' Karrion says with a chuckle.

'Roman?'

'You know, divide and conquer.'

'I see. It's helpful sharing the workload with someone.'

'I won't let you down, Yan.'

'I never thought you would.'

We regard each other. Karrion is the first to look away,

clearing his throat as he rubs his neck. It may be my imagination, but there seems to be a hint of heat on his cheeks.

'Shall we get to it? Despite your faith in me, I still want to prove myself.'

'Sure.'

I suggest Karrion takes my laptop for his research and he disappears inside, where the internet connection is more reliable. A pigeon that was watching him flies off. As I shift to a more comfortable position on my cushion, I catch a flicker of movement from the corner of my eye. The curtains in the window of the upstairs flat sway in the gentle breeze. Jans must be home early.

For the next hour, I browse through news articles about the Braeman murder and the judgement, looking for the name of the Paladin, without success. Even after a year with my smartphone, I am not altogether comfortable with all its functions. Technology had little place in the conclave and a phone that can access the internet is a novelty for me.

When the infinite world of the internet does not yield an answer, I settle for finding out the information the old-fashioned way.

A polite male voice answers my call. 'Good afternoon, Brotherhood of Justice, how may I help?'

'I was hoping you could tell me which Paladin was on duty at the judgement of Jonathain Marsh, please?'

'Hold the line.'

My ears are filled with flute music, which soon cuts off mid-note.

'Sorry to keep you waiting. The Paladin on duty that day was Brother Valeron.'

'Would it be possible to speak to him?'

'I'll try to put you through. Who's calling, please?'

I give him my name. This time the wait is longer before the voice returns.

'I'm sorry, but Brother Valeron is unavailable today. Perhaps you would like to try again tomorrow?'

'Yes, I'll do that. One final thing. Are there set visiting hours for prisoners housed at the Brotherhood?'

'Are you family?'

'No, I'm a… friend.' I hope he doesn't notice my hesitation.

'Non-family visitors can come between ten and noon. But an appointment must be made for them by a family member.'

I thank him and end the call. Perhaps I will begin tomorrow by visiting Marsh, and with any luck catch Brother Valeron while I am at the Brotherhood. My next call is to Ilana, and she promises to organise an appointment for the following morning.

When I go in, Karrion is busy typing on my laptop in the lounge. He looks up.

'Good news,' he says, 'the trial CCTV footage is on its way.'

'Any issues?'

'Not really. Scotland Yard in New London looks after the footage archives. Strictly speaking, any requests under the Freedom of Information Act take a few days to process through their system, but I befriended their archivist and she agreed to make an exception for me. Turns out she is a huge fan of Salvador Dali's paintings.'

'I'm glad to see all that flirting practice you got during your final university year hasn't gone to waste.'

'Maybe I'm just a natural.'

'I'll let others be the judge of that. Well done, anyway. Perhaps once this is over, you'll explain to me how you managed to steer the conversation from a murder judgement to paintings. Will she email you the footage?'

'The file sizes are too big for that. She'll put them online and send me a link. All we need to do is download the footage.' He sets the laptop on the side table between the armchairs and stretches, missing my tall reading lamp by inches. 'I also texted Mum to say I would probably be late coming home tonight and that they should eat without me.'

'Look at you being all organised.'

'I'm just being awesome.'

Resisting the urge to roll my eyes, I let him know what I found out while he was flirting with the New Scotland Yard archivist. Karrion seems keen to visit Marsh tomorrow morning, though I suspect it's because he is curious about the prison within the Brotherhood of Justice. Only those accused of murder pending a judgement and those awaiting execution are kept there. Otherwise, any prisoners with magical capabilities are incarcerated in purpose-built prison blocks outside of Old London.

By the time I have returned the blanket, cushions and papers indoors, the link has come through. Karrion turns the laptop around to show me the sender's avatar.

'She looks... artistic,' he says, altogether too pleased with himself.

Now I do roll my eyes. 'I'm sure the two of you will be very happy. But before you start naming your future children, perhaps you'd like to download that CCTV footage?'

We set the first file to download and go through the crime-scene photos. Although we have the key to the photos included in the case file, I find it more useful to begin by flicking through them without the list.

One thing that strikes me as odd is the bloodstain on the rug, and I say as much to Karrion.

'I know,' he says, zooming in on the photo. 'Wasn't he found lying on his back?'

I check the coroner's report even though I am certain I remember the answer. 'Yes. Lividity suggests that he fell on to his back and did not get up again.' A footnote catches my eye and I frown. 'There's also a mention that the lividity was unusually strong. Given the narrow time of death, the coroner did not expect the lividity to be that fixed when he first examined the body.'

'Could that tie in with the bloodstain? If he was stabbed in the back and he lay on his back, he should have been surrounded by a large pool of blood. Instead, this stain looks like he bled for a bit and then got up.'

I finish the thought for him. 'Which we know he didn't do. I suppose if something prevented the blood from leaving the body, there would be more of it to settle.'

'I don't think lividity works like that. The time it takes to fix is pretty constant, and if the coroner thinks it was unusually strong, then something in the timeline could be off.'

'Unless the coroner adjusted for that in determining the estimated time of death.' I brush hairs back from my forehead and stretch my stiff neck. 'I don't know. I never took a course in forensic pathology.'

'Well, between the bloodstain, the lividity and the Mage report mentioning that she thought there was some further magic at work, I would say there's something odd about the crime scene.'

'I agree, and it's not just that there's a bed in the study.'

Karrion sets the second video file to download. Ilana sends me a text confirming our appointment to visit her father at ten the following morning.

'And look,' I point at the next photo, 'there are dinner trays for two people on the side table. The staff must have known about the affair.'

'No, I think I have an answer for that.' He takes some of the pages from me and flicks through them. 'Reaoul, the PA, said that he and Braeman had dinner around five, while they discussed various documents that would need Braeman's attention that evening. The papers were on the second desk and they hadn't been disturbed.'

'Still, Reaoul must have known about the affair. I mean, if he was Braeman's PA, he must have spent most of his time with him. It would be hard to hide an affair from your PA.'

'Unless you're sleeping with the PA,' Karrion mutters, 'though I suspect it's unlikely in this case.'

'If you were sleeping with your PA, I'm pretty sure your PA would know about it. But I agree, I can't see Reaoul being Braeman's secret lover.'

'One of his lovers.' He shrugs. 'There could be more than one.'

'Perhaps that's something we ought to bring up with Reaoul. I'd like to talk to him about the events of that evening.'

Karrion starts another download, and we continue perusing the crime-scene photos. Even with the suspicion that something is not right with the murder, we glean little else. The police were thorough in their processing of the scene.

By the time we have examined each photo in detail, the downloads have finished and we switch our focus to the CCTV footage. There are four cameras in the courtroom. One offers an aspect of the viewing gallery from across the room, another looks out from the door that the public uses. The third is above the double doors that the court officials use, and the fourth is at the opposite end of the room. The camera angles are such that there are no blind spots.

We watch the judgement from each camera's viewpoint.

Ilana is easy to spot in the front row, next to a woman who can only be her mother. Ilana looks pale and drawn, her glance skittering from the iron pillar to the summoning circle to the seats of the officials and around the viewing gallery.

Tanyella sits in a different part of the gallery with a haughty expression that sets her apart. If Ilana knew her before the trial, she hides it well. While Tanyella's eyes linger on Ilana and her mother more than once, when Ilana looks in Tanyella's direction, her expression betrays nothing.

Two Paladins in full battle livery escort Marsh into the courtroom. Despite the chains of cold iron, true silver, and heart copper around his neck, wrists, and ankles, he looks calm and unperturbed. Nothing in his demeanour indicates that he is about to be judged for murder, and when he looks up at Ilana and his wife, he offers them a reassuring smile. The Paladins chain Marsh to an iron pillar next to the summoning circle taking up most of the space and leave him there.

The double doors open to admit the officials presiding over the judgement. A representative of the High Council of Mages is the first to walk in, wearing the grey robes of neutrality. He is followed by a detective inspector of New Scotland Yard, an Elder of the Circle of Shamans, and a Paladin who must be Brother Valeron. While the others take their places behind the officials' table, Brother Valeron faces Marsh on the opposite side of the circle.

With a word from the Mage, Brother Valeron kneels on the polished marble floor and begins a chant to summon a Herald. As the words he sings gain speed and confidence, the true silver symbols begin to glow. A brilliant wave of electric-blue light cascades outward from the circle and a portal shimmers into existence, casting dancing shadows around the room. In reality, the shifting colours are too bright to look at, but on the tape, the iridescent reflections on the marble floor offer a glimpse of the beauty of the gateway.

A figure steps through the portal, and in his wake the opening diminishes, shrinking into a pool of otherness at the centre of the circle. The Herald of Justice is clad in loose robes which shift through every shade of grey from black to white as they billow around him in a wind no one but he can feel. His features are too long to be human and his eyes are solid orbs of azure that cast a glow over his sharp cheekbones. The hair that streams behind him could be silver or white or black; as with his robes, it shifts and defies definition.

Even seeing a Herald through the CCTV footage sends a shiver through me.

The Herald steps towards Marsh. Brother Valeron pushes himself up and walks to stand next to the Herald. His head is bowed and his posture speaks of deep respect. In contrast, Marsh is studying the Herald's countenance with open curiosity.

Behind the officials' desk, the Mage unwinds a short scroll and reads from it. The footage has no audio, but I know from experience that the Mage is reading out the charges, which Brother Valeron translates for the Herald. I recall using my magic to hear the Paladin's words at the judgement I attended, but the language was so foreign that it did not seem possible a human mouth uttered the words.

Even when the Herald towers over him to peer into his soul, all Marsh does is tilt his chin up to allow better access. His composure does not change until the verdict is delivered, at which point he panics. From the desperation in his eyes as he speaks, I am guessing Marsh is protesting his innocence. In the front row, Ilana collapses into her mother's arms, while the older woman looks down with detached disapproval. Tanyella gets up and leaves the gallery.

Unconcerned by Marsh's reaction, the Herald turns away. Brother Valeron bows deeply, offering thanks for the justice imparted. The Herald steps into the reforming portal of shifting colours. A pillar of blue light shoots upwards and he disappears.

Two armoured Paladins come to take Marsh away and he struggles against his bonds. The officials leave after him, but Brother Valeron lingers next to the circle. He tilts his chin up to observe Ilana's grief and his own face reflects her sorrow. When her anguish changes to disbelief and she turns to hold her mother, he bows his head and leaves the courtroom.

Having seen Marsh's reaction for myself, I am more convinced of his innocence. His conduct throughout the judgement was that of a man confident of being acquitted of all charges. If he is guilty, he has the best poker face I have ever seen.

'What do you think?' I ask Karrion.

'He looks innocent.'

'And yet, we know that the Heralds are infallible, right?'

'Yes,' Karrion says, though the question was rhetorical.

'Let's watch it again.'

No matter the camera angle, we cannot spot anything amiss with the judgement. After the fourth viewing of the footage, Karrion switches on the lights. The nights are beginning to draw in. While he is up, Karrion also gets the leftover sushi from the fridge. We eat in impatient silence, caught up in the mystery of the case and keen to get back to it.

Once I have cleared the plates, chopsticks, and soy sauce away, we divide the case file in two again and go over the parts we did not read earlier. There is little to add to the particulars we have already discussed, but it allows us to go through the crime-scene photos with a fresh focus. When that yields nothing new, we turn back to the judgement footage. We loop through the camera feeds, certain that persistence will give us the answers we are looking for.

The moon has risen above the ragged clouds when my fatigue gets the better of me and my eyes slip closed. Sometime later, I stir when I am lifted off the armchair. Strong arms carry me a short distance before setting me on my bed. I try to speak, but sleep claims me instead.

TUESDAY

7

MISSING PIECES

The ringing of the doorbell banishes my dreams and I blink awake to see sunlight streaming through the lounge window. Karrion is asleep next to me, snoring softly. I slip out from underneath the blankets to find that I am still wearing my clothes from yesterday. All Karrion did was remove my fleece.

Rubbing sleep from my eyes, I hurry downstairs and into my office just as the doorbell rings again. At the sight of Detective Inspector Jamie Manning standing outside my door, my brain wakes up.

'Yannia. Good morning.'

'Jamie.' I nod. 'What time is it?'

'Eight thirty,' he says without looking at his watch. In his expression, I see the familiar longing. 'May I come in?'

'Sure.' I step away from the door, and he walks past me, carrying a narrow briefcase. While I close the door, he takes in the posters on the wall and his lips twitch. It is cold in the office without my fleece, and I shiver.

'Nice set-up you've got here.'

I shrug. 'What can I do for you?'

'I want answers.'

His directness throws me, but manners come to my rescue. 'Would you like a cup of coffee, or maybe tea?'

'Coffee, thanks.'

I lead him through the second door and up the stairs, remembering too late that Karrion is asleep on my bed. By then, I cannot turn back and we come through the lounge door to find Karrion standing, pulling on his jeans. As embarrassing as the situation is, I am amused to see him wearing boxer shorts with grinning skulls in various colours. At the sound of our footsteps, he turns.

'The doorbell woke me up. I was just about to come down to see what was going on.'

'Jamie, this is Karrion, my apprentice. Karrion, this is Detective Inspector Jamie Manning.'

Even as I perform the introductions, I can see the speculation in Jamie's eyes. There is no way to explain last night's sleeping arrangements without sounding like I have something to hide and I let him jump to the wrong conclusion.

My fleece is lying in a heap next to the mattress and I slip it on as I head for the kitchen. Jamie's statement about wanting answers has left me restless, and I pace while a pot of coffee is brewing. Through the doorway, I see Karrion straightening the blankets on the bed while an awkward silence fills the lounge.

Both Karrion and Jamie look grateful when I bring a tray through and set it on the side table. Karrion takes his coffee and goes to lean against the edge of the fireplace.

'What can I do for you?' I ask again as I motion for Jamie to take the other chair.

Jamie sips his coffee, sets his mug down and opens his briefcase. 'I have here a copy of the outstanding tests run on the murder weapon on the Braeman case,' he says, and takes out a clear plastic wallet of papers. 'Since I requested a copy of the case file yesterday, I was included in the notification to say the report had come in.'

'And you came all the way to Old London to deliver a copy? I'm touched.' I keep my tone light, but in truth, I am puzzled.

'Yes and no. Having seen the report, I went back to the case file and noticed another flag on it. Imagine my surprise when I found that someone had requested the CCTV footage for the Marsh judgement and given your name for the paperwork.'

I look in Karrion's direction, but he is busy studying the contents of his mug. I cannot blame him. This is my case, my PI business.

'I was curious.'

'Bollocks, Yannia. You're not just studying police procedures during a murder case. What's really going on?'

I stare at him as I consider my position, and he holds my gaze, steady and unperturbed. He is not going to give up until I give him something believable. I may as well go with the truth.

'Jonathain Marsh's daughter hired me to look into the Braeman murder.'

Jamie frowns, much the same way as I expect I did when Ilana first told me what the job entailed. 'Why?'

'Because she thinks her father is innocent.'

'But that's impossible.'

'I'm aware of that. But Marsh has an alibi, even though he never disclosed it to the police, and having seen the footage of the judgement, I think there's more to this case than meets the eye.'

'I agree.'

I stare at Jamie, but he ignores me.

'It wasn't my case, you understand, so officially I can't look into things. But unofficially, I've skimmed through the file and it seems Marsh was the obvious suspect.'

Karrion and I share a glance.

'That's exactly what we thought,' says Karrion.

'He might just have been incompetent if it wasn't for this.' Jamie points at the papers he has brought with him.

'The coroner wanted to run further tests on the murder weapon,' I say. 'What did they find?'

'The weapon found in Marsh's wardrobe wasn't the murder weapon.'

'What?' Karrion and I speak at the same time, and Jamie smirks.

'That was my reaction too. The coroner had a mould cast of the killing blow and the weapon is not a match to the ceremonial dagger with Braeman's blood on it. The killer used two weapons, one to stab the victim and the other for the curse.'

I nod. 'And because the curse required symbols carved on to the victim's chest, blood got on to the dagger.'

'Exactly. Why would Marsh take one of the weapons with him and not the other?'

'Is it valuable?' Karrion asks. 'The ceremonial dagger?'

'It's antique, but not worth much. What's more, it's not a family heirloom since it was one of Braeman's own daggers.'

'In that case, it doesn't make any sense,' I say, and finish my coffee. Between Jamie's news and the caffeine, I am now wide awake. 'Or it does make sense if the dagger was planted at Marsh's house to direct suspicion to him.'

'Did the tests identify the real murder weapon?' Karrion asks as he returns his mug to the tray.

Jamie rifles through the papers and pulls out a photo of a blade cast in dark-grey material. The weapon is narrow, curving to a point and with a serrated edge.

At the sight of it, I frown. 'Is it just me or does that look like a steak knife?'

'I was just thinking the same thing.' Karrion wakes up my laptop, which he must have forgotten to switch off last night, and flicks through the crime-scene photos until he finds what he is looking for. 'Here, check this out.'

The photo he has picked shows the far end of the study and the two dinner trays on the coffee table, the cursor hovering over the cutlery on the plates. Whatever the food was, it required steak knives.

'Both knives are there,' Jamie says, a crease appearing on his brow.

'True, but the mould looks pretty similar.' Karrion zooms in on a knife.

'Were they collected as evidence?' I ask before realising that Jamie would not know the details of the case. After flicking through the papers on the table, I find the list of evidence from the primary crime scene. There is no mention of steak knives. I say as much to the others.

'If there was no indication that the dinner trays had a bearing on the crime, they would have been left and released alongside the crime scene,' Jamie says.

'And the knives put through the dishwasher,' Karrion adds.

Jamie nods. 'It should be easy enough to compare one of the steak knives at the Braeman residence with the mould to see if it's a match. Any blood and fingerprints will have washed away by now, of course.'

'I'm guessing no one will follow up on this report, though, since the case is closed?' says Karrion.

'That's likely,' Jamie says. 'It doesn't matter that the weapon found at Marsh's wasn't the actual murder weapon since the guilty man is awaiting execution.'

'Could two weapons mean two killers?' Karrion asks. 'Maybe Marsh killed Braeman and someone else helped?'

'The Herald declared him guilty. Having an accomplice wouldn't change the verdict.'

While the men speak, I stare into space. Karrion notices this and rests his fingertips on my shoulder.

'Everything okay, Yan?'

'I was just thinking. If one of those steak knives is indeed the real murder weapon, how brave, how arrogant of the murderer to leave it there in plain sight.'

Karrion is taken aback by my words and Jamie's frown deepens. Neither says anything, and I continue. 'Everything about this crime screams premeditation to me, assuming Marsh is innocent. Nothing has been left to chance. But why choose a steak knife as the weapon? Why hinge all the planning on that evening's menu?'

'Maybe the murderer knew that the meal would be served with steak knives?' Karrion suggests.

'Or perhaps it was an attempt to make the whole thing look like a heat-of-the-moment sort of killing,' I say. 'I suppose it would be possible Marsh got so angry at the way Braeman treated Ilana that he grabbed the nearest sharp object and stabbed him.'

'If that's the case, why stop to carve a curse on Braeman's chest with a different knife, loot the spell cabinet, and wipe the steak knife clean enough that no one thought it might have been used in the murder?'

'I don't know. None of it makes sense.' I turn to Jamie. 'Now you know what I've been up to. Lots of things about this crime don't add up and I intend to keep digging for the truth.'

He nods. 'You may be on to something. At the very least, there are unanswered questions connected to the case. Officially, there's nothing I can do. I was never involved and the guilty person has been caught. But unofficially, if you need help, give me a call.'

'Thanks, Jamie. Do you mind if I ask something else?'

'Go ahead.'

'Do you know what happened to those stolen magical artefacts? Have any of them been recovered?'

'I don't think so, though I must admit, I only glanced through that section of the file. A pair of protection scarabs was sold online on Mana Net, but they were the ones that pointed the police at Marsh, since the money was transferred to his personal account. As far as I know, no flags have been raised in our system regarding the other items.'

'Other than the money, was there anything else linking the theft to Marsh?'

'Our cyber division traced the auction listing to Marsh's wireless network, though they didn't find the exact device that was used. The investigating officer assumed the theft was unplanned since the cabinet was unlocked.'

'That might be easier to believe with someone less wealthy than Marsh,' I say.

'Well, I can't say I'm up to date with the hidden debts and riches of Old London. That should be more your area of expertise.'

'Ilana said the family was not experiencing any sort of money problems.'

'Who's Ilana?' Jamie frowns.

'Jonathain Marsh's daughter, my client. She said her father would have no reason to steal magical artefacts, much less sell them online.'

'It seems you have another mystery to solve, Yannia. I'd best leave you to it.'

He snaps his briefcase shut and stands to leave. At the door to the stairs, he pauses and sends me a piercing look over his shoulder.

'You realise that if you are to prove Marsh innocent, you'll also have to demonstrate how the Herald could pass incorrect judgement. That's the real difficulty. And you only have three days to achieve the impossible.'

He leaves and we hear the front door close below us.

'He's not wrong,' Karrion says.

'No, he's not. But we'll do what we can.'

'Agreed. What are we doing first?'

'We'll go to the Brotherhood. By the time we've had breakfast, showered, and travelled there, it will be time for our appointment with Marsh. If we're lucky, we can catch Brother Valeron at the same time.'

'Sounds good.'

Karrion offers to clear away the coffee mugs and make breakfast while I shower. I am quick to wash and dress, eager to get on with the investigation. Jamie's parting words keep percolating in my mind, as relentless as a ticking clock. After a brief rummage in the cupboard under the sink, I find a spare toothbrush and leave it out for Karrion. His towel from yesterday hangs next to my dressing gown and it catches my eye when I wipe the mirror clear of condensation. The bathroom is a scene of domesticity. Funny how things turn out.

Outside, I come close to tripping over a box of apples. Footsteps above me draw my attention to Jans, who is at the top of the stairs. He turns and offers Karrion and me a vague smile.

'A friend had a glut of apples. She gave me too many and I thought I'd leave some for you.'

'Oh. Thank you. But are you sure you've left yourself enough?'

Jans and I have never exchanged anything other than polite pleasantries so this is unexpected. He stares at his feet, and I notice that his nails are bitten down to the quick, the skin around them red and inflamed. I wonder why, but then I wonder about a lot of things regarding him. What does he do for a living? Does he have any family? How does he spend his free time? What sort of dreams does he dream?

'Yes, I have more than enough. Let me know if you want any more. Us single people have to stick together.'

'I will, thank you.'

Karrion moves the box inside the office and closes the door. Jans hurries away, eyes downcast, leaving behind only a waft of cologne. I rub my nose to prevent a sneeze. Why Jans feels the need to wear so much cologne is beyond me, but even passing him in the street leaves me with aching sinuses. As a result, I have never managed to figure out if he carries any magical blood.

The Brotherhood of Justice is too far to walk, and we head for the nearest bus stop. The bus takes us as far as Blackfriars, and from there it is a short walk along the Thames.

There are streets in London that are meant for ordinary humans and streets that are meant for us. In some areas, such as near Blackfriars, the two overlap. If I squint, I see buildings that are dull and nondescript, covered in posters for rock concerts and gyms rather than remnants of spells and old symbols. The thrum of magic fades away into the rumble of traffic, the scents of the different beings become nothing more than fried food and rotting rubbish. Here at the border of Old London, magic competes with the mundane.

I know which London I prefer.

The Brotherhood's compound occupies prime real estate along the Thames. Behind wrought-iron gates looms the main building of grey stone. It houses the barracks of the Paladins, their communal areas, as well as the small prison wing. To the right of it, connected by a narrow corridor, is the circular courthouse. It has a façade of white marble and the entrance is flanked by marble statues of mounted Paladins. At the back are various other buildings, including small stables, though I understand that the Brotherhood has a large estate outside London where most of the horses are kept.

While New Scotland Yard has overall jurisdiction in Old London, the streets are patrolled by Paladins rather than human police. It is a common sight to see Paladins astride their mounts at street corners or trotting through a park. As a nod to the modern times, the Paladins' armour is made of Kevlar rather than steel, though they still carry swords as well as pistols.

An undecorated black door leads to the entrance hall, which is dominated by a large reception desk. At present, only one person sits behind a bank of monitors, though there is space for several. Inside the front door, two Paladins stand guard and they offer us a friendly nod as we walk past.

We pause near the reception desk and wait while a man is asking the receptionist to take a thin wad of posters. His teenage son has gone missing and he is hoping that the Paladins patrolling the streets can keep an eye out for him. The receptionist promises to pass them on to the captain of the barracks and the man leaves. As he walks past us, shoulders slumped, I catch the scents of ripening wheat, morning dew, and citrus fruit. He is a West Mage.

The receptionist turns her attention to us, and I tell her about our appointment to visit Marsh. After a quick phone call, a Paladin in full armour comes to meet us and leads us towards the back of the building. The processing of visitors is efficient, but the Paladins take every precaution. We have to sign in, provide identification, place all our belongings in a locker and get searched by the guards. Everyone is courteous and friendly, but there is no deviating from the rules. As a final step, before we are allowed in the cell, we both have collars fitted to prevent us using magic. They are similar to the one worn by Marsh during the judgement: cold iron, true silver, and heart copper forged together to bind our powers.

I feel the effect of the collar straight away. The world around me dampens and dims, as a barrier separates me from everything I know. It is disconcerting, and I shake my head to try to dislodge the detachment, to no avail. I have never realised how much I rely on magic to supplement my senses, even in London. Perhaps this explains why I am losing power far quicker than I should.

From the worried glance Karrion casts my way, I realise my distress is obvious. He appears unfazed by the collar, though I imagine he would feel differently if there were birds present. I offer him a reassuring smile and step towards the door.

The cell is not how I imagined it. One of the guards escorting us opens a heavy steel door, and I note the thin lines of cold iron, true silver, and heart copper running around the doorframe. My guess is that similar lines are embedded in the walls between the cells to keep out any spell that might target the area or anything within it. The window opposite the door is small and has no bars, only glass. One corner of the cell is taken by a bathroom cubicle; there are only a few reasons for a prisoner to leave their cell, and ablutions are not among them. There is a wooden bed with a proper mattress, pillow, and blankets, and a small wardrobe, table, and a single chair.

Jonathain Marsh looks no different from the man in the CCTV footage. Just like on the day of the judgement, he is wearing black dress trousers and a white-collared shirt. From his careful grooming, it would be hard to guess that he is imprisoned and waiting to be executed. Only the cell and the collar he wears mark him as a prisoner.

When we enter, he is sitting at the table, reading a paperback edition of Victor Hugo's *Notre-Dame de Paris*. Upon seeing us, he notes his place in the book, closes it, and stands.

'Ms Wilde, I presume?'

I shake his hand and introduce Karrion.

'My daughter said she had arranged your visit,' Marsh says, and invites me to sit on the only chair in the room. He perches on the edge of his bed, while Karrion remains standing near the door.

The first thing that strikes me about Marsh is that he does not act like a man who is scheduled to die in a few days. He appears calm and composed, just as he was during the judgement. Either he is an expert at hiding his emotions or he has more faith in me than I do.

Then again, even if he is frightened, would he show it to complete strangers?

'I was hoping we could ask you a few questions about the night of the murder and also about the judgement?' I take out a notepad and a pen.

'Of course, ask whatever you wish. I apologise for being unable to provide refreshments, but this place is not renowned for its waiting staff.' Although his voice carries genuine regret that he cannot meet his usual standards of hospitality, the sardonic twist of his lips shows that he understands the irony of his words.

'No problem.' I take a moment to gather my thoughts. 'I understand that Braeman called you on the night of the murder.'

'Yes, that's right.'

'What time was that?'

Marsh stares at the book while he thinks. 'About quarter to nine.'

'How long did the call last?'

'Two minutes, three at the most.'

'What did you talk about?'

'Braeman wanted me to visit him that night to discuss the situation regarding my daughter. I declined the offer. As far as I was concerned, if he ever approached Ilana again, I would expose his indiscretions to the Council and let them deal with it.'

'And that was it?'

'He tried to argue, but I had plans for the evening and had little inclination to continue the conversation. I hung up.'

'Was there anything about the phone call that struck you as odd?'

'Other than the fact that he was going over old ground?' Marsh pauses, eyes going to the book again. 'The line was poor. His voice sounded distant and distorted.'

'But it was definitely Braeman?'

Marsh appears puzzled by the question. 'Who else could it have been?'

I offer no response to that and jot down a note about the phone call. 'What time did you leave your home that evening?'

'Nine. I arrived at Tanyella's house shortly before half past nine.'

'And what time did you leave?'

'Just after six o'clock the following morning.'

That corroborates Tanyella's account of the night. Although I have no evidence to support the belief, Marsh's alibi appears genuine.

'Did you notice anything unusual,' asks Karrion, 'when you left your home the night of the murder or when you returned the following morning?'

Marsh thinks, resting his chin on the palm of his hand. 'Nothing when I left. The following morning, the only thing that struck me as odd was a bird's nest on the front step. It must have been dislodged from the gutter during the night.'

Karrion's interest is piqued, but there's little more Marsh can tell him about the nest.

'What about the judgement?' I ask, bringing the conversation back on track. 'Was there anything unusual about it?'

'Well, I can't say I have observed all that many judgements over the years, certainly not from the position of the accused. Truth be told, I found the experience most curious since I had no doubt I would be acquitted. A Herald is a magnificent thing to behold up close, and I could feel all of myself laid bare when he stared into my soul. That the Herald decreed me guilty troubles me a great deal.'

Although Marsh's choice of words is mild, in the furrow of his brow and the hands twisting in his lap, the composed character of a polite aristocrat cracks and his distress shows. I find it disconcerting that all my instincts tell me he is innocent, no matter how the Herald judged him. Can I really be that wrong about a person?

After a brief lull in the conversation, Marsh shakes his head. 'Apologies, I didn't answer your question. No, I noticed nothing unusual about the judgement. The only strange thing that has happened since I was declared guilty is that the Paladin from the judgement came to visit me.'

'Brother Valeron?' Karrion takes a step closer.

'Yes.' Marsh nods. 'Yes, I believe that is his name.'

'What did he want?'

'I am not certain. He came in on Sunday morning, stared at me for a while, and left without saying a word. Truth be told, I don't know what to make of the encounter.'

Me neither. The more I hear about Brother Valeron, the

more I want to talk to him. If anyone noticed anything unusual about the judgement, it must have been him.

'Can you think of anyone who might have a motive for killing Braeman?' Karrion asks into the silence.

'There are many people who did not think kindly of Braeman, but I am not certain the disagreements went deep enough to warrant murder.'

'What sort of people?'

'Families of other young women he harassed into his bed. His wife if she knew of his indiscretions. I've never been friendly enough with Viola to know if she is aware of her husband's appetites. Even his personal assistant, since there were some rumours about Braeman trying to seduce his wife. His political rivals, or rather, rival.'

'Lord Wellaim Ellensthorne,' I say.

'Indeed. Braeman and Ellensthorne were famous for disagreeing on most matters. And it was no secret among the Council that Ellensthorne coveted Braeman's position as the Speaker.'

'Which he has now taken,' I say.

'Yes. He's one person who won't have been unhappy to hear the news of Braeman's death.'

That makes him another to add to my list of people to see.

There is little else Marsh can tell us, and I jot down a few notes. Jonathain observes me as I put my notebook away.

The silence becomes awkward. It is time to leave. When Jonathain shakes my hand, his composure cracks again.

'I do hope you will be able to shed some light on this matter. As I'm sure you can appreciate, I'd rather not die in three days' time.'

It is as close to a plea for help as I am likely to get, but it affects me just the same. I give him my sincere promise that I will do everything I can, though I worry I have too little to offer.

Now I have met Jonathain Marsh in person, the enormity of the task of trying to save his life comes into sharper focus.

Karrion knocks on the door, and the guards let us out. As I step over the threshold, I glance back to see Marsh at the table, about to open his book. He seems smaller, more fragile than before, and my heart goes out to him and Ilana. No doubt he puts on a brave face when she visits him, and no doubt she can see straight through it.

We return to the reception desk and ask for Brother Valeron. The receptionist dials an internal number and has a short conversation over the phone.

'I'm afraid Brother Valeron is unavailable. Perhaps you would like to try again tomorrow?'

'Is there anyone we could speak to that might know how we can reach Brother Valeron? We have something urgent we need to discuss with him.'

'Just a moment.' The receptionist looks through a phone list, dials a number and asks the person at the other end to come down to the entrance hall. 'Someone will be with you shortly.'

I watch the crowds while we wait and notice from the corner of my eye as the receptionist points us out to someone. A Paladin dressed in the grey robes of the Brotherhood approaches us. Her lavender-blue eyes and steel-grey hair are telltale signs of old Paladin bloodlines. When she gets close enough, I catch a fleeting impression of the scents of true silver, steel, and oiled leather.

'You wanted to speak to me?' she asks, her expression polite.

'Yes and no. The person we're really after is Brother Valeron. Do you know where we could reach him?'

'What business would you have with Brother Valeron?'

'We were hoping to ask him some questions.'

'About what?'

'About the judgement of Jonathain Marsh.'

At the mention of the name, concern flickers over her features. 'Who are you?'

I introduce myself and Karrion and explain what I do for a living. The concern on her face intensifies. Glancing around the hall, she beckons us to follow her. She chooses one of the many corridors and ducks into a room on the right. A brass plaque on the door reads Palaeontology. The walls are lined with bookcases and at the centre of the room are two desks facing each other. A pen holder and a stack of blank notepaper sit on each desk.

Our guide closes the door behind us.

'This is our research wing, but few have time to delve into the mists of the distant past. We can talk here without being overheard.'

Karrion and I exchange a glance, puzzled by her cautious manner.

'Can you take us to Brother Valeron? And what's your name?' I ask, flashing her a friendly smile despite a growing sense of disquiet.

'My name is Sister Alissa. Valeron and I entered the Brotherhood at the same time and we have remained close. But I cannot take you to him because he's not here.'

'Do you know where he is?'

Alissa's frown deepens. 'No. He disappeared the day after the Marsh judgement and no one has heard from him since.'

'What?' Karrion paces across the room, and I sense the tense energy in him, like a kingfisher readying itself for a dive.

'Something is wrong,' Alissa says, slumping into a chair next to one of the desks, 'only I don't know what. And it's my fault.'

I notice for the first time that Alissa is barefoot and my legs ache at the mere thought of having to stand on the marble floor without shoes.

'When was the last time you saw Brother Valeron?'

'Sunday morning. We were in the dining room at the same time having breakfast, but he was preoccupied. After maintaining a one-sided conversation for a while, I gave up. He left the Brotherhood around noon that day and hasn't been seen since.'

'Does he have family or friends outside the Brotherhood that he could have gone to visit?'

'He has a wife and a daughter in Old London. I spoke to his wife yesterday and she said Valeron had told her that he was needed at the Brotherhood for the next week since we're short of Paladins. Which isn't true.'

'Any chance he's having an affair?' Karrion asks.

'No.' Alissa shakes her head. 'He's a devoted husband and father. His daughter has a rare form of blood cancer and all his free time is spent at doctors' appointments and in hospitals during various treatments.'

'It's an odd time for him to disappear, if his daughter is that sick,' I say.

'I agree. They were told a few weeks ago that there was nothing further the cancer ward could do for Elianora. Valeron was devastated. But his wife told me that on Saturday, she received a call from a private research hospital that is conducting drug trials for a new treatment for that particular blood cancer. A spot opened within the trial and their daughter was invited to take part.'

'That's quite a coincidence,' says Karrion. He shares my feeling on the matter. 'What did his wife say when you told her he was missing?'

'I didn't.' At my raised eyebrow, Alissa hurries to explain, 'I hoped Valeron would just need a day or two alone. It seems like his wife has enough to worry about with a sick child and I didn't want to give her more bad news.'

'But why do you think his disappearance is your fault?'

'Because he only began acting strangely following the Marsh judgement.'

Across the room, Karrion shakes his head, not understanding. Alissa notices this and runs both hands through her hair.

'He was not meant to serve at that judgement. It should have been me.'

'Why didn't you?'

'I got sick, some sort of food poisoning, and Valeron offered to take my place.'

My pulse quickens. We are getting somewhere. 'Is it usual for you to cover for one another?'

'We've done it a few times in the past. Anyone who isn't on duty can offer to cover for someone else.'

'Do you know what gave you the food poisoning?' Karrion asks, and I nod at him, confirming that my thinking is along the same lines.

'No, I ate in the dining room with everyone else. It must have just been bad luck.'

More design than luck, I think. I ask something that is intriguing me. 'Is it usual for a Paladin to visit the accused after they have been judged and are awaiting execution?'

'Quite the opposite. Any Paladin that has served at a judgement is not allowed to interact with or even guard the guilty.'

'Why do you think Brother Valeron went to visit Marsh on Sunday morning?'

Alissa frowns. 'He shouldn't have done. I'm surprised the guards let him through.'

'I don't suppose you saw the Marsh judgement?'

'No, I was in no condition to leave my chambers. Sunday morning was the first time I felt well enough to join the others for breakfast.'

Karrion leaves his post by one of the bookcases and walks to rest his hand on my shoulder. 'I was thinking, we could ask Jamie to track Brother Valeron's phone.'

Before I have a chance to agree, Alissa shakes her head. 'It won't get you anywhere. He left his phone in his chambers. I saw it when I went to check up on him on Sunday evening.'

'Did he take anything with him?'

'It's hard to say since he doesn't live here all the time, but my guess is only his wallet. He has a car, but his wife uses it mostly.'

'Is the Brotherhood looking for him?'

'Not yet. Summoning a Herald saps our strength, and after attending a judgement, we are given leave to recharge our magic. Valeron has not yet missed a day of work or given the Brotherhood any cause for concern. Unofficially, I have spoken to the various captains of the patrols and asked them to keep an eye out for him. None have come back with any sightings of him.'

'It's a start. And perhaps we can do our part to help find him. Could you let me have a photo of Brother Valeron, preferably by email? I also need his full name, date of birth, and home address. And if you know of any pubs, restaurants, and other places he likes to visit outside the Brotherhood, let me have a note of those as well.'

Alissa uses one of the notepads available and jots down a short list, together with Brother Valeron's personal details. She hands it to me with a promise that a photo will follow as soon as she has gone to her chambers to get her phone. I, in turn, give her one of my cards.

With the note safe in my pocket, I pause to ask one more question. 'Has anyone ever approached you regarding tampering with a judgement?'

The look on Alissa's face tells me I may as well be speaking in a foreign language. 'That would be impossible.'

'Are you sure?'

'Yes,' she says, 'I'm sure.'

She takes us back to the entrance hall, and we part with mutual promises to be in touch soon. As she turns to leave, I can tell from her expression that my last question has left her troubled. I cannot help but wonder whether it is because she has lied to me or because she has begun to join the dots.

8

SHADOW OF DOUBT

It is close to noon by the time we leave the Brotherhood, and the air has warmed. It's another beautiful autumn day. We jog across the road, dodging a pair of tourists on the pavement, and I lean against the railing overlooking the Thames. Low tide has passed, but the edges of the channel are still above the rising water level.

Casting my senses wide, I search for the wildlife supported by the river. Although the pollution in the water leaves me with a feeling of wrongness, there is plenty of life to be found. Gulls wheel above us, their cries sharp against the background of constant traffic noise. On the exposed sand, flies and worms search for food, only to become sustenance for starlings and sparrows. In the water, fish negotiate the murky depths. If luck was on my side, I may even have detected a dolphin or a seal in the river, but today I sense no such presence.

The Thames alone is not enough to recharge my power, not in the middle of London, but I find the existence of wildlife reassuring. If it can survive here, perhaps I can too.

In an effort to steer away from dark thoughts, I turn to

Karrion, who has mimicked my pose, elbows resting on the railing. A flock of pigeons nearby is cooing at him.

'That was an informative visit,' I say.

'Agreed. Interesting coincidence that the Paladin for the judgement changed at the last minute.'

From his tone, I can tell he is under no illusion that it was a coincidence.

'Imagine being told your child is going to die. What would you do to save her, even if the treatment had only a small chance of success?'

Karrion dips his chin. 'I'd do anything in my power, anything at all.'

'Exactly.'

The wind is blowing from the coast, and I lift my chin to sample the scents of silt, salt, and sea. It is tempting to follow the course of the river, to journey to the estuary and the waters beyond, to be free. But Karrion's presence anchors me to the pavement, to Old London and to the case. Reluctant to relinquish the feeling of nature just yet, I shift my focus to him. I hear the steady beat of his heart, every inhale and exhale. Were I to look closely enough, I know I would see the endless renewal and death of cells that leads to the decay of us all.

'You're doing it again.'

His words yank me away from my reflections, and I blink my eyes into focus. 'Doing what?'

'I'm assuming it's a Wild Folk thing, where you stare at me like I'm an ant under a microscope. You've never told me what you see. Can't imagine it's anything good.'

I shake my head, surprised by his perceptiveness. 'Sorry, I was just thinking.'

He nods and stares at the river. 'Do you think Sister Alissa is right? Is it impossible to tamper with a judgement?'

'Do you think she was telling the truth?'

'I... I thought she was. Do you think she lied?'

I take a moment to replay her reaction, to remember the disquiet in her eyes. 'No, my gut tells me she spoke the truth, or what she thinks is the truth.'

'Yet she may be wrong.'

'Yes. Chances are there is a way to fool the system, we just haven't figured out what it is yet. But I'm assuming it has something to do with a Paladin desperate enough to forsake his vows to uphold justice above all else.'

'All the more reason for us to find Brother Valeron.'

'Indeed.' I unfold Sister Alissa's list and glance through the names. There are a few I recognise, and a quick search on my phone pinpoints the others. 'Let's get to it.'

We begin with a nearby pub, which also provides a convenient place for lunch. Later, we visit restaurants, bookstores, a soft play centre where Valeron used to take his daughter, a bakery, and another pub. In each case, we show around the photo Sister Alissa has emailed me, asking whether Brother Valeron has come by in the past couple of days. In each case, the response is the same. No one has seen him since last week, though a few suggest other places we could try. Those turn out to be just more dead ends.

By late afternoon, I am all out of patience and energy. We find a small café near the Museum of London and take a break. I choose a table by the window, while Karrion gives our order to an elderly lady behind the counter. The mixture of cinnamon, coconut, and clouds heavy with rain identify her as an East Mage. Her greeting carries genuine warmth, and I wonder whether humans are equally welcome. The chimes hanging by the door are designed to detect magical blood, though she has no way of knowing what we are. Such detection systems are common throughout Old London, though hers is less subtle than some.

Karrion brings a tray with cups of tea and slices of carrot cake. Before he takes a seat opposite me, he also places a tall glass of water next to my tea.

'I figured you'd want to take some painkillers.'

My eyelids flutter closed at his gesture, though it is out of gratefulness rather than frustration. When I open my eyes, I see uncertainty in his expression and I reassure him with a smile. 'It's just what I needed. Thank you.'

His relief is palpable as he watches me extract two pills from a medication strip and take them with half the water. A forkful of the cake and the rest of the water follow. I straighten my legs under the table, careful not to kick Karrion, and luxuriate in the feeling of sore muscles stretching. In half an hour I will feel better, but for now I am content to rest and enjoy the break.

'It's been a pretty useless afternoon,' Karrion says, and attacks his cake with more force than is necessary.

'I wouldn't say so. It's frustrating, but we've established that wherever Brother Valeron is, he is taking great care to avoid all his usual haunts. Time, I think, to cast the net a little wider.'

Taking a sip of my tea, I pull my phone out and scroll through the contacts. I score the cream-cheese icing on my cake with the fork while I listen to the dial tone.

'Manning.'

'Jamie, it's Yannia.'

'Back in contact already? I'm beginning to feel popular.'

'Surely as a detective of Scotland Yard, you are popular?'

He laughs. 'What can I do for you?'

'I was hoping you could run a name through your databases and see if anything comes up?'

'What are you hoping to find?'

'Anything, really. I'm looking for a Paladin who has gone missing from the Brotherhood. No one seems to have seen him for a couple of days. I wondered if you have a missing person's report filed for him, if any unidentified bodies have been logged in the system that match his description, if his name has been connected to any illegal activity in Old London or outside it. As I said, anything.'

'All right, send me the details and I'll see what I can find out.' There is a pause, and I hear the creak of a chair. 'And Yannia, I don't suppose this Paladin you're after has anything to do with the Marsh judgement?'

'As it happens, he was the Paladin on duty in the courtroom that day.'

'Are you on to something?'

'I think so, but without talking to him, all I have is speculation and a hunch.'

'I'll want to be kept up to date.'

'Of course.' I nod even though he cannot see me. 'As soon as I know something, I'll let you know.'

'Good. Send those details through and I'll start some searches for you.'

'Thanks, Jamie. I owe you. Again.'

'Just keep me in the loop and we're even.'

I promise to and end the call. It takes a matter of moments to forward the email from Sister Alissa to him, together with Brother Valeron's details. I hope Jamie has more luck than we did.

While I close my email, I wonder at Jamie's helpfulness. The first time I met him, I provided his prime suspect in a murder case with an alibi. At the time the victim was shot, the suspect had been with his mistress in a hotel and I had the photographs to prove it. Jamie seems to have forgiven me, and in the papers, I later read that the guilty person had been caught and judged. Though now, in light of our present investigation, I cannot help thinking that without the photos, my then-client's estranged husband could have been convicted of the murder. Is there a fundamental flaw in the justice system or is it just the Marsh judgement that was corrupted?

We finish our tea and cake in silence. Some of the tension leaves my body as the medication kicks in, settling a cloud between me and the pain. As I draw in a deep breath and let the air escape in a steady hiss, I understand why people get addicted to painkillers. I both love and loathe the numbness encasing my brain, robbing me of some of my intellect even as it gives my body a fraction more functionality. But what is life if not an endless series of small compromises?

'What's next?' Karrion asks. Behind the counter, the elderly woman hums a tune while she knits what looks like a cardigan for a baby.

'I wonder if we might get an audience with Braeman's rival in the Council to see if there was as much enmity between them as Marsh intimated.'

'His house isn't far from here. But do you think he'll speak to us?'

'He might, if our story is good enough.' After a brief internet search, I find the telephone number I require and hit dial.

'Lord Ellensthorne's office. How may I help?' A cultured voice pronounces every word with extreme care.

'Good afternoon, I was wondering if it might be possible to visit Lord Ellensthorne today. I'm writing a blog about the Council and it would be wonderful to get a first-hand view on the future of the Council now that Lord Ellensthorne has been appointed as the Speaker.'

'Your name, please?' It may be my imagination, but the secretary sounds a fraction friendlier than before.

The question catches me off guard, though it shouldn't, and I curse the effect of the medication. My only option is to tell the truth because the silence lasts too long.

'Yannia Wilde.'

'Hold the line.'

It feels like she is gone an eternity, but in reality, it must only be a minute before the line clicks open again.

'Lord Ellensthorne is a busy man, but if you can get to his Old London residence for five o'clock, he can spare you half an hour.'

I glance at my watch. We should be able to make it.

'That suits me fine. Thank you.'

After the call ends, I put my teacup on to my plate. Karrion takes his cue from me and does the same.

'We are to be at Ellensthorne's by five.'

He too glances at his watch. 'A bit tight, but should be okay. How's the pain?'

I push myself up and my muscles protest. But the ache in the joints remains a nagging presence in the background rather than dominating my thoughts. 'I'll live.'

On our way out, we call a thank you to the café owner, who smiles but continues her humming. As we walk past the window, I see her coming around the counter to clear the table, the knitting tucked into a pocket of her apron.

———

Lord Wellaim Ellensthorne lives along one of the wide residential streets in Old London. His townhouse has a white front that gleams in the afternoon sun. There must be spells on it to keep it that white.

The house looks to have three storeys, and the upper floors have narrow balconies edged with black wrought-iron railings.

Wide window boxes line the ground-floor windows, filled with purple geraniums in bloom. Two columns flank the stairs up to the black front door. There is an intercom panel to one side, with a camera above it.

I give myself a moment to feel intimidated and then press the intercom button. After I announce us, there's an electronic buzz of a lock disengaging and the door swings open. Standing on the doorstep is an older man in full butler livery. He invites us in.

We find ourselves in a tall entrance hall dominated by a sweeping staircase leading to the upper floors. The floor is made of dark polished marble, which creates a stark contrast with the cream rug and matching walls. Along the walls is a series of portraits depicting stern men in suits. On the left and right sides of the hallway, double doors lead to other rooms.

The butler takes us up the stairs and along a corridor of dark doors, which are all closed. At the far end, he knocks on a door and admits us into Ellensthorne's office, which appears to double as a library.

Lord Ellensthorne is dressed in a rumpled, ill-fitting suit of pale grey, which clashes with a purple shirt. His hair is unkempt and in need of a trim; the ends brush against his glasses. I suspect the glaring red-and-gold frames are a deliberate ploy to deflect attention away from his dark eyes. The lines around his mouth give him a permanent sneer and the tilt of his chin reinforces this. Slouching back in his chair behind a huge mahogany desk, he is clearly a man who knows his own worth and judges the rest of the world to be beneath him.

I dislike him straight away.

Casting my senses out, I search for an animal and find a rat scuttling within the walls in the basement. I borrow its nose and inhale. At first, I catch nothing but the scents of a regular person. It is not until I am beginning to think I am mistaken about the identity of the man before me that I detect the faintest trace of shadows on a moonless night, the soft velvet feel of the deep dark. He is a Shadow Mage, the natural rival of the Light Mages.

But is it too obvious?

Ever since we stepped into the room, he has been watching me with an amused glint in his eyes and I wonder if he knows what I just did. To stop the silence growing any tenser, I force a smile and step forward to offer him my hand.

'Lord Ellensthorne, thank you for taking the time to see us.'

His handshake is weak, his narrow hand like a limp fish. I resist the temptation to wipe my hand on my trousers and instead introduce Karrion.

'Let me guess, this is your photographer,' Ellensthorne says. Even his voice carries an edge of arrogance.

'My apprentice, actually.'

'Indeed?' He points to two chairs in front of the desk, and we sit down. There is an uncomfortable moment while he scrutinises us before the corner of his mouth lifts into a smirk. 'Yannia Wilde. You're no more a political blogger than I am a Bird Shaman.'

Karrion bristles at this, but I shoot a warning glance in his direction. Ellensthorne is looking for a reaction and Karrion is a little too eager to oblige.

'I didn't realise you knew who I was,' I say, uncertain how to approach this interview. He has got me on the defensive, which I imagine was his intention all along.

'There's only one Wild Folk PI in Old London. One of the Wild Folk staying in the city temporarily would be newsworthy enough, but you look like you are trying to build yourself a life and a business here.'

'And yet you agreed to see us.'

'Consider me curious. What would a second-class private investigator possibly want from me?'

Before I have a chance to explain the reason for our visit, he leans forward on his chair. 'Here is something else I am curious about: how much power have you sacrificed by living in the city?'

'I haven't thought about it,' I reply, unable to hide a flinch. I wonder about that very thing most nights, when sleep eludes me.

The lie hangs between us, obvious to both.

'Fair enough,' Ellensthorne says after a while. 'If you want to donate your power to the Leeches, who am I to judge you?'

There are rumours circulating around Old London that speak of people who have no power of their own, but who can steal magic from others. They have been given a fitting name: the Leeches. The rumours also say that beings away from their element are more susceptible to having their power stolen.

I do my best to hide my discomfort, but Ellensthorne's smirk deepens. It seems I cannot fool him. But can he fool me?

Eager to get to the point of the visit, I clear my throat. 'I was hoping I might ask a few questions about Gideor Braeman and your relationship with him.'

'Relationship? I believe the term you're looking for is political rivalry.'

'If that's what you wish to call it.'

Ellensthorne brushes locks of hair from his face, but soon the lanky lengths are back, hanging over his eyes. 'Why would a private investigator be interested in a murdered politician? The case is closed, the judgement carried out, the sentence known.'

'My client has an interest in the case, therefore I'm interested.'

My answer appears to amuse him.

'Very well, ask away.'

'I gather your views on the role of the Council are different from Braeman's?'

'Indeed. The fool thought the use of magic should be restricted, monitored, and controlled. Had he got his way, Mages in England would never cast a single spell.'

'And you feel the Council should serve a different purpose?'

'The Council has all the tools it needs for the betterment of Mages. We are already superior to the other magical people, but careful breeding could only strengthen our blood and thereby our magic. Interbreeding with other races should be limited as much as possible, and interbreeding with humans should be banned altogether.'

Something of my shock must show on my face, for Ellensthorne chuckles.

'You know as much about keeping the blood pure as I do. Is your kind not extremely strict about tainting the Wild Folk bloodlines with other magical beings, or worse yet, with human blood?'

I fidget, more uncomfortable with every passing minute. It is true that I am a product of an arranged union for the strengthening of the old bloodlines within the conclave. It is likewise true that in time, I will be expected to mate with someone from one of the old families. That knowledge, the recollection of *who* is to be my mate, is yet another reason why I am in Old London instead of the conclave up north.

As he seems to sense my discomfort, a gleam appears in Ellensthorne's eyes. 'In fact, I have long admired the way your elders have maintained the pure bloodlines and dealt with the taint of outside blood. Your kind has grown strong despite the relatively small gene pool and your powers have amplified over the generations. And if primitive people like the Wild Folk have managed it, Mages should be able to do the same.' He taps the desk. 'That is what the Council will do under my leadership.'

'And Braeman disagreed.' I choose to ignore the insult to my people, recognising it as another one of his attempts to bait me.

'Very much so. He actually thought the lesser races and humans were equal to Mages. With a little time and care, I intend to show Old London just how wrong Braeman was. It's only a pity that he's not around to witness my proving him wrong.'

'Pretty convenient for you that he was murdered,' says Karrion. Ellensthorne does not spare him even a glance, but rather directs his answer to me.

'Convenient, yes. I can put my plans into motion quicker than I had anticipated.'

His eyes bore into mine, and I feel a fleeting certainty that he knows why I am asking these questions. But without tipping my hand, without revealing the extent of my investigation, I cannot ask if he has an alibi for the night of the murder or whether he killed Braeman. I have no authority to question him. Indeed, we are only here because he invited us into his home and has volunteered his answers.

'Do the other Council members agree with the direction you are planning to take?'

'The consensus is not there yet, but it will only be a matter of time, and skilful persuasion.'

I believe he has all the right skills to persuade the rest of the Council. I wonder what Marsh thinks of Ellensthorne's plan.

'What about outside the Council sessions? Did you know Braeman well?'

'Well enough to know that he was beneath my attention. His wife is from old blood but she lost all respectability when she married Braeman. Money must have played a part in that match, but Viola could have done much, much better. Just look at the children they produced. Two girls, and only one with magic. Makes you wonder about the parentage.'

His smirk widens at the last statement; his enjoyment in some private joke is clear, even if we have little notion of what is amusing him. My guess is he derives just as much pleasure from keeping us guessing.

Choosing to ignore the subtext, I stick to my line of questioning. 'But you must have come across them in Old London.'

'Naturally. But it didn't mean I had to tolerate them. We spoke enough to be civil, no more.'

'I see,' I say, though I am not certain I do. The political manoeuvrings of Old London are beyond me.

Ellensthorne glances at a clock on the mantelpiece and straightens in his chair.

'As fascinating as this audience has been, I am afraid your time is up. I have other matters to attend to this evening.'

'Thank you for your time,' I say, trying to sound grateful.

A mocking chuckle rings out in the room. 'It has been most entertaining.'

Karrion freezes, and I shoot another warning glance in his direction. With a nod at our host, I cross to the door, eager to escape. My hand is resting on the door-handle when Ellensthorne calls out to me.

'Watch out for the Leeches, Ms Wilde. With power as unique as yours, I imagine you're an irresistible morsel to them. If you're not careful, one of them might decide to eat you up.'

9

THE BEAUTY AND THE PRINCE

By the time the front door closes behind us, I feel the anger coming off Karrion in waves. He stalks down the road, hands balled into fists, and I have to hurry to catch up with him.

'Are you okay?' I ask after we have been walking side by side for a couple of minutes, and he has yet to acknowledge my presence. Karrion seems to have a destination in mind, though I am not certain where he is heading.

'No, I'm not.' He whirls to face me and I collide with his chest. The arm that steadies me is gentle, so his anger is not directed at me. 'Was he threatening you?'

'Ellensthorne? I don't think so. Why?'

'Because it sure sounded like that to me.'

'Do you mean that talk about the Leeches?'

He nods.

'It's just an urban myth. I don't know anyone who has ever come across a Leech.'

'Me neither, but it seemed like Ellensthorne was doing more than just alluding to an old wives' tale. Besides, I didn't like the way he was looking at you like you were a rare creature he wanted to possess.'

'I doubt he has much interest in me, beyond perhaps analysing my blood to see just how pure it is.' I offer Karrion a wry smile. 'That man is an arse and he went out of his way to rattle our cages.'

Karrion chuckles, the tension leaving his body. He flexes his fingers. 'I guess I was an easy target.'

'In our line of business, you need to learn to keep your cards a little closer to your chest. Rein in your emotions, use logic instead of your heart.' It is my turn to chuckle. 'That said, I didn't fare particularly well against Ellensthorne.'

'He'd done his homework about you.'

'Yes. I'm beginning to realise that when it comes to Old London, I would have attracted less attention if I had signed up to join a circus as the bearded lady.'

'Your career would be short-lived,' Karrion says with a grin. 'Your beard leaves a lot to be desired.'

'What a shame.' I roll my eyes. 'In any case, it was interesting to get the measure of Braeman's political rival.'

'What's your take on him? Other than the fact he's an arse, which I agree with.'

'I think he is intelligent, ambitious, and determined to realise his plans for the Council. As far as enemies go, Ellensthorne would be a dangerous man to anger.'

'But you're not frightened of him, are you?'

'No, I'm not,' I say, my words slow, 'though I wonder if I should be.'

We walk in silence for a while. Although his anger has gone, Karrion is still frowning.

'Don't worry about his comments about Mages being superior to the other magical people.' I nudge him with my shoulder. 'That's typical Mage rubbish.'

'I know. Shamans are under-appreciated, I've always known that. I don't think he realises that I could get every single pigeon in Old London to dive-bomb him whenever he leaves his house.'

'Best not. I doubt it would take him long to make the connection between all the pigeon attacks and the Bird Shaman he insulted in his home.'

'I won't, but it's a nice thought.' Karrion takes my arm and steers me to a bench. I am glad to sit down and he perches next to me, elbows on his knees. 'Is it true what he said about the Wild Folk striving to keep their blood pure?'

Wild Folk have understood the importance of genetic diversity for centuries. There is something in our instinct that causes us to shy away from mates too closely related to us, and our Eldermen have taken the instinct a step further. Despite our communities being small and isolated, the Eldermen meet on a regular basis to consider matings between conclaves. They can trace each Wild Folk family's roots back through at least a dozen generations, and the work is done by hand on animal hides and sheets of polished wood. Often the Eldermen choose a child to be fostered in a different conclave with the understanding that a mate for the child will be chosen from there.

Personal freedom and choice have little room in a society like ours.

'Pure bloodlines are prized within the conclaves. Not that keeping the blood pure always works well. My illness is genetic and I've often wondered if a wider gene pool might have helped with that. Though I understand that it's an illness both humans and magical people can have, so perhaps I would have been unlucky anyway. But as much as the Eldermen are concerned with keeping our blood pure and inbreeding to a minimum, none of them have a degree in genetics. If I told them I have Ehlers-Danlos Syndrome, they wouldn't know what to do with the information.'

'Couldn't they look it up?'

Shaking my head, I lean back. 'Why would they, when it's nothing but a product of modern medicine? And that doesn't concern them.'

There is little Karrion can say to that, but his curiosity is not yet sated.

'What happens if one of you chooses a partner that is not Wild Folk?'

'That depends. If a mating results in children, they will be tested to see if they carry our magic. If they do not, the child will be disavowed and banished from our lands. If they have the gift of magic, depending on the bloodlines of the Wild Folk parent, the taint could be bred out of the blood in a few generations.'

'And if you chose to mate with a non-Wild Folk man?' The question is hesitant, and I see that he is concerned with overstepping boundaries.

I shrug. There is no reason not to tell the truth. 'I would be recalled to the conclave and put under house arrest for a time. My bloodlines are as close to pure as they can be and any child of mine would be retained within the conclave on the assumption that they would have the Wild Folk magic. Unless I mated with a human.'

'Why would you want to do that?'

'I wouldn't. But I don't much want to mate with anyone.'

'And Dearon? Is he from the old bloodlines as well?'

At the mention of the name, I flinch and glance around at the steady stream of people hurrying home in the evening rush hour. Names have no power of summoning and yet that is what I fear. Silence hangs between us until I can bring myself to answer his question.

'His blood is almost as pure as mine, his magic stronger than mine.'

'Is that why–?'

My phone rings. I have never been so grateful to see Jamie's name flash across the screen.

'Hi, Jamie.'

'I ran those searches you asked me about but nothing turned up, I'm afraid. If your Paladin has crossed over to New London, he's kept his head down and not got himself killed.'

'It was always a long shot, but worth a try. Thanks for your help.'

'No problem. I hope you find him.'

We end the call, and I relay Jamie's news to Karrion. He looks as disappointed as I feel.

'What do we do now? How do we find Brother Valeron?'

'I honestly have no idea. Unless you happen to know a Dog Shaman with a pack of bloodhounds, that avenue of enquiry may be a dead end for now.'

'What's next then?'

With a glance at my watch, I stand. 'Well, it's not even six o'clock yet. Why don't we see if we can have a quick chat with Braeman's personal assistant, Reaoul? I want to ask him about his employer's lovers, confirm his alibi, and also follow up with that offhand comment Marsh made.'

'The one about Braeman being after Reaoul's wife? I meant to ask you about that earlier.'

'It would be quite a twist if Braeman's lover turned out to be his personal assistant's wife. Talk about a motive.'

'Doesn't Reaoul have an alibi?' Karrion asks as we head towards the nearest bus stop.

'He does, but so does the man convicted of Braeman's murder. I'm disinclined to believe anything at the moment.'

'Fair enough. Do you know where he lives?'

We reach the bus stop, and I check when the next bus is due to arrive. 'The case file had the address. Mr and Mrs Pearson have a penthouse flat near the Brotherhood.'

In the evening rush hour, the journey takes twice as long as it would normally, and I have plenty of occasions to mutter that it would have been faster to walk. But for all the complaining, my legs appreciate the rest, and I feel less sore and tired when we alight near the river to walk the last few hundred yards.

From the location alone, it is clear the Pearsons have money. The building is old, but it was refurbished a few years back to become one of the most sought-after riverside locations in Old London. Since then, even human celebrities have been known to visit the occupants for glamorous parties that go on all night. Or so Karrion explains to me during the walk. Much of it happened before I moved to Old London and I have little interest in famous humans.

We are greeted by a doorman, and while he phones the Pearsons about our arrival, I note the security cameras covering the entrance to the building and the hallway area. Reaoul's alibi becomes a little more believable.

Soon we are in the lift on our way to the top floor. Reaoul is not home yet, but his wife, Eolande, is willing to speak to us while we wait for her husband. Even the lift has a marble floor, and from the way Karrion shifts his weight, I can tell he is as uncomfortable with the luxurious setting as I am.

I have barely finished knocking on the door when it opens and we set eyes on Eolande Pearson for the first time. Even without the scent of nectar, cherry blossom, and meadow grass rolling out to greet me, I would know that she is Feykin. Her eyes are deep pools of spring water, her hair a cascade of the brightest autumn colours, and her skin as pale as a midwinter moon. She carries herself with a natural poise that no human ballet dancer could ever hope to emulate, and even though she has been caught out by unexpected guests, her skirt and white blouse are smooth as if just ironed.

'Good evening,' she says in a voice to rival a nightingale, 'I gather you wish to speak to my husband?'

'Both of you, actually.' I offer her my hand. 'Yannia Wilde.'

When we shake hands, it is obviously not just me who feels the compatibility of our powers. Her magic brushes against mine, as tentative as the first unfurling of the spring. I neither reciprocate nor discourage the exploration, and she soon loses interest.

Karrion stammers out his name.

Her magic hangs around her like a shroud of summer mist. I feel its presence, but it defies definition; ephemeral like her Fey relations. My guess is she is first generation Feykin, the blood of the Fair Folk strong in her veins. She is also more powerful than Tanyella, or that is the impression she is giving. With Feykin it is impossible to tell where the deceit and manipulation give way to honesty.

She leads us to an enormous lounge dominated by windows affording a view of the Thames. The décor is all whites, greys, and sharp angles, which together with the marble floor give the rooms a cold, hostile feel. Nothing is out of place. To me, the flat looks more like an interior decorator's showroom than a home. How could anyone live in such a place? How could one of the Feykin live so far removed from nature?

Large abstract paintings and canvas prints of Eolande hang on the walls. They match the colour schemes of the flat and my eyes are drawn to the only splash of colour in the room: a pink gerbera Eolande holds in an otherwise black-and-white photo. I know she is a model and the photographs on display look like modelling shots. There is no sign of wedding photos, holiday pictures, or anything that suggests she is not the sole occupant of the flat.

When she seats herself on the sofa, one ankle tucked behind the other, and with perfect posture, I understand the purpose of the clinical décor of the flat. It has all been designed to draw attention to her: the living, breathing thing of beauty occupying the space. Everything else pales in comparison, which is no doubt her intention. Even armed with the knowledge, I cannot tear my eyes away.

How has a Light Mage of moderate standing convinced a Feykin like her to marry him?

There is a pregnant pause while we sit on a sofa opposite her, and I gather my thoughts. She watches me with impassive eyes, even as her lips maintain a polite smile.

'I've been hired to go over certain aspects of Gideor Braeman's tragic death and there are a few things I want to check with you and your husband.'

'Ask away.' Some of the politeness in her expression changes to boredom.

'I understand your husband came home about nine thirty that evening, is that correct?'

She nods.

'Is it usual for him to work such long hours?'

'My husband was there whenever Gideor wanted him.'

It could be my imagination, but an edge of chill seems to have crept into Eolande's voice.

'Was there anything unusual about that night or about your husband's demeanour?'

'No, everything was normal.'

'Did you know Gideor personally?' I ask, choosing my words with care. It would not do to jump straight into accusing her of adultery.

'Enough to engage in small talk at various functions. Gideor was not one to socialise with staff, but our paths did cross at events which Reaoul and I attended due to my career commitments. That said, recently my husband began receiving invitations in his own right, which I believe was a reflection on the rumours that Gideor intended to name my husband his successor as the Head of the Light Mages.'

This is all news to me, but I keep my expression neutral.

'I've heard it said that you and Gideor were... close.'

Eolande laughs and the sound is devoid of mirth. 'I wondered if you might bring up the gossip that I was having an affair with Gideor. I wasn't. He certainly would have wanted to, but my reciprocation never went beyond light flirting in public. While I don't expect you to believe me, of course, you should know this: the wedding vows I took were most specific. Any infidelity on my part would have unpleasant consequences.'

I have heard of such clauses being inserted into a marriage ceremony. They are promises sealed with magic, and acting contrary to them would indeed be unpleasant. To me, such inclusions show a fundamental lack of trust between the spouses, but the Feykin are not known for fidelity.

My attention is diverted to the sound of a door opening and closing. Footsteps approach the lounge and the mystery of how Reaoul has married a Feykin like Eolande is resolved.

The man who enters is tall and slender, with the sort of innate grace that, while it is not on a par with his wife's, can still put most humans and magical people to shame. Heavy locks of flaxen hair frame his oval face and cornflower-blue eyes lock with mine as he smiles a greeting. He is dressed from head to toe in black as a sign of mourning, though his suit looks tailor-made and the different materials create stylish contrasts without detracting from the overall impression of solemnity. Karrion and I stand to greet him.

'Reaoul Pearson,' he says as he offers me his hand. The scent of new dawn envelops me, even stronger than the cologne he is wearing. 'The doorman said you have some questions for me.'

I introduce myself and Karrion, and explain the purpose of

our visit. Eolande rises from the sofa in one fluid move and comes forward to press a chaste kiss on her husband's cheek.

'Have you offered them something to drink, my dear?'

'Why would I?' Eolande frowns. 'That implies I'd like them to stay and they're not guests.'

Consternation flashes across Reaoul's face, but he is quick to cover it up. 'Offer them a drink.'

When she turns to us, Eolande is all cool politeness. 'Would you like something to drink?'

I am tempted to decline the offer, but from the tightness in Reaoul's jaw, I surmise he would take it as an insult.

'Coffee would be lovely, thank you,' I say, and Karrion is quick to echo the request.

As Eolande heads for the open-plan kitchen, her stiff back is the only outward sign of her irritation. Meanwhile, Reaoul takes his wife's place on the sofa opposite us and motions for us to sit.

'I hope my wife has been helpful in answering your questions.' Reaoul's eyes flicker towards the kitchen, where cups are being set on a granite counter with a little more force than is necessary.

'She has indeed. And thank you for taking the time to speak to us.'

'What is it that I can do for you? I must admit to being rather curious about why a private investigator is looking into my employer's murder after the verdict has been delivered. Aren't you a little late?'

'It is unusual, but my client wishes certain aspects of the case to be clarified.'

'I see.' Reaoul leans back and smooths his silk tie. 'Gideor's death was a great tragedy and if there is any way I can help, I will do so.'

'What time did you leave the Braeman household on the night of the murder?'

With a tilt of his head, Reaoul stares past us, eyes unfocused. 'It would have been about seven thirty. I left through the main house and informed Simon, the Master of the House, that Gideor did not wish to be disturbed for the remainder of the evening. He had a Council meeting to prepare for, and I understand he also wished to continue his spell research.'

'Was that usual?' Karrion asks the question before I get the chance to. No doubt he too is wondering whether Gideor had a different reason for not wishing to be disturbed.

'Fairly usual. Between being the Speaker and the Head of the Light Mages, Gideor had a great deal of work to do. He was at his most efficient in the evening, in part because people were less likely to phone him after the usual working hours.'

'Was the study warded to ensure privacy?'

'Yes. There are a number of wards in place around the study. Some were always active, such as those preventing the room being viewed from afar, but you would have to ask Simon which wards were engaged that night.'

I jot a quick line in my notebook to add that to a list of questions I have for the Braeman household staff.

'I understand that you arrived home about nine thirty that evening,' I say, checking through my handwritten summary of the case. 'Where did you go between leaving work and getting home?'

There is a pause while Eolande returns with a tray of coffees. She sets cups in front of us on the coffee table, together with a small plate of chocolate truffles. The coffee is hot and strong, perhaps because the brewer was angry, and I add a little milk to dilute the taste. Eolande takes a seat next to her husband and sips her coffee.

'I walked to the river and stopped at a whisky bar for a drink.'

Setting down my coffee cup, I jot down the name of the bar,

should I need to go there later. It is academic anyway, given that Reaoul was home at the time Gideor was stabbed. The police have confirmed the alibi.

'Did you notice anything unusual about Gideor on the night of his murder? Was he troubled, particularly happy, or stressed?'

'No. He was busy, but there was nothing unusual about that. His wife had got him involved in a charity function she was organising and he had more on his plate than usual.'

'Was he expecting any visitors that evening or was he due to go out again?'

'I'm not aware of anyone due to visit him.'

I try to maintain my neutral expression while I study him. Of all the people close to Gideor, it would be Reaoul who knew about any affairs.

'Did Gideor spend nights in the study? I understand there is a bed in the room.'

'There were occasions when he would sleep there if he had stayed up late to do research and didn't wish to disturb his wife.'

There is no change in Reaoul's open expression, and I cannot tell whether he is lying. Time to be more direct.

'Do you know whether he was romantically involved with someone other than his wife?'

'As far as I was aware, my employer was faithful to his wife.'

Reaoul's face remains fixed in a half-smile, but Eolande gives something away. When he denies any affairs, her eyebrows flick up before her expression returns to haughty boredom. So he is lying and his wife knows it.

'Did Gideor ever mention his disagreement with Jonathain Marsh?'

'In passing. From what I know, it was a misunderstanding that was blown out of all proportion.'

That is a new way to describe it, but there seems little merit in challenging Reaoul over the point.

'Do you know if he had trouble with anyone? Anyone who might have borne a grudge against him?'

'He was well-liked. Although,' Reaoul hesitates, 'I suppose it's common knowledge among the Council members that Lord Ellensthorne and my employer disagreed over the direction the Council should take.'

'Yes, I understand that was a source of tension.'

'You could say that.' Reaoul hesitates again. 'Last time they argued, a few days before the murder, a whole corridor full of people heard Lord Ellensthorne tell my employer that unless Gideor changed his views, Lord Ellensthorne would destroy him.'

Karrion and I exchange a glance. This is new to us, and it is interesting that Lord Ellensthorne did not mention it earlier. Then again, the impression I got was that he thrives on being obtuse.

'The thing is,' Reaoul continues, 'Lord Ellensthorne was singular enough in his pursuits that I could well imagine him following through with the threat. Only Marsh got there first.'

He sets his cup down and stands. The interview is over.

'Thank you for taking the time to see us,' I say as I, too, stand and offer him my hand. Karrion finishes his coffee in one long swallow, coughs, and thanks our hosts.

'If there is anything else you need to ask me, please do get in touch,' Reaoul says as he walks us to the door. My feeling is that there is nothing sincere about his offer. Eolande stays in the lounge, all notions of politeness forgotten.

The door closes behind us with a note of finality and I wonder what Reaoul and Eolande will say to one another. Will they compare stories or move on without another thought?

We take the lift down in silence, and once we have left the building, I steer us across the road to the riverbank. The cooling air is wet, and I draw it deep into my lungs. Even with the pollution of Old London, it tastes great after the sterile feel of the Pearsons' home.

Eyes fixed on the brown water, I ask, 'What do you think?'

'A PA who doesn't know about his employer's affairs? Bollocks.'

'Reaoul was lying. His poker face is pretty good, but Eolande's dropped when Reaoul said he didn't know about any affair.'

'Faithful employee even beyond death,' Karrion says, his tone disbelieving.

'Perhaps, or maybe Reaoul is hiding something bigger and an affair is only a part of it.'

'Do you think he knows who killed Braeman?'

'At this point, I have no idea. It was interesting to hear that Lord Ellensthorne was threatening Braeman in public. The more we dig into things, the more inconsistencies we seem to find.'

'Isn't that the nature of murder investigations? Personally, I'm looking forward to the high-speed car chases and stalking bad guys through darkened alleys.'

A grin tugs the corner of my mouth as I shake my head. 'You watch far too much television. Doesn't your mum give you enough chores to do?'

Karrion's reply is a disgusted snort, and I laugh. He joins in and we stand side by side on the bank of the Thames, lost in the moment. Once again, I am struck by a feeling that this case would be far harder without Karrion helping me. This apprenticeship is proving to be good news indeed.

10

___

WISH UPON A HEARTH

O ur laughter subsides to comfortable silence, which Karrion breaks as he nudges my shoulder.

'What next?'

'Why don't you go home? It's getting late and I'm sure your mother will be anxious to hear how your apprenticeship is going. I'll formulate a plan for tomorrow and we can catch up first thing in the morning.'

'Fine. I need to grab my rucksack from yours, though.'

We walk to the nearest bus stop and catch a bus going in the right direction. During the journey to my flat, we are both lost in our thoughts. I suspect Karrion, too, is going through all the conversations we have had, trying to identify anything we may have missed before.

'Will you take some apples?' I ask when we walk into my flat and I spot the box.

'Sure. Mum will find plenty of use for them.'

I find a plastic bag and transfer most of the apples into it. Karrion tries to object, but I point out that his family will go through five times as many as I will.

While Karrion jogs upstairs to fetch his bag, I get the office chequebook from my drawer. By the time he returns, I have written the cheque and I hand it to him.

'Consider this your first pay cheque.'

'It's only been two days,' he protests, and then he looks at the figure. 'Are you sure?'

'Ilana is paying me well, so I can afford to do the same. We'll have to sit down and figure out something more official when we get a chance, but let's go with this for now.'

'Thanks, Yan.' He steps closer and gives me a quick peck on the cheek. Before I can be embarrassed by the gesture, Karrion wishes me goodnight and leaves.

I climb upstairs and set the kettle to boil. My laptop is still on the side table and I switch it on while the tea brews. My first task is to write an email to Ilana updating her on the progress we have made so far. It is my intention to continue reviewing the judgement footage in light of everything we have learned today, but after a while, I realise I have not taken in anything that is happening on the screen and my tea has gone cold. Restlessness forces me off the armchair, and after pouring the tea down the drain, I grab my keys and leave.

Whenever I need a change of scenery but cannot leave the city, I go to the Open Hearth. It's a pub five minutes from my flat, and for some time now, I have considered it to be my local haunt. I know the regular bar staff and they all greet me by name. Most of the regular clientele have magical blood, but the landlord, a Dog Shaman, welcomes humans and non-humans alike. No device detecting magical blood hangs by the door; everyone who enters is treated the same.

The Open Hearth is longer than it is wide, with the bar dominating the centre of the room. Wood panelling and copperplate engravings on the walls hark back to an older era, but the wi-fi signal is strong and the cash register modern. Tables are dotted around with sofas against the walls, and at the far end, patio doors lead to a small paved garden, which is popular during the summer months. The pub is named for the enormous fireplace along one of the long walls. The hearth is always set with logs and a fire burns there on all but the warmest days. More often than not, an Irish wolfhound snoozes in front of it.

Beyond the fireplace, the corner at the back of the room is darker than the others. Only one table is kept there, and it is reserved for a regular customer. It is his habit to sit with his back against the wall, obscured by the shadows. The black mariner pea coat he wears around the year, with its collar turned up against his angular face, only adds to his air of mystery. A constant smell of smoke hangs about him, and when he laughs, sparks flash in his dark eyes.

When I first began frequenting the Open Hearth, I was impressed and intimidated by him in equal measure. I have since learned that his image is carefully cultivated. That corner of the pub should be no darker than the others, but he insists on removing some of the bulbs from the light fittings above his table, with the blessing of the landlord. Tables that should stand nearby have been pushed away. His message has been received: the corner is his and his alone. The landlord and the staff allow his proprietary quirks because he is a long-standing regular and a valued visitor.

His name is Wishearth and he is there now, sitting in his shadowed corner. He raises his pint of Guinness as a greeting and motions at the chair opposite him. I pause at the bar to order myself a brandy and ask the bar staff to bring Wishearth another pint when his current one is finished. While one of the regular bar staff is measuring my brandy, I hear a thumping sound from near the fireplace and I bark out a short greeting.

'My Boris, I think he likes you better than me,' says a voice behind me. I turn to see Funjabun, the owner of the pub, step out of the kitchen. Although he has lived in Old London for decades, his thick Russian accent remains. Funja is a short, rotund man with a receding hairline and a ponytail tied back with a rubber band. With his deep-set eyes and heavy jowls, he reminds me of a bulldog rather than a wolfhound. Still, he and Boris are a perfect match.

'Why ever do you think he likes me better than his master?' I ask with a grin as a nose nudges my hand. Boris has risen from his favourite spot by the fire and has come to greet me. My fingers find a specific spot behind his ears and he leans against my side with a sigh.

Although I share a kinship with all aspects of nature, the affinity is only skin deep. I could never bond with a dog like a Dog Shaman, or understand a horse like a Horse Shaman. While I borrow elements from nature, I keep nothing for myself.

'I think perhaps you bribe him, no?'

We both know it would be impossible to break the bond between a Dog Shaman and his dog, but I play along, as I have many times before, and fashion my expression to one of innocence.

'I have no idea what you're implying, Funja.'

He shakes his head and gives me a critical look. 'You always too skinny. Visit more often at dinner time and we will feed you properly. Boris, he will keep an eye on you.'

'Now that would be a way to bribe Boris,' I say, and we share a laugh. Funja pats my arm as he goes past and waves away my money when I try to pay for the brandy.

Boris follows me as far as the fireplace and curls up on a thick rug that is there for him. Wishearth has been watching the interaction with a smile and I roll my eyes at him as I cross to his table. When I take the seat he indicated, I lean forward and breathe in the smells of fresh logs, wood smoke, and cooling ash. Ever since our first meeting when he sat next to me at the bar, I have known what he is. How strange that only upon moving to Old London have I found the truth behind the prayers and offerings of childhood. Here, in Wishearth, I have proof of my beliefs and fuel for my faith.

'Fancy meeting you here,' I say with a sardonic twist of my lips.

'Where else would I spend my evenings?' The warmth of his smile softens the sting of his words.

'I don't know. Do you not have a home to go to?' It's something I have often wondered about, and the fire of the brandy appears to have loosened my tongue.

'I get around.'

It is a point I want to press, but laughter erupts at the bar and my attention is drawn away from Wishearth. Boris too has lifted his head to observe a group of young men, but he appears unconcerned. A chair creaks, and I turn back to see Wishearth leaning further back in his seat.

'At a dead end, are we?' he asks, pushing locks of black hair from his face. My eyes stray to his slender, graceful fingers. I am struck by the familiar thought that they would be perfect for building fires and binding together elaborate offerings.

My eyes flick back up to meet his. 'Is it that obvious?'

We rarely speak beyond pleasantries, and yet he seems to know a great deal about me.

'Yannia, you only come here for two reasons. Either you are stuck with a case or something is bothering you. Given that I know you drove out of the city on Sunday, I'm inclined to think the former. So tell me, why are you stuck?'

I do not bother asking how he knows about my trip to the coast. 'I'm trying to find a man. He's vanished from Old London and his colleagues have no idea where he could have gone. He hasn't turned up in New London either, at least as far as New

Scotland Yard is concerned. If he has left Old London, tracking him down is going to be tricky.'

'It sounds to me like you need someone who can find people.' Wishearth drains the rest of his pint and leans back in his chair again. His long legs poke out next to me from under the table.

'And you know of such a person?' I sit up straighter, cupping the brandy tumbler in my hands.

He waits while one of the bar staff delivers his next pint and collects the empty glass before responding. 'Might do.' Sparks flash in his eyes as he grins at me.

'Are you going to tell me?'

'Might do.' His grin widens.

I roll my eyes. 'What do you want me to do? Beg?'

'That would be weird. I'll settle for the magic word.'

'Regular offerings of fir boughs?'

'That works too, though I did say a word. "Please" was what I had in mind.'

The urge to roll my eyes again is overwhelming, but I resist the temptation because I know that is what Wishearth is expecting me to do. So I watch him in silence, knowing patience is my greatest weapon against him.

He lasts under my stare for almost a minute, a new record for him. Then he laughs and leans in for a conspiratorial whisper. 'Have you spoken to Lady Bergamon?'

'Lady Bergamon?' The name means nothing to me. 'Who is she?'

His sigh is part exasperation, part amusement. 'Time to widen your contact list, Yannia. Go to see Lady Bergamon and discover for yourself. She lives on Ivy Street and may be able to help.'

I get no further than thanking Wishearth when Funja comes out of the kitchen and sets a plate in front of me. On it are a gammon steak, two fried eggs, fried pineapple rings, and a mug of chips. He returns a moment later with cutlery wrapped in a napkin and a bottle of ketchup. What makes him an exceptional pub landlord is his ability to memorise the likes and dislikes of his regulars.

'Less talking, more eating, *da*? Funja's food is good for the body, good for the spirit,' he says with a brief glance at Wishearth, who dips his chin.

'There was no need, Funja, but thank you,' I say.

'Boris, he keep an eye on you.' He wags his finger at me. 'No cheating, no bribery.'

Summoned by his master, Boris abandons his post by the fireplace and comes to sit next to me. Given his height, our eyes are level. His gaze is even as he watches me eat and never once does he drool, whine, or beg. Although being a Dog Shaman's companion gives him no exceptional intelligence, he seems to know that the food is not for him. Knowing Funja, Boris probably eats like a king.

Once the initial edge of hunger has dulled, I glance up to see Wishearth watching me, flames in his eyes. Heat rolls off him in waves, and I embrace the warmth as it soothes tension and aches from my muscles and joints. Boris begins to pant, but he does not move away from his post. From the corner of my eye, I notice a woman at a nearby table unbuttoning her cardigan, seemingly oblivious to the source of the sudden rise in temperature.

Having dinner in the company of Wishearth and Boris, I feel warm and protected. The frustration and niggling questions about the case fade into the background, as does the memory of Karrion's questions about Dearon. For a little while, the world eases away until it consists of a friend, a dog, a good meal, and the heat of a hearth fire.

WEDNESDAY

11

PLANT PATHWAYS

I dream of a chase through the forest, my forest. This dream has occurred increasingly often of late. I have come to fear it. A part of me knows it is because someone is looking for me. Every step I take in the forest brings him a little closer, yet I cannot help but flee from him. With every form I take, he is there. I am a dormouse, seeking to hide in the undergrowth, but he is a horned owl who hears my heartbeat. When I, as a vixen, dash off in a flash of fiery fur, a he-wolf pounces. Spreading wings, I head for the sky as a swift, but he, a gale-force wind, forces me back to the ground. A fallow doe's long legs eat the distance to the forest edge, but a hound pursues me, silent and determined.

There is a gap in the trees and I know I am close to freedom. My muscles burn in a final burst of speed, and the hound cannot keep up. Just two more strides and I will be free. Hope springs within me, only to be dashed when the trees move to block my path, denying me my freedom. I turn around, human once more, and watch as he stalks towards me. His dark eyes burn me and he is cloaked in the power of the Wild. I tremble with fear and yearning. My heart races and I feel my resolve fraying. If he reaches out, if he touches me, I will yield to his claim.

It is always at that moment that I wake.

As I sit bolt upright on my mattress, his name is on my lips. I dare not speak it aloud for fear of summoning him to me. What would I do if he came to Old London? If he came to seek me out, to take me home? Would I have the strength to defy him? Could I resist him after such a long absence?

Hugging my knees close, I stare at the embers of the fire and wonder. Is the dream a result of Karrion asking questions about Dearon or is there a deeper meaning to it? Names have no power to summon people, but can they summon dreams, memories? Could he be looking for me? Is it time?

The good mood I fell asleep in has been chased away by restlessness, and I have no desire to stay in bed. We are another day closer to Marsh's execution.

It is still dark outside, but when I open the lounge window to let the cool air in, I smell the breaking of dawn. The temperature has plummeted during the night, and I taste moisture with every breath. Once the sun rises, the garden will be grey with dew.

My flat is cool enough to tempt me to rebuild the fire from the remaining embers, but instead I choose a thicker fleece from the wardrobe in the corner of the lounge. As I hug the soft fabric close, I dread the coming of another winter. How wonderful it would be to hibernate like a bear and only awaken at the emergence of spring.

Feeling warmer, I am driven to the kitchen by my growling stomach. A glance in the fridge indicates that I should shop more often. I fix myself a bowl of porridge and add slices of apple. I eat by the lounge window. The world pales from black to blue to grey until colours bleed into the landscape. As I expected, the grass is grey with dew, and spiders' webs in the bushes gleam like strings of pearls when the first rays of the rising sun touch them. I am struck again by how much beauty there is in the middle of Old London. The thought brings a smile to my face.

A shower and a mug of coffee get my exhausted brain going, and I text Karrion, asking him to meet me at the bus stop nearest to Ivy Street at nine thirty. While I wait for the rest of the world to wake up, I type up the notes I took at the Brotherhood yesterday, adding as much detail as I can recall. I also summarise the conversation we had with Lord Ellensthorne, omitting the insults.

I reach the meeting point early. The streets are still busy with the tail-end of the morning rush hour, and I tuck myself against the wall of the building behind me. It keeps me away from the press of people. Even after all this time living in Old London, I am still not good with crowds, although I no longer have an urge to flee from them. But the instinct is hard to suppress and I am watchful for any signs of danger, of anything unusual or of any interest to me. I see nothing out of place.

A bus pulls up at the stop, disgorging a load of people. I spot Karrion hurrying towards me through the crowd. His hair is smoothed back, still wet, and I wonder if he overslept.

'Morning, Yan,' he says when he is within speaking distance. 'Sorry I'm late. I walked Wren, Jay, and Robin to school so Mum could run some errands before work.'

'You're not late, I was early.'

'Good. Mum wants you to come round for dinner soon.'

'I'd be delighted. What's the occasion?'

'She said it's her way of thanking you for taking me on as an apprentice.'

'Will she give me a medal as well?' I ask, and grin at his scowl.

'Funny.'

'I thought so.'

Karrion chooses to rise above the teasing. 'Where are we going this morning?'

'I mentioned our missing Paladin to a friend last night and he suggested we go and talk to a woman called Lady Bergamon.'

At the mention of the name, Karrion's eyebrows shoot up. '*The* Lady Bergamon?'

'Do you know her?'

'I know *of* her. She's as much an urban legend as the Leeches Ellensthorne mentioned. From the stories I've heard, she sounds like a Plant Shaman, except they don't exist.'

'That we know of, anyway.' At his confused expression, I smile. 'Not everything magical resides in Old London. I would imagine that for some people here, Wild Folk are little more than creatures of tales and songs, yet we are as real as you are. Who knows what else resides in the remaining wild places, in the caverns under the island, in the sheltered coves along the coast? And don't forget, Britain holds no monopoly over magical blood. It's a big world out there.'

'Point taken. But what I'm saying is that all I know of Lady Bergamon are vague rumours.'

'Let's go and see if there's any truth in those rumours.'

We turn a corner and I pause to look ahead. There is a pub on the corner across from us, but otherwise, we are on a residential street. I lead on, glancing at each house we pass.

'I take it you have an address?' Karrion asks.

'No, all I got was the name of this street. My friend said I'd recognise the house when I found it.'

'Who is this friend of yours?' There is curiosity in his eyes and perhaps a hint of protectiveness.

'He's one of the regulars in the Open Hearth. I know him, a little. I was preoccupied, he noticed and I explained about trying to find Brother Valeron. He knows what I do, so looking for people is nothing out of the ordinary.'

'Did he tell you how he knows Lady Bergamon?'

'No, but he always gives the impression he knows a lot more than he lets on.'

'Who is he?'

I consider how best to answer, knowing my reply will be cryptic. 'He's Wishearth; nothing more, nothing less.'

Karrion has further questions, but my attention is drawn elsewhere, and I let them remain unanswered. We have walked almost the length of the street when I feel threads of power beckoning me. There is something ahead of us, something I have not encountered before in Old London. My steps quicken until I am running. Karrion follows, calling my name, but I ignore him in favour of racing towards the last house on the left.

I come to a breathless halt in front of a property bordered by a wrought-iron fence that twists into branches and leaves. An arch in the middle admits access to what, perhaps, was once the driveway. It is now covered in rows and rows of plant pots. Larger pots line the edges of the space, and the pots get progressively smaller towards the middle. In each, a plant of some description is growing, and I cannot see two that are alike.

My eyes are wide as I take in the chaotic organisation of the pots and the plants they contain. The house itself, a two-storey detached family home built of pale bricks, looks warm and welcoming. Leaves press against the net curtains in all the windows, and I guess that the inside will be as full of plants as the scene before me.

'Wow.' Karrion has caught up with me and is looking at the potted garden over my shoulder. 'I'm not imagining this, am I?'

'No.'

'I know I've walked down this road before. How have I not noticed this?'

'Perhaps you weren't meant to?' I am not sure what makes me utter the words and yet I am certain there is truth behind them. With a property this distinctive, how could Lady Bergamon be little more than a myth? If I am right, does that mean that she wants to be found and wants me to find her? Is that the reason why this place feels welcoming to me?

There is a narrow path leading to the front door, just wide enough for one person. I head down it, Karrion right behind me.

'I feel sorry for anyone having to deliver anything bulky to this house,' I say over my shoulder.

'The plants are in pots. It should be easy to move them out of the way.'

'Move them where?' I gesture at the area around us. 'There's not a spare inch of ground anywhere.'

'Maybe there's a back gate.'

The right side of the property, where it borders an alley connecting to Ivy Street, is separated from the pavement by a brick wall. It is tall enough for me to suspect it has been built deliberately to block prying eyes. But why then is the front fence built of open wrought iron rather than closed with bricks?

Before I can present the mystery to Karrion, I reach the front steps. As I do, the door opens. A woman, tall with a wiry physique, stands in the doorway. Her white hair cascades in curls to her shoulders and she is wearing a blue summer dress adorned with white flowers. The blue eyes regarding me would be severe, were it not for the warm smile tempering their edge.

'I wondered when your path would lead you to my door,' she says as she steps out into the morning sun.

Taken aback by her words, I borrow the nose of a nearby hedgehog and take a deep breath. She smells of rich soil, nectar, fresh green shoots, and rotting plant matter. It is the scent of life and I am drawn to her straight away. I have never met another like her.

I make deeper use of my power to examine her more closely. I find she is like an ancient oak tree: her roots burrow deep into the ground; her branches are strong and free of decay; the sap flowing in her veins is potent and full of magic. She is far, far older than she looks, and my impression of her confirms that I found the house only because she willed it so.

Her gaze never wavers as she waits with patience for my answer. Relinquishing the threads of magic, I respond to her smile.

'I had no idea you knew of me, yet you wondered when I would come.'

She reaches out and tilts my chin up to examine my face. Her fingers are all at once soft as marigold petals, smooth as acorns, and rough as spruce bark.

'There have been many whispers of something wild in the city, something that lingers longer than just a fleeting visit. You may not have been aware of it, but you have been noticed wherever you've gone in Old London. The plants were right to have told me about you, for you are a reminder of the old days when there were many wild places in England.'

'Some still remain.'

'Some, yes, guarded by your kin. But they have become too few. Many of the voices I grew up with have faded into faint whispers, while others have gained prominence. The language of the plants is changing, just as the world is changing. Those of the wild will struggle to adapt.'

I nod without breaking her hold, though I am left with an impression that she speaks more about herself than about the Wild Folk. In the city, adapting to change must be far harder than in the open countryside. Yet she has chosen Old London as her home. I hope in time I will find out why.

'But guests should not linger upon the threshold. Come through to the garden and there you can tell me what brings you to my world.'

She ushers us in, through a long corridor with doors on both sides and into a spacious kitchen. Everything is clear and ordered, but the faded floral wallpaper and the avocado-green sink look thirty years out of date. Another door with a frosted glass window framed by frilled curtains is open to the back garden. She invites us to go on out while she brews a pot of tea.

As I step over the threshold, the world shifts focus and a ripple of magic washes over me. Shaking my head, I rub my eyes. Karrion does the same next to me. We share a confused glance, but before I have a chance to say anything, his focus is drawn to something beyond me. His expression goes slack. Now concerned, I look out into the garden.

The tall brick wall continues along the right edge, disappearing in the distance behind fruit trees. It is a garden too large for central London. I become aware that I can no longer hear the constant rumble of traffic; I can no longer smell cars and dust and too many humans living in close quarters. Wherever we are, it is not the back garden of a house on Ivy Street. And yet it is.

Lady Bergamon is more powerful than I appreciated.

Green lawn rolls into the distance, dotted with trees of all varieties from a tall pine to a maple sapling. Along the edges of the garden, borders of flowers create a chaotic display of colour. The air is heavy with their scents. There is a narrow patio area next to the house, but that too is dominated by plants of all kinds in pots of all sizes. A wooden table and chairs take up what little space is available amid the pots. Away in the distance, beyond the fruit trees, I catch a glimpse of a vegetable plot and a greenhouse.

An incongruous detail strikes me. The variety of flowers I

see blossoming is odd. Along the edges of the nearest border, primroses and snowdrops compete for space with daffodils and hyacinths. A buddleia bush is full of butterflies, while foxgloves reach their long stems over the grass, and bumblebees are swarming to feed on the lavender bushes that grow alongside the camellias in bloom. Further along, asters, verbena, and dahlias grow side by side with climbing roses and winter jasmine.

The ordered sequence of seasons is lost here. All exist together, no matter how impossible that is.

I look up, expecting to see the city skyline around us. Instead, there is only blue sky with wispy white clouds. The sun seems brighter than before, no longer obscured by the polluted air.

The garden is teeming with life, and I let it rush to greet me. Earthworms inhabit the soil, a family of field mice has made a nest in one of the bigger pots, slugs inch between blades of grass, and I hear the shuffling of a hedgehog hunting them. Birds sing in the trees, and a cat suns himself on top of the garden table.

I have found a haven in the middle of Old London.

'What is this place?' Karrion murmurs.

'I don't know, but I trust we're about to find out.'

Lady Bergamon emerges with a tray laden with a teapot, a smaller tea infuser, a Victoria sponge cake, and crockery. When she sets the tray on the table, she picks from it a flower with narrow blue petals and a striking yellow centre and hands it to Karrion. I recognise it as an aster from a cluster I noticed growing nearby.

'It may be somewhat presumptuous, but this reminded me of you.'

Karrion takes the flower, stammering a confused thank you, and Lady Bergamon turns to me.

'I have no plant for you, for all plants are you and you are all plants.'

I incline my head, accepting the truth of her words. I suspect her statement applies as much to herself as it does to me, and in her eyes, I see a glimmer that suggests she knows this too.

The moment passes, and she smiles. 'Now, I believe some introductions are in order.'

'Of course, excuse my manners,' I say, and point at Karrion. 'This is my apprentice, Karrion Feathering, and I am, as I gather you know, Yannia Wilde.'

'It is a delight to meet you both. You will no doubt have concluded that I am Lady Bergamon.'

'Where are we?' Karrion asks, unable to contain his curiosity.

'This is my garden.'

'We're not in Old London anymore, are we?'

'We are.' Her eyes sparkle with amusement. 'But perhaps it is Old London as it once was, rather than how it is now.'

Karrion's eyes widen. 'We've travelled back in time?'

'Oh, nothing as simple as that,' Lady Bergamon says. 'Think of my garden as a memory, a remnant of old times, which has been sustained by the plants and their magic.'

'Don't you mean your magic?' Karrion seems emboldened by her answers.

'Is there a difference?'

At Karrion's astonished expression, I hide a smile behind my hand. Once again, his youth shows.

'Come now,' she beckons us towards the table, 'let us take tea.'

We choose seats opposite her and she pours tea into two of the porcelain cups. Each is decorated with delicate flowers of different species. Lady Bergamon places one of the cups in front of Karrion before offering him a small milk jug and a matching sugar container. The other cup she leaves at her elbow.

She turns to me. 'I took the liberty of preparing something a little different for you.'

My response is a hesitant smile. She pours a pale-amber drink from the separate tea infuser and stirs in two teaspoons of honey without asking.

'It will help with the pain,' she says, and places the cup in front of me.

I must look as astonished as Karrion did moments ago, for she chuckles, though I detect a softness in the melodious sound.

'It's in your eyes, in the tightness around them. But fear not, it is not obvious unless you know what to look for.'

Her words reassure me, and yet I feel a flash of disquiet at how much she has read from me. It proves my impression of her wisdom is correct. I suspect there is little she does not see and deduce.

While she cuts slices of cake, I take a sip from my cup. Ginger dominates the taste, though I also detect clove and something different. Feverfew, perhaps, and willow bark. There is an undercurrent of bitterness, almost masked by the honey. Ginger, clove, feverfew, willow bark: these are all herbal remedies for pain, and I take a long sip, touched by her thoughtfulness. Some of my disquiet eases away as a warmth takes root in my stomach and I relax against the cushioned backrest.

Once we all have a piece of cake in front of us, Lady Bergamon leans back in her seat, a teacup in her hand.

'As much as I enjoy the occasional visitor, I doubt this is a social call. What is it that brings you to my door?'

'The life of an innocent man. We're investigating the possibility that he has been framed for murder. The execution is set for two days' time, at noon on Friday. There's someone, a man, who might be able to tell us how the Herald could be fooled into convicting an innocent, but he has disappeared and no one seems to know where he could have gone. Someone suggested you might be able to help.'

'Wishearth sent you, did he?'

Karrion chokes on his piece of cake, and I let out a surprised laugh. Lady Bergamon's smile widens.

'You have a smell of wood smoke about you, Yannia. It seems someone has taken an interest in you.'

I am not certain what Lady Bergamon is hinting at with her words. From Funja's passing comments, I had gathered that Wishearth preferred to drink alone. When we did share a conversation, I assumed it was an acknowledgement of my following the old ways. There cannot be too many people still honouring Hearth Spirits in Old London. But Lady Bergamon suggests a connection that goes beyond the old rites; a connection I cannot grasp as yet.

If Lady Bergamon guesses anything of my thoughts, she gives no indication of it. Instead, she refills our cups and adds more honey to mine. I take a forkful of cake, which is a perfect combination of fluffy sponge, sweet strawberry jam, and fresh whipped cream.

'Yes, I may be able to help you,' Lady Bergamon says. 'You will need to tell me a few things about this man you seek, and with the right combination of flowers, blood, and magic, I can find him. Even if he does not wish to be found.'

I open my mouth to give her a brief account of Brother Valeron, but Lady Bergamon shakes her head. 'Not yet. First, we must finish our tea; then we shall see about finding the man.'

A bumblebee lands on my plate, and I extend a finger towards it. After partaking of a smear of jam, it climbs on to my finger. I stroke the soft pile covering its body while it explores my hand. There is something about bumblebees that I cannot help but love. The sight of them buzzing between the berry bushes never fails to put a smile on my face.

I now watch as the bumblebee, having concluded its exploration, takes flight and makes a beeline for a cluster of tall fireweeds growing on the edge of the patio. Lady Bergamon follows my gaze and nods towards the plants.

'Bumblebees love the rapscallion roses.'

Her name for the plant catches me by surprise, and I offer her a puzzled frown as a response, which makes her laugh.

'A rather unsuitable suitor once offered me them in lieu of roses in the hopes of winning my heart. I'm afraid the name has stuck.'

I join her in laughter, delighted by the image and the personal touches which add to the richness of her garden. Every moment, I feel more at home in her domain.

By the time our cups and plates are empty, the warmth has spread to my limbs and some of the ache in my joints has eased. The effects of the herbs are familiar from my past when they were all I could use to alleviate the pain, but their impact is far greater when combined with my regular medication. While it would be wonderful to manage with herbal remedies alone, it is simply not feasible for me.

We stack the crockery and cutlery on the tray, and Lady Bergamon takes it inside. When she returns, she is carrying a shallow metal bowl that glints of copper in the sunlight. The blue and purple reflections within the metal tell me the bowl is cast from heart copper, making it extremely valuable.

'Walk with me,' she says, and steps off the patio on to the grass.

I follow her example and take off my shoes and socks. As I feel the softness under my feet, the power of the garden washes over me. It is alarming to find how much my magic has depleted in just a few days, and with a chill of fear, I realise it is happening increasingly quickly. How soon until a trip to the coast every two weeks will no longer be able to sustain me?

A few paces ahead, Lady Bergamon stops and turns to look at me.

'Tell me three things about the man you are looking for.'

I push my fears aside and catch up with her, Karrion matching his pace to mine.

'He is a Paladin.'

She steers us past a weeping willow to the brick wall, which is covered in a creeper plant. I recognise the distinctive blossoms as passionflower. It may just be my imagination, but the leaves and flowers seem to reach out to greet her. While I watch, she runs her fingers along the stem and over the leaves, until she finds the base of a flower. With a gentle twist, she detaches it and places it in the bowl.

'He is a conduit for the Heralds of Justice,' I say, sensing that she is waiting for me to continue.

We duck under low branches of an elder tree and the sweet fragrance of the flowers envelops me. The scent transports me back into a memory of lying in the shadow of such a tree, the sky above me a mottled patchwork of delicate white flowers and green leaves. A long blade of grass appears in my field of vision and tickles my nose. I laugh, swatting it away, and the timbres of another voice join me.

How old was I? It feels like a long time ago. I may have been fourteen, perhaps fifteen. My love for Dearon was still pure, untainted by what was to come. I was happy that afternoon under the elder tree. A traitorous part of my mind thinks that perhaps he was too.

Beyond the tree, the scent of elderflowers gives way to cherry blossoms and the memory fades. I had forgotten all about that summer afternoon and I wonder what other memories this garden may reawaken. Will all of them include Dearon?

Lady Bergamon has walked some way ahead of me, and I quicken my steps. She is heading for a small black cauldron sitting on a patio stone. It is full of bright-yellow flowers that have domed black centres. Showing as much care as before, she cuts one of the flowers and adds it to the bowl.

'He has left the Brotherhood,' I say, 'and is lost to his Brothers and Sisters and to his family.'

A nod is her only response as Lady Bergamon takes us to the left border, to another brick wall. Even before she stops, my eyes are drawn to a cluster of tall flowers leaning over the row of white stones marking the edge of the flowerbed. Each flower has two sets of petals: the purple outer ones taper to points, while the five inner ones are rounded and white, save for an area of deep blue at their base. From the centre, yellow anthers reach out. Again, Lady Bergamon adds one of the flowers to the bowl.

The greenhouse and the vegetable patch are ahead of us and both are larger than I first appreciated. Beyond them is a small copse, and I realise that the garden is also far wider than it should be. I can no longer see the brick walls on either side of us.

In the dappled shade of the nearest trees is a well, built of grey stones and weathered wood. When we reach it, Lady Bergamon sets the bowl on the wide edge and turns a winch to raise a bucket of water. The liquid is crystal clear and smells of deep earth, hidden springs, and winter rains. While we watch, she pours water into the bowl, deep enough for the three flowers to float in it. She leaves the bucket on the edge of the well and motions for us to continue into the woods.

Under the trees, the season appears to be late summer. The leaves on the ash and rowan trees are beginning to change colour, but for now, green still dominates. Here, the power of the garden is the strongest I have felt yet, and I wish I could curl in the shade of an oak tree and take a nap while my magic recharges. As it is, my steps lighten. I look around with the keen senses of a squirrel and revel in the presence of the unspoilt forest.

Karrion slows so he is walking a few steps behind me and I feel him staring at me, but here I am not concerned. Here it feels like I could take to the high branches.

Once again, my sight has misled me and the copse is larger than I thought. A worn trail winds between the trees and opens into a clearing in the middle of the woods. Amidst a wild flower meadow is a stone, perhaps six feet in diameter, sunk into the ground. It is a perfect circle, weathered and covered in moss. Carved into its edges are runes, though I recognise neither the style of them nor the individual symbols. They alone are free of the moss and their sharpness suggests that they were carved yesterday. In the centre of it stands a short stone pillar, and as Lady Bergamon steps on to the circle, she places the bowl on top of the pillar.

Karrion and I pause at the edge of the stone. We have neither invitation nor permission to step on to its surface. Whatever its purpose, it is not for us, not for our magic.

Lady Bergamon dips her hand into a pocket in her dress and pulls out what I first think is a knife. A closer look reveals it to be a short length of obsidian fitted into a bone handle. The blade gleams black in the sun, casting light into the bowl and along its rim.

Raising the knife, Lady Bergamon runs it along her palm. Blood drips into the bowl. Each of the three flowers receives at least one drop.

'A flower for faith, a flower for justice, a flower for desertion,' she says, lifting her eyes to meet mine. 'Now give me his name.'

'Brother Valeron Fidelis.'

I feel the gathering of her power, but it is no brash surge of magic. It is the rustle of dry leaves; the whisper of a breeze in the long grass; the cascade of rain on spring flowers. It teases at the edges of my power, so familiar, so alien.

Summer heat washes over us, followed by a bite of winter frost, and Lady Bergamon drops her gaze to the bowl before her. It is hard to tell in the dazzling sunshine, but the whole bowl appears to be glowing, magic pulsing from the flowers within.

The power ebbs away, fading like the colours of day at dusk. Sunlight seems a little less bright, the day a little less warm. Lady Bergamon lets out a shuddering breath, bracing her uncut hand against the stone pillar. I see beads of sweat sliding down her temples and a grey tinge to her otherwise rosy skin. Whatever magic she has wielded, it has taken a lot from her.

'He is in the Wayfarers Inn, just outside Hertford.' The words are soft but full of conviction.

Intent upon helping her, I step forward, but Lady Bergamon stops me with a raised hand.

'No, you must not step upon the stone. I shall be all right in a moment.'

She stands in the pool of sunlight, head bowed. Little by little, I become aware of whispering and I glance around to seek the source. Karrion does not appear to have noticed anything out of the ordinary, so it must be from the magic particular to this garden. The trees above us are reaching towards Lady Bergamon, lending her strength and vitality.

Encouraged by the power swirling around me, I open my senses to the garden. My nose identifies the scents of Karrion and Lady Bergamon, as well as the smell of fresh horse manure and a hint of fresh water. I cock my head, and somewhere ahead of us, I catch the sound of running water and the rustle of reeds. For a fleeting instance, I fancy there is something large moving in the forest, but it is gone before I can be certain of what I sensed.

At length, Lady Bergamon straightens up and I see the lines

of fatigue have faded from her face. Here, in her element, it does not take long for her to regain her power.

'Let us go back,' she says, and indicates the path we followed to the clearing.

'What's that way?' Karrion asks, and points towards the woods ahead.

'Gardens. Woods. Meadows.' Lady Bergamon smiles, picks up the heart-copper bowl, and steps off the stone.

'How far does it extend?'

'Oh, quite a distance.'

Karrion looks like he wants to pepper her with more questions, but he must have realised he will get little from her. I can see he is burning with curiosity and I duck my head to hide my smile. In truth, I am grateful for his questions, for I am as curious as he is.

As we turn to leave, I notice the forest around us appears to have grown while Lady Bergamon was working her magic. A narrow game trail winds between trees to a smaller clearing. At the edge, a rose bush has crept up an elder tree and across a low hanging branch. It forms a living arch over the path, inviting me to step through.

'May I?' I ask, pointing towards the game trail.

'Of course. While you are with me, the garden is perfectly safe.'

The implication is clear. As benign as Lady Bergamon's domain appears, hidden dangers lurk within its flexible borders.

I follow the path, drawn by my curiosity. As I walk closer to the arch, the ground beneath my bare feet grows wetter. By the time I am standing in the shade of the roses, the moss is waterlogged.

With a clearer view of what lies beyond the arch, I see that what I thought was a large clearing is only a couple of square metres in size. It too is carpeted in thick moss, with a small spring in the middle. The blue sky and border of trees above are reflected in a dark pool. From it, a narrow stream skirts the larger clearing before disappearing into the woods.

Something about the spring draws my attention, and I open my senses to it. The scent of water is strong, more prominent yet more diverse than it should be. Mixed in with the deep spring scent are those of meandering rivers, wide lakes, and sheltered sea coves.

This water carries power that differs from that of Lady Bergamon. But how could someone else be contributing to this place which exists only because of her? And who or what could weave their power with hers so that at first glance they appear as one?

At the edge of the pool, I dip my toes, sending ripples across the still surface. The clear water reveals dark depths, and were I to step in, I would be completely submerged. There is, in this spring, a distinct feeling of hostility. I am not welcome here. The feeling is in direct contrast to all else I have felt in this garden, which reinforces the notion of there being two distinct sources of magic at play, and only Lady Bergamon welcomes my presence.

Are all visitors targets of suspicion, or is there something about me specifically that offends the being? My imagination runs rampant with possible answers.

The feeling of hostility intensifies and I whirl around, certain someone is staring at me. All I see are trees and the distant shapes of Lady Bergamon and Karrion.

As I hurry back to them, I notice a bare patch of soil under a birch. Embedded in the wet earth is a hoof print. Other than the faint smell of manure I picked up earlier, I have seen no evidence of a horse in the garden. There was nothing near the house that could be a stable. Can this place sustain wild horses? If that is the case, I would expect to see more evidence of their existence. Or does Lady Bergamon have a single horse? But why? And where is it?

Lady Bergamon's expression is inscrutable when I return to the main clearing. From the steady way she meets my eyes, I know she can sense the dozens of questions spinning around my mind. As curious as I am, they will remain unasked. Perhaps in time I may return to this garden and get to know Lady Bergamon well enough to voice my questions and have them answered.

We walk through the garden in silence, and I feel a tinge of sadness when I put on my socks and shoes. My power has recharged, but a part of me yearns to linger, to explore the limits of this haven. I could run through the woods as a wolf, soar over the meadows as a swift, and speed through the brooks as a trout.

The heart-copper bowl that Lady Bergamon sets on the garden table reminds me of why we are here. Only one question remains.

'What do we owe you for the information you have provided?'

'Nothing.' She shakes her head with a smile. 'The pleasure of assisting some of Old London's younger inhabitants is payment enough. I hope you succeed in your attempt to prove the impossible.'

'As do I.'

Stepping forward, she brushes her fingers over my cheek. 'You're welcome to visit whenever you wish. I imagine you need to recharge your powers on a regular basis and running in my garden is an easy way to do so.'

'Are you sure?' She has offered me a valuable gift. 'I wouldn't want to lessen the power of the gardens.'

Her laugh is deep and rich, with the vitality of the dark soil nourishing the plants around us. 'It is an exchange, is it not? Something given for something received. No, you cannot diminish the power of this place simply by visiting me. In fact, I believe you would prove to be beneficial; an edge of Wild always has a place in my garden.'

'In that case, I'd be honoured.' Following an instinct, I bow and she chuckles.

'Come and see me when you have solved your case. I shall look forward to hearing all about it. Perhaps then you will also tell me how one of the Wild Folk has come to make Old London her home.' Taking two steps to the side, she twists a short branch free from a cypress. 'Give this to Brother Valeron's wife.'

I have no inkling of its significance, but I tuck the branch in my pocket. 'Thank you, for everything.'

'I wish you the best of luck. Give Wishearth my best when you next see him. He has earned his offerings tonight.'

With that, she guides us through the house and out to the front garden. Her smile is warm when she bids us farewell, but I am left pondering the significance of her words.

12

BROTHER VALERON

Stepping through Lady Bergamon's front gate feels like waking up from a deep slumber. As the sights, smells, and sounds of Old London assault my senses, I yearn for the serenity of her domain. From Karrion's expression, he shares my feelings. The visit to the garden has been a short, welcome reprieve.

Can I really prove the impossible?

As if sensing my doubts, Karrion bumps shoulders with me.

'Don't worry, Yan. I knew you were special the moment we met. That's why I stopped you plunging to your death by jumping from roof to roof.'

'Was that the reason? I always thought it was because you wanted to know how to get bat wings so you could be Batman.'

'You've got to admit, being Batman beats being an unemployed artist any day.'

'If it's the leather suit you want, we could always stop at a fetish shop.'

I grin. Karrion pulls a face.

'I think I'll pass. Besides,' it is his turn to grin, 'you lack the necessary social skills to be Alfred.'

'Funny.'

I do my best to remain straight-faced while he laughs, but in truth, the banter has lifted my spirits.

As much as it feels like we have spent days in Lady Bergamon's garden, it is still Wednesday. A glance at my watch tells me I have forty-seven hours to save Jonathain Marsh.

We catch the bus back to my flat, get the postcode for the Wayfarers Inn, and head out in my car. The A10 will take us most of the way there, and it should be an easy drive once we leave London.

The border of Old London on the A10 is just past Liverpool Street station and I feel a subtle shifting in reality when we drive over the invisible line. A background thrum of magic fades away, and the colours around us become muted. My car runs a little more smoothly, as if the presence of magic was adding extra air tension the engine had to struggle against in Old London.

Next to me, Karrion's brow furrows. While I know he is not as sensitive as I am to changes in background magic levels, leaving behind the one place where he knows he belongs does unsettle him. Since my power is tied to nature, I am grateful for a reprieve from the stink of cars and streets crammed with people, no matter how short that reprieve may be.

Besides, I left behind the one place where I belong over a year ago.

As expected, the traffic eases once we leave Central London and we make good time to Hertford. Neither of us says much during the drive or our lunch break, content to dwell on our own thoughts. After our visit to Lady Bergamon, we both have plenty to think about.

The Wayfarers Inn is a red-brick building on the outskirts of the town, designed to attract travellers from the A10 and A414. There are two floors above the ground floor and two separate wings stretch away from reception. A paved courtyard and blue awning over the glass double doors are an invitation for guests to enter.

Both the car park and the strip of green between the hotel and the road are bordered by maple trees and trimmed rose bushes. While the plants appear to be flourishing, I find the straight lines and lack of variation irritating. It is a classic example of humans attempting to control nature.

As we cross the car park and walk towards the reception, Karrion's attention is drawn to the left, where trees line the side of the building. When he stumbles on the kerb, I reach out to steady him, but his eyes remain focused elsewhere.

'Is everything okay?'

'Huh?' With effort, he glances at me. 'Yes, fine.'

His attention remains fixed until we pass through the glass doors and into an average hotel lobby.

A young man standing behind the reception desk smooths his suit jacket and straightens his posture when he spots us. We make a beeline for him and I flash him my best smile.

'Hi there. A friend of mine is staying in this hotel, but I can't seem to get hold of him over the phone. His daughter is unwell and I was hoping to take him straight to the hospital.'

'I'm sorry to hear that. What is your friend's name?'

'Brother Valeron Fidelis.' Thinking his title cannot hinder, I add, 'He's a Paladin of Justice in Old London.'

The clerk spends a few moments tapping away at the computer and nods. 'Yes, he's staying here. He arrived on Sunday and requested a room in the magic users' corridor.'

'You have separate areas for magic users and non-magic users?' I find the idea vaguely offensive.

'Yes. I mean no disrespect, but some of our clients... well, they get a little nervous about magic. This arrangement keeps everyone content.'

I am tempted to point out that we are all just people, but getting into an argument with the clerk will achieve nothing. It would be my time and breath I would be wasting.

'Could you ring the room, please? Or could I do that?'

'No problem, I'll try for you.'

We wait in tense silence while he dials a number. After a minute, he sets the phone down.

'I'm afraid he's not picking up.'

'Would it be possible for me to go up to his room and knock on the door, just in case he's in the shower and can't hear the phone?'

'I'm not allowed to give out a guest's room number,' the clerk says, looking uncomfortable.

'Perfectly understandable. Is there someone who could take us up? At the very least, then I'll know for sure he isn't there and can slip a note under the door.'

When the clerk hesitates, I add my trump card. 'I get that this is unusual, but Valeron's daughter has cancer. She's six years old and she really needs her father. The doctors don't think she's got long to live.'

'I... I'll call my manager.'

'Thank you.'

We step from the reception desk to give him a measure of privacy. My conscience twinges at the deception, but what I said was not strictly a lie. Brother Valeron's daughter is sick and a life does hang in the balance. It is imperative that we speak to him.

After a few minutes, an older man dressed in a suit hurries to the reception desk. His name tag identifies him as Michael.

'I understand you need to speak to one of our guests?' he asks.

'Yes, that's right. I've tried phoning him dozens of times, but

I can't get hold of him. His daughter is in hospital and I need to take him to her.'

'I'll take you up.' He motions towards the lifts and we follow him.

'Thank you, Michael. I really appreciate this.'

On the second floor, we step out of the lift and turn right through a set of glass double doors. This is the magic users' corridor. It looks no different from the rest of the hotel, but it's not as though we have a habit of leaving pet imps in the corridors or resting our broomsticks against the doors. Even so, I catch an impression of power, like an itch between my shoulder blades I cannot scratch, which goes beyond the subtle sense that others with magic are nearby.

Something is not right.

As we stop outside Brother Valeron's room, Karrion's eyes lose their focus again. He stares at the door as if he can see through it and his expression grows troubled.

'There's a tree just outside the window of this room,' he says, his words slow, 'and it is full of crows and magpies.'

'So?' Michael shrugs. 'We often see birds here.'

'But a tree full of birds, each of them waiting?'

'What are they waiting for?' I ask, as concern grows at the back of my mind.

'Food.' Karrion turns to meet my eyes.

'We don't feed the birds,' Michael says, but we both ignore him.

Tugging at the threads of my power, I find a rabbit asleep underneath a nearby rose bush. It lends its nose to me that I may smell what humans cannot. I hear Michael's astonished gasp as the ripple of magic passes over my face. I pay him no heed as I focus on the room in front of me, leaning closer to the door.

The smell is faint, but there is no mistaking rotting meat.

'I can smell decay.' I turn to Michael. 'I suggest you open the door. Your guest is not well.'

He fumbles with the key card and finally gets the door open. I feel a fleeting caress against my cheek; gone before it fully registers. The moment the door moves inwards over the threshold, there is a snap of the ward that was in place. We are hit with a wall of stench, the metallic notes of blood all but overwhelmed by the odour of decomposing flesh.

While Karrion and Michael gag and recoil, I step into the room. The human in me finds the smell as repulsive as they do, while the wilder side of my nature is whispering that there is meat, a little spoilt, just right, not overripe. A hunger rises within me, the instinct of a predator to gorge on meat when it is readily available.

I am glad we ate lunch along the way, otherwise I may have given in to the hunger.

The return of a body to the elements of nature is a powerful process, and here it has been compounded by the enclosed space and the ward. A pulse of power runs through the room and calls to me, tempting me to give in. Without thinking, I reach out to it, my wildness reacting to a natural process. In doing so, I get far more than I bargained for.

Karrion sensed the birds through the open window, but the crack is only wide enough to let in air. Insects are always the first to arrive at a carcass, but in this case, they have had exclusive access. When I reach out with my power, I am swept away by the feeding frenzy of flies and maggots. Through them, I taste the iron tang of blood, the sweet and sour of rotting flesh, and the rich notes of the less spoilt meat. I am surrounded by the decomposing body, immersed in the decay, and now I do gag, severing the threads of magic that connect me to the insects.

I need to learn to have more care.

Bracing my hands against my knees, I take a moment to

recover from the overwhelming sensation. Even now, power is tugging at the edges of my consciousness, urging me to give in and join the feeding. To have any chance of figuring out what happened here, I need to control my wilder side. Breathing in the stench of decomposition does nothing to help.

Looking around, I see small symbols glittering on the carpet in each corner of the room, underneath the window and next to the door. They will be made of heart copper and they mean that the ward to contain the smell was premade. The power was forged into the symbols and all someone had to do was to set up the ward area and activate it. But how did they get out of the room without breaking the ward?

A quick glance tells me there is no way. Whoever set the ward never left.

There is nothing remarkable about the hotel room itself. The small space contains a double bed, a wardrobe, a table and an armchair. Other than a wallet on the bed, there is no indication that the room is occupied.

I cover my thumb with the sleeve of my jacket and flip open the wallet to reveal a driving licence belonging to Brother Valeron. This is the right room.

With nothing seeming to be out of place in the room itself, the source of the stench must be in the bathroom. The door is open a crack, blocked from closing by a hand towel, and the lights are off. I pause to steady myself, flip on the lights and push the door open with a covered hand.

Even though I was expecting the worst, the sight still unsettles me. The shower curtain has been pushed to the far end of the rail, offering an unobstructed view of the body in the bathtub. He, for I assume it is Brother Valeron, is dressed in the grey robes of his Order, although I note strips of black fabric tied over the eyes and around the wrists and ankles. They are a mark of shame among the Brotherhood. The front of the robes is dark brown with dried blood, and a dagger with a jewelled hilt rests against his chest.

In his left hand, Brother Valeron holds a photo of people who can only be his wife and daughter. Given that his chin is resting against his chest, I cannot see any wounds, but from the pattern of blood, the logical assumption is that his throat has been cut.

All these details register almost on the periphery of my consciousness, while most of my focus is on the decomposition.

While I am no pathologist, it is clear that Brother Valeron has been dead for some time. His skin is covered in large blisters and bloated to a point where it looks like it may rupture at any moment. Whereas his face is a blackish-green colour, the backs of his hands show a marbling effect that is unsettling. A swollen dark-red tongue hangs out of his mouth, flanked by dried residue from bloodied foam.

Insects are all over him. Flies buzz in and out of the open mouth, competing for space with writhing maggots. Every few moments, a couple of maggots tumble out of his mouth and land on his robes, where they begin the long climb to reach skin once more. From the way the strip of cloth covering Brother Valeron's eyes is moving, insects must be eating through his eyeballs. A wasp crawls out of his ear, trailing orange liquid, followed by another, and I suppress a shudder. More flies and maggots are swarming over the purged fluid leaking out of the body.

Seeing the decomposition process awakens my predator instinct once more. There is power here, power I can claim for myself if I only give in to the temptation. But what will be the price? Will I prove everyone who says that the Wild Folk are savages right? Worse yet, will I truly become a savage?

'Yan?'

Karrion calling my name interrupts my thoughts, and I back away from the bathroom, eyes still fixed on the body. Karrion has not entered the hotel room, and when I turn to face him, he takes a step back. Alarm is written across his face.

'What's wrong?' I ask. Focusing on something other than the writhing, buzzing, swarming power in the bathroom helps me ignore the magic tempting me.

'Nothing.' The alarm eases into a frown. 'It's just, your eyes looked like you had borrowed the sight of a fly. That's a pretty freaky look. *Lord of the Flies* doesn't really suit you.'

His humour is forced and it is clear my actions have unsettled him. I cross over to the threshold and put a hand out when he tries to enter the room.

'Don't.'

'It's bad, then?'

'Really bad.'

The stench has spread to the hallway, and I see Michael speaking to a couple of guests who have opened their doors to find out what is happening. In the circumstances, I have no chance of discovering which sort of magical blood they possess. I doubt I will be able to smell anything other than rot for some time.

'Is it Brother Valeron?' Karrion asks.

'I think so. But the decomp is too far gone for me to say for sure.'

Pulling my phone out, I find Jamie's number. While I wait for the call to connect, I ease the door towards me until it is only a fraction ajar. It does little to help with the smell, but at least it is less obvious which room the stench is coming from.

'Yannia, I'm really feeling popular now.' Jamie must have saved my number to his phone to begin with such a familiar greeting.

'Hi, Jamie.' I hesitate for a moment. 'Listen, I've found the missing Paladin.'

'Yeah? Where is he?' The edge of laughter disappears from Jamie's voice as he responds to my flat tone.

'A hotel bathtub in Hertford. He's been dead for days.'

'Shit. Give me the address and I'll send the local police to secure the scene until I can get there with a crime-scene unit and a Mage.'

Reciting the address, I hear the tapping of a keyboard in the background.

'Done. Keep everyone out of the hotel room until the police get there. I'm sure you know the drill.'

'I do. And to be honest, the smell is so bad, no one in their right mind would want to go in.'

'But you did, I bet. Though if the smell is that bad, why wasn't the body discovered until now?'

'The room was warded. Your Mage will be able to confirm it, but my guess is that the ward was designed to contain strong smells. Pretty handy for decomposing bodies.'

'That suggests premeditation. Was he murdered?'

The question surprises me. I had expected Jamie to tell me to leave police work to the professionals, but he seems genuinely interested in my opinion.

'I'm not sure. At first glance, it looks like a suicide, but it could have been staged. There's not much else I can say without disturbing the scene and I figure you'd kill me if I did that.'

'A private investigator with common sense and respect for the law? You really are a rare breed.' There is laughter in Jamie's voice again, and I find myself smiling in response.

'Don't go spreading scandalous rumours, you'll ruin my reputation.'

'Duly noted. I'll see you soon.'

We end the call, and I explain the gist of it to Karrion. All the while, the smell of decomposition and the pulse of power from within the room call out to me. The distraction is so great I jump when Karrion lays a hand on my arm.

'Do you want to go outside for some fresh air? I can stay up here with Michael and make sure no one goes in the room.'

My first instinct is to decline his offer, but on second thoughts I see the wisdom of it.

'That sounds like a good idea. Call me if you need me.'

'Will do, Yan.'

Getting away from the stench is a relief, and I pace in the lift, impatient to be outside. On my way past the reception desk, I flash the man there a tight smile, but offer no explanation as to why I am in such a hurry to leave.

Once outside, I gulp in fresh air, eager to rid my nose of the lingering rot. The smell seems to have seeped into my pores and clothes, and it stirs the primal hunger within me. I move from the main entrance to the side of the building, where a few picnic tables and a trimmed lawn lead to a narrow stream. Restlessness drives me to keep moving; hunger summons memories from my time at the conclave.

As I pace, I recall hunts through the forest, the taste of warm blood, and the scent of fresh meat. There was satisfaction in the meal the hunt provided, in another turn of the predator-prey dance, and in co-operation so seamless it was as if we were one mind, one body. But the satisfaction was always tinged with an edge of bitterness that none of it was my choice.

At the snap of a branch, I whirl around to find the blue eyes of a young boy staring at me. His lips are stained purple from the lollipop he is holding.

'Are you going to turn me into a toad?'

My thoughts are still elsewhere, and I struggle to process his question. 'What?'

'Are you going to turn me into a toad?' The boy's tone suggests that he relishes the prospect.

'No. Why would I turn you into a toad?'

'My brother Charlie says that's what witches do. Are you going to turn yourself into a toad?'

'No. No one is going to get turned into a toad. I'm not a witch.'

'Oh.' His expression falls, but not for long. 'If you're not a witch, what are you?'

Before I have a chance to figure out what to say, a voice calls out, 'Marcus, will you stop bothering the lady.'

A woman with the same blue eyes hurries towards me, another boy in tow. Both children are wearing matching school uniforms and there looks to be only a year or two between them.

'Mum, I was only asking her if she was going to turn me into a toad.' Marcus's voice implies that it is a reasonable line of enquiry and that his mother is fussing over nothing.

'I'm sorry about him,' the woman says, cheeks flushed with embarrassment. 'Ever since a little Shaman girl joined his class, he has been convinced that everyone has magical blood. His brother only encourages him, I'm sure.'

'But Mum, she is magical, I saw her.'

I have had no chance to contribute to the conversation, but now I wonder what the boy saw. Was I so affected by the crime scene and the memories of past hunts that I let my guard down? Can he smell the metallic tang of death and the musky sweat of my hunting partner, conjured from my memories? Did he catch a glimpse of the wilder side that I keep tucked away at the back of my mind?

The woman steps forward to take her son's hand and inhales deeply. A cautious look crosses her face, and with an apologetic smile, she steers her children away. Before they go beyond earshot, I hear her explain that magical folk are like someone in a wheelchair: they may be different, but it is not fair to point at them or treat them any differently from normal people.

Normal people. I turn away, shaking my head. How would I even begin to explain to that family that we consider ourselves the norm and humans as lacking something fundamental? There is ever a divide between us and the humans, and I doubt any amount of educating them about our magical capabilities and limitations will bridge that gap.

Keeping an eye on the front of the hotel, I wander towards the stream. It flows through a large pipe under the main road before emerging in the sunlight. The dark waters seem foreboding and part of me wonders if the tunnel is an entrance to another world. What would I find there? Who would inhabit such gloom? Or is light there and it is we who live in the dark?

A splash behind me interrupts my ruminations, and I turn to see six cygnets waddling towards me. They are this year's brood, and most of their grey feathering has given way to brilliant white. I greet the drift, relieved to borrow power from something other than insects immersed in rotting flesh. The cygnets surround me, unafraid and curious. I expect the visitors and the hotel staff feed them. One of the parents swims upstream, but appears unconcerned when I reach out to the nearest cygnet. Under my fingers, the solid beak gives way to soft down, and I wonder at the fineness of the feathers.

Another cygnet prods my side in search of food. When none is forthcoming, it and the others lose interest and return to the stream.

After the brief distraction, my thoughts return to the body in the tub and I pull my phone out and open the web browser. There is something I want to look up, and the answer comes as no surprise.

The sun disappearing behind a cloud heralds a sudden drop in the temperature, and I angle my face upward. Darker clouds are rolling in, and there is a hint of rain in the air. The beating of many wings draws my attention to the hotel and I watch a flock of birds rise from the distant trees. They are black silhouettes against the afternoon sky, uneven in shape and disorganised in their flight. Did something scare them, or did Karrion dismiss the birds holding their hungry vigil outside Brother Valeron's room?

As if summoned by the fleeing wings, a police car stops by the main entrance. One officer steps out and waits there while the other drives off to park the car. I take advantage of the delay, put my phone away, and hurry to introduce myself to the waiting officer. Jamie has told him about me.

Once his partner joins us, we head inside. On our way past reception, I ask the young man to direct any further officers straight to the second floor. He stammers a promise to do so.

The lift ride upstairs is silent and uncomfortable. How do you make small talk when you're guiding two police officers to a crime scene? One of the men catches my eye and offers me an awkward half-smile. It appears I am not the only one wondering.

Karrion is standing guard outside Brother Valeron's room. I see from the tightness around his eyes that he would rather be somewhere else. Given the smell, who can blame him? He looks relieved when he sees our approach. Michael is talking to three women further along the corridor.

One of the police officers takes Karrion's post by the door, while I step inside the room with the other one. In a low voice, I recount why our concerns were raised, what caused Michael to open the door, and what I touched when I went inside. The smell is bad enough to make the officer look pale and nauseated. Knowing what to expect, I have gone in prepared and am able to control the hunger within me better than before. Still, it is a relief to return to the corridor.

The officers roll crime-scene tape across the doorway, and Michael makes a trip downstairs to fetch a key card for the room. Karrion and I are grateful to retreat to the hotel's café to wait for Jamie's arrival. As we are waiting for our order, I wonder whether I ought to phone Sister Alissa now or wait until the scenes of crime officers have done their job.

We are still sitting by the patio windows, nursing our cups, when Jamie strides in half an hour later. His eyes find us across the quiet café, and when we rise, he waves at us to sit back down.

'I'm going to check things over upstairs,' he says once he is close enough not to have to shout. 'Wait here. I'll need to talk to you.'

While he goes upstairs, Karrion gets us new coffees from the counter. I still have a half-eaten brownie on my plate, but every time I go to take a bite of it, my mind flashes back to the wasps crawling out of Brother Valeron's ear and bile rises in my throat.

I saw my fair share of deaths at the conclave, where bodies were nothing more than another turn in the wheel of nature, but the sight of our missing Paladin in the bathtub has left me shaken for reasons beyond the potential power I experienced upstairs. Karrion is understandably upset by what we stumbled across. Looking at his pale face and glazed eyes, I fear he has been exposed too soon to the ugly side of my work. Not that I have any experience in discovering dead bodies either.

My thoughts keep turning to Brother Valeron's wife. Who will tell her the awful news? How will she cope with the loss of her husband, when their daughter is fighting cancer?

Karrion interrupts my thoughts when his coffee cup clatters on the saucer. Deep furrows line his forehead, and I reach out to rest my hand on his. He responds with a forced smile.

'Do you think I should have gone in? Do you think I should have looked at the body?' he asks.

'No, I don't.'

'But if I'm to be your apprentice, I should get used to that sort of sight, shouldn't I? I mean, it's part of the job.'

'My job is a lot less gruesome than you may imagine. This is my first body, too.'

'Really? But I thought—'

'Real life rarely parallels an Agatha Christie novel.'

'Just as well. Neither Poirot nor Miss Marple is really you.' This time, his smile is a little more genuine.

'I agree. As much as I've tried, I can't get either a moustache or knitting needles to work for me.' Growing more serious, I continue. 'Look, this case is likely to be the exception rather than the rule when it comes to my work. Most of the time, I follow paper trails rather than suspects. There is very little that's glamorous about it. And the only car chases I've been involved in were the ones where people were chasing me to renew my insurance or organise the car to be serviced. It's pretty boring, really.'

'I'm okay with boring, I just don't want you to be disappointed with me.'

'And you think I'll be disappointed with you if you don't rush in to gawk at a corpse?' The flash of uncertainty in his eyes suggests that is exactly what he is worried about. 'There are certain things in life that you should be in no rush to experience. Decomposing bodies is one of them.'

'Was that your first decomposing body too?'

'No. Back at the conclave, we had a different way of dealing with our dead from most people.'

'What do you mean?'

Crumbling the edges of the remaining half of my brownie, I wonder how to explain. Karrion watches me and then steals the brownie. With youthful exuberance, he eats it in two bites.

'We owe everything to nature: our existence; our power; the sustenance and shelter we need. From nature we are created, and to nature we must return. So when one of the Wild Folk dies, the body is given back to nature.'

'I have a sneaking suspicion I can see where this is heading.'

I nod. 'Each conclave has a specific area, usually a small clearing, where the body is placed. It's wreathed in flowers or vines, depending on the time of the year, and shallow cuts are made at various points in the body for better access. It's the duty and privilege of the deceased's family to hold vigil over the offering and to make sure most of the body parts remain in the clearing. We remember while nature takes what belongs to her. That is what it means to be of the Wild Folk.'

A memory pulls me to the past until I am sitting in a clearing bordered by white stones. Not a single tree grows within the area, and being deep in the forest, it offers access to a variety of wildlife. My legs ache from hours spent kneeling; my untrained power is focused on inviting animals to partake of what is offered. Opposite me, on the far side of my mother's body, my father is likewise engaged. And behind me, on the edge of the clearing, I feel the dark presence that has been in my life since the day I was born, watching, waiting, knowing.

Does he ever go there, to the grove of memories where his own adopted parents were given back to the world around them? Does he ever recall the vigil held many years ago, when he was desperate to sit by my side, but was barred from entering the grove because he was not family? Or has Dearon forgotten it; forgotten how I cried in his arms afterwards?

Gradually, I become aware of Karrion staring at me and I realise my explanation remains unfinished.

'When most of the body is gone, we bury the rest so the bones may nourish the soil. Our dead remain within the boundaries of a memorial grove, with us even though they are gone.'

'That,' Karrion swallows, 'that sounds kind of nice.'

'We're pretty big on traditions.'

'It's nice to know where you come from and that you'll be remembered after you're gone. I mean, I'm a Bird Shaman. But how did I come to be? What is it that gives a man an affinity with birds, a power over them? Or how can someone summon a Herald from another dimension? Or shape raw mana? Or channel all of nature? How can it be?'

'The power is in the blood, Karrion.'

'I know that, but what does it mean? Why did we get this power, when so many others didn't?'

He is not the only one who has asked me those questions, but I am not sure how to explain. All my instincts say that the power is in the blood and that is how it should be. It is the gift of magic that makes us complete and it feels natural; it feels right.

Before I have a chance to formulate an answer, Jamie returns.

'Yannia, we need you upstairs.' Turning to Karrion, he continues, 'I understand that you didn't go in the room. Is that correct?'

Karrion nods and agrees to wait in the café while I follow Jamie out. Once upstairs, we dodge the scenes of crime officers and duck under the police tape into the room. A young grey-haired woman is standing by the bed with a distant expression. My guess is she is a Mage of some kind, but the decomposition is too strong for me to attempt to figure out her exact type.

For the two of them, I recount my story, what I observed and touched. The woman confirms my theory regarding the ward and asks detailed questions about the powers I used. It is clear she has never met one of my kind and has little idea of our capabilities. We end up going outside so that I can demonstrate borrowing the nose of an animal and the sort of magical traces it leaves. Jamie's eyes burn holes in my back.

When we have returned to the room and the Mage has

tested the power residue there, we move to the bathroom. A coroner is there, examining the body, though it has not yet been moved from the tub. The black strip of cloth covering the eyes has been removed, and I now see the empty sockets crawling with maggots. Instead of the earlier hunger, a stab of pity runs through me. There's little dignity in the advanced stages of rot.

'My preliminary analysis indicates that the death was a suicide,' the coroner says, and turns Brother Valeron's head to expose the neck wound. Dried blood cracks and flakes as the skin stretches. 'There are shallow cuts near the main wound, which I expect a closer examination will reveal to be hesitation marks. Cutting your own throat is a terrible way to die, but there's little chance of failure once the blade has sunk in.'

'So Brother Valeron left the Brotherhood the day after the Marsh trial, came here, set up a ward against smells and committed suicide.'

Both the coroner and the Mage cast a curious glance in my direction, and Jamie steers me out of the bathroom.

'Let's talk downstairs.'

Jamie orders a tea from the counter. Caffeine is buzzing through me and I pass on the offer of a third cup of anything. Karrion has bought himself an orange juice.

There are no other customers occupying the nearby tables, but we keep our voices down while Karrion and I fill Jamie in on everything we have discovered so far. He listens with a grim expression as the inconsistencies and questions mount up. When we fall silent, he rubs his eyes.

'What a mess, and now we have a dead Paladin on our hands.' Jamie drains the last of his tea.

'Though he's been dead all along,' I say.

Something in my voice causes Karrion to frown. 'You were expecting this?'

'I was.' Now Jamie is also looking at me. 'Lady Bergamon

gave us a cypress branch. Her tone gave me a sense of foreboding, and the dead body didn't come as a complete surprise. And finding out what cypress symbolises only confirmed my feeling.'

Karrion leans forward. 'What does it symbolise?'

'Mourning.'

'What about the flower she gave me?'

A smile offers a reprieve from my doubts. 'Patience.'

Karrion chuckles and scowls simultaneously.

'What's your next move?' Jamie asks.

'I'd like to talk to Brother Valeron's widow. It can't be a coincidence that their daughter received a place on a cancer drug trial on the day of the Marsh judgement. If we can find out who arranged it, we'll be one step closer to finding out who murdered Braeman.'

'If you two don't mind waiting here until we have finished upstairs, you can come with me when I go to deliver the bad news.'

While I am keen to continue the investigation, Jamie's suggestion makes sense. He returns upstairs and we wander out of the hotel. Karrion goes to greet the swan family and I call Ilana. When the call connects, I hear traffic noise in the background and opt to keep the call brief. We agree that Karrion and I will drop by later that afternoon to interview the household staff. I promise to call her again with a full update on the case.

As I am putting the phone away, Karrion returns with a small notebook and pen in hand. He shows me a page of illegible scrawl and I laugh. For an artist, he has terrible handwriting.

'I made a list of things I think we need to do,' he says, ignoring my amusement.

'Go on.'

'First of all, talk to Brother Valeron's wife. Then interview the Marsh household staff. And we should also try to see if we can speak to the household staff at Braeman's townhouse. Maybe we can even have a word with his widow. And I thought perhaps we should ask Marsh about the enmity between Braeman and Lord Ellensthorne.'

'I agree for the most part, but I think we'd best speak to Lord Ellensthorne himself about the threats he made in public. Assuming he'll grant us a second audience.'

'Oh.' Karrion's expression sours.

'Sorry, but I think it's best if we hear that particular story from the horse's mouth.'

'I'm sure you're right. I just can't stand that man.'

'You were quick to reach that conclusion, having only met him once.'

'There are some people you dislike straight away.'

'I get it,' I say. 'I wasn't that enamoured with him myself.'

'Knew it.' Karrion grins. 'You looked like you had a steel rod holding you up, you were that tense. Had the conversation not been so infuriating, it would have been funny.'

'I'm glad I managed to entertain you.' My attempt at looking stern fails when my lips twitch and we laugh together.

Nudging me with his shoulder, Karrion waves his scrawled list. 'What do you think?'

'It looks good. We'll do as much of it as we can today.'

'You know, if you want to leave Lord Arrogant-Thinks-He's-Better-Than-Everyone until tomorrow, I won't be heartbroken about it.'

'I'll take that into consideration,' I say with a grin as Jamie walks out of the hotel.

'The others are still processing the scene, but I'm free to go and be the bearer of bad news.' As he speaks, Jamie looks old and reluctant.

'At least you won't be going alone if that's any consolation.'

'It helps,' he admits, and glances around the car park. 'Listen, any chance of a lift back to London? I came in the van with the rest of the team and it didn't occur to me at the time that I might escape the crime scene early.'

'Sure, no problem. My car's this way.'

There is a moment of shuffling as Karrion tries to offer Jamie the front seat, which he declines, folding his long legs in the back seat without a protest. I apologise for the lack of space; it is rare for me to have any passengers at all, let alone two at once.

During the drive back to London, Karrion and Jamie make awkward small talk about football, but it only goes so far. I know Karrion is more interested in the low-key league we have in Old London than the national competitions. After that, we comment sporadically on landmarks we pass, but otherwise the drive is silent. From something Jamie says, I discover that he is divorced. The information surprises me.

Jamie's colleagues at New Scotland Yard have tracked down the hospital where Brother Valeron's daughter is receiving treatment and he reads the address out from a text message. It is near St Paul's Cathedral and the area gets busy in the afternoon. We manage to avoid the worst of the traffic and duck into the hospital's underground car park.

As we get out of the car, Karrion and I share a concerned look. Here we are, heading for more uncharted territory.

Just how do you tell someone their husband has committed suicide?

13

BEARERS OF BAD NEWS

A receptionist in the main hospital lobby directs us to a children's ward on the sixth floor and gives us a room number. In the lift on our way up, Jamie seems to sense our growing nervousness.

'Let me do the talking,' he says, and makes a valiant effort at a smile. 'Once she's had a chance to let it all sink in, I'll introduce you and see if she can answer some of your questions now, or whether it would be better if you met later.'

'Sounds good, though we don't have a lot of time to spare.'

The lift pings to announce our arrival at the children's ward. The doors open, and we are met by a small alcove with a door in front of us, an intercom unit next to it. Jamie introduces us and the door is unlocked. Beyond it, I expect to see yet another clinical hospital corridor, though perhaps adorned with a few balloons or flowers to accommodate the younger patients. Instead, the yellow walls of the reception area are decorated with jungle scenes and flocks of colourful birds. A television opposite a comfortable-looking sofa is showing cartoons, and toy boxes litter the area. Even the nurses are wearing uniforms adorned with flowers, animals, and various toys, and everyone greets us with a smile.

As we walk past rooms, I see children in their beds, playing with toys, building jigsaws, drawing, or using games consoles. Those who are more mobile are engaged in similar activities elsewhere in their rooms, sometimes alone and sometimes under the watchful eye of a parent or staff member. Everything about the place speaks of easing the suffering of the children and genuine efforts to make their stay on the ward as pleasant as possible. It is a stark contrast to the conclave and my kind's way of dealing with illness. I push the thoughts away; the present is hard enough without painful memories clouding my thoughts.

We stop at a pale wooden door bearing the right number. Straightening his posture, Jamie knocks. When a voice answers, Karrion and I take a few discreet steps away from the door and Jamie goes in. As he does so, I catch a glimpse of the room.

The walls are decorated in the theme of an underwater coral reef, with curtains to match. From its size, it is clearly a private room. Most of the space is taken up by a hospital bed and two armchairs. The girl in the bed is hooked up to an array of machines and seems far too small under a blanket covered in turtles. A scarf decorated with colourful fish is wrapped around her head. Despite the dark circles under her eyes, she is looking towards the door with a smile. Our eyes meet and I look away for fear of betraying the news we are bringing.

Jamie and Brother Valeron's wife exchange a few quiet words. Whatever he says causes her to rise from the chair by the bed and leave the room. She closes the door and leans against it, hand on the door-handle. Her expression is one of caution as if she is already bracing herself for more bad news.

There are no animals here to lend me their noses and I have to dip into my inner reserves as I inhale. I know Karrion's and

Jamie's scents well enough to ignore them and only focus on Brother Valeron's wife. From her, I catch hints of citrus fruit, patchouli, and make-up, all but obscured by the harsh smell of disinfectant. My eyebrows rise; she is human. How awful must it be for her, living in Old London surrounded by magic when none of it can heal her daughter?

When she and Jamie shake hands, I catch her introducing herself as Megan Fidelis. She looks to be in her early thirties, slim with shoulders that are a little stooped. Her auburn hair and green eyes are at odds with the common colourings for the Paladins and her daughter appears to have inherited her looks from her father. Does she carry the blessings of the Heralds, I wonder? Will she live long enough to find out?

Megan's eyes flicker to me and Karrion before focusing on Jamie again, and I realise I have been staring at her. Jamie's tone is low so I cannot hear the individual words, but from the way concern changes to horror on Megan's face, I can guess that he has got to the purpose of our visit. My heart clenches in sympathy when Megan's eyes fill with tears.

'No,' she says, careful to keep her voice down, 'it can't be true. He can't be gone.'

'I'm terribly sorry for your loss, Mrs Fidelis,' Jamie replies.

'How will I tell Elianora? How will I explain to her that her father isn't coming home?'

She breaks down then, face buried in her hands and shoulders shaking from the force of her sobs. Jamie watches her, helpless and uncomfortable, before turning to me for help. I spot a box of tissues on a nearby table and fetch it. Megan thanks me with a watery smile and uses a handful of tissues to mop tears and streaks of mascara from her face. No sooner has she regained her composure than tears well in her eyes again.

We stand by her in silence, waiting until the first wave of

grief has ebbed. When it does, she looks from me to Jamie and back. Jamie takes the hint and introduces us.

Megan frowns. 'Has someone hired you to investigate my husband?'

'No, but I had hoped I could speak with him regarding the judgement he served in last Saturday. That's why I tracked him down and I... discovered his body.'

Megan turns to Jamie. 'Are you sure it was a suicide?'

Instead of answering the question, Jamie points towards a small alcove nearby, where a sofa and three chairs have been arranged around a small table. On the table are a tray of cups, a jug of water, and a plate of biscuits.

'Why don't we sit down? There are some questions that myself and Ms Wilde would like to ask you.'

After a hesitant glance towards the door behind her, Megan agrees and Jamie steers her to the sofa. He sits down next to her, while Karrion and I pick armchairs. After he has poured her a cup of water, Jamie returns to her question.

'The preliminary findings of both the coroner and the Mage at the scene indicate that it was suicide, although the official reports will take some time to prepare. Your husband's wrists and eyes were bound with black strips of cloth, which I understand is a mark of shame among the Brotherhood. Can you think of any reason why he might have taken his own life out of shame?'

'No.' Megan shakes her head, twisting a clean tissue in her hands. 'Valeron is a good man and he has always taken pride in serving the Heralds and the people of Old London.'

'When was the last time you spoke with your husband?' Jamie asks.

'Sunday morning. He was supposed to come home to rest after Saturday's judgement, but there was a mix-up with the staff numbers at the Brotherhood and he had to work over the weekend. On Monday, he returned to duty as normal.' She pauses, grief threatening to overwhelm her. 'I mean, he should have returned to duty as normal.'

I set the box of tissues on the table next to Megan's cup. 'How did he sound during the conversation?'

Megan thinks for a moment. 'Distracted and tired, like he was carrying a great burden. I assumed it was because of Elianora and because the judgement had fatigued him.'

'Was it usual for him not to contact you for several days?' I ask.

'No. If his duties meant that he had to spend nights at the Brotherhood, we spoke at least once a day. But with this new treatment for Elianora, I have all but lost count of the days. My phone has been switched off for the most part. Even if he had rung me, I might not have known about it.'

'We spoke to Sister Alissa at the Brotherhood and she told me a little about how sick your daughter is. Am I right in thinking that you weren't expecting the treatment Elianora is receiving at the moment?'

'Yes, that's right. Her doctors at the main hospital told us a few weeks back that there was nothing more they could try and the only remaining options concerned giving Elianora as painless an ending as possible. The call about this new experimental cancer drug came out of the blue.'

'When did you get the call?' Karrion asks.

'Saturday afternoon. They said a research trial had an opening and Elianora was a perfect candidate. All the hospital fees and everything else had been paid for.'

'That sounds like a real blessing,' Jamie says. 'Is the pharmaceutical company covering the costs or does the trial have an outside sponsor?'

'My understanding is that a charity stepped in to help with

the costs. They are doing a great deal of work with sick children in Old London and they have a big fundraiser coming up in the next few weeks. I thought the gala evening might be cancelled because Gideor Braeman died, but apparently it will still go on.'

Karrion and I exchange a glance.

'Why would his death make any difference to the gala evening?' I ask.

'His wife, Viola, is the driving force behind organising it.'

'The Lifelines charity?'

'Yes, that's it.'

My pulse quickens. Now we are getting somewhere. Jamie, too, understands the significance of Megan's revelation and leans forward.

'Just out of interest, did you contact the charity regarding the drug trial?'

'No.' Megan shifts to look at Jamie. 'We didn't even know about the trial until I got the call on Saturday.'

'Then how could the charity have known about Elianora's illness?'

Megan pauses. When she replies, her voice is hesitant. 'You know, I'm not certain. Unless it was because of an event Valeron and Elianora took part in six months ago. Lifelines organised a day at a butterfly world for young cancer patients and their parents. I had to work and Valeron took Elianora. I think the charity wrote an article about it for their website and one of the photos featured Valeron and Elianora. We have a copy of the photo framed in her bedroom, which is why it stuck in my mind.'

'Did you tell many people when the doctors indicated that there was little else they could do for Elianora?'

'Only family, though I think Valeron might have mentioned it to a few close friends at the Brotherhood.'

'Do you have family in Old London?' I ask, trying to keep my voice impassive.

'No, my family lives in Manchester. And my husband's an only child and his parents died in his youth.'

'That means only a few people knew?'

'Yes.' Megan frowns. 'Why? Why is that important?'

I hesitate and glance first at Karrion and then at Jamie. 'It could be important.' She deserves more, but I am unwilling to explain.

'I don't think many people knew. It's not exactly the sort of news we wanted to share with everyone and their dog. Although,' Megan pauses again, 'now that I think about it, Valeron might have told Lifelines. They followed up with the children from time to time.'

So Lifelines knew. The very same charity that arranged for Elianora to get into the drug trial. Coincidence? I think not. We need to look into Lifelines further. But although there is an apparent connection between the victim and the dead Paladin, that does not bring us closer to figuring out who killed Braeman.

Or does it?

While my thoughts are elsewhere, Jamie picks up the threads of the conversation.

'Do you know if your husband was having any problems at work? Did he have any enemies at the Brotherhood or outside it?'

'No. He was a devout, faithful Paladin, and well-loved for it.'

'Have you noticed any change in your husband's behaviour of late? Has he seemed depressed to you, irritable or somehow different?'

'The last few months have been tough on us both. We've tried to maintain a brave face for Elianora's sake, but I think she suspects just how bleak her situation is. Her illness led to something of a crisis of faith for Valeron. I think he felt he should have been able to do something to save her because he has magic. He felt helpless in a way that I didn't because I've always placed my trust in technology and modern medicine.' Megan takes a sip of her water, eyes distant. 'I reminded him that he serves the Heralds of Justice and that is beyond the life and death of a little girl. The disease is beyond justice, as are many other things in life. And perhaps God loves our daughter so much, He wants to take her home.'

As she bows her head and reaches for another tissue, Jamie's hand finds the small silver cross that hangs around his neck. He has faith, I know that much. But can even the most devout of prayers help a child being eaten away by a disease?

Megan regains her composure. 'If Valeron seemed depressed or distant of late, it was no more than I would have expected. We had fought a long battle against cancer and were having to find a way to say goodbye to our little girl.'

The brief interlude in her vigil at Elianora's bedside is over. As she rises and plucks one more tissue, Megan says, 'I cannot think of a single reason why Valeron would commit suicide. Not now, while Elianora is still here and each day is precious. Why would he choose to miss her smile or the little songs she sings to us? It's inconceivable.'

There is nothing any of us can say to that. We shake hands and offer her our condolences. Jamie wishes the family all the best with the new drug trial and we are happy to hear that the doctors are quietly optimistic.

When Megan heads back towards Elianora's room, a final question jumps into my mind and I hurry after her.

'Mrs Fidelis, one final thing. Did your husband ever mention the possibility of manipulating a judgement to condemn an innocent?'

'No, and he would never do that,' Megan says over her

shoulder. 'Valeron would rather die than pervert the course of justice.'

With an attempt at a smile, she returns to her daughter, and I am left in the corridor, frozen in my tracks by the significance of her words.

14

TO CATCH A THIEF

J amie takes a taxi back to New Scotland Yard with a promise to call us if the investigation into the death of Brother Valeron yields any new insights. We locate my car among the desolate echoes of the parking garage and join the early evening traffic. Our next destination is the Marsh residence.

Ilana's family lives near Lord Ellensthorne's Old London residence on another road lined with beautiful houses and expensive cars. Maple and ash trees cast dappled shadows on the pavement and offer a degree of privacy to the upper floors. Looking up at the pale-grey façade of the building, I try to imagine someone breaking in to plant evidence. Perhaps it would be easier through the back.

We have to drive almost to the far end of the road before we find a parking spot. As we walk back, Karrion's head swivels from tree to tree. His whole appearance becomes more attentive, and I feel him opening himself to the magic in his blood.

'There are plenty of birds in these trees,' he says, head cocked. 'Magpies, pigeons, parakeets.'

'Do you think they saw anything?'

'Birds' memories don't work like ours do, nor do they perceive time in the same way. Still, it wouldn't hurt to try, I suppose.'

We agree that he will stay outside to talk to as many birds as he can, while I speak to the household staff. A young woman with an open, friendly face lets me in. She is dressed in a navy-blue trouser suit and a white blouse, but I get the impression that fifty years ago she would have been wearing a maid's outfit. Ilana is visiting her father, the woman tells me, but she has arranged for me to talk to everyone who was working on the night of the murder. I feel a fleeting pang of disappointment at not seeing Ilana, but I push it aside. She is not the reason I am here.

The members of the household staff are all eager to help their master, but there is little they can tell me. Marsh left around nine, which is in line with his own story, and did not return until the following morning. No one at the house saw or heard anything out of the ordinary, except for a maid who remembers that the parakeets were making a lot of noise in the trees. While they are known for calling out to each other, that night the birds seemed upset by something. Another maid recalls clearing a bird's nest from the front step the following morning when Marsh pointed it out to her upon his return. Like Marsh, the maid does not know what sort of bird built the nest.

Having spoken to the staff, I am taken upstairs to Marsh's study by one of the maids. Here, as with Gideor Braeman's study, the room appears to double as a bedroom. The maid, while staring at her feet, tells me that the master and the mistress have slept in separate bedrooms for as long as she has been employed there. As Ilana said, the marriage is one of appearances only.

The room is large, with high ceilings and tasteful décor

throughout. A pair of French windows leads on to a small balcony overlooking a well-kept garden. While I take in the view, Karrion walks along a narrow alleyway at the back of the gardens, two parakeets perched on his arm. His head bobs with each step and his free hand is folded close to his body in a way that resembles a wing. His hair, the piercings, and the black clothes all seem to form a part of an elaborate plumage, which suits him perfectly. I wonder if he is aware of how different he looks when he is focused on his magic.

Shifting my attention away from Karrion, I look around the balcony. Although the air is still warm, there are no chairs or a table for taking afternoon tea outside. My guess is that if Marsh uses the balcony, it is for thinking or for fresh air. The tiled floor is clear of leaves and other debris, and it is impossible to tell whether someone has been out here recently.

I step back inside the study and inspect the door with the help of my phone's camera zoom. While I am no expert when it comes to locks, it seems to me that there are faint scratches around the keyhole. Anyone living here would have no reason to lock and unlock the door from the outside. The lock was picked.

According to the case file, the police found no evidence of a break-in here. But how thorough was their search, when they had been handed a suspect on a silver platter?

I go out on to the balcony again and look up. The edge of the roof is not far above me, and someone standing on the railing could reach it without a problem. I am briefly tempted to see if I can climb on to the roof, but the long drop to the paved patio below soon dismisses that idea. Instead, I fetch a chair from inside, kick off my shoes and climb on to it. Standing on tiptoes, I can just reach the guttering above me and I run my hands along it.

On the left, next to the railing, my searching fingers find something soft snagged on the join between two sections of the guttering. With a bit of patience, I ease it free. On my palm is a small strip of fraying black cloth, soft to the touch. It still retains its colour, and I estimate that it cannot have been there longer than a few weeks.

Someone climbed down from the roof, accessed Marsh's bedroom, and then climbed back up again.

On the far side of the house stands a maple tree. The closest branches are ten feet from the house. It is not a jump most people would want to make in either direction, but perhaps someone with the right sort of magic would brave it. But who was it and how do I find them?

The room and the balcony yield no further insights and I return downstairs where I thank the staff for their help. Part of me was hoping that Ilana would have returned while I was here, but I have no reason to linger. I console myself with the thought that I did promise to call her, even if meeting her in person would have been preferable.

Karrion is waiting for me outside, leaning on a tree near the front door. As I descend the steps, an elderly couple walking past gives him a suspicious glare. I half expect them to start accusing him of loitering, but they deem a withering look to be the extent of their civic duty. Once they have moved on, Karrion rolls his eyes. He too must know that in this area, he stands out like a sore thumb.

As we head for the car, I give him a brief summary of what I found and show him the scrap of cloth. When I express my frustration at not knowing who the burglar was, Karrion grins.

'I may be able to help with that.'

'Do tell.'

'Well, that broken bird's nest proved to be the key. Birds don't have a linear memory like we do, right?' I nod, but he is focusing on the birdsong coming from the tree above. 'Right. Like a bird's memories about nesting are separate from his memories of feeding. The two memory clusters also have separate senses of time, and a bird cannot link a memory of finding a great deal of food with the day her chicks hatched, even if they happened on the same day.'

'This is not making me feel optimistic, Karrion.'

'I'm getting to the good bit. The blackbirds told me a cat destroyed their nest. The parakeets told me that a cat took one of their fledglings. Even the pigeons said they fled one night because of a cat.'

While that is interesting, I cannot see how it helps us. 'There are cats roaming free in Old London, though I admit not many.'

'On its own, not too convincing, I agree. But what if I told you that they all nest in the trees surrounding Marsh's house? And that the pigeons were in his back garden when the cat attacked them?'

'If that's the case, maybe there is a connection. Who knows, the burglar might even be a Cat Shaman. But none of that gets us any closer to a name.'

'That doesn't,' Karrion's hand dips into his pocket, 'but this might.'

Dangling from his fingers is a small fabric collar with a metal tag. The red colour is faded and the fabric worn in places. The front of the collar has the words *'Felix Felis'* engraved on it and the back shows a phone number.

Turning the collar in my hand, I ask, 'Where did you get this?'

Karrion's grin widens. 'As it happens, the cat also went after the magpies living in the tree at the end of the house. They were prepared to fight, and in the process, the cat lost its collar. The magpies kept it because of the shiny tag.'

'Good work.' I am impressed.

'I'm not quite done yet,' Karrion says, obviously proud of

himself. 'While I was waiting for you, I looked up "Felix Felis" online. It means "the lucky cat" and it's a cat rescue shelter near Holborn. I wouldn't be at all surprised if the woman running the place turned out to be a Cat Shaman.'

'Fancy that.' I glance at my watch. 'There's still time to talk to her today.'

'Okay, let's get going.'

'No. You're going to sit this one out,' I say with a shake of my head.

'What? Why?' All the excitement leaves Karrion's expression and straight away I regret my tone.

'Taking a Bird Shaman to accuse a Cat Shaman of being a thief doesn't seem like the wisest of ideas.'

'I'm not afraid of a Cat Shaman,' Karrion says with a defiant look in his eyes.

'It's not about fear or about my doubting your courage. The thief has information we need and I'd like to go into the situation as neutrally as possible. There's natural conflict between Bird Shamans and Cat Shamans which we don't need in our situation. It's best if I confront the Shaman alone.'

It looks like he wants to argue further, but then his shoulders slump. 'I guess that makes sense.'

I take his arm and steer him towards the car. 'There will be many times when you want to rush straight into a situation, but you need to learn to pause and think about what you're about to do. Who are you up against? What are their strengths and weaknesses, and how do they compare with yours? How can you approach the situation with the maximum advantage?'

'I guess I'm not very good at that.' His lips twist into a rueful smile.

'Neither am I.' I laugh at his look of surprise. 'But the way I see it, we can practise together.'

'Yeah, that sounds good.'

'And no matter how annoying it will be for you to sit on the sidelines for a bit, we wouldn't have caught this break without you. I really mean it when I say that you've done a great job today.'

Karrion seems to grow an inch taller and I am certain his feet never touch the ground as we make our way to the car. I watch him with a smile, pleased by his enthusiasm and his easy enjoyment of the work we do. The gruesome discovery at the hotel and having to tell Megan Fidelis her husband is dead seem to have slipped from his mind, and for that I am grateful. Let him maintain his innocence for as long as possible, especially in light of how hard his life has been so far.

It takes us so long to drive to Holborn that I regret not having walked. When I finally find a parking spot, I suggest Karrion goes home. There is little else we can do that evening and I still need to have a long conversation with Ilana. Karrion agrees to come to my place first thing in the morning so that we can plan our final full day of investigation. We must make significant headway tomorrow if we are to solve the case, and the knowledge sends restlessness into my limbs.

Having retrieved his rucksack from the boot of my car, Karrion waves goodbye and jogs towards the nearest bus stop. I watch him go before walking in the opposite direction in search of Felix Felis.

The cat shelter is based next to St Andrew's Church. Built from irregular light-brown bricks, it has a pointed roof over the façade, with a circular tower on the left dominating the open space between the court house and the church. Lead decorations divide each windowpane into rows of small squares, and although they are dark with age, I can see light streaming out from several windows. A tawny cat is sitting on the window ledge of one of the upstairs windows, looking down at me.

A green door is set back from the rest of the façade in a tight archway and a small plaque on it shows the opening times for Felix Felis – a home for homeless cats. When I push it, the door opens without a protest, and I step inside.

The entrance hall is brightly lit and a stone floor is covered with a worn rug. Much of the noise of traffic is muffled by the thick walls, and it feels like I am stepping into a different world. The air is cool but dry, and I smell fresh coffee and cake rather than the distinct smell of many cats living in a small space.

To my right, the entrance hall leads into a long room, which looks to be a mixture of a cat café and a charity shop. The items on sale are mostly books and children's toys. Two grey cats are fast asleep on a faded sofa, while a white cat is sitting on a table, watching a customer eat a slice of red velvet cake. A plump elderly woman dressed in a frilly floral dress smiles at me as she comes around the counter and clears away empty cups and plates from one of the tables. She is unlikely to be my thief.

The sound of a pen dropping draws my attention to the left, where a small sitting area has been set up near an old counter. From the cat-related posters on the walls, I take that to be the actual shelter. A woman of my age straightens behind the counter, pen in hand, and our eyes meet. She has a tight bob of chestnut-brown hair and pale-hazel eyes that regard me with a mixture of wariness and curiosity. Her build is slim and athletic; perfect for a cat burglar.

Maintaining eye contact, I walk towards the counter. When I am close enough, I borrow the nose of one of the many cats I sense nearby. One sniff confirms what I already suspected to be true. She smells of catnip, soft fur, and paws dipped in a saucer of cream: a Cat Shaman.

'Selina Kyle, I presume?' I say as I relinquish the threads of magic.

The woman's expression is blank before irritation flashes across her face. 'Funny.'

'Perhaps. True? I think so.'

'Do you want to adopt a cat?' she asks, eyes hard and voice cold.

'No, but I do want to talk to you about one of your cats.' I pull my hand out of my pocket and let the collar dangle between us. 'Seems someone here has lost a collar.'

'Where did you find it?' She moves to take the collar, but I pull my hand back.

'At a crime scene.' It is not quite true, but close enough.

'Who are you?'

I introduce myself and give her one of my cards. She studies it before slipping it into the back pocket of her jeans. Only then does she tell me her name is Fria Knutson.

'What do you want from me?' she asks to fill the silence that settles between us.

'Is there somewhere we can talk in private?'

She hesitates, glancing between the front door and the café. It is clear she would prefer to get rid of me straight away. I put the collar back in my pocket, and her eyes narrow.

'We can talk in my office,' she says, and motions to me to wait. Having spoken briefly with the woman minding the café, Fria leads me out of a door behind the rescue counter. We walk through a small veterinary clinic, past a couple of closed doors, to an office small enough to be a glorified broom cupboard. The desk crammed at the far end is covered in piles of paper, as are the two chairs in front of it. Fria sweeps the papers on the nearest chair into her arms and drops them carelessly on to the desk. She motions for me to sit while she remains standing.

'What do you want?' she asks again without a preamble.

'Information. I want to know about the night one of your cats lost its collar and you left a piece of your clothing in the guttering of the house you broke into.'

'I don't know what you're talking about.' Fria crosses her arms and glares at me.

Choosing silence as my weapon, I tilt my head and say nothing. We stare at one another for a long moment, neither wanting to be the first to break. In the end, she looks away and back at me.

'You have no proof.' The lift of her chin screams defiance. 'Finding a cat collar nearby is hardly damning.'

'That's true.' Her eyes widen in surprise, but I am not yet done. 'I don't have proof. But I do have enough to sow suspicion, to send unwanted attention your way. And maybe the police won't find anything, but how long will they detain you, comb through your life, and disrupt the shelter you're running here? Won't it be your cats that ultimately suffer?'

'And you would do that?' There is a note of accusation in her voice.

'Look, I don't care about the theft from Braeman's house. I don't care if the items are sold on the black market. It doesn't matter. What I do care about is the possibility of an innocent man having been framed for a murder he didn't commit. And as far as I'm concerned, you're my best shot at finding out what really happened that night.'

Fria paces across the cramped office and back again. With each step, her toes touch the ground first, giving her the grace of a ballerina. It is easy to imagine her with a tail and the aloof posture of a cat. She already has the arrogant look down to a fine art.

While she paces, I become aware of a growing sense of hostility from her. With her hard eyes and set jaw, I half expect her to unsheathe claws and bare her fangs. We are of equal height, but she is not hindered by aching joints and sore muscles. Reaching for my magic, I prepare to defend myself.

The arrival of a tortoiseshell cat distracts Fria and her

shoulders relax. When she turns to me, she no longer looks murderous, only unfriendly.

'If I tell you what I saw, you'll keep quiet about any potential link to the stolen goods?'

'As far as I'm concerned, any information you give me has come from a source that chooses to remain anonymous.'

'Okay.' She perches on the edge of her desk and straight away the cat leaps on to her lap. Her hand reaches to stroke its fur even as her attention appears to be elsewhere. 'That night, I got a call on my burner phone informing me of a unique opportunity to acquire certain rare items that were possessed by Gideor Braeman. His collection has quite a reputation.'

'What time was that?'

'About nine.'

That does not fit the timeline, but I let it pass. 'Did you recognise the voice?'

'No, but it sounded distorted. I'm assuming the caller used a masking spell.'

'Could you tell whether it was male or female?'

'Male.' The cat pushes its head against Fria's side, and she smiles.

'Did he say anything else?'

'He told me to use the door to the study, that it would be left unlocked for me. The items would be in a cabinet that would also be unlocked.'

'And this Good Samaritan just told you all this?'

Fria laughs and the sound reminds me of a purr. I like it. 'Of course not, nothing comes without a price.'

'And in this instance that price was...?'

'Odd.' The cat distracts her again and she rubs heads with it, as two cats would do. Her mannerisms are appealing, though I imagine Karrion would be outraged if I ever voiced the thought to him. 'All he wanted in return was for me to put a set of two protection scarabs up for sale using the wi-fi connection of a specific house. Hacking it was a breeze. I also had to break into a study at that address and hide a bag in the wardrobe. The bag was left for me in Braeman's study.'

'Let me guess,' I say, and recite Ilana's address.

'Yes, that's it. That's where I went.'

A surge of relief washes over me. This is the first concrete proof that I am on to something. Despite all the odd inconsistencies, there has been a little voice at the back of my mind wondering whether the whole thing is a wild goose chase. Now, I think Ilana may be right about her father's innocence.

'What happened when you went to Braeman's house?'

'The door was unlocked, as the caller had said it would be. I sneaked up the stairs, but the whole wing of the house was quiet. In the study, the spell cabinet had its doors wide open. Braeman was lying in front of it.'

'What time did you get there?'

'Maybe half past nine.'

There it is again, a nagging inconsistency. I think back on the timeline for the night of the murder. 'Wait, Braeman was on the floor? But he wasn't killed until later.'

She frowns at that, and the cat fixes me with a piercing stare. 'I think you mean he didn't die until later.'

'I don't follow.'

'Braeman was already dying when I got there.'

'What?'

'He had been stabbed. At first, I thought he was dead, but as I was stepping over him, he drew a breath and nearly gave me a heart attack.'

I shake my head. 'Why didn't you call for help?'

'Other than the fact that I was there to rob him? Because he was beyond saving.'

'How do you know?'

'I watched him for a moment, puzzled by how little blood there was around him. Whoever stabbed him worked powerful death magic that prolonged the dying process. No will in the world could have reversed that. If the spell had been broken, Braeman would have died in an instant. There was nothing I could do for him.'

Fria's lack of concern is just what I would associate with a cat. The troubles of strangers cannot touch her.

'That means he was stabbed earlier than the police thought.'

'Yes.' She nods. 'Braeman was murdered earlier that evening, it just took his body a few hours to catch up.'

The image is powerful enough to send a shiver down my spine. 'That's a terrible way to die.'

'I agree. Whoever killed Braeman wanted him to suffer.'

My mind reels at the new possibilities. If Braeman was stabbed earlier that evening, that eliminates Marsh's alibi for the murder. Ilana is not going to be pleased to hear that. It also means that the whole timeline for the evening is wrong and I have a great deal of work ahead of me.

'So someone, most likely the murderer, phoned you at nine that evening to tip you off about an easy robbery. You got there half an hour later to discover Braeman dying. In all likelihood, he had been stabbed before the phone call and he was still bleeding out. You took the artefacts from the cabinet as well as the bag and left?'

'That's right.'

'Did you notice anything else unusual?'

She cranes her neck to stare at the ceiling, eyes unfocused. 'I thought it was odd that Braeman had a bed in his study. There were some vials and jars on the table next to the cabinet, but I didn't pay much attention to them. Mage spells don't interest me and none of the ingredients were valuable.'

'Did you look in the bag that you were told to hide at the other address?'

At first, I am certain she will say no, but then the corner of her mouth lifts into a small smile. 'They do say curiosity killed the cat.'

'What was in it?'

'A white shirt with blood on it. Based on the weight of the bag, there was something else in it as well, but I felt it would be foolish to root around too much. The last thing I needed was to get a murder victim's blood on my clothes.'

According to the case file, the police found Marsh's bloodied shirt and the ritual dagger in a bag at the back of his wardrobe. But if the shirt was there waiting for Fria, chances are it was not one of Marsh's after all. Anyone who knew Marsh and was a little observant could buy a shirt matching his.

But is Marsh innocent? If what Fria has told me about Braeman is true, Marsh no longer has an alibi. Could all of this be an elaborate double bluff to cast doubt over the infallibility of the Heralds? But to what end? And how do I fit into the picture? These mere thoughts cause a throb behind my eyes.

'What happened when you went to the address you were given?'

'Not much. I hacked into the wireless network, posted the scarabs for sale and broke into the study to put the bag in the wardrobe as instructed. The upstairs was mostly dark, and I didn't see or hear anyone while I was there. One of my cats accompanied me and there was a scuffle with some birds, which is where I assume he lost his collar. That was careless of me.'

'And thus a man was framed for murder.'

'Yes, that was strange, wasn't it?' Fria rubs the cat's ears, a frown on her face. 'I assumed my actions were meant to lead the police astray, but then Jonathain Marsh was declared guilty of

Braeman's murder. That business with the bag must have been a double bluff.'

'Perhaps.' I look away, wishing to hide my doubts from Fria, but she is too quick for me.

'But you don't think so.'

'Wouldn't you rather get a third party to dispose of the murder weapon than hide it in your wardrobe?'

'A Herald declared him guilty, therefore he must be the murderer. Our justice system is infallible.'

'So I keep hearing.' Frustration does battle with doubt in my mind. If I know something to be true but everything indicates it is otherwise, how do I find proof?

'I don't know who hired you and what for, but it sounds like you have your work cut out.'

I stand and offer Fria a wan smile. 'Thank you for your honesty. What you've told me changes everything. Or, perhaps, it changes nothing.'

'What about me?' Fria also stands and the cat leaps on to her shoulder. It stares at me, unblinking. 'What about us?'

I shrug. 'As I said, I have no proof, only a source that wishes to remain anonymous.'

'Thank you. I appreciate that.'

With a nod, I head for the door. When I reach the threshold, Fria calls my name. It is her turn to offer me a card, which shows nothing but a mobile number.

'If you ever need anyone to take a look at a place with utmost discretion, give me a call.'

A private investigator can never have too many allies. I thank her for the card and leave. As I close the front door behind me, I wonder how Karrion is going to react to my adding a beautiful cat burglar to my contacts.

15

MEETINGS AT THE OPEN HEARTH

I opt to leave updating Karrion until tomorrow and make my way back to the car. The shadows between the tall buildings are deepening and street lights are beginning to glow. It is another reminder that the nights are drawing in and the death brought by winter is just around the corner.

Once I get in the car, I switch to hands-free and dial Ilana's number. Just as she picks up, my growling stomach makes itself heard. Lunch seems like a lifetime ago.

Ilana speaks a breathless greeting, and once again I hear traffic in the background. When we try to exchange pleasantries, it becomes clear that we are struggling to hear one another and she suggests that we meet in person. I give her the name of the Open Hearth, and she promises to be there in half an hour. That gives me just enough time to drive home and take a shower.

Having dressed in clean jeans and an aubergine turtle-neck, I pause to check myself in the bathroom mirror. Serious brown eyes stare back at me, betraying a hint of nerves at the prospect of meeting Ilana again. My hair is swept back and I have twisted it into a loose braid. A few strands have come loose and are framing my face. Staring at my plain reflection, I wish I could apply a flawless, understated make-up, but I push the thought aside. This is not a date.

A glance at my watch tells me I need to go, so I switch off the bathroom light and grab a coat and my bag on the way out. I hurry for fear of being late, until twinges of pain in my knees turn into a throb and I have to slow down. It is only a short walk, I reassure myself, and take a few deep breaths to steady my nerves.

Warmth washes over me as I push open the door to the Open Hearth. The pub is filling up and many voices form a continuous sound of human communication. I look around the bar and the dining area, but cannot see Ilana. The thought of having got here first pleases me.

It seems wisest to wait at the bar. I slip out of my coat and step into the space vacated by another punter. A familiar girl comes to take my order and I stick to a cola until Ilana arrives.

I am just taking a sip when I realise someone is watching me.

'Did you find your Paladin?'

As quiet as he is, Wishearth cannot sneak up on me because of his scent. I inhale the heady combination of wood and smoke, trying to purge from my memory the metallic tang of congealed blood. He comes to lean against the bar next to me and straight away a pint of Guinness is placed by his elbow.

When he suggested I speak to Lady Bergamon, I never mentioned the missing man was a Paladin. His question now is bait, which I choose not to take. In all likelihood, he has spoken to Lady Bergamon, although a nagging voice at the back of my mind reminds me that Wishearth always seems to know a great deal about me.

'I did. He was dead, though.'

'Shame,' he says, his tone unconcerned. I often wonder how

his mind works, but it is not a question I dare to ask for fear of offending him.

'I wish there was a way for me to talk to him regardless. This is not a dead end I needed.'

'If you want to make wishes, you ought to get in touch with a genie. Maybe find an antique store and start polishing lamps?'

My glare is met with a familiar grin, and some of the tension leaves my shoulders. If nothing else, Wishearth has an unerring talent for distracting me from my problems.

'I don't know, I think you'd look pretty good stuffed in a bottle,' I say, and my smile widens at his outraged protest.

'I'll remember you said that.' He tries to hide his smile by taking a sip from his pint, but I catch it just the same. 'At least now I know where your loyalties lie.'

'You've always known, haven't you?' I say. An edge of seriousness creeps into the conversation, and I watch him with unguarded eyes.

'A few more offerings wouldn't go amiss, just to make that doubly clear.' Warm embers glow in his gaze, and I wonder at the beauty of them.

'I'll bear that in mind.' I reach to rest my hand on his arm. 'Thanks for the tip. Lady Bergamon was most helpful.'

'Good.' His hand covers mine and his fingers carry the heat of a hearth fire. It has the power to sear and singe, but in this instance, all it does is ease the ache from my bones. But it is not long-term relief, that much has been clear from the start of our tentative friendship.

We are still standing there, sipping our drinks in comfortable silence, when the door opens and Ilana walks in. I stand a little straighter, turning towards her, but not before I have seen Wishearth's smile widen into a knowing grin. In response to my eye roll, he sees me off with a low chuckle.

Ilana is dressed in black slacks, a matching blazer and a

navy-blue shirt. Her hair is down, framing her face in locks of gold. When her eyes find me across the crowd, she smiles, but I see the worry and fear weighing her down. What I am about to tell her will do little to alleviate that.

Having weaved through the crowd, we meet near the middle. Ilana surprises me by kissing my cheek, and I am too late to reciprocate before she pulls away. The scents of a North Mage, coupled with the pheromones that are unique to her, fill my nose. I blink, worried that my slowness has offended her, but she only laughs at my astonishment.

There is an empty table near the fireplace, and I steer her to it, choosing for myself the seat closest to the heat. Ilana sits opposite me and glances through the short menu. While she chooses, I greet Boris, who settles next to me with a contented sigh. From the corner of my eye, I watch as Wishearth returns to his table.

A waiter comes to take the order, and I greet him with a nod. Ilana orders a venison pie and asks if I want to share a bottle of red. The suggestion catches me by surprise. It seems to me that wine adds an edge of familiarity to this meeting, shifting its parameters. But since I am unwilling to put my hesitation into words, I nod at her suggestion and she chooses a bottle from the wine list. The name means nothing to me, but she appears to know what she is talking about.

When it is my turn to order, I simply ask for "the usual" and the waiter nods. He leaves, and I find Ilana watching me.

'I take it you come here often?' Ilana asks, breaking the silence before it turns awkward.

'It's the nearest pub to where I live and the staff have become friends of sorts.' I pat Boris to emphasise the point. 'The food is great and I like the atmosphere.'

'I can see why.' Ilana looks around. It may be my

imagination, but her gaze seems to linger on Wishearth. 'There's something about this place that suits you.'

There is little I can say in response to that and I simply smile. She returns it and my pulse picks up speed. It must be because I am hungry, I tell myself.

The waiter rescues me while I am trying to think of something to say when he returns with two glasses and a bottle of wine. Once he is gone, I sip from my glass and take a moment to consider the rich, earthy tones of the wine. Ilana has chosen well and I say so.

'In my family, knowing wines is as important as knowing the family trees of the aristocrats in Old London,' she says, with a twist of her lips. I am left with the impression that she is not entirely happy about it, though I know not why.

To save us from another awkward silence, I launch into an account of everything Karrion and I have discovered. I have just finished summarising the meeting with Lord Ellensthorne when Funja comes out of the kitchen with a tray and heads in our direction. There is a bit of shuffling while he serves us our food and finds space on the table for Ilana's gravy jug, a bottle of ketchup, and a selection of other sauces. When his tray is empty, he cups my cheek with his free hand.

'I told you, you come here and Funja will feed you, *da*? You came yesterday and now you come again. It is good. Boris, he will keep an eye on you.' Boris barks his assent and Funja laughs. 'No cheating, no bribery.'

Ilana watches Funja go before turning to me with a grin. 'He's great.'

'The best pub landlord in Old London,' I say, and squeeze a dollop of ketchup on to my plate. 'Make that in all of London. Funja is unique and he's made it his mission to feed me. Though with food like this, I'm not objecting too much.'

Encouraged by my words, Ilana breaks the pastry lid on her

pie and takes a forkful of steaming filling. She blows on it and gingerly eats it. A quick sip of wine later, she nods.

'You're right about the food. It's delicious.'

'It's probably not quite what you're used to—'

Ilana interrupts me with a shake of her head. 'Trust me, there are only so many gourmet meals I can eat before wanting something a little more substantial and down to earth. There's a time and a place for everything, and tonight, this is exactly the sort of food I need.'

'Good.' Why am I feeling relieved?

'Now, you were telling me about Lord Ellensthorne, who is well known for being pompous and arrogant. And everyone knows he and Gideor hated each other.'

Her words bring me back on track with my account of the case and I continue with our visit to Reaoul Pearson and his wife. When I reach the point where Karrion and I discovered Brother Valeron's body, I sketch over the details to avoid ruining Ilana's appetite. I likewise gloss over Fria's identity by merely saying that we managed to track down the thief.

We have finished our food by the time I am done with the story. Ilana's expression has grown troubled upon hearing that her father no longer has an alibi.

'After an early dinner, my father was in his study all evening until he left to see Tanyella,' she says, picking at the edge of her napkin. 'He could have slipped out without anyone noticing.'

'True, but if he did kill Gideor, instructing the thief to plant evidence in his wardrobe seems nonsensical.'

'Do you think he killed Gideor?' There is naked fear in Ilana's eyes as she regards me. My response is delayed while a waiter clears the table. We both decline the offer of desserts, and instead, Ilana pours the last of the wine into our glasses.

'Having met your father and having discovered various facts about the case that don't add up, I'm inclined to think he is innocent. But I can't as yet prove it, nor do I know who the real murderer is. I'll do my best to find out, though.'

'I trust you,' Ilana says with conviction. 'I've trusted you from the moment I first met you, though I cannot say why that is.'

Her words touch something within me, and I fervently hope I can solve this case. More than anything, I want to save her father and banish the shadows from Ilana's eyes. There is so much sadness in her, so much weight that she bears on her slender shoulders. And still I wonder whether I am what she was looking for that day on the beach.

Silence stretches between us, and I realise I have been staring at her. She does not appear perturbed by this, but rather watches me with unabashed interest. There is something in her expression, something I have had no problem identifying on the face of others, but which I dare not define on hers. Can her look really mean what I hope it does?

It is possible her scent might give me a clue, but if I were to use my powers here, my senses would be overwhelmed. There are too many people, magical or otherwise, in close confines. That is yet another reason why Wild Folk are not made for city life. What use are our powers if invoking them renders us blind to the world around us?

'Do,' I have to clear my throat before I can go on, 'do you want to order anything else?'

A roar of laughter erupts from a nearby table, and I wince at the loudness of it.

'While I wouldn't mind a cup of tea, it's getting a little loud to hold a conversation here.'

Ilana leaves her statement hanging, a challenge in the way her eyebrow curves. Does she want what I think she wants? I swallow and find my courage.

'I could make us tea back at my place if you'd like?'

'That would be lovely, thank you.' Ilana flags down a passing waiter and asks for the bill.

Despite my objections, she insists on paying for the meal. Her reminder that my bringing her up to speed is part of my assignment is like a bucket of cold water on me. So the charge I had sensed between us was a mere figment of my imagination. For her, this is nothing but business.

When we rise to leave, Wishearth lifts his pint in greeting. More than once during the meal, I glanced in his direction and he looked to be nodding off, which is unusual. Now he is awake and watching me with a hint of a smile.

As I pull my coat on, I realise how hot I am. The fire in the hearth is on the small side and not capable of this much heat. I nod my thanks to Wishearth, who acknowledges it with his pint glass.

I turn to Ilana to find that she has been following the silent exchange with open curiosity. Casting one last look in Wishearth's direction, she follows me out of the pub.

'Is he a fellow regular?' she asks once we are outside. We both take a moment to breathe fresh air, and I feel the first hint of chill after the warmth of the fireplace.

'Wishearth? Yes, he is.' I steer us towards my flat.

'There's something about him,' Ilana shakes her head, 'something familiar that I can't quite place.'

'You may have met him somewhere. He's a Hearth Spirit so he gets around.'

'A Hearth Spirit?' Ilana's expression grows thoughtful. 'I always assumed they left Old London a long time ago. Not many fireplaces still in use, and even fewer people who venerate the old spirits.'

'Most of them may have moved to places where people still follow the old ways. Wishearth is the only Hearth Spirit I've met in Old London and he's never spoken of others like him.'

'It must be lonely, being the only one of his kind in the city.' I feel her eyes on me. 'That said, the same applies to you.'

'I suppose so.' With my hand on her arm, I guide her to cross the road. 'Here we are, my place is just around the corner. Which you know, of course.'

If she objects to the change of subject, she makes no comment. The comparison with Wishearth has left me unsettled. Is that why I feel such a strong kinship with him? Lady Bergamon is also the only one of her kind in Old London. Is that why Wishearth put me in touch with her? Perhaps we can alleviate each other's loneliness, though I have little evidence to suggest that Lady Bergamon is lonely in her garden domain.

Lost in my thoughts, I come close to walking past the stairs leading down to my front door. It is only the small plaque showing the name of my business that catches my eye. There is a moment of shuffling while I look for my keys in my bag, only to find them in my pocket.

With a smile to make up for my quietness, I invite Ilana into my home.

16

JUST A CUP OF TEA?

I lead Ilana through the office and up the stairs. Nervousness washes over me as I wonder what she will think of the way I live, but it is too late to suggest an alternative. At least my early start to the day means that upstairs is tidy.

After I switch on the light in the lounge, I watch while Ilana takes in the double mattress by the fireplace, the faded armchairs, the narrow wardrobe, and the sparse contents of the bookcase in the corner. Everything is clean, but worn. Between my home and having seen me gathering driftwood on the beach, she must think me poorer than I am, but I offer no explanation about preferring a simple way of living, or how this is luxury after growing up in the conclave.

'What kind of tea would you like?' I say, breaking the silence. 'Regular or herbal?'

'Regular would be lovely.'

My guess of milk but no sugar turns out to be correct. Before I head to the kitchen, I kneel by the fireplace and stack branches and logs in the hearth for a fire. The chill from outside has crept in and the prospect of a cold night worries me.

Once the fire is alight, I reach for a length of fir and speak the ritual words to accompany the offering. All the while, I am conscious of being watched.

'It doesn't come as a surprise that you should follow the old ways,' she says when I lean back and position the spark guard in front of the fire.

'No one has ever accused the Wild Folk of being modern,' I reply, my tone defensive.

'I didn't mean it as a bad thing, far from it. The thought of you and the old rituals fits, just like this place fits you. Or at least, it fits my impression of you.'

She is more perceptive than I have given her credit for, and the realisation pleases me. I scoop a pile of papers and my laptop off one of the armchairs and leave them on an empty spot in the bookcase.

'Please, sit.' I motion towards the chairs. 'I won't be long.'

There is a natural lull in the conversation while the kettle boils and I prepare two cups of tea. I am aware that we are both observing each other in passing glances through the kitchen doorway. Ilana has opted to stay standing as she examines the detail of the fireplace and then the contents of the bookcase. There is little she can learn about me from the room; there are no photos anywhere, no childhood mementoes on display. When I left the conclave, I took nothing more than a bag of clothes and my savings.

A sharp crack has Ilana whirling around just in time to see a burst of purple flames in the fireplace.

'That's quite a trick,' she says, walking closer to the fire.

'No trick. Don't go too near the smoke, it's toxic.'

'What?'

I offer her a small smile as I hand her a cup of tea. 'The salt in the driftwood releases toxins when on fire.'

Taking a sip from her mug, Ilana looks at me with open

curiosity. 'What's with the driftwood? Is it part of some sort of Wild Folk ritual?'

'Nothing like that. Part of it is practicality. Why buy firewood when it's readily available on the beach? As for the other part...' I take my mug to the fireplace. The corner of my mattress is perfectly positioned so that I can sit down and enjoy the warmth from the fire. Staring at the flames, I try to find the words to explain. 'Driftwood is of the land and of the sea.'

It is clear from her expression that Ilana does not understand.

'The wood comes from the land, from the forests, and yet it is also part of the sea. It straddles two worlds.'

'Just like you,' she whispers as she approaches and sits down on the mattress next to me. Her designer slacks look out of place against the worn hearth stones.

'Yes, I suppose.' I feel her eyes on me and I fix mine on my feet.

'Why are you living in Old London?' Ilana clears her throat as if surprised by her own question. 'I mean, it seems like an odd place for one of the Wild Folk to live.'

'It is.' I continue to stare at my feet, uncertain what, or how much, to tell her. I have known her less than a week, I know very little about her as a person, and yet I have a feeling I can trust her. But am I willing to share with her something I have only ever told Karrion? Perhaps I will start with something simpler. 'There are various reasons.'

'Yes?'

When I look up, her smile is a cautious invitation to say more.

'In the conclave, everyone has their place, their role. The Elderman determines the role for each individual, and what the Elderman says is the law. I was born into a role, I was brought up in that role, but I... I wasn't sure I could fulfil it. So

I left, to find out who I would be if stripped of that role, that place in the conclave. I wanted to see if I could achieve something just by being me.' I inch my feet closer to the fire, enjoying the feel of heat easing some of the nagging ache in my ankles. 'That's why I'm trying to establish myself as a PI here.'

'It seems you're doing just fine with that.'

'Maybe.' I hesitate. 'I'd be lying if I said it isn't hard, that I don't miss home, but at least out here I can breathe freely. In Old London, I can be me and not what's expected of me.'

'I think I understand. Other people's expectations aren't always easy to live with.'

'Don't I know it.'

She waits in silence while I try to find the words to continue.

'The other reason for my coming to Old London is that I'm sick.' Her eyes widen and I see all sorts of terrible options running through her mind. 'Not sick as in I'm dying, but I have a connective tissue disorder. Hypermobile EDS, it's called. My joints aren't supported properly because the collagen in my body is defective, which leads to frequent injuries and a lot of pain. There's no cure, only management.'

'Yannia, I'm sorry.'

'It's not your fault, it's not anyone's fault. It's all to do with genes, I'm told. But the problem is that my kind believes only in natural remedies, and no amount of willow-bark tea takes away chronic pain.'

Now she is truly shocked. 'You had to leave your home to get proper pain relief?'

Although I have ranted about that very point many times in the past, all of a sudden I feel the need to defend my people. 'No community is perfect. In some sense, I understand the need to accept only that which is given directly by nature, but I'd be lying if I said that the first dose of proper painkillers didn't feel like heaven.'

'And are you doing fine now?'

'I'm okay. I have meds, I know my limits, and I've learned to pace my activities. Things could be a lot worse and I'm grateful for every okay day I have.'

'That's a pretty amazing attitude.'

I shrug, uncomfortable with her sympathy. While she watches me, I play with my empty mug and a memory of dark eyes and a crooked grin floats to the forefront of my mind. It is not something I care to share with Ilana and I banish the memory before I remember Dearon's touch, his laugh, and his scent. I am running from more than just pain and restrictive roles. When the Elderman dies, Dearon will come for me and I must honour the promises our parents made the day I was born.

'Are you in pain now?'

'Yes, it's there every moment of every day.'

'Is it bad?'

'I'm aware of it, but it's not bad enough that I need to take extra pain meds.'

'What's it like, living with constant pain?' There it is, the question I get asked whenever I speak to someone about my illness. It is the one aspect of my life that no healthy person can understand.

'There's no alternative.' I pick at a loose thread on the hem of my shirt. 'I can't remember any other way of being.'

A soft gasp escapes her lips and my muscles tense. I would like to pace across the room, to get away from the look of pity that I imagine on her face. Instead, I keep talking at my knees.

'After a while, you forget. I suppose it's a coping mechanism. My concept of normal has changed to include the pain. Now I can't remember what it feels like to not be in pain.'

'We are masters at adapting.'

'That's true.'

'Thank you for telling me. Thank you for trusting me with something so personal.'

Gathering my courage, I look at Ilana. Instead of pity, I find sympathy and understanding in her eyes. An unforeseen implication of my words dawns on me and fear chills my insides.

'I can still do my job,' I rush to say, stumbling over the words. 'The pain and the medication don't affect that.'

'I know.' She lays her hand on my arm. 'Nothing you say could convince me otherwise. Just hearing all you've accomplished in three short days is enough to show that you're the perfect person to help my father. To help us all.'

Relief washes over me. 'I'll do all I can.'

'If anyone can succeed in solving the case by the day after tomorrow, it's you.'

Her confidence pleases me, and I smile. At length, I become aware that her hand is still on my arm. Warmth is spreading outward from it and my pulse picks up speed until I am certain Ilana can feel the erratic beating of my heart through her hand. She seems out of place in my home, and yet I feel comfortable in her presence.

Little by little my eyes creep up until they find hers. She appears calm as she watches me and now I am certain there is desire in the depths of her gaze. The flames turn her hair into shifting hues of copper, silver, and gold. I could watch her all night.

'You know, when I first watched you on the beach, channelling your magic freely,' Ilana says in a low tone, stroking my arm with her thumb, 'I thought you were the most beautiful being I have ever seen.'

'Oh,' is all I can think to say.

My focus is on the movement of her thumb and heat is

beginning to pool low in my stomach. It feels like a lifetime since a mere touch evoked such a reaction. In many ways, it has been a lifetime, and it happened in a different existence. I turn my thoughts away from those memories for fear of ruining the moment.

'My feelings haven't changed since then,' Ilana says, and leans closer to kiss me.

The kiss is over before I can react and I am left with the fleeting impression of soft lips on mine.

'That's probably the most unprofessional thing I could have done,' she says, and to my surprise, I notice that she is blushing.

Still speechless, I leave my empty tea mug on the floor and bring my fingers up to touch the spot where her lips were. They felt even softer than they look.

'Oh God, did I misjudge the situation?' Embarrassment floods her eyes and I drop my hand to cover hers.

'No, you didn't. I just didn't expect... I never thought you'd be interested in me. Especially not after I told you I'm sick.'

'What you've told me tonight makes me want you more, not less. If you're interested, of course.'

'I am. It's not professional, but I have been all along.'

'Well, in that case.' She smiles and kisses me again.

We end up in a tangle of limbs on the bed, clothes discarded without a thought. I take Ilana in my arms and she comes willingly, drawing me into another deep kiss. It is an invitation to explore the expanse of her creamy skin, and I apply myself to the task without hurry.

Her hair smells of frost and I imagine waking up to a world blanketed with fresh snow. Her neck smells of moss and I feel my hands braced on the damp edge of a forest stream. Her shoulder smells of autumn and I imagine myself running through a cloud of dry leaves, laughing as they dance in my wake. In everything I imagine there is someone with me, someone by my side. But it is not Ilana.

The thought, the memory threatens to take me away from Old London and away from her. I reach up to kiss her, to drown all my senses in her. Why dwell in the past when she is here with me? She is soft, gentle, careful; nothing like I experienced with Dearon the night before I left the conclave. This could be something different.

For a few blessed hours, her touch, her scent, and her sighs create a place where I am safe, warm, and content. As time blurs into pleasure, I forget who it is I am running from.

THURSDAY

17

LEECH

The sharp crack of igniting sap yanks me from empty dreams. Ilana is curled against my side, her hair a pale halo in the flare of flames from the dying fire. I reach up to tuck a blanket over her shoulder and settle back to my previous position, enjoying the feel of warm skin against mine. It has been quite some time since I shared my bed with a lover.

Sleep beckons me until I hear a creak. As the sound registers, adrenaline chases away the fatigue. That creak came from the staircase, third step from the bottom.

There is someone in the flat.

Reaching out with my mind, I find a fox sniffing for mice in the alleyway and I borrow its keen ears. It takes little more than a whisper of power, but the progress of the footsteps on the staircase stops. Can the intruder detect my magic? I let out what I hope is a convincing snore and roll over, hoping that the sound will carry to the hallway.

With my enhanced hearing, I follow the progress of footsteps as they climb the stairs. The intruder takes more care now. I picture him pressed against the wall of the staircase, easing forward. His breathing is fast, erratic, and to my ears, it sounds like gusts of storm wind.

If my memory serves me correctly, the door to the stairs is closed. Careful not to wake Ilana, I roll over to face the fireplace. By cracking my eyelids open a fraction, I can see the door. At the same time, I shift the blankets so that they cover most of me but can be kicked aside.

The footsteps halt on the landing, and for a long moment, nothing happens. Were it not for the fact that I can still hear his breathing, I may think I dreamed the intrusion. But then my eyes catch the door-handle inching down and I know that someone is about to enter the room.

I should have called for help. How could I have been so foolish? I could have sent a text to Karrion or Jamie. Now it is too late. He will hear me speak, and typing a message takes too long. Why was that not the first thing that sprang to my mind, instead of waiting for whatever is about to happen?

The door inches open. With the sense of the fox, I smell pungent cologne. The scent is instantly familiar. Why is Jans breaking into my flat?

After a pause, the door eases open. Jans steps in. He moves forward with a hunched posture. I hear the staccato of his breathing, and beneath it the murmur of words. Risking a little more magic, I sharpen my hearing. The words chill me.

'Too much magic.' Inhale. A shuffling step. 'I've been so very patient.'

He leans closer and sniffs us.

A Leech.

Lord Ellensthorne was not simply intimidating me. Nor was he speaking of an urban myth. Why didn't I ask him to tell me more?

How do I defend myself against something that feeds on the very thing that gives me my best defence?

My sleeping form betrays nothing while I track Jans's progress towards the mattress. A flame flaring in the fireplace causes him to freeze. Ilana remains asleep and I dare not move a muscle. Jans continues his approach.

As I consider my options, I curse myself again. I should have woken Ilana and conveyed the need to be quiet. Now she will wake up in the middle of a confrontation and is as likely to hinder as help me. Again, it's too late.

I ready myself to lash out.

Jans has crept up to the mattress. He bends over me and I feel the fatigue of a long run sinking into my bones. The weakness bypasses my muscles and begins shrivelling the edges of my magic. It is a stronger version of the loss of power I experience in the city. Jans has been stealing my magic. Time to put a stop to it.

Jans may sense the gathering of magic and I need to surprise him. My foot connects with his ankle, powered by my human strength alone.

The angle of the blow is awkward, but it sends him off balance. I miscalculated the direction of the kick and he falls on to us. His knee lands on my hip, causing pain to flare out and me to cry out loud. Ilana wakes up. She opens her eyes to a stranger's face inches from hers and screams.

Despite the throb in my hip, I roll off the mattress. The fact that I am naked barely registers as I grab handfuls of his shirt and shove him off Ilana. Jans lands on the floor and leaps up.

'You bitch,' he spits, face twisted in anger and eyes burning with feverish hunger. They lock on Ilana, lying frightened on the bed.

When he makes a move towards her, I leap to put myself between them. Drawing on my inner reserves, I borrow the claws of a cat and strike Jans. My hand lands on his cheek, the claws sinking in, but the magic falters. I still scratch him, but my nails leave red lines instead of bleeding furrows.

Jans smiles. 'Go on, use your magic against me. That way it will taste all the more delicious.'

Standing face-to-face with him, I appreciate for the first time that he is both taller and broader than me. Magic has always been my greatest asset, but now it is of no use. My only advantage is catching him by surprise again. He looks me up and down, noting the mark Ilana left on my shoulder, my nipples standing erect in the chilly air and the bruise on my upper thigh. A new sort of hunger in his eyes floods my insides with fear, freezing my racing thoughts.

I allow myself a moment of fear before hardening my resolve; I will not let him touch either of us.

The scent of crisp frost fills the room and power surges behind me. Ilana is preparing a spell, unaware of what the intruder is.

'No–' I begin, but Jans shoves me aside in his haste to get to Ilana.

My foot catches the edge of the mattress, and I stumble back. I fall across the bed, my shoulder catching the edge of the hearth stones. Pain flares and I gasp. Ilana's spell is disrupted when Jans launches himself at her, hands clenching around her throat. His nails lengthen into claws and score her skin.

Once more I sense the gathering of power, but this time it is jagged, and with it comes a sense of decay. Ilana's skin takes a grey hue as she struggles against Jans's hold. I don't know whether the draining of magic can kill a person and I don't intend to find out. Looking for a weapon, my eyes land on the basket of logs.

As I crawl towards the logs, hip and shoulder aching, I only hear Ilana choking. My fingers close around the nearest decent-sized log just as the room is filled with the heady mixture of moss, frost, and dry leaves. Jans is about to become even more dangerous.

I turn, swinging the log at Jans's head. Ilana goes still. The log connects with Jans's temple, all the strength I could muster behind the blow. He slumps on to Ilana, blood running over his forehead. I hit him again and push him on to the floor. Ilana scrambles away from him, holding her throat and drawing jagged breaths.

All we can do is stare at the man on the floor.

The pain pulsing from my shoulder forces me into motion. Handing the log to Ilana, I walk to the wardrobe and get a length of rope out of my backpack. My hands are shaking while I tie Jans's hands behind his back and press a tea towel against his temple to stem the flow of blood. The tremors worsen when I find my phone and dial the emergency line for the Paladins. Reporting the crime takes no time at all, but I am conscious of how foreign my voice sounds throughout the conversation. Afterwards, I cannot recall a single thing that was said and I hope I directed the Paladins to the right address.

Throughout my burst of activity, Ilana sits huddled on the mattress, a blanket wrapped around her. The grey pallor is gradually disappearing from her skin, but her eyes are empty. I set the kettle to boil, find a bag of sweetcorn and another of mango in the freezer and take them to her.

'Press these against your neck. It will reduce the swelling and bruising.'

Ilana stares at the bags for a while before taking them. She moves in slow motion, but the frozen goods end up against her neck. I watch her until the kettle boils, then with some reluctance leave her while I make both of us a cup of strong, sweet tea.

'Drink this,' I say when I return. 'And you'd better get

dressed. Any moment now, this place will be crawling with Paladins.'

A couple of swallows of the tea shakes her from the worst of her stupor and she dresses while I tidy away the clothes that were scattered across the floor. From the wardrobe, I dig out yoga pants and a vest top that leaves my shoulders bare. The cut begins to bleed again as I dress and I press a wad of kitchen roll against it. Half a mug of tea later, I tell Ilana I will go down to wait for the Paladins.

During the night, fog has rolled in from the sea and I taste the salt and moisture in the air when I walk downstairs. The front door is wide open, and from the intact lock, I assume Jans picked it to gain entrance. My office is cool, and tendrils of fog are floating down the steps leading to the front door. It is early morning and the street lights are not on. The hazy darkness outside seems uninviting, but I slip on a pair of trainers and climb the stairs to street level.

Old London never sleeps, but in the darkness of the night, it feels like I am miles from the melting pot of magic, people, and technology. In a moment of weakness, I long for the safety of the conclave, where even the darkest night holds no menace.

What would Dearon say if he saw me now?

The simple thought evokes conflicting emotions, but lights turning the corner bring me back to the present. When the headlights illuminate me, I wave at the Paladins. The van sends the mist dancing in its wake, colouring the wisps red and yellow. Fingers of fog caress my spine, whispering a promise of winter and pain. I shiver and stand my ground.

Although the Paladins patrol the streets of Old London on horseback, when they are responding to an incident, they arrive in vehicles. This time, given that none of the injuries we sustained are serious, they have come in a van capable of transporting a prisoner. Three Paladins get out, all dressed in standard patrol armour, and one of them shoulders a large medical kit.

A Paladin named Brother Eo takes charge of the situation and the next two hours pass in a blur. Jans has his head dressed and is taken to the back of the van, which has a containment unit for prisoners with magic. To my relief, he does not regain consciousness in the flat. Ilana's injuries consist mostly of bruises and scratches, which are treated with a healing poultice. My shoulder requires stitches, but I decline a trip to the hospital. Instead, one of the Paladins gives me an injection of local anaesthetic and sews the wound shut. I watch him work, fascinated by the needle passing through my skin and the tugging of the thread. Deep down, I know that I am in shock, but the thought does not yet penetrate my conscious mind.

We give the Paladins preliminary statements, though Ilana has little to add to mine. From her waking up to Jans being knocked unconscious, the whole incident lasted no more than a minute. The Paladins assure us that Jans will not be freed anytime soon and take their leave.

When I return after seeing them off, Ilana and I share a look. A heavy silence hangs in the room. Outside, a grey dawn is breaking. It will be some hours before the sun will burn through the fog, and some of the dampness has wormed its way inside. I shiver in my vest top and move the mattress aside while I clear the still-warm embers in the fireplace aside and build a new fire. It is another early morning for me, but I have no desire to close my eyes again. Not until I feel safer.

'It's lucky you woke up before he could drain us dry,' Ilana says as bright flames spread across dry wood.

'Lucky?' I repeat and frown. Was it lucky? Or was I warned?

The thought lingers as I replay the moment of waking and the flare of flames a little later. In hindsight, I doubt it was a coincidence. Perhaps tonight I have received a reward for my offerings, prayers, and faith.

Instructing Ilana to stay inside, I open the lounge window and walk to the woodshed, my feet getting wet with heavy dew. In one corner there are longer branches of fir, together with oak and birch. I take two of each and weave them together, binding the ends with a length of willow. As a final touch, I wedge dried lavender blossoms in between the branches.

When I return inside, Ilana looks at the bundle of branches with curiosity. I offer no explanation as I walk to the fireplace and kneel on the hearth stones. The dry branches ignite straight away and release aromatic smoke. Bowing my head, I offer my thanks.

'Hearth Spirit, we thank you for guarding our sleep, for the warning, and for safety. Accept this offering as a token of our gratitude.'

The offering is soon reduced to ashes and a warmth begins to penetrate the chill within me. Even here in Old London, someone is watching over me.

18

THE MORNING AFTER

Behind me, Ilana clears her throat. 'Do you really think it was a spirit that warned you about your neighbour?'

'I woke up because sap snapped in the fireplace. That it happened right before Jans stepped on the creaky stair could have been a coincidence, but I doubt it.'

'So if you follow the old ways, spirits will protect you?' she asks, her voice carrying a hint of awe.

'That's my belief.'

'Is it one spirit or a whole host of them?'

Replacing the spark guard in front of the fire, I linger to enjoy the heat. Tiny flames of lilac and green leap above the logs, but the impurities being ignited are minor. The wood is dry and burns fast.

'Opinions are split. Some say each house has a host of spirits attached to it, who grow strong or weak depending on the rituals observed, while others claim that only one spirit looks after several homes.'

'How about one spirit for the whole city? Or even the whole country?'

I shake my head. 'Now you're getting too close to human beliefs. Spirits aren't omnipotent.'

'I guess human religions aren't prominent among your kind?'

'We know spirits exist, we see their work everywhere. Why look beyond that for something to believe in?'

'What about the Heralds of Justice? Aren't they gods?'

'Who knows?' I temper my shrug with a smile. My shoulder twinges in protest; the local anaesthetic is wearing off. 'They could just as easily be spirits.'

'But they live on a different plane,' Ilana says with a frown.

'As do Hearth Spirits, Nature Spirits, and even the Fey. But they all have the same capacity to pass over and affect the world we perceive.'

'Note to self, never debate theology with one of the Wild Folk. You are too connected to the world around you.'

'But you also draw your magic from everything around you,' I say, 'even if it's not quite the same as how my kind receives its power.'

Before Ilana has a chance to reply, the doorbell rings. A glance at the clock leaves me puzzled. It is too early for Karrion.

When I open the door downstairs, I am greeted by the sight of Lady Bergamon on my doorstep. She is wearing a green cloak against the autumn chill and the weave is grey from the mist. If the cloak was red, I would fancy her as a grown-up Little Red Riding Hood; one who avoided the wolf's trap. She is even carrying a basket.

'Lady Bergamon, this is an unexpected pleasure.' I step aside to let her in.

'Wishearth told me you were attacked. I wanted to check whether you were hurt.' She sets down the basket to unclasp the cloak, and I hang it on the coat stand.

'I'm fine,' I say, ignoring the ache in my hip and shoulder.

She says nothing as she carries the basket upstairs. Ilana is sitting on the edge of an armchair with an expression of reserved curiosity. Lady Bergamon nods a greeting, but in her eyes I see disapproval. Is her objection to do with my having slept with a woman or is there something else behind it? If it is the former, I would expect her to extend the same disapproval to me, but warmth returns to her eyes as she offers me the basket.

'I prepared something for the pain. The Paladins dressed your shoulder?'

'They did.' It seems pointless to ask how she knows. Wishearth has been most thorough. 'The local anaesthetic is starting to wear off.'

'The Paladins have their healing magic woven through the thread, but a salve will enhance the spells already there.'

'I didn't realise you were also a healer,' I say, fatigue dampening my sense of curiosity.

'Not quite a healer, but I have found few ailments I cannot treat with my plants.' Lady Bergamon steps forward and touches my aching elbow. 'Though some illnesses are a challenge even for them.'

'That was my experience back at the conclave.' I look in the basket and see a Thermos flask, two earthenware pots, and a clay dish with a matching lid.

'I thought as much.' Lady Bergamon takes my hand. 'Come, let's get you something warm to eat and drink.'

Ilana has been watching the exchange in silence, but I can see the questions in her eyes. All I can do is offer her an apologetic smile as Lady Bergamon ushers me into the kitchen.

The Thermos flask contains the same pain-relieving mixture I drank yesterday and I accept a cup while voicing my gratitude. Lady Bergamon brushes my thanks aside and opens the lid of one of the pots, revealing dried mixture for the tea. She explains how to brew it, and I try my hardest to memorise her words. The other pot contains a lumpy green salve. I smell honey, aloe, and other herbs I do not recognise. But the purpose is clear: it will speed up the healing of my shoulder.

Lady Bergamon lifts the clay dish out of the basket and sets it on the stove. It looks heavy.

'After a shock, I find hot food will help, even more than a stiff drink or medication,' she says.

'I wouldn't mind all three.' The corners of my mouth lift into a brief grin and she laughs with me.

'Food and herbs I can manage, but with the drink, you are on your own.'

She removes the lid and takes a bowl I offer her. Tantalising aromas of chicken, root vegetables, and fresh herbs fill the kitchen as she serves me something that looks like thick soup.

'Perhaps you want to offer some to Miss Marsh.'

The note of distance is back in her voice and my curiosity is piqued. She knows who Ilana is without introductions. Lady Bergamon seems unwilling to explain herself, and I take the bowl to Ilana. When I turn back towards the kitchen, I see that Lady Bergamon has followed me. She hands me a second bowl.

'Eat, so the herbs won't make you feel sick.'

The stew is thick and warm, the pieces of chicken fall apart, and the vegetables are full of complementing flavour. As with everything else, Lady Bergamon clearly applies time and attention to detail to her cooking.

While we eat, Lady Bergamon adds a log to the fire, murmuring under her breath. When she turns to face me, I can see she is concerned.

'You must take care, Yannia. I told you yesterday that you have attracted attention wherever you've gone in Old London, but perhaps I ought to have phrased that as a warning. In this city, you are unique, and that makes you a target for people such as the Leeches. You must be cautious, for there is a dark, violent side to Old London.'

I set my spoon in the bowl. 'I thought Leeches were an urban myth. In hindsight, I should have realised the danger. Lord Ellensthorne tried to warn me, but I thought he was just being unpleasant.'

'He may have tried to intimidate you, but his words carried a kernel of truth.' Lady Bergamon's eyes flicker to Ilana and back. 'The Leeches are much like the Wild Folk: we hear stories of their existence, but few have ever met one in person. Your kind is just as elusive, if for a different reason.'

'But how can you tell if someone is a Leech?' Ilana asks, joining the conversation for the first time. Her hand rises to cover the bruises beginning to emerge on the sides of her neck.

'For the most part, we cannot unless they try to steal our magic,' Lady Bergamon says, her tone guarded as she avoids looking at me. 'But there are some who are... more perceptive to those around them. Their senses may alert them to something not being quite right with a Leech.'

Is it just me she is talking about or does she have such an ability as well? Regardless of the answer, it is clear Lady Bergamon does not wish to discuss the matter in front of Ilana. I respect that.

'You have an investigation to conduct, Yannia, and I won't keep you longer,' she says. 'Be sure to drink more of the tea I brought now that you have eaten. You can return the dishes when you next visit me.'

'Thank you. This was thoughtful of you.'

'Wishearth is rarely wrong.' Lady Bergamon heads for the stairs, glancing back at me with a smile. 'But don't tell him I said so.'

'My lips are sealed,' I say, and follow her down to the front door.

At the door, she tilts my chin up and regards me. I wonder what she sees, but dare not ask.

'You are the wildest thing in Old London. Don't let this city tame you.'

'I won't,' I reply, puzzled by her words.

'Good. I'll look forward to your visit when you have finished your case. Until then, if I can be of further help, you need only ask.'

I thank her again and watch as she walks up to the street level, disappearing into the mist that still lingers. After she has gone from my sight, I close the door and return upstairs.

Ilana is finishing her bowl of stew and she looks up at me.

'Who is she?'

'Lady Bergamon.'

At the name, Ilana's face registers shock and a little fear. '*The* Lady Bergamon?'

'I guess. I don't know of any others.'

When Ilana sets her bowl on the table, her hands are shaking.

'I thought she was a myth.'

'There's a lot of that going around,' I say, fatigue beginning to take hold of me again.

'They say she's a Plant Spirit, the most powerful of her kind in the whole country. Every plant in Old London is hers to command, and probably those outside the city as well.'

'Is that what the stories say?'

From my two encounters with Lady Bergamon, I believe Karrion was nearer the truth than Ilana is. Lady Bergamon is a Shaman, not a spirit, no matter how long-lived she may be.

Ilana looks at me, uncertainty in her eyes. 'I suppose your kind prefers the company of spirits and the Fey to the rest of us, even those with magical blood.'

'I can't say for certain since I've never met one of the Fair

Folk. But it is true that we Wild Folk keep our own company. We need space and wilderness, which doesn't lend us to city living or endear us to humans.'

'Yet here you are,' Ilana says.

'Here I am.' I take her bowl to the kitchen and pour myself another cup of Lady Bergamon's herbal tea. Just as I am about to offer Ilana a hot drink, the doorbell rings again.

'I'm beginning to feel popular,' I mutter as I head down as fast as my aching hip will allow me. At the door is a sight that is becoming familiar.

'Jamie,' I say as I let him in.

'Imagine my surprise when I woke up to an email alert about a disturbance at your address.' He steps in and shakes beads of moisture from his coat. He is carrying a Costa takeaway cup and a paper bag. I can smell a toasted sandwich inside. I inhale: cheese and ham. The tea is weak.

'You get email alerts about crime in Old London?'

Too late, I remember Ilana is upstairs and feel a sense of déjà vu. But Jamie is already going up.

'I set an alert for your address. Call it professional curiosity. I never thought something would come up in just a couple of d–'

I can tell the moment he spots Ilana. Hoping that I'm not blushing, I clear my throat and deal with the inevitable.

'Jamie, this is Ilana Marsh, my client. Ilana, this is Detective Inspector Jamie Manning from New Scotland Yard.'

Glancing back at me, Jamie smirks. 'Karrion on Monday, your client on Wednesday. You don't waste time, Yannia.'

My cheeks heat, but I bite my tongue. 'Thanks for stopping by, Jamie, but as you can see, we're fine. The Paladins took the Leech away and patched us up.'

'I'm glad you're okay,' he says, taken aback by the sharpness of my response. 'Anything new on the case?'

This is not the time to share news with Jamie. As soon as Karrion arrives, we will continue the investigation. Now that I am on to something, my curiosity is urging me forwards. Having spent a night with Ilana, the case has become personal.

'We've got a few leads to run down this morning, and given tomorrow's deadline, we're keen to do them as soon as possible. I'll call you with an update later.'

'All right.' Taking a sip from his tea, Jamie nods to Ilana and leaves. The silence while we listen for the closing of the door is awkward.

'Are you with Karrion?' Ilana hugs her arms around her torso, uncertainty in her eyes.

The question is absurd, and I laugh. 'No. We were up late going through the case file on Monday evening and he stayed the night. Jamie came to see me first thing Tuesday morning, saw Karrion here, and jumped to conclusions.'

'So you're unattached?'

I hesitate and then cover it with a smile. 'Yes.'

'Good.' She shares my smile. 'It's something I probably should have asked before I kissed you.'

'No harm done. I would have told you if the attention had been unwanted.'

'I did get the impression you were okay with it.' Ilana blushes, and I wish the day could have begun differently. Damn Jans! 'I should get going; you've got work to do and I have another meeting with the family solicitor.'

'Of course. Do you want me to call you a cab?'

'Please.'

I phone for a taxi and text Karrion, telling him to come here as soon as possible. We have plenty of work to do and I am eager to get started. While I wait, I call Lord Ellensthorne's secretary and arrange a meeting for late morning.

Once I get a text saying the taxi is about to arrive, I walk

Ilana downstairs. There is an awkward pause at the door when we both wonder how to say goodbye. Ilana resolves the dilemma by pressing a lingering kiss on my cheek.

'Thank you. This has been... interesting. I needed a distraction from everything that's going on.' She pauses on the threshold. 'Though the night would have been better without the intrusion.'

With a wave, she hurries up the steps and into the waiting taxi. I am left pondering her words. A needed distraction? Was that all the night meant to her? Would I want it to be more?

I close the door, shutting out the damp morning. The unprofessional one-night stand with my client is over.

19

PICKING UP SPEED

When Karrion arrives, I spend half an hour bringing him up to speed regarding my meeting with Fria yesterday and everything that has happened since. His eyes light up when he finds out that Ilana spent the night, but he gets no chance to tease me before the amusement is replaced by outrage. I've been preparing a cup of tea for him, but upon hearing that I am injured, he pushes me out of the kitchen and insists that I sit down.

He follows soon after with his tea, eager to find out our next steps.

'I've made an appointment with Lord Ellensthorne for eleven o'clock this morning,' I say, and Karrion grimaces.

'I hoped you'd forgotten about it. But needs must, I suppose. What are we going to do until then?'

'I need you to use your people skills and your telephone charms.'

'Who do I have to charm? Is she pretty? It is a she, right?'

'No idea. But I want you to see if you can find out why Lifelines funded the cancer-drug trial spot for Elianora.'

'I'll do my best.'

While Karrion scours the internet for contact details, I call Sister Alissa. News of Brother Valeron's death has already reached her, but she appreciates my offered condolences. Although I am reluctant to give out too much detail about the circumstances surrounding the body's discovery, I am able to confirm that it was a suicide.

This seems to anger her.

'No. It doesn't make any sense,' she says. 'Valeron was the least likely of us to commit suicide, especially while his little girl still lives. I don't believe that.'

There is little I can say, except to promise I will call Alissa if I find out anything further regarding Brother Valeron. She, in turn, promises any help she can offer, and we end the call. Karrion is still on the phone, and I update my notes on the case, hoping it will allow me to spot something I may have missed. Nothing jumps off the page.

When Karrion finishes his call, he looks displeased.

'Any luck?' I ask.

'They were lovely, all three members of staff I spoke to, but they wouldn't tell me much. All they said was that it was a private donation earmarked specifically for funding Elianora's place on that trial.'

'Who made the donation?'

'That's precisely what they wouldn't tell me. Something about donor confidentiality. That's a dead end. Sorry.'

'At least we tried. It's another item crossed off the list.' I perch on the edge of an armchair and rub my sore hip. 'Alissa doesn't believe that Valeron committed suicide.'

'Did you tell her your theory about the drug trials being a bribe?'

'No. I have no proof. But from everything I've heard about

Valeron, he would have found it hard to see an innocent man executed, even if doing so might save Elianora.'

Karrion takes our mugs to the kitchen and speaks over his shoulder. 'How did he do it? That's the bit I can't figure out.'

'Me neither. But I need that moment of clarity soon.'

'What now?' Karrion asks.

'I'm going to take a quick shower, and then it's off to Lord Ellensthorne's humble abode.'

'And I thought this morning couldn't get any worse.'

'Never say that, Karrion. Things can always get worse.' I leave him and head for the shower.

My shoulder is aching by the time I have washed and dressed, and I take some painkillers with the last of Lady Bergamon's tea. Today, I have little time for my injuries. I will rest tomorrow once noon has passed and we have saved Marsh.

As we head for the car, I spot the rotund figure of Funja following Boris along the adjoining street. After asking Karrion to wait for me, I jog towards them. Funja hears my approaching footsteps and stops, a smile lifting the jowls on his face.

'Yannia, good morning.'

Boris rubs his head against my side, and I bury my fingers in his rough fur. With my free hand, I pull a tenner out of my pocket and offer it to Funja.

'Can you do me a favour and buy Wishearth a couple of pints for me? I owe him big time.'

With a shake of his head, Funja pushes my hand away. 'At the Open Hearth, while Funja is landlord, Wishearth's drinks always on the house.'

'Why is that? I tried asking him once, but he wouldn't tell me.'

'He is modest, unusual for a spirit. I will tell you, but it is our secret, *da?*'

I nod, thrilled to be able to satisfy my curiosity.

'Many years ago, when I just take over the pub, logs were left too close to the dying fire. Ember jumps and starts a fire. My Borzoi companion, he asleep and smoke get to him. Wishearth wake Funja up, help contain the fire until the fire engine come. Wishearth, he save Funja, he save my Borzoi. Now Wishearth never pays for drinks, while Funja lives.'

'Wishearth is quite the hero.'

For someone seemingly unconcerned about others, Wishearth has done his fair share of heroic deeds.

'You tell him he is a hero, he very mad.'

'I've no intention of doing so. His ego doesn't need inflating.' We share a laugh, and I put the money away. 'I'll have to find another way of saying thank you.'

'You make offerings to him, he pleased.' Funja leans forwards, his voice dropping. 'Wishearth likes you. With you, he remembers the old times, when he has much power. Now his power less, but still he helps.'

Ever since I first met Wishearth, I have wondered whether he is the Hearth Spirit receiving my offerings and hearing my prayers. Funja's words seem to confirm this and I feel a flush of pleasure. My friendship with Wishearth is more reciprocal than I had appreciated.

Funja and I say our goodbyes and I return to the car, where Karrion is waiting. He is curious about my brief conversation with Funja, but I choose not to share. That and the prospect of coming face to face with Lord Ellensthorne again brings a scowl to his face.

Once we get going, Karrion rediscovers his good mood by teasing me about Ilana until I am relieved to park outside the Ellensthorne residence. At the sight of the forbidding black door, Karrion's cheerfulness evaporates and his face returns to a scowl.

'Don't look like that, Karrion. The less we antagonise him, the sooner we can leave again.'

'That's all well and good, but what about him antagonising us?'

I have no response to that so settle for ringing the doorbell. A liveried servant shows us in and takes us upstairs to the study. Lord Ellensthorne is lounging in his chair and greets us with a smirk.

'Back so soon, Ms Wilde? Did you perhaps want to discuss Leeches in greater detail?'

Either he has informants among the Paladins or the question is a wild stab in the dark. Whichever it is, I have no intention of rising to the bait.

'I have just a couple more questions, Lord Ellensthorne,' I say, and sit without invitation.

'Fire away, though you're no dragon.'

Karrion bristles with irritation and chooses to remain standing behind my chair.

'Where were you between seven and ten the night Braeman was murdered, and did you kill him?'

My questions catch Lord Ellensthorne by surprise and the mask of arrogance slips. He blinks and composes himself.

'I was at a dinner party all evening. There were plenty of witnesses, should the police wish to check my alibi. And no, I did not kill Braeman.'

'But you did threaten to destroy him shortly before he was murdered.'

'Is that what I said?' He steeples his fingers, his lips curling into something resembling a smile. 'I meant it, you know.'

'And yet you claim you didn't murder Braeman.' My tone is as unconvinced as I am.

LAURA LAAKSO

'For a private investigator, you're not terribly perceptive.' Lord Ellensthorne leans forward. 'The devil is in the details. I said I would destroy him, not that I would kill him.'

'I don't understand.' My confusion must show on my face as he chuckles.

'That much is evident, Ms Wilde. Let me explain: I had no reason to kill Gideor Braeman because he was worth more to me alive than dead.'

'How?' Karrion asks, as puzzled as I am. 'He was your rival in the Council.'

'Not for long. You see, it was only a matter of days before he was going to step down as the Speaker and offer his full support to me as his successor.'

'Why would he do that?' I ask. 'You hated each other.'

'Because I had certain facts in my possession that allowed me to be... persuasive.'

I finally see. 'You were blackmailing him.'

Lord Ellensthorne tuts. 'Blackmail is such a dirty word. But, in essence, yes.'

'What were you blackmailing him with?'

'That would be telling. Suffice to say it would have destroyed his career and his marriage had details of it been made public.'

'Do you know who killed him?' I ask.

'I rather assumed it was Marsh. But judging by your question, we are all, a Herald included, wrong about that.'

There is a hint of curiosity in his cold eyes, but I know he will not ask for details and I will not volunteer any. The interview is over, and I rise to leave. We have almost reached the door when he opts to have the last word.

'Might I suggest a visit to the Braeman household? Someone with your unique set of talents ought to be able to sniff out

Braeman's dirty secrets. Though I warn you, there'll be plenty of those in that house.'

Puzzled by his turn of phrase, I thank him, and we leave.

Back in the car, Karrion stretches his neck. 'That wasn't as bad as I thought it was going to be.'

'No. He must have had something else on his mind. Damn, I forgot to call him a liar.'

'You did accuse him of murder. That was pretty awesome.'

'Perhaps, though I have no proof and he seems to have a solid alibi.'

'Do you believe what he said about blackmailing Braeman?'

'I think so. While I'd like to say that I see no reason why he would lie to us again, the fact that he can do so might be reason enough for him. But he seems to think there's something incriminating at Braeman's place.'

'It's the one place we haven't been to yet.'

'Perhaps we should have gone there sooner, but we've had plenty of leads to follow. Only now they are fast running out and we're no closer to finding out who murdered Braeman.'

'We've still got twenty-four hours,' Karrion says, ever the optimist. 'We'll get there.'

'Not if we just sit here talking about it. We should head over to Braeman's now. It's not far, and hopefully someone there will be willing to talk to us.'

We drive in silence, but Karrion keeps staring at me until my patience wears out.

'What is it?'

'I was wondering, do you have some sort of Wild Folk magic that lets you detect people's secrets?'

'No. Should I?'

'Maybe. It was just the way Ellensthorne was looking at you when he said you might be able to sniff out Braeman's secrets. I wondered if he knows something about Wild Folk powers that I don't.'

'Hard to say. But I don't know what he meant.'

'I guess we'll find out.'

'Perhaps we will,' I say, though my voice lacks conviction. We need a lucky break.

20
_____

VIOLA BRAEMAN

The Braeman household looks twice as large as Lord Ellensthorne's Old London residence. From my internet research, I know that the Braeman family spends most of their time in Old London, though they do have a country manor in Berkshire. As the Speaker of the Council, Braeman would not have wanted to be absent from Old London for long.

The door is answered by the Master of the House, Simon Underhill. He is tall with greying hair and a deeply lined face. Beneath the scents of the man himself, I catch traces of ripening wheat, morning dew, and limes. A West Mage, though a weak one. Perhaps he lacks training. Perhaps he is unaware of his heritage, possessing the blood without the power.

Which is worse, to be unaware of one's potential or to be unable to reach it?

I give Underhill my card and explain why we are there. He stares at it, thick eyebrows joining while he considers the information. I am left with the impression that he is carrying a heavy burden.

'Please come in and wait in the hall. I'll enquire whether Mrs Braeman will see you.'

We step into a wide hallway decorated in muted pastel colours. Everything looks clean, and I smell fresh paint. The house is silent and I wonder if that was the case when Braeman was still alive. Or is this the mark death leaves on a Mage house?

Five minutes pass before Underhill steps in through a door to our right and holds it open.

'Mrs Braeman is waiting for you in the library.'

We thank him, but our smiles are deflected by his frozen expression. Is it our surprise visit that has left him perturbed, or is something else troubling the Master of the House?

The open doorway leads into a drawing room of sorts, from which another door leads into the library, which is the sort of room I have always imagined rich Mage houses would have. Dark bookcases reach to the high ceiling, which is domed and white enough to shine. Books are arranged in matching sets and tall ladders allow access to the top shelves. At the centre of the room is a circle of sofas and armchairs, with a small table bearing a reading lamp next to each.

Mrs Viola Braeman is sitting on a sofa facing the door. Her business suit is black, matched by a dark-blue shirt and understated make-up. She is in mourning. With her dark hair pulled back, she has a severe, uninviting look to her.

Does everyone in this household wear the same expression?

'Ms Wilde, Simon says you have some questions for me.' Viola's voice is cool, composed. With just one sentence she tells me I do not belong here.

'Thank you for seeing us.'

That is as far as I get before another door opens and a young woman dressed in a deep-green dress comes in, carrying a tea tray.

'Here we are, then. Simon said we have guests and I added a

couple of extra cups. You will have tea, won't you? We have Mrs Kennington's famous lemon drizzle cake, which is well worth trying. Our cook is the most marvellous baker. You won't find another cake as delicious in Old London.'

'Thank you, Felicia,' Viola says, the frost gone from her voice.

'I'm Viola's–' a quick look at Viola, 'Mrs Braeman's PA.'

I introduce us and we both accept the offer of tea and cake. It has been some time since I ate Lady Bergamon's stew. Felicia takes a seat next to Viola and we pick the sofa opposite them.

'What did you want to ask me about?' Viola asks.

'I'm looking into certain inconsistencies regarding your husband's murder. Do you know if your husband had any visitors that evening?'

'Reaoul worked with him for part of the evening and I think he was alone after that. I didn't go to his study, so I can't say for certain.'

'When he had visitors, did they use the main entrance or did they come and go through the study entrance?'

'The study entrance,' Viola says. 'We had the second entrance put in when my husband became the Speaker. He had plenty of visitors on Council matters, as well as in his capacity as the Head of the Light Mages, and he felt it best if the rest of us were disturbed as little as possible.'

'Do you know if your husband kept a log of who visited him?' Karrion asks.

Viola glances at Felicia, who shrugs. 'Reaoul might have kept some sort of records,' Felicia says, 'though I can't say for sure.'

'I don't know of any,' Viola adds. 'My husband's memory was excellent and it's unlikely he felt the need for written records.'

'Are you aware of any enemies he had, anyone who might

have wished to harm him?' I take a forkful of the cake, followed by another.

'No, everyone loved my husband. I understand he had a disagreement with Jonathain Marsh, but it must have been a misunderstanding. Politically, my husband considered Jonathain a valued ally. Even after the judgement, I cannot fathom that Jonathain could have killed Gideor.'

'Do you know the Marsh family well?' Karrion asks.

'No, not well. We met at various Council functions over the years, and I always felt that Jonathain was a quiet, gentle academic. That he is capable of murdering anyone seems completely out of character.'

Viola dabs her eyes with a tissue while Felicia refills her teacup. Mindful that Viola's emotions are running high, I change the subject.

'I understand you are closely involved with the Lifelines charity?'

'Yes, that's correct. It's a charity designed to help sick children in Old London, to provide respite for young carers, and to make good memories for families with a terminally ill child.'

'Do you know Brother Valeron Fidelis or his wife Megan? Their daughter Elianora has a rare form of cancer and has benefited from the charity.'

'No, I can't say I do,' Viola says, her words slow. 'Nor can I see how a sick child might be connected to my husband's murder.'

'Perhaps it's a coincidence, but the charity's name came up during my investigation. A private donation was made through the charity that got Elianora into a trial for a new type of cancer drug. It's her last chance of beating cancer.'

Felicia has been staring into her cup and now sits up straighter. 'That's where I know the name from!'

'What do you mean, Felicia?' Viola asks, looking puzzled.

'It was a day or two after your husband died. I was putting the post into envelopes and there was a letter from you to Lifelines asking them to sponsor a place in a specific drug trial for a child called Elianora Fidelis. It stuck in my mind because the accompanying cheque had been signed by your husband and I wasn't sure if the bank would honour it. The charity must have cashed it in before we sent a death certificate to the bank because the cheque never came back.'

'No, that can't be right.' Viola shakes her head. 'We haven't made any personal donations to the charity for some time, barring the bequest in my husband's will. I certainly didn't write a letter about helping with cancer treatment for a specific child.'

Karrion and I exchange a look. Reflected in his eyes, I can see my confusion. Why would the murder victim write a cheque that may have persuaded Brother Valeron to tamper with the result of a judgement? There is no way Braeman's death was a suicide.

'Are you sure the letter was in Mrs Braeman's handwriting?' I ask Felicia.

'It was written on her letterheaded paper,' she replies, stirring her tea until it forms an eddy in the cup. 'I glanced through the letter to check whether it needed any other attachments and then found a label for the envelope. Would I swear it was in Mrs Braeman's handwriting? No. But I wouldn't swear it wasn't, either.'

'Isn't the timing strange, too, if the letter didn't go out until a couple of days after Mr Braeman's death?' Karrion asks.

'I didn't think much of it,' Felicia says. 'I suppose I assumed Mr Braeman had signed the cheque shortly before his death and the police wouldn't let Reaoul back into the study for a couple of days to collect the outgoing post.'

'I assure you all, I did not write a letter accompanying a cheque,' Viola says. 'No more than my husband would make a donation out of the blue. Drug-trial places don't come cheap.'

'Is it possible someone else wrote the letter and signed the cheque?'

'No. There must be some mistake.'

While my focus is on Viola, from the corner of my eye I see Felicia open her mouth to say something then drop her gaze to her lap instead. Viola also notices.

'What is it, Felicia?' she asks.

Under scrutiny from several directions, Felicia blushes and her teeth worry her lower lip.

'Felicia?' Viola prompts her.

Leaning forward, Felicia sets her teacup on the coffee table. It looks like she is going to refuse to speak, but then her shoulders slump.

'Reaoul made me swear I wouldn't say anything.'

'Reaoul isn't the one signing your pay cheque,' Viola says.

'Mr Braeman got loads of post as the Speaker and he insisted on going through it all himself. He didn't have time for writing replies or for much else. With Reaoul's help, they devised a system whereby Reaoul would go through the post and select the items that required Mr Braeman's personal attention. Mr Braeman would draft a reply, which Reaoul would finalise, sign on Mr Braeman's behalf and send out.'

Viola tilts her head, her brow furrowed in confusion. 'I don't see the relevance of any of that.'

'I do,' I say. 'My guess is that over the years, Reaoul grew adept at faking your husband's signature.'

Felicia nods.

'And if he could imitate one family member's handwriting, it's not a big leap to suggest he might have learned others' as well,' Karrion says.

I smile at him to show that we are both heading towards the same conclusion.

'What possible reason would Reaoul have for signing a cheque on my husband's behalf and then faking a letter from me?' Viola asks.

It must be unfathomable to her since she does not know the full story, whereas I am beginning to wonder if anything Reaoul told us the other night was true.

'Would you mind if I took a look at your husband's study?' I ask. 'I've seen photos, but it might help to be there in person.'

I leave out the part about Lord Ellensthorne implying that there is something in this house for me to discover. My gut tells me that whatever it is, I will find it in Braeman's study.

'I suppose that's fine. Felicia, will you show them the way?'

'Of course.' Felicia rises and we set our cups on the tray. Karrion clears his plate of cake before standing, crumbs clinging to the corner of his mouth.

We say our goodbyes to Viola and follow Felicia out. I am close enough behind her to inhale her scent. Felicia is human. It surprises me. Why would a human choose to become the secretary of a Mage?

She takes us back to the entrance hall, through a long dining room, and into a small corridor. At the far end, she looks through a set of keys and unlocks a door. My ears detect a hum from within, but it disappears straight away.

'Here we are. I won't come in. The room has been giving me the creeps ever since the murder.'

I thank Felicia for her help and she offers to wait in the dining room should we need anything. One thing jumps to my mind straight away.

'Would it be possible to have a quick word with Mr Underhill when we're done in the study?'

'Of course. We'll wait for you in the next room.'

With a glance towards the door, she shudders and hurries away.

21

___

THE SCENE OF THE CRIME

I push the door open and we step into the study. It is dark inside, and I fumble for a light switch near the door. Finding none, I borrow the sight of a cat I sense dozing in an adjacent room and walk to the nearest window. Heavy velvet curtains take some tugging before light floods into the room.

As I take in the dark furniture and the stone walls, I see that I was searching for a light switch in vain. There are three light fittings hanging from the ceiling, lined with candles. On the windowsill are tall tapers. Mounted along the walls are more candles. There are no lamps.

The room is as I recall it from the crime-scene photos. From the door we entered, the two oak desks flank the room in the foreground, with the sofa set and the bed beyond them at the far end. To our right, at the beginning of the long wall is another door. The separate entrance. The décor is minimal, which fits with my image of Braeman as a pragmatic man. This is the seat of his power, obvious from the furniture and the feel of the room. It is a fitting study for a Light Mage.

My attention is drawn back to the matching desks. Both are constructed from polished oak, with intricate carvings of leaves and vines decorating the edges. The high-backed chairs are part of the set, the backrests formed of three elven figures caught in mid-revel, hair and garlands of leaves flowing around them.

I recognise the work of a Feykin carpenter. The Elderman of my conclave has a chair that was given to him by such a carpenter, though its details are less intricate. Feykin carpenters are rare among their kind and they use magic to tease out figures, leaves, and flowers from the wood without the need of a chisel or knife. Each detail emerges with a mere stroke of fingers and a burst of power, creating unique pieces of art that no human artisan could ever hope to match. They must have cost a fortune.

At the centre of the room, between the two desks, is a section of bare floor where a cream rug once was. That and the empty desk against the left wall are the only indications that the study is no longer in use. No one in the household has yet begun the task of clearing out Braeman's possessions or choosing another function for the room.

The sight of the crime scene gives us both a reason to pause. When we turn to look at each other, the first thing I do is brush the cake crumbs from Karrion's face.

'Sorry. I got carried away,' he says with a smile.

'It was a good cake.'

'I was going to say that Reaoul has an alibi, but then I remembered.'

I nod. 'He had an alibi for the assumed time of death. However, if we move that time an hour or two earlier, where are we then?'

To answer my own question, I pull out my phone and scroll through the case-file attachments until I find the page I need.

'It says here Reaoul spoke to Underhill at about seven thirty. He was leaving and Braeman didn't want to be disturbed for the rest of the evening.'

'Yet he didn't get home until nine thirty, if I remember right?' I confirm his memory. 'What did he do for two hours?'

'Murder his employer?'

'But why?' Karrion asks, looking around the room. 'I'm not seeing a motive.'

'Me neither. The only real thing pointing towards Reaoul is the fact that he may have forged a cheque and a letter. Which we don't know for sure and we can't prove.' A wave of despair washes over me and I turn away. 'Was I mad to take this case?'

'Come on, Yan. Think of everything we've achieved in the last few days. No way would another PI have got as far as this.'

'You don't know that.'

'I do. Because no one else in Old London works with a team of a Wild Folk and a Bird Shaman.'

'That's true. But it's another matter whether we can finish what we started.'

'Have faith.' Karrion turns me back to face him and gives me an encouraging grin. 'I believe in you.'

We stare at each other until I throw my arms around his neck and hug him. I catch him by surprise, but he soon recovers and squeezes me back.

'Thanks, Karrion. I needed to hear that.'

'That's what you hired me for, isn't it? That and my good looks.'

I laugh as I step back. 'Sure, keep telling yourself that.'

The mood is lighter as we walk further into the room. I pause where the body lay.

'That cabinet was unlocked when the body was found, so it's likely Braeman was standing roughly where I am now when he was stabbed.' I glance over my shoulder. 'He would have had his back to both doors.'

'They can be bolted from the inside, but I seem to

remember the police report saying that only the door leading to the rest of the house was locked from this side.'

'The killer had to get in and out somehow. As did Fria, our thief.'

'Are you sure she didn't kill Braeman?' Karrion asks, suspicion creeping into his voice.

'She's a thief, but I can't see her as a murderer. Besides, what motive does she have?'

'Plenty of valuable magical items in this room.'

'That's true, but most of them are still here. If Fria killed Braeman to rob him, she would have cleaned the whole study. And I don't think she knows the Council gossip well enough to have got wind of Braeman's disagreement with Marsh.'

'Good point. I hadn't thought of that.'

'The murder was personal,' I say as I turn a full circle, staring at the room. 'The North Mage death curse might have been cast to throw suspicion on Marsh, but I think it served another purpose: to ensure a painful afterlife. Another curse was cast to prolong the moment of death by some hours, which fooled the coroner about the time of the murder. But it would also have caused a great deal of suffering. The killer wanted Braeman to suffer.'

'A crime of passion then?' Karrion suggests. 'Was it love, money, or revenge?'

'Could have been all three. But I can't see Marsh committing such a brutal murder, not when all Braeman did was proposition Ilana. Things would be different if she'd been raped, but as it is, the punishment seems disproportionate to the crime.'

'But we've not found anyone who hated Braeman enough to make him suffer.'

'Could the answer be somewhere in this room? What is it that Ellensthorne wanted me to find?'

I inhale deeply, sifting through the smells of spell ingredients, wood smoke from the hearth, and dried parchment in the cabinet. The many scents from the work desk overpower all others. With the bloodied rug gone, I cannot even catch the iron notes of dried blood. There is no trace of the man who once worked here.

As I move closer to the sofa, the scents of dried herbs, heart copper, and true silver grow less prominent. Now I smell furniture polish, the leather of the sofa and the chemical residue left from a carpet cleaner. Underneath it all, there is a hint of something else, something that teases a memory on the edge of my consciousness. No matter which way I turn my head, the scent eludes me.

On impulse, I walk to the bed. The burgundy cover has been arranged with precision, decorative pillows placed against the headboard. Shifting the nearest pillow aside, I lift the cover. Karrion comes to stand next to me, but I ignore his question about what I am doing.

The sheets on the bed are clean, though the new-linen smell has faded. No doubt the sheets were changed in the days following the murder and no one has slept in the bed since. Ignoring a nagging voice at the back of my mind telling me that I have gone mad, I lean close to the pillow and inhale. The smell of detergent and fabric softener overpowers everything else. I cast my senses out, find the cat nearby, and with its nose, I inhale again.

This time, I am able to ignore the smells from the sheets to get at the scents that have seeped into the pillow itself. I smell the sweat from several people, though two stand out, and the faint aroma of new dawns I have learned to associate with Light Mages. But beneath it all is a pervasive sour odour of wrongness that sets my adrenaline coursing and my blood pumping.

I recognise that smell. It was only earlier this morning that I smelled it when I came face-to-face with Jans in my home. That sour tang must be a telltale sign of the Leeches.

As the implications hit me, my grip on the bed cover slips and I slide down to sit on the floor. With my thoughts racing, I take a few moments to realise that Karrion is kneeling in front of me, his eyes filled with concern.

'What's wrong, Yan? Is it the pain? Are you feeling sick? Do you want me to call someone?'

'No.' The word slips out, although I am not certain what I have said no to.

'What do you need?'

At the vague motions of my hand, Karrion helps me up and guides me to the sofa. I slump back, my mind still trying to process the implications of my discovery.

'He was not a Light Mage.' In my haste to speak, the words merge together into an incoherent mess.

'Sorry, what was that?'

'He wasn't a Light Mage,' I say, meeting Karrion's eyes. 'Braeman was a Leech.'

'What?'

'That's what Ellensthorne meant when he said I would sniff out the truth. He knows we can identify other magic users by their scent.'

'But wait. There is no way Braeman could be a Leech. He was the Head of the Light Mages and the Speaker of the High Council. There's no way.'

I straighten on the sofa, the worst of the shock passing.

'Think about it. How much spell-casting is involved in being either the Head of the Light Mages or the Speaker? For both jobs, all he needed to be was a good politician.'

'How could he have gone undetected this long?'

'I'm the only Wild Folk in Old London and it was unlikely my path would ever have crossed Braeman's. If he knew what my kind is capable of, he would have made certain to avoid me.'

'It seems unbelievable,' Karrion says, shaking his head. 'Who can pull off that sort of a con?'

'The best conman in Old London. Do you remember what Braeman's main policies were?'

'He wanted the use of magic to be better regulated...'

'What better way to make sure you don't have to cast spells in public than to make it a regulated activity?'

'Wait a minute. There's no way Braeman could have got himself promoted to the Head of the Light Mages without casting a single spell.'

He has a point. Resting my elbows on my knees, I let my head fall into my hands. Karrion is a reassuring presence next to me on the sofa as I force myself to relive this morning, from the first crack of sap to Jans falling unconscious. Bile rises in my throat as I remember his feverish eyes and the stench of his breath. I remember the moment when I realised just what he intended to do to us.

But amid the fear and horror, I also recall Jans's nails turning into claws. There is my answer.

'I'm sure he cast plenty of spells. Because he could. A Leech takes on the power of his victim. When Jans stole some of my magic, he could do the sort of things I can.'

'Are you saying Braeman drained Light Mages on a regular basis to be like them?'

My eyes are drawn to the bed, my thoughts to the sweat that has seeped into the pillow. Two scents are prominent, one of which I recognised as that of a genuine Light Mage.

'No. I think he stole power from one Light Mage on a regular basis.'

'But how could he do that without the Light Mage noticing? You said you felt the weakening of your magic straight away.'

'I suspect that the Light Mage knew all along, that the power was freely given.'

Karrion looks aghast. 'Who would willingly give their magic to a Leech?'

Who indeed? I only have a suspicion, but my instincts tell me I am right.

'A lover?'

'So he *was* having an affair.'

'Judging by the bed, he was having several. But there was only one recurring lover.'

'Who?'

'Think about it. Who's the only Light Mage we know who could come and go in this house as he pleased?'

'Reaoul,' Karrion says.

'His scent is all over that bed.'

'But Braeman was married. He was interested in young women. Doesn't that make him straight?'

'Does my night with Ilana make me gay? Sometimes it's about a person, not their gender.'

'Hey, I'm not judging. Not now, not ever.' Karrion stares at the bed. 'What I don't get is how Reaoul would have benefited from the arrangement.'

'Wasn't Braeman grooming him to become the next Head of their school of magic? From what I've read, the previous Head has a great deal of say in who is chosen as his successor.'

'It doesn't seem a high enough price for years of giving your magic to a Leech. And what about before Reaoul? Braeman was in a position of power long before Reaoul started working for him.'

'I expect there were others. Perhaps they were drained dry, perhaps not. Reaoul may have got something else out of the arrangement. If that's the case, we need to find out what.'

'Are we going to see him?' Karrion asks as he stands and helps me up. I walk to the bed and straighten the covers.

'Yes. He lied to us about the affair, and who knows what else? Perhaps he will be more forthcoming the second time, especially now we know about the letter and the cheque.'

'We can't prove he forged Braeman's signature on the cheque, though,' Karrion says. 'All we have is speculation.'

'You're right. We need a link between Reaoul and Brother Valeron, something solid to prove it was Reaoul who tampered with the judgement.' I think for a moment and motion towards the door. 'I have an idea, but it's a phone call I want to make from the car.'

As we head for the door, Karrion says, 'Braeman being a Leech has solved one mystery.'

'What's that?'

'All those mana gems he had and other artefacts that stored power. A Mage wouldn't need that many unless he was working on a huge spell, but for a Leech, they would have been a handy way to maintain his power reserves if he couldn't get a top-up from a suitable victim.'

'You're right. The pieces are falling into place.'

'Now all we need is a murderer and some solid evidence.'

Therein lies our challenge and the clock is ticking.

22

EMERGING PICTURE

True to her word, Felicia is waiting for us with Simon when we step out of the corridor leading into Braeman's study. She is in the middle of an anecdote, speaking fast enough to trip over the words, and I spot relief in Simon's eyes as we enter the room.

'Felicia says you wanted to speak to me,' he says, dodging around the end of the dining-room table to approach us.

'I wanted to ask about the wards in Mr Braeman's study.'

'The study has many layers of wards. Some are built into the walls, others are less permanent additions.'

'Who sets the wards?' I ask.

'Usually it was Mr Braeman or Reaoul. I have an item that can power the wards down and raise them again.'

Even with premade wards, like the one Brother Valeron used, activating them requires a small expense of power. Breaking them can be as simple as disrupting the borders of the ward or casting a spell that severs the threads of magic. To avoid having to redo a ward every time it is needed, there are items that allow them to be activated and deactivated with a word of command. If an item is powerful enough, even those with little magic can use them.

'Do you remember which wards were active when the body was discovered?'

Simon thinks, his hands smoothing the lapels of his suit. 'The permanent wards were all active: the ones that protect the study from outside spells and remote viewing. Of the others, only the ward for silence was on.'

I feel Karrion's eyes on me. 'Was it usual for the silence ward to be active?'

'Mr Braeman had it on whenever he was doing spell research. That way his experiments did not disturb the rest of the household.'

There are other reasons why he might have wanted the study protected. It is harder to get caught in bed with your PA if the sounds of sex do not carry to the rest of the house.

'Am I right in thinking you were the one to discover the body?' I ask, instead of voicing my suspicions.

'Correct. I knocked on the door the following morning to see if Mr Braeman wanted to take breakfast in the study or whether he would eat with his wife. When there was no answer and the door was bolted from the inside, I walked around to the outside entrance and let myself in. That is when I found Mr Braeman on the floor.'

'Did you notice anything unusual about the room, other than the dead body?'

'There was a strong smell of ozone and burnt true silver. The air felt charged, full of static electricity. Both sensations dissipated within moments of my entering the room.'

What Simon describes must have been the after-effects of the death curse. In a confined warded space, the physical manifestations would not have had anywhere to go until a door was opened. Simon was lucky the spell had not reacted with any of the more volatile ingredients on Braeman's work desk. The whole house could have gone up in an explosion.

'Was it usual for the dinner trays to be left in the study until the following morning?' Karrion asks, remembering something I had forgotten.

'I would have sent one of the maids to collect them, but Reaoul told me before he left that Mr Braeman was not to be disturbed for the rest of the evening.'

'Strange that Reaoul didn't bring the trays out when he left,' Karrion says.

Simon snorts. 'That would be a first.'

'What do you mean?' I ask.

'Reaoul would never clear dirty plates or fetch his own food. Tasks such as that were beneath him, and he had no qualms about letting us know that.'

'So Reaoul felt – feels – he is better than the rest of the household staff?'

Simon and Felicia exchange a glance.

'Certainly,' Simon tells me. 'He acted as though he was part of the family instead of staff.'

'Did he ever say why that was?' Karrion asks.

'No, but between his looks and his fancy wife, it was clear he thought he should be aristocracy rather than paid staff.'

'I heard a rumour that Mr Braeman was going to name Reaoul as his successor,' I say.

Felicia scoffs. 'We've heard that tale to death. If Reaoul was arrogant before, he became insufferable afterwards.'

Simon nods. 'Yet where's the proof? He's not the Head of the Light Mages now, nor is his standing as high as he has for years given us to understand.'

'Mr Braeman's death was a bit of a fall from grace for him,' I remark.

'More like an overdue tumble back to where he belongs,' Simon says, voice dripping with distaste.

'Thanks. Before we go, could you let me have a note of two phone numbers: the landline in Mr Braeman's study and Reaoul's mobile, if you have it?'

Felicia retrieves the numbers from her phone and I jot them down in my notebook. We move towards the door, but Simon's words halt us.

'Watch out for that one, Ms Wilde. He has learned a thing or two from that wife of his. As beautiful as they may be, there is only ice and stone beneath the skin.'

We thank Simon and Felicia. They see us out. I pause on the pavement and glance at my watch. It is just past lunchtime, but it feels like we have spent days in Braeman's study. A picture is beginning to emerge in my mind, but we need proof.

As I slide behind the wheel of my car, my phone rings. It's Jamie.

'I was just about to call you,' I say.

'Yannia, could you come to the Brotherhood? We need to take an official statement from you. Ilana has already been here.'

'How did she seem?'

'Shaken, but fine. She was visiting her father.'

'The execution is scheduled for tomorrow. Giving a statement today isn't ideal.'

'Consider it killing several imps with one lightning bolt. You can bring me up to date on the investigation and the Paladins can take your statement. Why were you going to call me?'

'To ask for advice and perhaps a favour.'

'There you go. Let's meet up; we can talk and deal with the attack on you and Ilana properly.'

'Okay, we'll be there.'

Jamie is waiting for us on the steps of the Brotherhood as we hurry from the car park. After brief pleasantries, he leads us into one of the corridors branching off the entrance hall. A group of three Paladins is waiting for us outside a room and we are ushered in. The Paladins try to suggest that Karrion waits for me outside, but he wants to stay and I insist on it.

One of the Paladins, Sister Erina, does the talking while the other two act as scribes.

'We've called you here rather than New Scotland Yard because the accused will be incarcerated here until his trial,' she explains. 'A Leech is a rarity in Old London, so we want not just to take your statement, but also to ask your advice on keeping him safely imprisoned.'

'I'll do what I can to help.'

Over the next half hour, Erina takes me through the attack again. I do my best to keep my voice steady, but after a couple of minutes, Karrion slips his hand into mine. His grip grounds me, and when Jamie casts a meaningful look at our linked hands, I ignore him.

When Erina moves on to Jans's imprisonment, I lean back in the plastic chair and try to force my stiff muscles to relax. The worst may be over, but Karrion does not pull his hand away, and neither do I.

'How far would you say his power-stealing ability extends?' Erina asks.

'Several yards. In hindsight, he must have been part of the reason why my power has depleted so fast in Old London. He can be subtle when it suits him, which makes him a dangerous opponent.'

'We'll keep him isolated and collared.'

'While I don't doubt the effectiveness of a collar on regular magic users, does it also prevent the gathering of power from external sources?'

'We believe so,' Erina says, but her eyes betray doubt.

'It might be best to keep him in a regular prison with humans where he has no source of power. But leave him collared so he cannot use any magic reserves he has managed to accumulate.'

'We'll take it into consideration.' Erina rises and the other Paladins follow suit. Before they leave, I have a question of my own to ask.

'There isn't any chance he could be released on bail, is there?'

'No. He will remain imprisoned until judgement, which will most likely take place next week. After that, he'll be transferred to another prison to serve his sentence.'

'Good. Thank you.'

'The room is yours to use as long as you need it,' Erina says to Jamie.

With a nod of thanks, the Paladins leave and Jamie comes to take a seat opposite us.

'Talk to me, Yannia,' he says.

Seated around a scuffed plastic table, Karrion and I bring Jamie up to speed on everything we have discovered since we parted yesterday. I keep my promise to Fria and leave her name out of the account.

When I reach the big revelation about Braeman and our speculation about the source of his magic, Jamie lets out a string of curses.

'Bloody hell. Did they hire you to sniff out all the major scandals in Old London?'

'No, but it stands to reason that the aristocrats would have the most scandals because they have the most to gain by keeping their skeletons firmly locked in closets.'

'Make that spare rooms,' Karrion adds.

'That the most influential man in Old London was an

impostor could have far-reaching consequences for the political stability of your community. If the papers in both Londons get wind of this, they're going to have a field day.'

'Probably best if they don't find out,' I say. 'As for the Mages, they have everything to gain by making sure the news never gets out. Look at Lord Ellensthorne. While blackmail is not something I would condone, he could have leaked the news to the press.'

Karrion leans back. 'Mages would become the laughing stock of Old London, instead of our sage leaders.'

'That could be a motive for murder,' Jamie says.

'Not for Reaoul.' I shake my head. 'He must have known about Braeman's true nature for some time if he allowed Braeman to feed off his magic. It doesn't seem logical that he would wake up one day and realise what a threat to our political structure Braeman was.'

Jamie's chair creaks as he moves to rest his elbows on the table. 'I agree. And yet you like Reaoul for the murder?'

'More than Marsh, for sure. Reaoul lied to us, and at the very least I'd like the truth. My problem is I have no evidence of any wrongdoing beyond adultery, which isn't a crime. And his motive isn't clear, either.'

'Could it be jealousy?' says Karrion.

I turn to him. 'Go on.'

'Let's assume Reaoul had been sleeping with Braeman the whole time he worked as Braeman's PA, and that Braeman had been using Reaoul as a power source since the beginning. For the affair to have lasted that long, it must have been mutually beneficial. We know what Braeman got out of it, but I can't see a simple job and a vague promise about being named the next Head of the Light Mages sustaining Reaoul's interest. What if there were feelings involved?'

'You think Reaoul was in love with Braeman?'

'Maybe. He needed a reason to stick around.'

A slow smile appears on my face. 'Ilana Marsh.'

'What's that?' Jamie asks, while Karrion nods.

'I was going to ask what changed, but that's the answer. Ilana was the catalyst. The other students Braeman took on may have been so charmed or intimidated by his persona and political standing that even if they didn't agree to sleep with him, they didn't mention his advances to anyone. But Ilana went to her father and Braeman's disagreement with Marsh became the worst-kept secret within the Council.'

'Reaoul would have got wind of it soon enough. It's one thing to be someone's lover, quite another to find out he has others, too.'

'And he did have others,' I say, remembering the scents that had seeped into the bedding. 'Perhaps Reaoul always suspected and here was his proof.'

'It still doesn't seem enough, somehow,' Jamie says.

'Maybe it was the straw that broke the camel's back. Years of having a Leech feed off his magic must have weakened Reaoul and he was no closer to becoming the Head of his school of magic. There may have been other tensions that we're unaware of.'

'But how do we prove it?' asks Karrion.

'That's where I need your help,' I tell Jamie. 'I need something tangible to connect Reaoul to the crime.'

'You said on the phone that you needed a favour.'

'Yes. This need for solid proof got me thinking. Reaoul didn't have to watch himself in the study because he was there every day. But if he did organise the cheque to Lifelines as a bribe for Brother Valeron, the two of them must have communicated. I can't see them putting any of it in writing, so letters and emails are out, and frequent meetings might have been noticed. My guess is they communicated using phones.'

'You want me to get my hands on Reaoul's phone records? Because I will need a warrant for that.'

I open my notebook and flip through the pages until I find the one I need. 'You don't have to, Jamie. You're still investigating Brother Valeron's death, aren't you?'

'It's more or less ruled as a suicide by now.'

'But is the investigation still open?'

'Yes, it is.'

'Great. Request Brother Valeron's phone records going back to the date of Braeman's murder. Check them against these two numbers.' I show him my notebook. 'One is the direct line to Braeman's study and the other is Reaoul's mobile. If either of them shows up, we have a connection.'

'It could be innocent,' Jamie says.

'It could, but it's not going to be. That would be too much of a coincidence and I've read enough detective novels to know there are no such things as coincidences when it comes to a murder investigation. Reaoul isn't involved in the work Lifelines does and he has nothing in common with Brother Valeron.'

'I'll make some calls, see what I can do.'

'Thanks, Jamie. You can add this to the growing list of favours I owe you.'

'At this point, I want to see this closed. You two have done one hell of a job in less than a week. Puts trained detectives to shame.'

'It was easier for us, given that we have fewer rules and regulations to follow.'

'Still, you should be proud of what you've achieved.'

A shake of my head dismisses the compliment. 'We're not finished yet, not by far. While I know the judgement was tampered with, I still don't know how, nor have I any proof. Likewise, I have no evidence to show that it was Reaoul, not Marsh, who killed Braeman.'

Jamie copies the phone numbers into his phone and stands. With the scrape of chair legs on linoleum floor, we follow suit. It is a relief to get out of the plastic chair and I massage my aching collarbones.

'When was the last time you ate, Yannia?' Jamie asks.

'We had cake at Braeman's.'

'I mean proper food.'

I check the time on my phone. 'It's been some time.'

'Go and get something to eat. It will take me a while to obtain the phone records anyway.'

'He's got a point, Yan,' Karrion says. 'I'm starving. I can't think when I'm starving.'

There are plenty of jokes I could make about his brain capacity, but none come to mind as fatigue washes over me. The early start to the day, together with all the painkillers I have taken and the lack of proper food since breakfast, has sapped my strength. As much as I want to continue at our current speed, the others are right. We need a break.

'Food wouldn't be a bad idea. Call me when you have something, Jamie.'

'Of course. I'll get this done as soon as I can.'

'Thanks. Your help means a lot to me.'

'You'd better watch out. Keep this up and I might try to recruit you for the Metropolitan Police.'

Although he joins in the laughter that follows his statement, Jamie's eyes remain serious as he leads us out of the room to the main exit of the Brotherhood.

23

SMOKING GUN

Karrion and I find an Italian restaurant near the Brotherhood and order enough food to last us several days. We eat in silence, my thoughts returning time and time again to the Marsh judgement and how it could have been rigged. The answer must be on the trial CCTV footage, and I curse myself for not having transferred the files to my phone.

'A feather for your thoughts,' Karrion says while we wait for coffee and tiramisu.

I explain about the files, but Karrion seems unconcerned.

'The way I see it, we should focus on one thing at a time. Let's get Reaoul to confess to the murder, and while he is busy giving his evil mastermind speech, he will let slip how the trial was rigged.'

'When you put it that way, it sounds easy.'

'It's all about your point of view.'

'Duly noted.'

A waiter brings us our dessert, and I take a sip of my coffee. It is dark and strong, just what I need. I took painkillers with my starter and they are beginning to blur the edges of the pain in my legs and shoulder.

The coffee spreads warmth to my limbs and the tiramisu is delicious and sweet. Karrion ends up with cream on his lip piercing, and I am reaching to wipe it off when my phone rings. In my haste to answer Jamie's call, I come close to knocking over my glass of water.

'What news?' I ask.

'You were right, and I'm no longer surprised about that. Brother Valeron called Reaoul's mobile the morning after the murder and they have been in regular contact ever since. The last call from Reaoul was made on Sunday morning, half an hour before Brother Valeron disappeared. It lasted less than a minute and Brother Valeron rang his wife straight after. That was the last call he ever made.'

'There's the connection. I need to speak to Reaoul.'

At my words, Karrion grins and motions for the waiter to bring the bill. He still has half a dessert left and he shovels it into his mouth. At the bar, one of the waiters casts a disapproving look in our direction.

'I would much prefer it if you didn't go accusing dangerous Mages of murder by yourself,' Jamie says. In the background, office noises change to sounds of traffic. He must have stepped out of New Scotland Yard.

'I'm not going to. I have Karrion with me.'

Although he has no context for the comment, Karrion grows an inch taller. The aura of magic around him expands, and where it touches me, I feel the brush of a thousand feathers on my skin. The sensation is soothing and a part of me wonders what it would feel like to have all of his magic directed at me.

When the bill arrives, Karrion is distracted and his magic ebbs.

'Karrion or no Karrion, I fear a Bird Shaman and one of your kind are no match for a Mage who's had time to recharge his power. You've been to see him once, he may be expecting you again.'

'What do you propose, Jamie? I can't march in there with a section of Paladins.'

'I could come with you.'

'Didn't you tell me on Tuesday that you can't investigate a closed case?'

'Not officially, no. But Reaoul won't know that, will he?'

'That's sneaky. Do you know the address?'

'Text me and I'll meet you there.'

We end the call and I send the text message while I get my credit card out. Karrion tries to pay for his meal, but I wave his money away and remind him that we are working. After I have paid, I usher him out and we call our thanks to the owner of the restaurant.

From where we are near the Thames, it is a short walk to where the Pearsons live. On the way, I try to formulate a plan. Should I be bold and direct, or circumspect and cunning? Can I even be circumspect and cunning?

We wait across the road from the block of flats, leaning on the railing. I keep one eye on the road and the other on the lazy movement of the river. The water I see here will go all the way to the sea, and perhaps the currents will carry a diluted form of it past my beach. I long to be there, or to visit Lady Bergamon's garden. After Jans's attack, I feel drained, worn out. But it is not the only reason my magic is low. This week, I have been using my powers with wild abandon.

Yet as much as I need to recharge, I have never felt so alive in Old London. In this moment, in the middle of my biggest case yet, I know what I want.

I have tears in my eyes when I look up at Karrion. A smile

spreads across his face as he reaches up to wipe something wet off my cheek. He lets his fingers linger there.

'You've finally got it, haven't you?'

'Got what?' I ask.

'I saw it the first time we met. All this time, you've been trying to figure out who you could be, when you've already found it. This is who you were meant to be. It's your time to shine.'

'Okay,' I say, and my grin matches his.

'Okay.'

'Am I... interrupting something?'

At Jamie's question, Karrion drops his hand and steps back.

'No, not really,' I reply. 'I just had a personal eureka moment.'

'Care to share?'

'Nope.' I motion towards the building across the street. 'A suspect is waiting. Shall we?'

Without waiting for an answer, I jog across the road, dodging cars. Behind me, I hear Karrion laughing as he follows. I assume Jamie is also coming.

The doorman calls the Pearsons' flat and then sends us up. In the lift, I turn to Jamie.

'Just in case she's up there, do you know who Reaoul is married to?'

'Yes, a model. I saw her photo on the bus a few months back. She's beautiful.'

'Right. That photo you saw?'

'What of it?'

'It doesn't do her justice. By a long shot.'

'Oh. Okay. Right then.' Jamie turns to the mirror and smooths his hair. Next to him, Karrion rolls his eyes and I duck my head to hide a smile.

My warning comes in handy because it is Eolande who opens the door for us. This time, she is dressed in a deep-red cocktail dress that accentuates her pale, flawless skin and the hues in her hair. Her magic reaches out to me like a breath of spring breeze and I allow the scent of blossoms and saplings to wash over me. The subtle meeting of our powers takes only a moment, but there is enough of a pause to make Jamie clear his throat.

I perform introductions. When Jamie stammers a greeting, I resist the urge to follow Karrion's example and roll my eyes. Eolande shows no sign of noticing Jamie's eagerness, and with a simple handshake, she charms him. As I watch his wide eyes and slack expression, I appreciate anew how dangerous the Feykin can be. Magical people have a level of innate resistance arising from our powers, but humans have no defence against the subtle ways of the Fey. I feel sorry for Jamie. As good as he feels now, it will be replaced by hollow longing when we leave.

Eolande shows us through to the lounge and seats herself on the same spot as she did last time we visited. Her expression is one of polite interest, but her shrewd eyes study me. Can she sense the void in my power, the blurriness caused by pain and fatigue?

'We were hoping to speak with your husband,' I say, glancing around the lounge. Nothing has changed. 'Is he here?'

'He's out.'

'Do you know when he'll be back?'

'No.'

My surprise must register on my face for Eolande's lips tighten into a wan smile.

'He has taken to spending his days elsewhere. Perhaps he is looking for new employment, perhaps he's found other diversions.' She shrugs.

Her disinterest shocks me and I am left speechless. Then honesty forms words of its own accord.

'I'm surprised you invited us up.'

'I thought you might provide a moment's diversion. Besides, you,' she points at me, 'you intrigue me. In your company, I find myself reminded of home, though it is a home I've never been to.'

'Our powers hark from the same source, though you are a direct manifestation of Nature at her most powerful.'

'You are not so bad yourself, Wild Woman. Though here you are at a disadvantage and must take all the allies you can find. If you do, perhaps you will survive Old London instead of the city taming you.'

Eolande's words mirror those of Lady Bergamon so closely that a sense of disquiet settles over me. How can she know what Lady Bergamon said only this morning? Or is my predicament that obvious?

Sensing my thoughts, Karrion shakes his head. 'No city could ever tame Yannia.'

'That remains to be seen,' Eolande says. 'Do you want something from me?'

'Do you know a Paladin called Brother Valeron?' I ask.

'I don't make a habit of associating with Paladins.' The way she says it implies that Paladins are akin to vermin and my hackles rise. Such is the changeable nature of the Feykin.

'What about your husband? Can you think of a reason why he would speak to Brother Valeron on a regular basis?'

'No.'

I leave the word hanging there for a moment, waiting to see if Eolande will elaborate. She chooses not to.

'Phone records indicate that your husband and Brother Valeron have been calling each other since Gideor Braeman was murdered. The last call was on Sunday and Brother Valeron committed suicide some hours later. He was the Paladin serving at the judgement of Jonathain Marsh.'

Eolande shrugs at this, but a hint of speculation creeps into her eyes.

'Were you aware that Braeman was being unfaithful to his wife?'

'Of course.'

Next to me, Jamie sits a little straighter. So far, he has been content to let me do the talking and I take full advantage of that. Direct questions appear to be the way to go with Eolande.

'Yet when we were last here, your husband told me that to his knowledge, Braeman wasn't having an affair.'

'He lied.'

'Why?'

'Damage control.'

I frown at her choice of words. 'What sort of damage control?'

'It suited several parties, my husband included, to maintain the illusion that Gideor died a devoted husband and father, a great politician whose legacy will endure in Old London for years to come.'

'Yet this wasn't the case, was it?'

Anger twists Eolande's face. Even in her fury, she is beautiful, but her beauty is that of a predator leaping at a prey's throat.

'He was a fraud.'

Again she surprises me and my brain is struggling to adjust to the new knowledge, considering the implications.

'You knew he wasn't a Light Mage?' I ask.

'I figured it out, yes.'

'How?'

'Sometime after he began working for Gideor, my husband started coming home low on power. At first, I thought it was because they had been working on spells all day and Reaoul's magic was sapped from constant use, but I soon learned to tell the difference between usage and drainage. It didn't take a great deal of intelligence to figure out Gideor was using my husband in more ways than one. There is only one type of creature in Old London who can, and must, do that.'

Eolande rises in a fluid motion and walks to the windows. The lounge offers a great view of the river and she stares at the brown water long enough for me to get restless. When she turns back to us, the anger is gone, replaced by a mask of cool disinterest.

'Over time, I grew to respect Gideor in a whole new way. What he did required extraordinary audacity, and the fact that he succeeded proved how determined he was. He wouldn't let anyone or anything stand in his way.'

'There's something I don't understand,' Karrion says into the silence that follows. 'How could your husband have an affair with Braeman when you told us last time that your wedding vows wouldn't allow adultery?'

Her face twists into a bitter imitation of a smile. 'I told you my wedding vows were... clear on the importance of fidelity. Alas, my husband is constrained by no such vows.'

Jamie lets out a soft curse and then murmurs an apology. Karrion and I are likewise shocked by the revelation, and despite her capricious nature, my sympathy goes out to Eolande. Did it cut her that day, knowing that the man she was about to marry did not trust her without magical vows?

'Such is the lot of the Feykin,' Eolande says. 'We are not trusted by anyone, and for a good reason.'

'Did your husband ever speak to you about the affair or his working relationship with Braeman?' I ask.

'Never.' Eolande lifts her chin as she regards us. With a nod, she continues, 'Though in the weeks preceding Gideor's death, he was often troubled when he came home.'

'Did he tell you why?'

'No. He did his best to hide it from me.'

'How did you know he was upset?' Karrion asks, his words rushed in his eagerness.

'Feykin are master manipulators. The ability to read others comes naturally to us.'

Jamie fidgets, and I know he is worried about what Eolande could deduce about him. He need not worry. There is little of value he could offer her.

'What about the night of the murder, what time did he get home?' I ask.

'Around nine thirty. The police already checked his alibi.'

The speculation is back in Eolande's eyes as she watches me. I am left with the impression that she is challenging me to go on, to reveal how much I know.

'How did he seem when he came home?'

'Calm and satisfied.'

'What did he do when he got home?'

'He took a shower, dressed, and went out again.' The answer comes without hesitation: a rehearsed response to an expected question.

'He went out again? When?' There was no mention of the fact in the police report.

'About twenty past ten. He was gone for twenty minutes.'

I do some quick maths. Twenty minutes is not long enough to get from the Pearsons' flat to Braeman's house and back, so Reaoul's alibi for the erroneous time of death is solid. But it would take about ten minutes to drive to the public phone from which the anonymous tip was made.

'The staff at Braeman's tell me that Reaoul left there about seven thirty. Do you know why it would have taken him two hours to get home?'

'Did he not tell you he stopped at a whisky bar on the way home?'

Now I am certain she is challenging me with her loaded questions and vague answers.

'Did he smell of alcohol when he came home that night?' I ask.

'No, he didn't.'

'Do you think your husband is capable of murder?'

Eolande steps forward. 'There is nothing my husband isn't capable of.'

While we are still processing her cold words, she asks a question of her own.

'Do you think Reaoul killed Gideor?'

I exchange a glance with the others and nod. 'Yes.'

'Have you any proof?'

In the pause before I answer, a thousand frustrations and bluffs flash through my mind. Once again, honesty wins.

'No.'

Eolande turns without a word and leaves the room. We are left sitting on the sofa, looking at each other in confusion. She is gone long enough for me to wonder whether she is calling Reaoul to warn him or to sneak out of the flat unseen. I am about to ask Jamie what we should do when Eolande returns, carrying a black bin bag.

'This may help.' She gives me the bag. It is light, and from the feel of it, contains some sort of fabric.

'What is it?'

'My ticket to freedom.' Upon seeing our looks of confusion, Eolande chuckles. 'My marriage to Reaoul had its benefits at the time, but that is no longer the case. I've grown tired of him and his ambitions no longer match mine. Time to move on, and you will ensure that I do so from the most advantageous position.'

Her blatant admission of using us is shocking, though it should not be. This is why the Feykin have the reputation they do. This is why they will achieve anything they set their minds to.

All politeness slips from her face as she crosses her arms.

'The execution is tomorrow, so you'd better hurry. Tick-tock, tick-tock.'

24

A CASE REOPENED

Eolande remains in the lounge as we walk to the door and let ourselves out. The ride down in the lift is silent, as is the walk to Jamie's car. By unspoken agreement, we all slip inside and I hand the bag to Jamie. He works open the knot and reveals a white dress shirt inside.

Borrowing the nose of a spaniel who is sniffing a lamp-post nearby, I focus on the shirt. In the periphery of my vision, I notice Jamie leaning closer. Karrion too must have noticed, for I sense his disapproval as the rustle of unseen feathers. I ignore them both.

Once I get past the dusty smell of the plastic, I catch a fleeting impression of a new dawn, of Reaoul, and of blood.

'I think it's Reaoul's shirt and there's blood on it,' I say, relinquishing the threads of power. 'Your lab will have to do the rest.'

'You can't tell whose blood it is?' Jamie asks, sounding disappointed.

'While my magic does lend me certain advantages, I'm no bloodhound. Besides, the blood is old.' I twist so I can see both

Karrion and Jamie. 'I suppose this is the point where New Scotland Yard gets involved in an official capacity.'

'Is this the end of the road for us?' Karrion asks, and I hear the disappointment in his voice.

'No.' I shake my head. 'We've found no evidence of Marsh's innocence, and given the Herald's judgement, the police are going to assume Reaoul was an accomplice, not the sole murderer. While they confirm the proof against Reaoul, we still have a tampered judgement to tackle.'

'Good. It would be a shame not to see this to the end.'

'Just because the police are going to get involved doesn't mean this isn't still your case,' Jamie says. 'The only reason we're reopening the file is because of what you two have discovered. The least I can do is keep you informed, even if I'm not supposed to do that.'

'Thanks, Jamie. We both appreciate that.' Behind me, Karrion nods.

'To set the ball rolling, I think it's best if you come with me to New Scotland Yard and give an official statement regarding your investigation.'

'Now?' I glance at my watch. 'Can't it wait until tomorrow?'

'Not if you want us to rush through a DNA test on this shirt.'

'In that case, we have no choice. So long as you appreciate that I gave my word to one of my sources that their name would not be mentioned to the police.'

'That's fine,' Jamie says, and starts the car. 'The Paladins may not like it, but that's up to them, not me.'

Our route takes us along the river, and I watch the scenery until we pass out of Old London and magic changes to mundane. The closer we get to the Houses of Parliament, the slower the traffic becomes, and I use the time to call Ilana. Her voicemail picks up the call. I leave a message saying that we have identified a suspect, that the police are processing key evidence for us, and that we are now focusing our efforts on figuring out how the process of judgement was corrupted.

After everything that happened last night and this morning, part of me is glad that she did not pick up. I cannot afford the distraction of an awkward telephone conversation that would no doubt linger in my mind. In hindsight, sleeping with Ilana may have been a mistake, especially as I am not certain whether it was a one-night stand or something more. I am not even certain which I would prefer.

When did life get so complicated?

Once we reach New Scotland Yard, Jamie takes us past the public entrance and into the heart of the building. He finds an unoccupied interview room and leaves us there. When he returns, he is accompanied by another human, Detective Allen, and a North Mage. Allen was in charge of the Braeman murder investigation, and it soon becomes clear that he is less than thrilled to be dragged away from his desk to speak to a private investigator who has proven his work inadequate. As we recount our week, his attitude shifts from hostile to sceptical.

It takes us several hours to go over every interview we have conducted, every lead we have followed and everything we have concluded. At one point, the Mage goes out to get us all coffees, but they go cold while we continue speaking. I do most of it, with Karrion interjecting with details or corrections when I misremember something. The only part of the investigation I am less than forthcoming on is Fria's involvement. I promised to keep her name out of it, and I do so, though it is clear from the coldness of the detective's expression that he knows I am holding something back. He remains sceptical until the Mage confirms that it is possible for a spell to delay the physical process of dying and that a powerful death curse could mask the magical residue it would leave behind. When she adds that the

Shadow Mages are known to possess such a spell, I shake my head.

'What?' Jamie asks.

'A Shadow Mage death spell and a North Mage death curse. Reaoul was diligent in directing the blame at others.'

'If Shadow Mages have spells like that,' says Jamie, 'I should think they would be the obvious choice as suspects.'

I tilt my head as I regard him. 'Why?'

'Aren't they sort of evil?'

'No more than I'm evil because I have the potential to borrow tiger claws and hurt someone. Shadow Mages aren't inherently evil, just like Light Mages aren't inherently good. They are simply people.'

'What about Lord Ellensthorne?' Jamie asks.

'He is a thoroughly unpleasant person, but that doesn't make him evil. Or a murderer.'

'A shame, really,' Karrion says, and I prod his bicep.

'As fascinating as this ethics lesson has been, some of us have work to do,' the detective says, and stands. 'Especially since you've given us cause to reopen a closed file.' He walks out without a goodbye and the Mage follows him.

'Don't mind Allen. He's grumpy with everyone who gives him work, and he doesn't much care for magical folk.'

I smile at Jamie. 'We'll live.'

'Good. We'll get the case officially reopened and send the shirt to the lab. I'll tell them it's a rush job. The DNA testing will take all night at least, though.'

My impatience protests at the delay, but there is little I can do to affect the lab backlogs. 'Call me when you get the results, no matter the hour.'

'Of course.'

Jamie walks us through the building and gives us a lift back to my car, which is still parked at the Brotherhood of Justice. We part ways with promises to be in touch, though my thoughts are already turning to the judgement. Time is running out for Marsh. Karrion seems to sense my concern, and together we hurry to my car.

As I am pulling out into the evening traffic, Karrion turns in his seat to face me.

'Can you really identify every type of magical person based on their scent alone?'

'Yes.'

'What do I smell like?'

'Like Karrion,' I say, enjoying a moment of being literal.

From the noise he makes at the back of his throat, I can tell he is less than impressed. 'You know what I mean.'

After a brief silence, I relent. 'You smell of wind and feathers.'

'What about you? I mean, do Wild Folk have a distinctive scent as well?'

'It's more a range. Different people smell of different things, but there's always an underlying wildness to them.'

'But do you know what you smell like? I'm just trying to imagine what it's like, having that sort of awareness of people and a whole different sense at your disposal. Ordinary people like me don't use their noses for much more than checking whether the milk is still okay to add to their tea.'

'That's not quite true, but I take your point.' I stare at the flow of traffic while I think about his question. He seems to sense this and does not press me further. 'Someone once told me that I smell like a mixture of soil, saplings, and sunlit meadows.'

'Sounds... nice.' He hesitates. 'Was it Dearon?'

This time I take even longer to answer. 'Yes.'

'What about him? What does he smell like?'

My heart clenches at the memory, and I look away to hide the anguish on my face. 'Please, don't.'

'I'm sorry, Yan.' His fingers brush against my hand on the steering wheel before he changes the subject. 'One task down, one to go.'

'Yes, and fewer than twenty-four hours left to accomplish the impossible. No pressure.'

'We can do it,' he says, and I love him for the optimism.

'How do you know?'

'Because you have a girl to impress.' Karrion follows his words with a laugh, no doubt in response to my cheeks heating.

'Are you ever going to let that go?' I ask, though I am grateful for the changed subject.

'Considering how much you've teased me about girls over the past few months, not likely.'

'Figures.'

The lighter mood lasts until I park outside my flat. I look at the stairs to my front door and my thoughts turn to last night. How long will it take for me to feel safe in my own home again, with or without Wishearth's protection? How long until I stop seeing Jans's manic leer every time I close my eyes? Personal safety is something I took for granted until I lost it. Now I cannot help marvelling at how easy it is to unsettle the foundations of someone's existence.

Karrion must have noticed my trepidation, for his hand finds mine. 'I wish I'd been here to keep you safe.'

'I should be able to take care of myself. I did, even if I got hurt in the process. What's unexpected is the sense of violation. Not of me personally, but rather in relation to my home.'

'I get it. Your home is where you're safe and no one should be there uninvited.'

'Exactly.'

'At least the Hearth Spirit was able to warn you,' he says, and in his voice I detect jealousy. However much it bothers him that he was not there to protect me, it bothers him even more that someone else was. I expect it would be worse if he knew the Hearth Spirit who warned me was Wishearth, who also directed us to Lady Bergamon.

'Yeah, I got lucky.' I nod towards the building. 'I suppose we ought to get this over and done with. Even if we didn't have a case, I can't put off going home for ever.'

We head down the stairs, and my only concession to my lingering trepidation is to allow Karrion to go in and upstairs first. He has a look around, but of course there is nothing to see. Jans is in Paladin custody and no one else has reason to break into my home. Still, Karrion's presence does allay some of my discomfort.

While my laptop boots, I brew a pot of coffee. It is too early to think about dinner and I dig out a packet of custard creams from the cupboard. We get our mugs of coffee and head to the lounge.

'Okay,' Karrion says, taking a seat in the armchair opposite mine, 'let's solve this case.'

FRIDAY

25

CONFRONTATION

By the following morning, we are no closer to figuring out the truth. Coffee and sugar have kept us up all night, but I am not certain either of us still has a functioning brain.

We have gone over the judgement footage countless times from every angle, but I cannot see anything wrong with it. Every aspect of the procedure is as expected. We have scrutinised the reactions of the officials and the audience, and only two things stand out: Marsh's shock when the verdict is delivered and Brother Valeron spending a moment watching Ilana right before he leaves the courtroom.

As for how the judgement was tampered with, we are still in the dark, and each passing minute diverts more of my attention to worrying about failure.

A night spent huddled in front of a laptop has taken its toll. My legs ache and the pain in my pelvis has flared to a point where it feels like my sacroiliac joints are filled with ground glass. Every movement sends shooting pain through my body. The only upside of it is that I doubt I could fall asleep even if I wanted to.

The ringing of my phone interrupts the despondent silence in the room. My hand shakes when I reach for the phone. I see Jamie's name on the screen. When I greet him, my voice is hoarse.

'Care to come and witness the fruits of your labour?' he asks. I hear people speaking in the background and the sound of a car door slamming.

'Does that mean the DNA came back a match?'

'Braeman's blood on Pearson's shirt.'

A thought floats through my sleep-deprived mind and my brain struggles to formulate it into a coherent sentence. 'And there's no danger of him claiming that the blood got on his shirt because of a separate incident?'

'Not unless they practised North Mage death curses together. The lab found traces of the spell ingredients mixed in with the blood.'

'We nailed Reaoul,' I say, and next to me, Karrion grins despite his fatigue.

'You certainly did. I'm heading over there right now with a section of Paladins to arrest him. Do you want to join us?'

'Are we allowed to come?'

'It's already been cleared with the people higher up the food chain. The offer is there if you're not too busy.'

I drink the rest of my cold coffee while I consider the offer. 'Not too busy as such, but we still haven't figured out how Reaoul and Valeron changed the outcome of the judgement.'

'Who knows, maybe Reaoul will confess all?'

'Maybe. It's no worse a plan than sitting here, staring at the judgement footage we know by heart. Count us in.'

'I'll swing by to pick you up. The Paladins will head straight there and secure the area.'

As I end the call, Karrion rises and rakes a hand through his hair. There are dark circles under his eyes.

'Are we going to arrest the bad guy?'

'Jamie is,' I say, 'but we get to watch.'

'Hopefully it won't take too long and we can get back here to continue with the judgement footage.'

'At this point, I'm hoping that your earlier comment about Reaoul spilling the beans as part of his evil mastermind speech ends up being correct.'

Karrion stretches and winces. 'What sort of a world do we live in, if we can't even rely on evil mastermind rants?'

'I suppose a world without evil masterminds would be too much to ask for?'

He begins clearing the table of plates and cups. I hurry to take a cold shower. The water temperature increases the ache in my body, but it also refreshes me. I need refreshment more, and I can relieve the pain when this is all over. Given how much putting on a pair of socks hurts my pelvis, midday cannot come soon enough.

By the time Jamie arrives, we are outside waiting for him. I have had more forethought than yesterday and transferred the footage of the judgement on to my phone. It keeps me occupied as we drive across Old London, and Karrion leans forward to watch it over my shoulder. We are none the wiser when Jamie parks outside the Pearsons' flat behind an armoured Brotherhood van.

Jamie ushers us into the entrance hall, where we are met by three Paladins in full Kevlar armour. The jewelled swords the Paladins carry may look outdated, but they are charged with enchantments and wielded with great proficiency. The doorman on duty sits behind his desk, looking lost and annoyed at the Paladins who have taken occupation of his domain.

We exchange greetings with the Paladin in charge, Sister Jonya, who informs us that the Pearsons are both upstairs and that she has Paladins stationed on their floor to ensure they do not leave the flat. She accompanies us into the lift with another Paladin, who is carrying the magic-nulling chains used on all magical prisoners. At the sight of them, I take a step back; our visit to the prison wing of the Brotherhood still fresh in my mind.

Upstairs, the corridor is quiet. Jamie squares his shoulders before knocking on the door, and I wonder if he hopes or fears that Eolande will open it. Perhaps both.

It is indeed she who answers. Her eyes scan us all and she gives a small nod. Instead of inviting us in, she steps out into the corridor and leans against the wall, arms crossed. The door remains open.

Her actions have thrown Jamie, who looks from Jonya to me. When neither of us has an insight to offer, he shrugs and enters the flat. We file in after him.

Reaoul is sitting on the sofa, an espresso cup in hand. In a pale-grey suit, he is as eye-catching as his wife, but now that I know what to look for, there is coldness to his beauty. He says nothing as two Paladins enter behind us, only a quirk of an eyebrow acknowledging our presence.

Jamie clears his throat and pulls a folded piece of paper from his suit's inner pocket. Next to Reaoul, he looks drab and mundane. It is not just that his clothes are cheaper and ill-fitting, but he lacks the glow of power magical people have. No wonder humans are drawn to us; there is little that separates them from moths dazzled by brightness.

'Reaoul Pearson, I have here a signed decree for your arrest. The Paladins will detain you until such time as you will be judged for your crimes.'

Leaning forward, Reaoul places the cup on the coffee table. He looks neither concerned nor interested by Jamie's words.

'On what charges am I to be arrested?'

'For the murder of Gideor Braeman, your employer and the First among your order. For orchestrating a theft of magical artefacts from your employer's residence. For seeking to pervert the course of justice.'

'How curious. I have been labouring under the impression that Jonathain Marsh has been judged guilty of that murder.'

'The judgement was rigged,' I say, 'and you know it.'

Reaoul looks at me as he stands and I catch a glimpse of cunning in his eyes. 'Prove it.'

'We can link you to the Paladin who served at the Marsh judgement,' Jamie says.

'There are plenty of reasons to speak to a Paladin. I may have been concerned for my spiritual welfare.'

'Bullshit.' Karrion takes a step forward. 'You bribed him into tampering with the judgement in return for you funding his daughter's place on a drug trial.'

I lay a hand on Karrion's arm to rein him in. Though I understand his anger in the face of Reaoul's indifference, he has given away more than I wanted. This conversation is a game and our only chance of winning is catching Reaoul by surprise. That will not happen if we tip our hand too early.

'Bribery is such a dirty word,' Reaoul says, tilting his head. It occurs to me that he and Lord Ellensthorne must get along very well.

'We know about Lord Ellensthorne blackmailing your employer,' Jamie says.

'Do you now? Well done, it's reassuring to see that my tax money is being well spent on upstanding officers such as yourself.'

It is Jamie's turn to bristle, but Reaoul ignores him in favour of studying me. How will he bait me?

'I can't help wondering about your professional competence, Ms Wilde,' he says. 'Shouldn't you be saving your client's father instead of spending time with humans and the rabble of the magical world?'

Karrion's magic flares with his anger, a capercaillie male spreading his plumage in preparation for a fight. I too am caught by surprise, for I never told Reaoul who my client was. It would appear that gossip spreads like wildfire among the aristocrats of Old London.

'I'm fulfilling my brief as we speak,' I reply, keeping my expression neutral.

'Is arresting an alleged murderer more important than saving a man's life?' Reaoul tuts and shakes his head. With sunlight streaming into the room, his flaxen curls create a fleeting halo around his head. 'Seems the stories about Wild Folk savagery are true after all.'

'What makes you think I can't do both?' I ask, refusing to be thrown off balance by his taunting. His opening move was too predictable. I know full well the sort of stories told about my kind. Some may be exaggerated, but most are true. We can no more claim to be sophisticated citizens of the world than Paladins can claim to be atheists.

Reaoul makes a show of checking his gold Bulgari. 'The execution takes place in under three hours.'

'I am aware.' Resting my hands on my hips, I lean forward a fraction. 'Why do you think it's still going ahead?'

At this, Reaoul's cool exterior fractures, affording me a glimpse of uncertainty. Although he is quick to regain his composure, some of the haughty derision has gone from his voice.

'You've managed to persuade the Paladins to postpone the execution?'

I shrug, feigning nonchalance. 'Why postpone when we both know Jonathain Marsh is innocent?'

'You got them to call off the execution?' This time, I offer no reply, too focused on keeping my expression neutral. He shifts, more of his confidence chipped away. 'You figured out how the judgement was rigged?'

There it is, the first admission of guilt. He is not yet accepting blame, but he has just confirmed what I already know to be true. The judgement was corrupt. Reaoul was involved in its corruption.

All of this I keep from my face as I smile. 'If the judgement can be corrupted, then that corruption can be detected.'

'How did you figure it out?'

'Brother Valeron. He told me all I needed to know.' I am betting that since he was involved, Reaoul will have kept a close eye on the news of Old London.

'Didn't he commit suicide last Sunday?' he asks, confusion joining uncertainty on his handsome features.

'He did,' I agree, allowing my smile to show just a hint of smugness.

'So how could he have told you anything?'

'Even the most savage among us have their ways.'

A look of speculation takes over his features and I can almost hear him wondering whether he miscalculated when he dismissed me as one of the forest folk: unimportant and ineffective. He did. But then he glances around the room and the glint of cunning returns to his eyes.

'You're bluffing. You have no more figured out the truth about the judgement than you have found proof to connect me to my employer's murder.'

'That's where you're wrong,' I say. 'There's a van full of

Paladins waiting for you and they wouldn't have turned up without solid evidence.'

From the way he glances around, brows furrowed in concentration, I am guessing he is trying to figure out what possible evidence we could have unearthed. I marvel at his arrogance in thinking that he has committed the perfect murder and got away with it, and cannot help taunting him a little.

'Next time you kill someone, you should do a better job of getting rid of your bloodied shirt.' I grin, taking a step forward. 'Except, it's really not going to be an issue for you going forward, is it?'

Anger twists Reaoul's features into those of a stranger and I feel the gathering of power. As I open my mouth to warn the others, I hear a whisper of steel from behind me as one of the Paladins draws their sword. Reaoul takes several quick steps to put the sofa between him and us.

Light is pouring into the room, streaming through the window and pulsing from Reaoul himself. My eyes water from the assault of brightness, and next to me, Jamie recoils, shielding his face. Karrion cries out in pain. Invoking my power, I shield my skin by turning it into the scales of an adder and close my eyes to prevent damage. Behind me, the Paladins activate the spells on their swords and the air crackles.

I stand in the eye of a magical storm, my senses all but overwhelmed by the power. From somewhere to my right comes a cracking sound and I realise that the huge windows are about to buckle in the face of the magic expanding away from the spell-casters. It is dislodging small items from the counters and pressing outward, seeking an outlet for the explosion that is about to happen.

Reaoul's magic grows focused, gaining definition from the words of the spell he is uttering. Although identifying the spell is beyond my ability, I know he cares nought for the people in this room. I do, and what spurs me forward is the thought of Karrion, no match for a Light Mage, and defenceless Jamie.

Channelling the strength of a wolf leaping at its prey's throat, I launch myself forward, over the sofa and across the space separating me from Reaoul. Unable to see, I let my other senses guide me as I hit solid flesh. Taken by surprise, Reaoul staggers back and falls down, the cadence of the spell broken. I land on top of him. My left wrist twists on impact and pain flares, but I ignore it.

Up close, the light still emanating from Reaoul burns with the heat of the sun and my skin prickles, then blisters. As my fingers, pressed against his upper arms, morph into claws that dig into his flesh, I become aware of a roaring sound. It takes me a few moments to realise the sound is coming from me. Yanking my head down, I prepare for a kill, my canines elongating.

'Enough!'

The word cuts through the noise and the magical storm, bringing with it the calm of authority. No longer assaulted by a blinding glare, I open my eyes. Inches from my face, pressed against Reaoul's throat is a glowing sword. The symbols carved into the steel pulse and I feel the dissipation of Reaoul's power even as my claws and fangs retract. Soon only Paladin magic remains in the room, and I let Reaoul go.

Nausea washes over me when I realise how close I came to tearing open Reaoul's throat. Am I really capable of killing a person? One look at Karrion and Jamie is all the answer I need: to protect those I care about, I will do anything. They are both staring at me. Jamie's expression is one of shock, whereas on Karrion's face I see awe.

'Chains, please.'

Sister Jonya keeps the sword against Reaoul's throat until he is chained and hauled up between two Paladins. Blood has stained the torn edges of his suit where my claws cut him, but I offer no apology for his injuries. All civility disappears from Reaoul's face, leaving only rage behind.

'You'll pay for this,' he spits in my direction.

'Not before you pay for your crimes,' I say, struggling to stand. My body is a mass of pain and focusing on anything for more than a few seconds requires a great deal of effort. Karrion comes to rest a hand on my elbow and I am grateful for the support.

The Paladins tug Reaoul towards the door, but I hold out my hand.

'Wait. Why did you frame Marsh?'

A cruel smile twists Reaoul's lips, marring his beauty. 'Whoever said I framed him? After what Gideor did to his daughter, he was the perfect accomplice.'

Karrion makes a disbelieving noise at the back of his throat, but I silence him. Eyes fixed on Reaoul, I step closer.

'Why did you kill Braeman?'

As he stands between the Paladins, it looks like he is going to ignore the question, but then he lifts his chin and straightens his back. His eyes are mirrors of ice.

'I am nobody's fool. Least of all that of a lowly Leech.'

We watch in silence as the Paladins lead him out.

26

A MOMENT OF CLARITY

Once Reaoul is out of the room, adrenaline fades from my blood and I sway at the onslaught of pain. Karrion catches me and leads me to the sofa. Over the pulsing pain, I am dimly aware that Jamie leaves and returns soon afterwards with a Paladin.

'Let's get you some first aid,' the Paladin says.

'I can't. We need to save Marsh.'

'You're in no shape to save anyone if you can't walk without help.'

The Paladin has a point, and after a token protest, I follow his order and lie down. My eyes close of their own accord, fatigue dragging me under.

His fingers against my cheek feel like sandpaper, and I shy away from his touch. Hands on my shoulders steady me, and when I force my eyes open, I see Karrion hovering over me. Next to me, the Paladin is spreading the contents of his first aid kit on the coffee table, which has, by some miracle, escaped the maelstrom of magic that raged in the room.

'Your magic saved you from the worst damage,' the Paladin says. 'I'll see what I can do about the rest.'

He snaps on a pair of latex gloves and unscrews a jar of vile-smelling unguent. The paste is cool against my skin and my eyes flutter closed. I feel the salve hardening, followed by a whisper of Paladin magic. The healing spell feels like spring water over feverish skin, bringing numbness in its wake. It dries the blisters and draws the damaged layers of skin into the paste. When he peels the paste back, the skin that remains feels raw but whole. He repeats the process on my neck and on my hands, which also came into direct contact with Reaoul's light.

When I look down at my clothes, I see that their colour has faded, as if they have been left in the sun for too long.

I protest when the Paladin takes out a syringe, but he insists on giving me a shot of painkillers while he sees to my arm. His words alert me to the wetness near my shoulder; the stitches must have burst during the struggle. He helps me out of my jacket and pushes up the sleeve of my T-shirt. At the sight of the needle, I am forced to look away due to nausea from the pain and fatigue. Karrion remains nearby, his expression one of concern. We share a smile.

'That was quite the leap,' he says, and kneels to rest his chin on the back of the sofa.

'You saw it?' I ask, my words slurred from the medication.

'Just about. You went all wolverine on him.'

'I wish. If I had a wolverine's body, I wouldn't hurt this much.'

'It looked like you were going to change into a bear or something. From what little I could see, your outline went blurry.'

I shake my head and the pain between my temples intensifies. 'I don't have that kind of power. The Eldermen do and a few others. For the rest of us, it requires the collective power of the conclave, and even then the effort to maintain another form is huge.'

'Can Dearon do it?'

In my peripheral vision, Jamie shifts closer and I curse both his and Karrion's curiosity.

'Of course. Only the Elderman has more power than Dearon. He's the damn golden boy of the conclave.' The words are meant to be bitter, but numbness encasing my mind leaves them sounding weary instead.

'Who's–?'

Karrion cuts Jamie off with a shake of his head. The Paladin wraps a fresh bandage around my arm and packs away his kit.

'Take it easy for a few days and you'll be fine,' he says. 'Now you can carry on with the saving.'

I try to offer my thanks, but Karrion beats me to it, and I struggle to sit up instead. The room spins and then settles. Looking around, I wonder where Eolande is, but I cannot summon the energy to ask someone. Perhaps she is already shopping around for husband number two.

'Do you think Reaoul was telling the truth when he said that Marsh was his accomplice?' Karrion asks, and sits next to me on the sofa.

'No,' I say straight away. 'I think it was a last-ditch attempt at misdirection. He'd already admitted that the judgement was rigged. If Marsh had been his accomplice, the verdict would have come back guilty without the need to tamper with it.'

'Okay.' From Karrion's frown, I can tell something is still bothering him. 'I was just thinking, if Braeman did... hurt Ilana, that would give Marsh a pretty good motive for murder.'

'It would, but remember how Viola described Marsh? She said he was a "gentle academic". Why would he have murdered Braeman instead of calling the police? The scandal would have ruined Braeman's political career.'

'You're right, it doesn't make sense.'

'Besides, I don't think she was raped. When Ilana told her

father about Braeman's advances, Marsh acted immediately. There's no reason to think Marsh wouldn't have believed Ilana if she'd told him Braeman had raped her.' Aware of Jamie's presence nearby, I hesitate before continuing, 'And I sensed no tension in her when we made love. I believe Ilana spoke the truth when she said Braeman only propositioned her.'

Having checked the time on my phone, I shake my head to clear some of the numbness that is weighing me down.

'We should go. Sitting here isn't bringing us any closer to saving Marsh.'

Karrion helps me up and Jamie follows us out. I look for Eolande in the corridor, but she is no longer there. Several scenes of crime officers step out of the lift, dressed in white overalls and carrying their kits. I watch them head towards the Pearsons' flat while we wait for the lift doors to close, grateful that our part here at least is over. A glance in the mirror shows that the skin on my face is pink but not burnt. The Paladin spells were potent.

'Where do you want to be dropped off?' Jamie asks me when we get to the car. Karrion glowers at the flock of pigeons ambling around the pavement.

'My place, please.'

I have my phone out to go over the footage of the judgement even before the car has joined the morning traffic. Nothing short of a miracle will save Ilana's father now, and yet I cannot bring myself to stop trying. The slow movement of the car has a soporific effect on me, and my eyelids grow heavy as I watch the Mage reading out the charges. I blink as Brother Valeron turns to speak to the Herald. Trapped between being asleep and awake, I stop looking for what is not there and see instead what is.

Then I know.

Clarity sends a shaft of energy through me, and I jerk

upwards, sending my phone flying into the footwell. My sudden movement startles Jamie and the car swerves before he brings it under control. He curses, but I ignore him as I pat around the floor in search of my phone.

'What was that all about?' Jamie asks.

At the same time, Karrion speaks out in the back seat. 'Are you okay?'

'Turn the car around,' I say, closing the video and scrolling through my list of contacts.

'What?' Despite his confusion, Jamie indicates left and turns into a narrow side street where he executes a three-point turn.

'We need to get to the Brotherhood as soon as possible.'

'Why?' Karrion asks, leaning forward.

'I know how the judgement was rigged, but I need a Paladin to prove it.'

'How?'

I smile and shake my head at Karrion while I wait for the call to connect. Sister Alissa answers and asks for news about Brother Valeron. I have little to tell her and instead ask a favour. All the while, I keep an eye on Karrion, waiting for understanding to dawn. When it comes, his grin matches mine.

Alissa promises to meet us at the main entrance as soon as she has tracked down the Paladin I need. We end the call and I tap another name in my contacts.

Ilana answers after just one ring, and from her tone I call tell she has been waiting for my call.

'What news?'

'Are you at the Brotherhood?'

'Yes. It is less than two hours until the execution.'

'I know. We are heading there now. I know how the judgement was corrupted, but I need the help of a particular Paladin to prove it. Do you want to be there for that?'

'Of course. Does this mean you caught the real killer?'

'The Paladins arrested Reaoul Pearson half an hour ago.'

'Reaoul did it? But he seemed so distraught at the funeral.' Ilana's voice is a mix of surprise and disbelief. 'Did he say why?'

'It's a long story, and sensitive. I'll fill you in later, but for now, can you meet us at the main entrance in about five minutes?'

Ilana agrees to do so and says a hasty goodbye. Before the call disconnects, I can hear the sound of high-heeled shoes hurrying along marble corridors; an echo of a daughter's concern for her father. Refusing to think about my own father, I turn to Jamie.

'Doesn't this car have a siren and flashing lights?'

'We're only allowed to use them in an emergency,' Jamie says, switching lanes.

'Doesn't an innocent man facing execution count as an emergency?'

'Not when the execution isn't due to take place until noon. Relax, Yannia, we'll be there in a couple of minutes.'

'Time is of the essence. We can't just burst in at the last minute and demand a stay of execution.'

'Fine. What's one more bent rule?'

Jamie switches on the sirens and I wince at the loudness of them. How the police can stand them for any length of time is beyond me. But they have the desired effect and cars give way to us as we speed through a red light. In the rear-view mirror, I witness Karrion's excitement.

Even with the sirens, it feels like the journey takes ten times longer than it should, but the clock on the dashboard indicates that it is only two minutes later when we reach our destination. We turn through the main gates of the Brotherhood, and Jamie parks in one of the spaces allocated to the Metropolitan Police. I am out of the car before he has switched off the engine, and both he and Karrion have to jog to catch up with me.

'What's the rush?' Jamie asks. 'We've got plenty of time.'

'Perhaps, but the Paladins aren't just going to take my word that their infallible justice is, in fact, fallible.'

'You said you have proof.'

'I do, but I expect they'll still take some convincing.'

'So let's go and convince them,' Karrion says, and pushes open the heavy doors into the Brotherhood.

As we step past the guards into the great hall, my eyes scan the sparse crowd for familiar faces. Ilana is hurrying towards us from the wing leading to the prison cells. The collar of her shirt is high enough to conceal any bruising on her throat, but I look out for any other signs of the night we spent together. I find none. Only when she reaches us and lays her hand on my arm do I get an affirmation of what passed between us.

'You did it,' she says, and to my pleasure, she includes Karrion in that statement. He grins with pride at this and I notice that his magic no longer diminishes in Ilana's presence.

'Almost,' I reply. 'Though the hard part will be convincing others.'

'I'll help with that. Trust me, I can be quite persuasive when my father's life is at stake.'

Movement catches my attention, and I turn to watch Sister Alissa approach with two other Paladins, all clad in the grey robes of the Order. As I step towards them, I push the pain and the fatigue to the back of my mind.

'Let's end this.'

27

THE PRICE OF JUSTICE

Sister Alissa introduces the other Paladins as Sister Serah and Brother Themas. While she speaks, Brother Themas's eyes are fixed on her lips. When it is his turn to greet everyone, he does so by signing while Sister Serah translates.

'He says it's a pleasure to meet you and he hopes that he will be of assistance to you.'

'I hope so too,' I say, and turn to Alissa. 'Do you have the laptop?'

'Yes, right here.' She hands me the bag she was carrying.

'Great. Is there somewhere we can go to do this in private?'

'Follow me.'

Sister Alissa leads us to the research wing where we conversed once before. We can hear voices through the Palaeontology door and we choose the Ethnoarchaeology room instead.

Alissa boots up the laptop and together we connect my phone to it. When I have called up the judgement footage and found the relevant section, I address Brother Themas.

'Would you take a look at the footage and tell me what the charges presented by the Mage are?'

Brother Themas nods and focuses his attention on the film. When the Mage sets down his scroll, Themas begins signing and Sister Serah provides us with a translation.

'The charges read as follows: Jonathain Marsh, you hereby stand accused of the murder of Gideor Braeman, the Speaker of the High Council of Mages and the First among the Light Mages. You are further accused of profiting from your crimes by way of auctioning certain artefacts of power taken from the victim's abode. Stand ready to receive the judgement of the Herald.'

I nod. Although I did not know the exact wording, the gist of the charges is as I expected.

'Would you now watch the charges Brother Valeron presents to the Herald and tell me what he says?'

Again, Themas watches the footage I play him, and from the shock creeping across his features, I know I am right. When he attempts to sign the answer, his hands are shaking too much and he has to start from the beginning.

Sister Serah frowns. 'Wait, that can't be right,' she says, and Themas signs again, more insistently. All colour drains from Serah's face.

'He says that the charges presented to the Herald were as follows: this man, Jonathain Marsh, stands accused of being unfaithful to his wife. Please cast your judgement as to his guilt or innocence.'

Several people begin speaking at once, but I only nod. Ilana throws her arms around me and whispers a thank you. Jamie grins at me over her shoulder and steps back to lean against the door. When Ilana and I step apart, Sister Alissa rests a hand on my shoulder. She looks pale and frightened.

'How did you know?'

The murmur of voices dies away as everyone waits for my answer. Feeling self-conscious, I pick up my phone and slip it into my pocket.

'Well,' I say, shifting from foot to foot, 'I knew that if someone wanted to tamper with a judgement, it would have to be subtle, given how many people were watching. And Brother Valeron's suicide indicated that it was something he did, that he specifically influenced the judgement. So I watched him, over and over, until I knew every moment of the judgement by heart. But the problem was, he didn't do anything unexpected; he never hesitated or gave any indication that he wasn't following the standard procedure. It wasn't until after we arrested Reaoul that I realised I should have been looking for a weakness in the system. From there it was obvious. There was only one point when Brother Valeron spoke so that only one other person in the courtroom could hear him: when he translated the charges to the Herald.'

'Do you think he whispered the charges?' Karrion asks.

Ilana shakes her head. 'He didn't whisper, I remember hearing him speak.'

'He didn't have to,' I say. 'Heralds aren't human; they don't speak English or any other human language. When the Paladins communicate with them, it is using the Heralds' native tongue that only the Paladins understand.'

Karrion remains confused. 'But how come no one realised he changed the charges?'

'Valeron was the only Paladin in the room. The Mages, Shamans, and Metropolitan Police all had representatives present. Brother Valeron represented the Brotherhood. Even the guards left the courtroom once they had secured Marsh to the pillar.'

'There was no one there to hear the charges, no one except Valeron and the Herald,' Karrion says, finally understanding.

'Afterwards, it would take a Paladin able to read lips to discover the truth.'

Brother Themas smiles.

'Marsh's affair with Tanyella was one of those secrets among the aristocracy of Old London that wasn't a secret at all. Between that and Marsh's disagreement with Braeman, Reaoul had an ideal scapegoat. It's the perfect way to fool an infallible justice system.'

'But it couldn't fool you,' Ilana says, and hugs me again.

'We need to see the Paladin General immediately,' Sister Alissa says, and closes the laptop lid.

I nod. 'Agreed. There's an innocent man about to be executed and only the Paladin General has the power to stop that.'

As I move to leave, Ilana touches my hand and gives me a cheque.

'It's the outstanding part of your fee, plus an estimate for the expenses you have incurred.'

A glance at the figure leaves me frowning. Even with a generous estimate for the expenses, she has paid me for an additional day.

'This is too much,' I say. 'By default, my employment ends today at noon.'

'Given everything you have done for my family, it doesn't seem enough,' Ilana replies. 'Take it, with my gratitude.'

'Thank you.' I fold the cheque and slip it into my back pocket.

'Like you said, let's end this.'

The Paladin General's assistant tries to stop us marching into the General's office, but the Paladins leading the way listen to no protests. Sister Alissa knocks on the door, and upon being granted permission to enter, opens it for us. The Paladins bow, while the rest of us file in, uncertain how to greet the Head of the Brotherhood.

A tall man sits behind an imposing oak desk. His robes are embroidered with blue symbols and his grey hair rests on his shoulders in tight curls. Shrewd eyes regard us beneath thin eyebrows and his dark skin is a roadmap of lines. When he stands, I feel the edge of his magic against mine, questioning, assessing.

'Sister Alissa, what is the meaning of this?' His deep voice holds an edge of authority that demands acquiescence. The auras of power around me shrink and diminish.

'My apologies, Paladin General, but this could not wait. The life of an innocent is in danger.'

Before he has a chance to reply, I step forward. 'Your justice system is flawed. I have proof.'

Dark eyes fix me on the spot, and I regret my hasty words. But every minute takes Marsh closer to execution, and at least with that opening I now have the Paladin General's undivided attention.

'Close the door.'

Behind us, Sister Serah hurries to obey.

'Speak.'

I take one of the seats in front of his desk, uninvited, and his frown deepens. A wave of magic washes over me, more assertive in its assessment, and I hide nothing from it. Whatever the Paladin General learns about me causes him to indicate the other seats, and Ilana, Karrion, and Jamie sit. The Paladins remain standing behind us, shoulder to shoulder.

Taking a moment to gather my thoughts, I begin an abbreviated account of how Karrion and I were hired and where the investigation has led us. At the first word, a different kind of magic envelops me, leaving me with the feeling that I am breathing in a mist so thick it qualifies as water. I have heard of the spell, but never experienced it myself. It is the truth aura the Paladins use. From here on, the Paladin General will know instantly if I speak any untruths. With the façade of an infallible justice system crumbling around us, I have to wonder how effective the spell is.

When I get to the point involving Brother Themas, the focus of the Paladin General's spell shifts to the line of Paladins behind me. Sister Serah translates Brother Themas's statement, and with it comes the finality of belief. The Paladin General slumps down on his chair, his features twisted by shock. His spell dissipates like morning mist faced with the rising sun.

'This cannot be,' he says, his words slow. 'For centuries, we have relied on the Heralds to impart justice.'

'The Heralds are still infallible,' I reply, feeling a surge of sympathy for him. 'It's the human element that has let you down.'

Silence permeates every corner of the room, while the Paladin General stares at his desk, chin down. Next to me, Ilana casts a discreet glance at her watch, ever mindful of the passing time. As much as I wish to hurry the Paladin General, I dare not speak. Being tactless once was enough.

Ilana, however, is braver than me.

'So you see, my father is innocent.'

The Paladin General lifts his head, and although his expression is blank, I am struck with a sensation akin to the calm before a storm. I shudder.

'No. Your father was judged guilty by the Herald.'

'Yes, but of adultery. That is not punishable by death, it's not even a crime.'

I can tell from her tone that Ilana does not yet understand. I do, and I stare into the yawning gulf of failure.

'No,' the Paladin General repeats. 'The Herald declared

your father guilty of Gideor Braeman's murder before the presiding officials and a gallery full of people.'

'So? A new judgement would see the verdict changed to innocent.'

'That may be, but there won't be a new judgement.'

'You will release him without a second judgement?' Ilana asks.

'I cannot do that. A Herald has delivered a verdict and justice must be served.'

My heart clenches at the dawning horror on Ilana's face. 'I don't understand. My father is innocent.'

'Not in the eyes of the world outside this room. They know with absolute certainty that he murdered Braeman and that he will be punished for his crime. And that is what matters the most.'

Ilana jumps up, her face red. 'You can't do that!'

The Paladin General also rises, but I can see he is burdened by this new knowledge. He no longer towers over us as an imposing authority figure. Instead, I see a troubled leader trying to make us understand the impossible.

'I not only can, but I must,' he says, emphasising his words by placing his palms flat on his desk. 'For centuries, the Heralds have served us infallible justice. They are never wrong and that has been the assurance we have offered humans. None of us, no matter how powerful, can use magic to conceal our crimes.'

'It wasn't a Herald that made a mistake, it was Brother Valeron!'

'Correct, and that very act drove him to commit suicide. He must have understood, as I now do, the full implications of his betrayal. For he not only condemned an innocent man to die, but destabilised the very foundations of our society. The magnitude of his crime is inconceivable.'

'Then blame him, make his mistake public,' Ilana says, anger continuing to fuel her words.

'That I cannot do. For no one outside this room can ever find out the truth. Your father must die so that the world can see him punished for his perceived crimes. Our justice system must remain infallible.'

'My father is paying for Brother Valeron's crime. Where's the justice in that?'

'Justice has been imparted and we must bow to its will.'

'That's horseshit. You're hiding behind platitudes and meaningless phrases, all the while choosing not to help my father. He is as much an innocent as those you claim to be protecting.'

'Alas, that is not true. Had your father honoured his vows of marriage, the Herald would have found him innocent.'

'It must be nice, judging others from the pedestal you've set yourself on.'

Behind us, I sense the growing disquiet and anger of the Paladins. I reach out to calm Ilana but she dodges my hand.

'It is true that I hold people to high moral standards, in particular those who are the leaders of our community. We should all lead by example, should we not?'

Ilana flinches. Before she has a chance to reply, the Paladin General runs a hand over his face.

'Despite my harsh words and the difficult choice I've had to make, I'm not without compassion. If there was a way to save your father and preserve the reputation of our justice system, I would gladly take it.'

'You were quick to decide that your only option was to kill my father.'

'I will forgive you your naivety, given your youth. There has been enough deception. Time to put an end to it.'

'What makes you think I won't tell the world about what

you are proposing to do?' Ilana steps forward so her legs are touching the desk, and she balls her hands into fists.

'First of all, you have no proof. Only a Paladin able to read lips can translate the charges presented by Brother Valeron, and every Paladin here has taken an oath of allegiance to the Brotherhood. They will not betray the Order or deviate from their task of protecting the citizens of Old London. But more importantly, consider the implications of what you are proposing.'

'The peace we have with humans is largely based on our ability to police our own kind,' I say quietly, and the Paladin General nods. 'Casting doubt on it would resurface every disagreement, every perceived slight between us and the humans. It would lead to rioting, or worse.'

'She's right,' the Paladin General tells Ilana, who glares at me. 'As much magic as we possess, we are no match for humans and their weapons because there are too many of them. Think about how many lives will be lost, needlessly. The aristocrats are well protected and the lower classes would bear the brunt of those losses. Is that the outcome you would want?'

'So that's it?' Ilana asks. 'You're just going to execute my father anyway?'

'What would he say? If I presented him with the choice of living with the consequences or being executed, how would he choose?'

Ilana's shoulders slump. 'He would say that the lives of many are worth more than a single life, even if that life is his.'

'Your father is a good man,' the Paladin General says. 'And you should know that choosing not to cancel the execution is not a decision I take lightly. But protecting the people of Old London, as well as those who live outside our city's boundaries, must always be my priority. That is the oath I took and that is my burden to bear.'

'It's not fair.'

'No. Brother Valeron has left us all in an impossible situation. Justice should serve everyone equally, with equal impartiality, and Brother Valeron took that away from your father. As much as I would like to right that wrong, I cannot do so.'

Although Ilana says nothing, I watch as she digs her nails into her palms and I admire her bravery in the face of defeat. The Paladin General must share my thoughts, for he walks around the desk and rests a hand on her elbow.

'Go to your father, make peace with his passing,' he says. 'Out of respect for your family and for your father, I will come and present him with the choice. I've no doubt he will see there is no choice. Afterwards, the Paladins will ensure that your father will feel no pain.'

Ilana turns and I see her eyes brimming with tears. She walks towards the door, her steps unsteady, and I jump up. I get to her as she is pushing open the door and reach for her hand.

'I'm sorry.'

She recoils away from my touch and the tears find paths down her cheeks. Her knuckles turn white while she gains control of her emotions and a crimson droplet slides down her finger. The stain is shocking against the white marble floor; the first of the innocent blood about to be spilt.

'You were my father's last hope,' she says. 'But you failed us. Just like the rest of the system.'

'Ilana–'

I get no further before she leaves. As I watch her hurrying away, I know I was not what she was looking for after all.

28

AFTERMATH

Silence hangs heavily in the car as Jamie drives us home. After Ilana stormed off, we stayed in the Paladin General's office long enough to swear that we would speak to no one about our discoveries. He, in turn, assured us that steps would be taken to ensure that such a catastrophic failure of the system could never happen again. While I appreciated the sentiment, I could not help wondering how long it would take for someone to find another chink in the armour. I also asked him what would happen to Reaoul, and with a darkening expression, the Paladin General promised that Reaoul would receive a just punishment for his crimes.

Having parked the car outside my flat, Jamie twists in his seat to look at me.

'Don't let Ilana's words get to you. They were spoken out of anger and despair, without any truth in them.'

Karrion tries to echo the sentiment from the back seat, his words thick with emotion, but I shake my head.

'I don't know. I keep thinking that maybe I should have been able to find the answer quicker, do it better somehow. If I had, this could have ended differently.'

'No.' Jamie leans forward. 'It was Ilana who was misguided. If she had paused to consider the task she was setting you, she would have realised that there could only be one possible outcome. No matter how quickly you discovered the truth, the Paladins would never have allowed such a fundamental flaw in their justice system to be made public.'

There is truth in what he says, and yet I struggle to hear it. He must realise this, for he sighs.

'You did exactly what you were hired to do and you did it damn well. The rest of it was all beyond your control. Remember that, Yannia. And if you ever need help with another case, give me a call.'

Forcing a smile, I thank him and get out of the car with Karrion. Wind tugs at my clothes as we watch Jamie drive off, and I shiver. Cold has settled in the void within my power, in the numbness left by pain and lack of sleep.

'There's one thing I don't get,' Karrion says. 'On Monday, Ilana said she accepted that you might not be able to save her father, that he might have been guilty all along. Why say that you failed now?'

'If it'd been your father's life hanging in the balance, wouldn't you have said anything, done anything to ensure someone would help? We were her last option.'

'She lied.'

'That's perhaps too harsh. It was easier to accept the possibility of failure when there was still a chance her father could be saved. As much as she may hate me now, we gave her five days of hope. Perhaps one day she'll come to appreciate the value of that.'

'What do we do now?' Karrion asks.

'Now?' I look at my watch and see that it is two minutes past noon. Sadness, disappointment, and anger war within me. 'Go home. Spend time with your family. Be grateful for them.'

Karrion wraps an arm around my shoulder and hugs me close. My shoulder wound twinges, but I stay in his embrace.

'What about you?'

'Me? I'll be fine. With a dose of painkillers and a good night's sleep, I'll be as good as new. Better, even.'

From the look he gives me, Karrion is far from convinced. I turn to face him and take his hand.

'Don't worry about me. It's been a tough week, but life goes on. Of course, I would have liked a different outcome, but it wasn't up to me.' I squeeze his hand. 'But I want you to know that regardless of how this ended, you did good. I couldn't have asked for a better assistant.'

Some of the shadows lift from his face, and I am struck by how similar my words are to Jamie's just now. Will Karrion believe me, even though I am not yet ready to believe Jamie? I suspect Karrion will, like me, not be satisfied with doing his part well if the case as a whole ends in failure. All I can hope for is that this will not deter him going forward, and together we will be able to find closure in time.

'Thanks.' His hand slips free and he looks like there is more he wants to say. I have an inkling of what it might be. After a brief hesitation, he settles for something safe. 'Call me if you need anything.' With a wave, he heads for the bus stop.

'Hey, Karrion,' I call out after him, 'about this apprenticeship trial.'

'Yes?' As he turns back to me, I see concern and uncertainty in his expression.

'I think we're on to something great here.'

A smile lights up his whole face and I have to wonder if I am truly that difficult to read.

'Really?'

'Really. I'll see you Monday morning.'

'Thanks, Yan.' In two strides, he is in front of me and pulling me into a hug that causes something in my spine to crunch. He lets go straight away. 'Sorry.'

'I'll live. Have a good weekend and give my best to your mum.'

He promises to do so and walks away, a spring in his step. Even a pigeon landing on a fence nearby cannot sour his mood and he coos a greeting. Let him enjoy a small victory while he can. Soon enough, he will recall that Marsh has died and Ilana is in mourning. Knowing Karrion, the memory of Marsh asking us to prove his innocence will keep him awake. In this, he and I are the same.

I watch Karrion go until he rounds the corner before turning to face my front door. The blackness of it seems uninviting and beyond it are empty spaces, ready to echo with my doubts and thoughts of failure. I am not ready to face that just yet.

Without a conscious thought, my feet take me away from the door to the Open Hearth. The pub is busy with the lunchtime crowd and the bar staff have only time for a quick greeting between pulling pints and taking money. Beyond the bar, I can see Wishearth sitting in his usual spot.

Sensing my stare, he looks up. Our eyes meet and I am struck with a certainty: he knows. He knows what has transpired this morning and the burden I am carrying. Above all else, I find I am relieved.

Instead of joining the crowd to order a drink, I walk around the bar, greet Boris, and sit down opposite Wishearth. The familiar smell of wood smoke and ash soothes my troubled thoughts.

As if reading my mind, Wishearth's eyes soften and the scent intensifies.

'Congratulations.'

The word catches me by surprise and he chuckles. Looking past me, he points at both of us and mimics drinking.

'"Congratulations" isn't quite what I was expecting,' I say.

'Why ever not? You've just proven the impossible. A murderer has been arrested because of you, and I'm pretty sure this time they've got the right man.'

Wishearth offers no explanation for the extent of his knowledge, and I know it would be pointless to ask. But there is another question I cannot resist voicing.

'Did you know? Did you know who the real murderer was?'

'How would I have known that?' He relaxes back in his chair, his boots resting against the side of my right ankle. 'I rarely concern myself with the troubles of the mortals.'

'Except when it suits you.' The skin of my ankle tingles at the contact that feels strangely intimate.

Sparks flare in his eyes as he grins. A waitress chooses that moment to deliver Wishearth another pint of Guinness. I accept a tumbler of brandy and hand her a tenner in return.

'I can't help wondering whether there is something more I could have done, some way for me to have saved Marsh.' The words tumble out unintended and I bite my lip.

The pressure of his boot against my ankle intensifies and warmth spreads to my toes.

'Did you follow every lead?'

'Yes.'

'Did you hold back on any information or did you delay sharing your findings with the authorities?'

'No.'

'Did you sleep last night, knowing that you didn't yet have all the answers and that you were running out of time?'

'No.'

'Given the kind of week you've had, the injuries you've sustained, was there anything further you could have done?'

'I don't know.'

Wishearth tilts his head as he regards me.

'No.'

'Then you did your best.'

'But Marsh died.'

'Saving him was never your job. Only the Paladin General has the power to halt an execution.'

I am thrown by the comment and his perspective on my assignment. In my haste at first to prove myself and later to solve the case, I never paused to consider where the remit of my assignment began and ended. Perhaps Ilana did not either.

Taking a sip from his pint, Wishearth cocks his head. 'I would tell you that you have proven yourself to be more than capable, but you already know that. Perhaps one day you'll even come to accept it. Others have already seen it.'

How is it that this man, this Hearth Spirit, knows me so well? I have made offerings all my life; could it be that he was always listening, always watching over me? Does he know everything I am running from?

'And here I was, thinking you were going to tell me it's not my fault.' The lightness in my tone is forced. As much as I want to believe him, Ilana's contempt is still fresh in my memory and it robs meaning from Wishearth's words.

'It's not my place to say so. You'll have to find a way to make peace with today's events yourself. No one has the power to do it for you.'

'Shame,' I attempt to joke, even though I know he is right. I would not have taken heart from his reassurance any more than I did from Jamie's. My failures, perceived or real, are mine to accept. I can share the burden with friends, but they cannot carry it for me.

Something of my thoughts must show on my face, for Wishearth nods. 'What's next for Yannia Wilde? Other than sleep and pain relief because, frankly, you look terrible.'

'Thanks. You're quite the charmer.' I roll my eyes at him

and more sparks fly from his eyes. One almost reaches the floor before fading away. 'I'm not sure. I have some paperwork to catch up on, a few prospective jobs I need to follow up, but nothing major. A few days' rest would be nice.'

'Before your next big case, you mean?'

Something in his tone has me glancing up, but his expression gives nothing away.

'Sure, whenever that might be.'

'Plenty of opportunities out there for a private investigator of your calibre, in Old London or even in New London.'

'I'm not sure humans are really my thing.'

'You'd be surprised.' Wishearth rests his elbows on the table, pulling his feet back. I miss the contact. 'We don't live in a separate world from humans. The sooner we accept that, the safer it will be for everyone.'

I nod, puzzled by his warning. It feels out of place, given that he derives all his power from magical people honouring the old rituals. Or does he? Could it be that humans too can feed him, that their belief sustains him just as ours does?

'Go home, Yannia,' he says, reaching to brush his fingers across the back of my hand. 'Rest, reflect, and regroup. You'll need your strength.'

There it is again, some hint of a premonition. In a fleeting premonition of my own, I know our fates are connected. To what purpose, I cannot tell, but the thought reassures me. I know I can trust Wishearth and I nod again, my thoughts turning to the empty house waiting for me. As if sensing some idea that is only half-formed in my mind, Wishearth smiles and shakes his head.

'Go home. And don't forget to light a fire. The weather is turning.'

Wishearth does not have to be physically present to look out for me. I am comforted by the thought and drain my brandy in one swallow, relishing the burn of alcohol. When I rise, instead of turning away, I walk around the table and press a kiss on his cheek. Heat envelops me and the terrible ache in my bones eases.

'Thank you,' I whisper, and leave him to his pint, my heart lighter than it was when I walked in.

The lightness lingers until I reach home and then it dissipates like the final wisps of smoke from a dying fire.

As soon as I open my front door, I know: there is someone in the flat. Easing the door shut behind me, I cast my senses outward. There is nothing out of place in my office, nor can I hear anything from upstairs. Yet I am positive I am not alone, the certainty borne out by some sixth sense I cannot explain. I should be frightened, but instead of fear, I feel apprehension coiling in my stomach.

The quirks of the flat are familiar to me, and I avoid the creaky floorboards on my way up. By the time I reach the top of the stairs, my heart is hammering in my chest and my palms feel clammy. I bite my upper lip to keep my breathing under control, puzzled by my reaction to an intruder. Even my magic seems to be pulsing, recognising something beyond my other senses.

I take a moment to steady my nerves and then push open the door to the lounge, ready for anything except what I find on the other side.

He is standing by the window, looking out into the garden. Although his back is turned, I recognise him straight away. I would recognise him anywhere, anytime, and my breath catches. His senses are sharper than mine, but he remains where he is. In that moment of stillness, my eyes find all the little details that have changed since I last saw him. His black hair is brushing the collar of his shirt, falling in thick waves that I have always envied. He seems taller than I recall, his shoulders broader than in my dreams. With a flash of consternation – or perhaps pleasure – I notice that the jumper he is wearing is one I knitted for the communal clothing supply before my departure.

As ever, he radiates power and my magic responds to it. I recall what it felt like to be suffused with that power until nothing else existed but him and his magic. It is the heat of a summer sun, the cool of deep spring water, the richness of fresh meat, and the sweetness of apple-blossom honey.

Longing wars with fear in my heart as my eyes drink in the sight of him. There was once a time when I wanted nothing more than to get lost in his eyes, the touch of his long fingers and his laugh. But that desire has long since been tainted with anger, disappointment, and bitterness. Yet even now, I am drawn to him.

'Dearon,' I whisper.

I smell him before he turns around. My heart clenches. He smells of wind over moors, of rainwater gathered in puddles, of wet moss under bare feet, of campfires, and clear nights. He smells of power, desire, freedom, but most of all, he smells of home.

A tremor runs through me as his dark eyes find mine. I know what he is going to say before he utters the words.

'Your father is dying. It is time for you to come home.'

THE END

ACKNOWLEDGEMENTS

First of all, a huge thank you to Louise Walters for seeing the potential in my novel and for giving me an incredible publication experience. I have enjoyed every step of the way and have learnt a great deal. Thank you to Jennie Rawlings, Alison Jack and Leigh Forbes for their part in making this book happen. I couldn't have asked for a better Team FJ! And thank you to Amanda Saint at Retreat West for bringing *Fallible Justice* to Louise's attention.

This book would not be here without two of my writer friends, Andrew Rogers and Johanna Saariluoma. I'm forever grateful for your comments and critique on the various drafts, as well as your general support and guidance. Even when I lost faith, you never did. You guys rock and you are my rock. Thank you.

Thank you to my family for their support and belief in me. And, because I promised I would include this in the acknowledgements, thank you to my niece Ada-Sofia for being annoying. I wouldn't have it any other way!

I have been blessed with a fantastic bunch of friends who have cheered me on every step of the way and who have been happy to answer really random questions with little or no context. You know who you are.

To the man who inspired Wishearth, thank you for your friendship.

To K and S, who can never reveal they know me, thank you not just for healing me but for teaching me how to heal myself.

Finally, thank you to Sinta and Halla for love, joy and cuddles on the sofa.

A NOTE FROM THE PUBLISHER

Thank you for reading this book. If you enjoyed it please do consider leaving a review on Amazon to help others find it too.

We hate typos. All of our books have been rigorously edited and proofread, but sometimes mistakes do slip through. If you have spotted a typo, please do let us know and we can get it amended within hours.

info@bloodhoundbooks.com

Printed in Great Britain
by Amazon

54010100R00189